PENGUIN HANDBOOKS

MS. PINCHPENNY'S
BOOK OF KITCHEN MANAGEMENT

Born in Reading, Massachusetts, and educated at the
University of New Hampshire, Dorothy Parker has
worked in book publishing for more than thirty
years and is now cookbook editor with a New York
publisher. She has taught courses on writing and
publishing at the New School for Social Research,
at Columbia University, and at New York University; her book reviews have appeared frequently in
the *Christian Science Monitor*. Books by her include
Home Preserving Made Easy (written with Vera
Gewanter), *The Wonderful World of Yogurt,* and
Feeling Fine, Looking Great. Besides cooking and
preserving, Ms. Parker likes gardening, furniture-
refinishing, "decorating," sewing, swimming, skiing,
rock-climbing, and singing—and is, she adds "an
amateur ecologist and conservationist, and a passionate animal-lover." She lives in Connecticut with
her novelist husband.

Ms. Pinchpenny's Book of Kitchen Management

〜‧‧

not the Dorothy Parker

PENGUIN BOOKS

For Carla, Ben, and Maya,
future penny-pinchers

With special thanks to Bill Trowbridge,
without whom this book (or one chapter of it anyway)
would have been a lie

Penguin Books Ltd, Harmondsworth
Middlesex, England
Penguin Books, 625 Madison Avenue
New York, New York 10022, U.S.A.
Penguin Books Australia Ltd, Ringwood
Victoria, Australia
Penguin Books Canada Ltd, 2801 John Street
Markham, Ontario, Canada, L3R 1B4
Penguin Books (N.Z.) Ltd, 182–190 Wairau Road
Auckland 10, New Zealand

First published in the United States of America 1977

LIBRARY OF CONGRESS CATALOGING IN PUBLICATION DATA

Parker, Dorothy, 1922–
Ms. Pinchpenny's book of kitchen management.

(A Penguin handbook)
Includes index.
1. Cookery. 2. Marketing (Home economics) 3. Recipes.
I. Title.
TX652.P296   641.5   76–48086
ISBN 0 14 046.262 7 (pbk.)

Printed in the United States of America by
Offset Paperback Mfrs., Inc., Dallas, Pennsylvania
Set in Linotype Times Roman.
Acknowledgment is made to Bantam Books Inc. for "Natilla"
from *The Spanish Cookbook* by Barbara Norman.
Copyright © Barbara Norman, 1969.
Reprinted by permission of Bantam Books, Inc.

CONTENTS

v

INTRODUCING
MS. PINCHPENNY . . .

Over the years I've spent a shocking amount of time trying to explain to disbelieving friends and family that my wife's frugality has nothing to do with the condition of penury, and is historically unrelated to the annihilating inflation of recent years. And it certainly has nothing to do with any lack of open generosity. In fact, her frugality and our income, if plotted on a graph by the Bureau of Labor Statistics, would prove to stand in an inverse relation, to wit: the larger the income, the more obsessive her thrift. By all the usual standards, we are far from improverished; the B.L.S. would even go so far as to say we're prosperous, everything considered. No, the sources of her enchanting eccentricities must be sought elsewhere.

Frankly, I've never been able to plumb the mystery in which her motives, or some of them, must forever remain shrouded. Some components are clear enough, however; and even if they don't seem clear to some of you, they would have been clear as window panes to her Puritan forebears, going back, if not the *Mayflower*, then to the boat directly behind it. Spendthrifts, to put it simply, are of the devil's party; frugality is a sign of grace, and those who practice it are obeying the Lord's command. It all has something to do with loaves and fishes, or casting bread upon the waters, or something. Whatever it was, "our kind of people" are very careful of their treasure; the others are likely to end up in the county poorhouse, gnashing their teeth and cursing their fate.

Habits transmitted from generation to generation for some three hundred years must finally enter the genetic code —or at least impress themselves heavily on the mind, stamp the soul. Stern ancestors, hovering unseen but very much sensed in the air around us, watch every move we make as we hesitate before the window of the gourmet shop. Something like that.

But that's not it at all. It's not a matter of pain and guilt dogging our days and haunting our nights. Nothing gloomy and crabbed about it. The point is that frugality as practiced in these pages is a joy, a positive pleasure. The point is that every time my wife creates one of the meals described here, it's not only a victory of the spirit but a triumph of the flesh as well, for the meal is superb, as comely to look at as it is lovely to ingest. Piquant, imaginative, various, subtle. What may begin with a desire to beat the system on its own terms —to keep afloat in these dire times, stay abreast of the spiraling cost of everything under the sun—becomes a pleasure in its own right, a continuing sense of self-mastery and mastery of a chilly, bleak world.

Yet mastery may be too ponderous a term, though certainly some part of the pleasure derives from a sense of taking control of one's own destiny rather than submitting to a fate of someone else's contrivance. You're not being priced out of the market; you're manipulating the market to your own ends—*your* own ends, not theirs. However important this is for the soul (and the pocketbook), the larger part, perhaps, is playing the game for the game's sake, and the sheer delight this bestows. By ingenuity and flair, inventiveness and low cunning, devious—almost occult—knowledge, and sophisticated know-how, this lady has created a space, a kind of island or small sovereignty, in which we can live *our* kind of life, which, while it is of course related to and partly dependent upon the life of the larger community, is nevertheless *our own*. An exuberant sense of freedom results.

Within limits, naturally, we've created our own economy—at a sharp angle to the larger one. We've given ourselves the incomparable gift of autonomy. And behold, it is good—born not of necessity, but of our own free will and desire. Money does not alter it in essential respects. If great clouds of greenbacks were suddenly to descend from the sky and land on our compost heap, we would not scrap what we have evolved and order a barrel of Iranian caviar, Scandinavian sturgeon, Peruvian piranhas, pâté of bluebird tongue. In fact, I'm not sure what we'd do with that green mist, but I'm sure it would not change our lives in any essential way. We prefer conducting our own life to having it programmed for us by computers.

If anything gladdens my wife's heart more than a really good tag sale, it can only be a really good landfill on a bright sunny morning during the height of the orgy—or mass madness—known as spring cleaning, when Americans, like whirling dervishes in the grip of the spirit, go into a frenzy, a passion, an ecstasy of flinging away their last season's unused or scarcely used treasures in order to fill the attic with this season's identical treasure. (The literally unused objects that Americans discard—everything from silk purses to leather coats to stuffed chairs to you-name-it—would raise the Atlantic's water level by several feet.) Much of this treasure, in truth, my wife acquires in order to give it to one or another of her many charities or beneficiaries, personal or institutional; but much of it has filled her friends' and her own drawers and closets and has furnished several of our residences over the years, as well as those of innumerable former skeptics.

And, again, the skeptics I'm talking about are the very people designated by that same Bureau of Labor Statistics as comfortable or well-heeled; in fact, not a few of them are more than that, and some are flat-out rich—eccentric, perhaps, by prevalent standards, but rich. They came to scoff and stayed to pray—and are now zealous converts.

Besides, town dumps—landfill projects (at least those we

know)—are convivial places: sort of open-air Grange Halls, town meetinghouses, marketplaces, flea markets, PTAs, church bazaars—all these and more. In our neck of the woods you're likely to meet acquaintances and neighbors there whom you don't see anywhere else for months on end. News is exchanged, and more worldly goods. The men who work there tend to be amiable characters who, once they come to know you and your requirements and interests, are apt to keep an eye out in your behalf and put things by for you. One man who works in our dump rebuilds discarded television sets as a hobby. That's how we got ours. A large family of cats resides in our dump, and they are fed regularly by the visitors. Recipes are often exchanged there.

From what I can observe, what might be called "parsimonious chic" is a growing movement. It certainly is among the young, the "kids," those who fled to the hills when the pressures in the polluted valleys below grew too intense. But more and more it appeals to the rest of us, regardless of age, background, or condition of servitude. It appeals equally to ourselves and our friends and to our children and their friends. If a generalization based on extensive personal observation is possible, it's this: "parsimonious chic" is a movement of the sophisticated, the well-educated, and those for whom money as such is not the pressing problem. Which, to repeat, doesn't mean these people are indifferent to the savings involved—the economic factors; but as much as or more than that, they enjoy flouting the consumer society—the deadly pressure to Buy, Buy, Buy, to live beyond one's means—and the heady sense of freedom and independence it brings.

Try it. If for no other reason than that the suffocating inflation of recent years is a *permanent* condition of our lives—a fact no serious economist doubts, whatever a vote-seeking politician might promise—you should try it. And having tried it, my guess is you'll like it. It feels good.

Join the party.

Mr. Pinchpenny

1

THE CROCK POT
IS A RIPOFF

What you need to know about the kitchen before anything else is how to equip it, how to set yourself up for cooking in the cheapest possible way.

Although books devoted to recipes for electric crock pots seem to have outsold everything but Rod McKuen and the Bible in the last year or so, this expensive gadget really has no claim on that part of your household budget allotted to furnishing the kitchen. Or to keeping up with the Joneses, who probably got their nifty slow-cooker when they opened a bank account anyway. The attraction of the crock pot, I guess, is that you can rise early in the morn, cut up the ingredients and toss them in along with some liquid, plug it in with the heat down low, and go off to your eight-hour job. Then return in the evening with your stew or ragout or cassoulet all ready for you to eat. The same result can be achieved with any sturdy Dutch oven or covered casserole, plus a source of heat that can be maintained steadily at a low level (while you're not looking). The *pot-au-feu* on the back of the wood-burning stove that heated the peasant or pioneer home is the crock pot's obvious predecessor. One of my United Kingdom correspondents has just sent me a clipping from a British newspaper that pictures a "fuel-saving fodder box," in which a meal can be slow-cooked over a period of hours without any heat at all, other than that retained by the covered pot. You heat up your rabbit

1

stew very thoroughly on top of the stove, boil it a few minutes, then wrap it in cloth and sink it in a bedding of straw inside a wooden box with a cover. Or you can use any other good insulating material—newspaper, a sleeping bag, or a quilt. "When it starts to cool down," says the article, "which is usually after about four hours, you take the container out, heat it through again, and put it back in the box." So this would probably work for part-time job-holders. In any case, if you are about to move into a house or apartment with a gas or electric stove, test the burners to see if there's one that can be kept to a *very* low heat. If there is, you're in business; if not, you can go to the dump (or walk the sidewalks on the night before city "collection" day) and find a discarded metal grill or trivet that will keep your Dutch oven from sitting directly on the flame or heat coil. And *voilà*, you have a perfect operating crock pot. In which you can make *boeuf bourguignonne, bouillabaisse, arroz con pollo, ratatouille*—or whatever plain or fancy combined-food dish you desire. And earn your salary at the same time.

Actually, if you have some spare cash to spend on some trendy sort of special kitchen equipment, you would be best advised to get an unglazed terra-cotta pot, which, presuming a good baking oven to put it into, will introduce you to a wonderful new-old method of cooking foods in their own liquids, achieving sauces at the same time, losing none of the food value or flavor. This is something of a luxury item —it breaks more easily than other kinds of roasting-braising pots and has to be replaced; and it doesn't conserve all that much time, energy, or heat.

Be sure that your stove is not a heat-waster, that the oven is well insulated so that all the heat poured into it *stays* in, and you will waste very little energy-money that way. If you have a large oven and a small family (or are a modest cook), your one investment in extra electrical equipment might well be a small oven-broiler (sometimes offered as a premium by depositor-seeking banks). This device will

2

save you thousands of kilowatts over a year of baking four Idahos or a two-and-a-half-quart casserole. An effective "oven" for the baking of one Idaho, for example, can be made by putting a tin pie plate on an electric burner; cover the potato with a thin aluminum loaf tin, one of those items you get free in the supermarket—or pick up in the town dump.

If meal size is not the problem, then my nomination for the one piece of "heavy" kitchen equipment that pays for itself many times over in low utility bills, time-saving, and elbow-grease conservation, is a good electric blender, one with a strong motor and hardy canister. You needn't open a bank account in five figures to come by one of these useful machines; like the American automobile, they come from the manufacturers in new models so often that the gadget-crazy retire them to their local thrift shops or charity-benefit junk sales with surprising regularity. Don't be afraid of a secondhand mixer or blender; the saving in cost is truly phenomenal, and you don't have to buy it if it doesn't sound right to you on its plug-in trial run. General Motors and Cuisinart notwithstanding, a plain serviceable blender is still the *sine qua non*.

The mixer, with a dough-hook attachment, would probably be my second-place nomination—if I didn't enjoy the physical acts of stirring and kneading bread so much. (For a mixer you should not pay full retail price either.) Things like the electric can opener and the electric carving knife spill over from gadget-craziness into decadence, in my mind, along with the electric toothbrush. Don't be decadent: open your cans, if any, with a manual can opener (cost 69 cents) and a sawing motion that is one of the best exercises around for keeping your joints limber. And if you buy an electric ice-cream freezer, you will make and eat more ice cream than is good for you.

Another point in keeping the fancy electrical gadgets to the minimum is worth mentioning. Not only are they tricky and subject to whim and breakdown, but the power that runs them is very costly—and likely to grow more so as time goes on. Moreover, you can injure yourself on some of them if you use them incorrectly or attempt to repair them yourself without proper knowledge or training. Your own two hands are still the best implements known to man, and this applies to cooking as well as other crafts. I have still to understand why the electric dishwasher is the ultimate desideratum in so many American minds; and the electric laundry washer-drier, it seems to me, deprives us not only of a low monthly electricity bill, but of one of the most satisfactory forms of exercise our lives afford.

So does the electric juicer, a fixture in many an American kitchen. Squeeze your oranges on an old-fashioned glass manual juicer and you'll get your isometric exercise for the day. In depression glass, these juicers are now claiming fancy prices, but you can still get one in the five-and-dime for under half a dollar. (By the way, you'll get more juice out of citrus fruit if it is warmer than refrigerator temperature when you squeeze it.)

The deep-fat fryer (which could, of course, be constructed of a large saucepan plus a slightly smaller strainer) is probably an item most kitchens should be *without*. French fried potatoes and other vegetables deep-fried in batter are purely once-in-a-while, luxury items in terms of the nutritive value you can derive from them, as well as in the amount of high-fat eating they encourage. Besides, the exquisite (and exquisitely cheap) potato-peeling chitlins found on page 201 can be made in any skillet.

Descending one step in cost, here are some further examples of kitchen equipment the economy-minded gourmet can do without. (If you just like the *look* of them, pick them up at auctions or secondhand shops for pennies and hang them around the kitchen for decoration.)

EGG SEPARATOR: One of my favorite uselessnesses. The shell of any fowl's egg performs this function admirably.

AUTOMATIC SALAD-GREENS DRIER: Rinsing greens

under the cold-water faucet, then wrapping them in a turkish towel does perfectly well.

CORER: A small, sharp knife and twist of the wrist is the ticket.

KNIFE SHARPENER: There are stones lying around your yard, or in the nearest city park or empty lot, that will do the job.

ELECTRIC ICE-CRUSHER: What's the matter with a heavy-duty cotton bag plus a little hammer or mallet?

COOKIE CUTTERS IN FANCY SHAPES: Your fingers, and funnels or jar tops, do just as well, and leave more room for creativity.

PASTRY BLENDER: Two knives or the tines of a fork are not inferior for this.

ENGLISH MUFFIN BREAKER: This keeps turning up in hardware stores and catalogs; I can't imagine why. Fingers and forks were made before English muffin breakers.

If you're going in for ethnic specialty cooking, then obviously you'll want to acquire some pieces of equipment that go with the national cuisine you're adopting. A pasta machine can save you hours of laborious cutting by hand; a *crêpe* pan should be bought and kept for *crêpe*-making only, and is a handsome wall-hanger. But a wok for stir-frying will be useful to the Chinese cooking aficionado only if accompanied by one of those collar-shaped stands. The burners on conventional stoves are not designed to support a wok, which is not a great advantage for the occidental cook over a plain cast-iron skillet. A soufflé dish, no matter what you've been told, does not have to possess absolutely perpendicular sides; a foolproof soufflé is made perfectly in an ordinary round Pyrex baking dish—and by now knows no nationality.

One of the secrets of equipping your kitchen efficiently and economically is not to buy anything that is not a versatile tool, that does not have a wide variety of uses. It may seem manifest, but you'd be surprised how often a person setting out to equip his newly acquired kitchen will—entranced by a department store he's entered for the first time (the "Gourmet Cook" department, naturally) or a fancy shop's fetching catalog—fall prey to a semi-soft-cheese mill (when the only semi-soft cheese he'll ever eat grated he'll buy that way) or a spaetzle and dumpling maker (because it's such a well-designed, handsome instrument), shooting the works on that very special utensil before he's even got a saucepan or skillet, the basic implements without which one can't begin to get a meal together. A jellyroll pan is hardly a necessity if you're not going to be a mad jellyroll maker. Even if you are, a jellyroll can be fashioned nicely in a general-purpose oblong baking pan, which you can use for anything from a roasted turkey to lasagne to cookies (a cookie sheet is not a must either, you see).

Another secret to keep in mind is that there's nothing wrong in using your fingers for any number of operations that tools have been made for: butter-molders and rubber scrapers being two utensils that leap to mind. For some processes in food preparation, fingers are the *only* utensils that work: bread-kneading, for example, or the tearing up of salad greens. I was going to add removing the pits from cherries, when lo and behold, I turned a page of a mail-order catalog and came upon—you guessed it—a sterling silver cherry-pitter.

If you plan to become a Preserver, there is a new *world* of equipment just waiting for you to weaken and buy. Home preserving is an excellent way to save food money. It's not only for the country person with a garden; even the city-bound can take advantage of seasonal bargains by purchasing produce in quantity and putting up some of it. More and more people are doing just that every year in these inflationary times. Don't, however, go out and buy yourself an electric smokehouse, a jelly thermometer, six dozen canning jars (if you can find them), a cheese wedge, and a sausage-stuffing machine, until you have thought the problem through and decided what kinds of preserving you're likely to start

6

in on. Even then, you ought not to launch yourself into this realm without reading a good book on the subject (for example, *Home Preserving Made Easy* by Vera Gewanter and Dorothy Parker). In such a book you can learn how to fashion your own equipment for the specialty you are going to try your hand at.

Surrounded as I am in my present living circumstances by ripening apples and grapes, I plan within weeks to make tons of grape-apple jelly, jam, wine, and syrups and butters, as a means of keeping these delightful fruits far longer than the few weeks of their perfect ripeness. All I'm going to need for these endeavors is a bunch of cheesecloth, a canning kettle (inherited from my mother), a collection of fruit jars that I've eaten the bought food from and will sterilize, and a few empty wine, soft drink, and ketchup bottles. Plus the usual all-purpose utensils such as pots and pans and spoons and string that are in every kitchen. And more than the usual complement of sugar—which I will have to buy, because that questionable commodity is what will do the job of preserving. (During other seasons of the year, the only sugar in my house is that which comes home from my once-a-week restaurant meal plus occasional coffee-wagon patronizing when I am on my day-and-a-half-in-the-office weekly work stint.)

The key is to pick tools with several functions, and to come by them in any way you can, short of purchasing them in some posh shop. The next time someone asks me what gift I want, in honor of some occasion or other, I'm going to put in a request for either a fruit press or a large copper bowl. The latter will, I'm told by good authority, produce a far greater volume of beaten egg whites. I don't know whether to believe this or not (I do know that adding a bit of vinegar to them does); but that gleaming copper moon will be so spectacular a decoration hanging in my kitchen next to the old blue enamel frypan I found in the dump. The former—the press—is probably too expensive for any of the gift-givers I know, so I'll doubtless just go on using

7

the small wooden salad bowl against the rigid plastic colander, plus a lot of elbow grease. Besides, there is in my locality a commercial press, a shop to which you can take your bushels of apples to have them pressed into cider. I hope there's one in your town, too, for this is a much cheaper way to get your autumn supply of cider than buying it in the markets.

Distributors of largesse being in short supply, you may have to rely on your own ingenuity to outfit your scullery in the fashion to which you'd like to become accustomed. Every writer of food books has his own notion of what the absolute essentials are, depending on his or her characteristics as a cook. I promise this: never will you have read a list so pared down but so capable of such a wide range and variety of cooking, accomplished at so low a cost. To support the last part of this contention, I shall append copious notes on the acquisition of these basic tools—and such other fascinating lore as occurs to me.

Necessary tools, implements, equipment. A list, sort of.

A LARGE DUTCH OVEN OR STOVE-TO-TABLE CASSEROLE DISH: Cast-iron will last the longest, cook the most evenly; glazed ceramic may look the spiffiest on the dining table. Buy cut-rate or find in the town dump. I keep looking for one in *my* dump. No luck yet . . . however I do have two large, cast-aluminum, covered skillets that I found there. Can't understand why my benefactor threw them out—almost brand new. They have cooked many a chili or stew for a crowd of eight or ten at my house.

A LARGE COVERED SKILLET: If I had to choose, I'd choose cast-iron. Buy cut-rate. Or find in rummage or garage sale.

TWO SAUCEPANS WITH COVERS: Again, cast-iron is best, but don't refuse aluminum if offered you for Christmas. Opaque tempered glass is even possible, though shorter-lived—can be secured in groups of two or three with a modest bank deposit sometimes. Just be sure to put a trivet between this sort of saucepan and direct heat. They can double as baking dishes. Should you come across two saucepans minus covers, grab them. You can always find lids that nearly match; somewhat larger lids work fine for most purposes. Pot covers are among the principal throwaways on the streets of major cities.

AT LEAST ONE OBLONG ALUMINUM BAKING PAN: This is the guy that cooks everything from turkey to fudge (unless you want a smaller one for sweets-making, which is a good idea). Mine came from East 12th Street, New York City, where it was waiting for the refuse collector, having been discarded after a batch of lasagne had been cooked in it (there was a little bit still adhering—that's how I know). It quickly soaked clean and left me with one of my most-longed-for pieces of equipment.

TWO OR THREE ROUND METAL PIE PLATES: Easiest thing in the world to acquire without paying for. People consider them disposable and will tell you to keep the one under the pie they brought you as a house gift. Or you clean and reuse the one in which you bought a frozen dessert. These can double as cake pans.

GLASS BAKING DISHES: One rectangular loaf-shaped, one round, are what I bake bread in weekly. One cost under a dollar years ago, the other was a street-find. If you try not to drop them on the floor, they'll last forever.

A GLASS OR ALUMINUM COFFEE POT: Again can be picked up for pennies in secondhand and thrift shops. If you're an instant-coffee type, unnecessary. But fine for cooking asparagus (stand it up in the pot, so the tips get steamed while the bottoms boil).

A DOUBLE BOILER: Essential if you make puddings and other such desserts, some sauces, candies. My nearly retired one, of aluminum, was a wedding present; my smaller "new" one achieved by floating in water an enamel saucepan from the dump.

A FRENCH STEAMER: Since steaming most vegetables is the way to render them edible while retaining the optimum nutritional value, you may be tempted to buy one of those cute little items with the holes, flip-flop fins and all. Why not get the same effect by combining a metal strainer (the kind with "ears" to rest on edges of things) and a large saucepan?

METAL STRAINERS: Two sizes will do it, the larger for such uses as mentioned above, the smaller for tea and tinier strainings. A five-and-dime-store item. Though some mail-order houses illustrate in their catalogs a handsome four-size set that would make attractive hanging decorations, for $2.98.

A COLANDER: Indispensable for getting certain foods to the table hot (drained and served before they have a chance to cool). Metal is more expensive than rigid plastic, which mine is, given to me by a friend breaking up housekeeping.

MIXING BOWLS IN SEVERAL SIZES: Obviously, any number of the items mentioned above can double for mixing. But this gives me a chance to tell you about the multicolored plastic set (with covers) I got free, which has been among my most treasured implements for years. The set of six in graduated sizes was a premium from a mail-order house trying to sell me a fake leather briefcase or something on a "trial basis." Naturally I found the leatherette item unsatisfactory and returned it—but have enjoyed the gaily colored plastic bowls ever since! They have been doing triple duty as mixers, storage containers, and lunchtime serving bowls.

STORING CANISTERS: Wooden firkins are charming and attractive but cost more than they should. Plastic-topped coffee cans, on the other hand, cost only a few pennies more than buying your coffee fresh-ground in a bag (and on sale can cost less). If painted or covered with sticky-backed paper, they make a useful set of matching canisters.

REFRIGERATOR STORAGE DISHES: Anyone who buys these must be throwing away a lot of immortal glass and plastic that gets paid for at the grocery store every week. Dairy items are an especially good source of covered plastic storing dishes, as is the delicatessen department of your friendly neighborhood supermarket. Cut-off milk or juice cartons of waxed cardboard make excellent freezer-storage containers, their square shape allowing you to utilize more space than the round plastic ones.

A HARDWOOD CUTTING BOARD: Butcher block is peachy, of course, but it's become so fashionable of late that it's prohibitively expensive. If you have a butcher block top on something, you're in. If not, hang around a road crew at work on a tree-lined street after an electrical storm or some other natural disaster that has made it necessary to cut down some trees. Ask for a slice from their chain saws. That's how a friend of mine obtained her decorative and useful round kitchen cutting board. Mine, believe it or not, of stout hickory wood, showing all its growth rings and still bearing its rugged, nubby bark, was picked up off the sidewalk on West 11th Street in New York City. (Just don't let the highwaymen foist on you a section of old felled telephone pole—they tend to be soaked with creosote or some such substance. Though they can't be used in preparing food, they do make dandy plant stands, doorstops, and bed legs.)

SMALL WOODEN BOWL: Mine was a "reject," so it cost only pennies at a wood objects shop in Vermont. Such seconds often display prettier wood pattern and more interesting shapes than "firsts." In addition to its function as part of a fruit press (see pages 7–8), it is half of a . . .

MORTAR AND PESTLE: Of which the other half is a little wooden gavel, left over from my stint as presiding officer of something or other. Works fine as mortar and pestle, though the heavy metal (brass or bronze?) pestles are very decorative in an old-fashioned way, and the porcelain ones are sleek and moderne.

GRATER-SLICER: Mine is a French Mouli-Julienne, a metal object with several sizes of blade, that resembles one of the machines that landed on the moon. *Very* useful, but a gift from a grateful cookbook author—and so a cheat for this list. The oblong stainless steel one with the handle top still costs less than two dollars and will give years of rustless service.

A SWIVEL-TYPE VEGETABLE PEELER: A good thing to have, even if you have an oblong grater-slicer. Costs only eighty-nine cents in my dime store, less from a sidewalk vendor.

KNIVES: In various sizes and shapes for their various purposes, are always assembled by the developing cook and money-saver, by fair means or foul. Carbon steel,* though long-lived, is not essential to efficient chopping, slicing, boning, peeling. Look for some kitchen knives in the carpentry workshop of your home. A cleaver by any other name fells as neat.

POULTRY SHEARS: Can definitely be found in the toolbox, where they are known as wire-cutters.

NUT CRACKERS: Are called wrenches or pliers, and can double as . . .

SHELLFISH HANDLING IMPLEMENTS

LONG STEEL NAILS: While you're raiding the household workshop to outfit your kitchen, you may as well pick up some of these, which can be used as skewers for shashlik-like dishes, for baking root vegetables and potatoes faster, for trussing birds, etc.

A SMALL HAMMER: From the same place, for crushing ice, tenderizing meat, making cutlets.

STOUT UNDYED THREAD AND LARGE-HEADED NEEDLE: From your sewing box, for doing up those stuffed birds.

MEASURING CUPS: One for dry, one for liquid. Are

* Never use carbon steel on strawberries—it will turn them black. Unless of course, you favor black strawberries.

12

usually acquired at household showers or other modest-gift affairs. Mine were bummed from my mother, who for some reason had about eight of them.

MEASURING SPOONS: If you're fussy about exact measurements. If not, your soup spoon, teaspoon and demitasse spoon will do quite as well. This was another department in which my mother was unaccountably well supplied, so I have two sets, graduated sizes, strung together for hanging. One tin, one copper. Quite decorative.

SPATULAS AND OTHER HOT-FOOD HANDLING TOOLS: Wooden ones are handsome, especially ensconced like a bouquet of flowers in a mug or jar by your stoveside. But metal ones do just as well for most purposes, and seem to be discarded with abandon by weary owners. My own favorite slotted spatula is aluminum and lacks its handle, which I find no disadvantage. I found it in a city apartment building incinerator room.

A PAIR OF TONGS: Essential for most cooks. Mine are left over from a formula-bottling set presented to me on the birth of my son twenty-seven years ago.

WHISKS: Are necessary to the would-be saucier; but not in six graduated sizes. Get *one*, unless you want them for decoration. Mine was bought for pfennigs, along with some coupons saved from home-baking materials.

OTHER STIRRERS: Bring home chopsticks from a Chinese restaurant, or save them from the Chinese take-home meal you resort to on a tired Friday night. Also good for digging stuck raisins out of boxes and such. One of my favorite stirrers is a fat wooden crocheting needle, with which my sister once made herself a porous sweater-dress, before she switched to needlepoint.

OTHER BEATERS, WHIPPERS: I have in mind the good old-fashioned hand-operated rotary eggbeater. It

13

went out of style (and hence can be picked up for peanuts in any flea market or country auction) when the electric mixer became a *must*. It is still the best way to whip eggs, whites only or entire. My own rotary eggbeater was given to me by a friend who was redecorating his kitchen pegboard.

APRONS: Though you may not think them chic, they really do save clothing from spots and stains. Of course you never buy one, you are given them by people who frequent church bazaars, gift shoppes, and such. You can also tie a discarded old shirt around your waist, or simply wear it if it's large enough to function as a smock. My own favorite apron is a very utilitarian-looking one with a row of pockets spelling out *Newsweek*.

POTHOLDERS: Never make the mistake of using a loosely crocheted one—you'll burn your hands through the holes. Easiest thing in the world to make from old discarded towels and other scraps of fabric.

COOKING CUFFS: If you save money in winter by keeping the heat low, you will find yourself cooking in long sleeves. Protect them from wetting and staining with a pair of cuffs left over from a shirt or dress you altered from long- to short-sleeved. Or run some elastic through one end of some denim tubes.

METAL FOIL: Without which most ongoing kitchen operators can't live. Should never be bought. If you don't have a large roasting pan with a cover, you'll need foil to cover the tops of certain birds and beasts while roasting. It just comes to you in all kinds of ways: wrapped around foods you bring home from restaurants, for example, around certain cereals, and so on.

WAX PAPER: Ditto. Look inside the boxes in which you buy cereals, gelatins, bread, crackers, and some other products. Sticks of butter and margarine come wrapped in it; once you've spilled the sticks out, these wrappers should be stowed in the refrigerator for greasing baking dishes and pans.

PLASTIC STRETCH WRAP: This may seem a bit more difficult to come by for nothing. But the next time you buy a small quantity of some vegetable in the supermarket, look and see what it's wrapped in. Peel it off carefully. It may even be the sort of stretch wrap that seals to itself. Don't ever fall prey to that seductive TV advertising again!

PLASTIC BAGS: Yes, *necessary* to the economy-minded cook, who wraps leftovers in them, covers dishes for the refrigerator, sends people to school or work carrying lunches, freezes separate portions of wholesale-cooked meals in them, etc. They come to you in all sizes, weights, shapes, colors, and consistencies, every day: on foods you buy, magazines you subscribe to, books you order, many articles of clothing, hardware, or gadgetry. Save every one you get, and you won't ever have to buy *plastic bags*.

This concludes my list of essential equipment. Except for three items that I have on my "maybe" list:

LONG-HANDLED BOTTLE BRUSH: An item that bit the dust in one of my house moves. You *can* make do with hot water and a supply of tiny pebbles—but it's not the same.

MUFFIN TIN, WITH CUPS: The one "extra" kitchen item I regret giving away when paring down, and I must soon find another in the dump or on the street, which is where my original one came from. Corn muffins and all sorts of biscuits and cupcakes can be made just as well in a flat square baking pan, then cut into serving pieces. But not popovers, which are fun.

GARLIC PRESS: One item I don't know whether to include in essential or nonessential equipment. Mine is such a good-looking object (Italian-made) that I have it hanging on the wall over my kitchen sink. I notice that I don't very often take it down. This is because I've long since discovered that minced garlic (or shallots) is just as proper in a recipe that calls for pressed garlic. It's easy to mash a clove of garlic quickly with a fork, putting the skin into your soup bag—and that way, there's no chance that the garlic press will lend a metallic flavor to the garlic.

There now, with all the money you've saved equipping your kitchen, you'll be able to lay in a year's supply of staples like flours, grains, salt, pepper and other spices, herbs and other seasonings, coffee beans, teas and other exotica, baking soda, and vinegar.

EQUIPMENT POSTSCRIPT: Should you be persuaded to go all out for beautiful hands, invest in a pair and a half of rubber gloves (that's how they're customarily sold: one left and two rights). Use one, the double number, for your principal working-cooking hand (presumably the manufacturer doesn't discriminate against left-handed persons, and you can get two lefts and one right), one this year, the other the next. The single one can be kept handy for a wraparound jar opener. Then you won't have to buy one of those inexpensive but nonessential (and highly perishable) little items called jar-openers. And you can put the sixty-nine cents into a good corkscrew-can opener.

2

"I SET THE BEST TABLE
IN MALDEN, MASSACHUSETTS"

A quotation from my maternal grandmother, a modest and retiring dowager when I met her, in reduced circumstances and dreaming of the days when she was the reigning hostess in what was then a suburb a long way from Boston. This was no idle boast; to help her charm and nurture her family and frequent guests, she had in her employ—not to mention the "upstairs" staff—a cook, a serving-maid, and a butler. With that formidable array of minions, who couldn't set the best table? Or have it set *for* her.

The dining room in those prehistoric days was a place to be reckoned with. Filled to bursting with overbearing furniture—tables that paneled out to enormous size, buffets and serving tables and tea wagons and dozens of chairs and who-knows-what—the dining room was a space where huge amounts of money could be spent on appointments and embellishments. Think of the fortunes in silver service alone that were squandered by our forebears in order that Madame should not be embarrassed at tea; of the thousands of dollars in lace and damask and such, so that a dining table should be properly "dressed." (Consider, too, the man- or woman-hours spent weekly on keeping that silver gleaming, that napery spotless and wrinkle-free!)

Today we should all be thankful that the dining room, if indeed it exists at all, is usually tucked into one corner of the living room, or at one end of a large "country kitchen"

17

where informality is the keynote. When dining with friends, we are likely to find not a footman in livery behind every chair, but a pair of hosts cooperating on the meal and its preparation, serving, and cleaning-up after. A different imported wine with every course has very likely given way to one good bottle of domestic red, white, or rosé. Indeed, if any alcoholic beverages are on hand, they may have been made by the friends themselves (see Chapter 9). Rather than a linen tablecloth starched within an inch of its life, we very often find we are eating from a bare oak table top—and what's more handsome and fun to eat from than a scrubbed wooden table? I say praise the Lord for this simpler life.

Place mats, if something in you recoils from good honest wood, are part of dressing up your dining surface. They can be fashioned from all sorts of materials that you just naturally have in your possession: leftover quarter-rolls of wallpaper, all those scraps of fabric that you stowed away in the patchwork-quilting bag, clothing you're about to give away, old curtains or windowshades. One clever place mat I recently ate supper on was a square of fake-brick linoleum. Place mats don't have to be cork from Spain, woven grass from mainland China or Taiwan, or plastic from J. C. Penney's—let your imagination go and see what you have lying around that is no longer performing the function for which it was originally obtained. One of my cheeriest sets of mats was formerly an orange corduroy skirt! But then, one of my most festive hostess skirts used to be a Mexican tablecloth. Never get stuck with a fabric object serving a limited function if you don't like, or have tired of, it as *that*. Change it to something else. My current set of potholders was for years a blue cotton paisley blouse; I stuffed them with several layers of aging terry cloth towel, and they hang up by some excess drapery rings fastened into their corners.

To get back to the dining table and its seductive pitfalls for the would-be economizer: one cardinal rule to follow if you are going to buy your own glassware, china, and other eating accessories is to avoid buying a "good" set for company only. One set of dishes, simple in design and decoration, is the ticket. Plain white "seconds" from a cut-rate ceramics outfitter are mine, because I like the shapes and colors and textures of the food I put on them to provide the visual (as well as olfactory and gustatory) interest of the meal. The wine goblets are from the five-and-ten-cent store, plus a couple swiped from a wine-tasting party that was a promotion scheme for the debut of some book or other years ago. The flat silver is not silver at all but the remains of a set of stainless steel eating tools bought from a mail-order house years ago for something like five dollars, bolstered by some silver plate picked up from here and there. They don't match, but the *coq au vin* or *moussaka* tastes just as good from them.

After-dinner coffee is drunk from a tea set left over from my childhood (the cups and saucers are demitasse size), and those silly enough to want to add sugar stir with an unmatched (naturally) set of tiny souvenir spoons that my grandmother used to collect, plus a couple "borrowed" from an airplane meal.

The appetizer course, when there is one (and when there is, dessert is usually omitted) is served (if it's soup) in a set of coffee mugs—four were a Happy New Home gift from a visiting friend, the others brought home from offices or dumps. If it's something like shrimp cocktail, I serve it in—guess what—shrimp cocktail glasses, twenty-three of which I once found abandoned in a glass-recycling center where I had taken my old bottles and jars. These remarkable objects also double as parfait glasses, or hold fruit compotes and other desserts. We also take our morning fruit juice from them.

If you don't have an obliging glass-recycling center near you, or yours is the kind where the excess glass is shattered upon deposit, I recommend that you canvass your incinerator room, the sidewalks you walk every day, or the town dump for your set of dinner plates, butter dishes, salad bowls, goblets, and mugs—people throw away the oddest things! My set of complete luncheon place settings for three—large and small plates, cups and saucers, sauce dishes and soup plates—weren't even chipped! (Chipped or nicked or discolored or minus their cups, saucers are among the most easily come-by items—and they make good flower-pot holders.)

Sometimes hors d'oeuvres (and once in a while a side dish or a dessert) are eaten from individual scallop shells—you know, those natural objects that look like the Shell Oil trademark. This is an idea I picked up from a Hostess-with-the-Mostest (in fact, she had just completed a cooking course with the late Michael Field, *chef extraordinaire*). She was giving a large soignée party for about twenty-four people, who milled around conversationally, eating a divine mussels-in-sour-cream out of scallop shells with plastic spoons, as their first course before sitting down to dinner. No one seemed any the less impressed with the rightness of things because he had picked up his appetizer from a tray passed around by the host, and no one seemed to notice that he wasn't eating it from a crystal dish with a silver spoon. Need-less to say, I soon thereafter picked up, from a seaside where I was strolling, enough scallop and clam shells of a nearly uniform size to use at my next dinner party.

The appropriateness of eating some foods from recep-tacles related to them in nature—if not, indeed, their own perfect containers—is indisputable. It is also often the least expensive method of providing yourself with dining room ware. Can a lobster shell be said to be its perfect "dish"? Yes. And likewise melon rinds, which we eat melon out of. (The unique perfection of the egg's pristine container is one to watch out for—Europeans seem to be better than Ameri-cans, for some reason, at eating soft-boiled eggs directly from their shells.) "Fingers were made before forks," as the old ones sometimes remind us. The skins or rinds or shells seem so obvious a means of serving some foods that we would laugh if a guest, on being offered his choice from our centerpiece bowl of fruit, selected a banana, then peeled it, discarded the skin, and proceeded to cut it up with his knife and eat it with his fork.

Have you ever thought of serving a warm or cold soup from a hollowed-out pumpkin or winter squash? Or a combined-fruit dessert from the shell of the half watermelon that provided some of the fruit? What can be more attractive, and more chic, than putting mayonnaise, sour cream, or some other cold sauce on the table for serving in scooped-out halves of green or red bell peppers?

Speaking of flowerpot holders (as we were a few paragraphs back), my first experience of really good, non-burn-your-tongue-up chili was served to me by a sculptor friend, on a dishtowel place mat, in one of those earthenware flowerpot saucers, fairly large size. (A group of these was her "company" dinnerware, brought home to the city from her country greenhouse, where the previous tenant had left lots of flowerpots behind.) With the large unglazed terra-cotta tureen that was put directly on the table as centerpiece, and accompanied by glass mugs of beer or water, it was an unbelievably tasty, attractive, and nutritious one-dish meal.

The size and shape of my dining table are such that my centerpieces tend to be the One Dish of a one-dish meal, or one of the dishes of a more-than-one-dish meal. Or a fresh-baked loaf of bread on a cutting board for people to help themselves to. Providing still-warm breads in two colors (one for the white-bread holdouts), with a slicing knife laid between, will save you a good deal of money, since you need serve almost nothing else for supper—and will make your reputation, too, as a splendid home cook.

Joking aside, one whole-grain plus one white loaf of steaming just-out-of-the-oven bread, plus a hearty soup or chowder (see Chapter 7) and a salad afterwards, need no apology as a company supper on any night of the week. It is far cheaper than the roast you were thinking of but

21

found you couldn't afford. The salad should be put on the table at the same time as the soup; let your guests decide in what order they want to eat—some may want to do the whole thing together. Now you have two centerpieces, the soup tureen and the big salad bowl. Let them mix their own dressing, if it's a simple oil-and-vinegar deal, by decorating the table with those handsome glass bottles given to you by a chemist friend—a sneaky way of informing you that *my* oil and vinegar stays decoratively on my kitchen counter in a handsome (free because a gift) pair of glass lab bottles with glass stopples. On the table, too, of course, are your salt and pepper shakers or grinders. (A stunning wooden pair of which is currently being advertised as a premium for a dollar and several of the proper labels. If I weren't already rich in salt and pepper shakers, I'd have sent for them long ago, as that's a very good price.)

Sometimes the centerpiece can be the food you're going to eat for dessert, as in a lovely arrangement of fresh fruit, cleaned and shining, displaying its various colors and forms, with nuts and flowers-in-season added if you wish. Or use the zucchini you're not going to cook until day after tomorrow, with some yellow and red tomatoes grouped around it for color contrast. Borrow a flowering plant for the occasion from its accustomed place in the window. Even your potted herbs can be called into service, or a bouquet of herbs on their stems in a vase. Don't think that a vase of roses from the posh florist, or carnations from the subway station, are the only floral decorations that will grace your "company" dining table. One of the prettiest I've been treated to lately was a bowl sprouting fresh green leaves of Swiss chard with a few coreopsis from the host's garden among them.

Don't imagine, either, that the only way that flowers can decorate your table is in a carefully arranged center-piece. A few daisies and clover blossoms picked from the side of the road and arranged in shot glasses between each two place settings cheerfully enhanced the dining pleasure of a table where I recently feasted. When this particular couple comes back to my house, I'm going to surprise them with an empty red rifle shellcase at each of their plates, with the tiny, perky snow-white blossoms pinched off my flowering basil plant pouring their incomparable aroma into the air. (It seems the best use I can think of for those unhappy remnants I found in my patch of woodland.) Beside each shellcase-vase will be a candle (homemade, thus inexpensive) in a candleholder found in the home workshop: a large-size silver-colored nut, from the nuts-and-bolts department of the garage shelf.

Another miniature bouquet for the individual place setting could be made of some forget-me-nots or bachelor's buttons from your lawn, put into a few thimbles which have been fixed in a bit of candlewax or modeling clay so they won't topple over.

If these costless decorative notions strike you as a bit cute, but your entertaining budget remains peasantlike, you may want to put on the dog by moving some ceramic piece or sculpture usually found in another location to the dining table for the occasion. A friend of mine uses her children's plaster-of-Paris schoolroom efforts for centerpieces whenever company is coming. This serves the double purpose of providing conversation pieces and pleasing her offspring, who seem more willing to remain in their rooms for the party's duration. I have a red-feathered cardinal, a model bird, whom I may soon induce to perch colorfully among the pieces of whitened applewood and the hickory and maple leaves in their full spectrum of autumn colors on my table. Needless to say, all the parts of this table decoration are "found objects" and hence costless. If you live near the shore rather than an orchard, driftwood can make an effective centerpiece, perhaps with some beach plum leaves. The small round red crab apples, each attached to a twig and a leaf or two, with which another friend recently decorated her evening dining table, were effective. But for that you have to *own* the orchard, or live next door to someone who does.

The apple-sporting hostess, by the way, created a heroic confusion when it came time for everyone to sit down at a largish dinner table and convinced me of the occasional necessity for that archaic convention, the place card. I think she prides herself on being very up-to-the-minute, but things would have gone far more smoothly at her fete if she had placed small cards with large letters on them at each place setting. Any time you are seating more than six at dinner, this old-fashioned device is "in" again. If you want pleasant choreography rather than traffic jams around your dining room, place cards are a favor to your guests. They needn't cost anything either. Spring-type clothespins, standing on their non-business ends, holding little pieces of cardboard sliced out of throwaway mailing pieces, can perform the function very well. Or a lump of modeling clay borrowed from your infant's toy chest, into which you've stuck half an old greeting card, reversed. When the number of guests approaches crowd size, there's nothing like an orderly procession around the table in search of one's place to promote a feeling of serenity in the host's or hostess's heart, without which you may flub what might otherwise have been a dandy party.

Many homemakers go broke with a tradition of the season for going broke: yuletide table decorations. The kitchen economizer can somehow manage homemade Halloween adornments, home-cooked items for the Easter-Pesach season, a cornucopia of later-edibles during Thanksgiving, even red-white-and-blue flowers or icings in July. But something says "spend money" when it comes time to do things up for Chanukah or Christmas. A silly little fake pink or white Christmas tree and a brace of plastic reindeer must be purchased at larcenous prices, and gobs of cotton batting fussed around it on the dining table. When a handsome branch of fir or cedar or pine picked up beside the road or from under the city vendor's ranks of Christmas trees would look (and smell) far superior.

If you're gaga for those highly perishable spherical baubles that hang from many a Christmas tree, who can blame you? I am too. And I'm always shocked at the number of these ornaments that get cracked or fractured by the end of any yuletide season. *Don't* throw them away and start all over again next year; a very gala centerpiece for next Christmas can be achieved by arranging the damaged ornaments (if they're not smashed into a million pieces), broken side in, in a transparent bowl or vase. This arrangement has been my favorite holiday season centerpiece for years, and I can never bear to pack it away at New Year's time. With the result that friends have come into my house in March or April and wondered at the large clear-glass vase full of Christmas tree ornaments and tiny pine cones. (Pine cones, by the way, store well and can be packed away after New Year's Day with your other tree ornaments and used again next year.)

Holiday or not, a dinner for guests is a time for you to cook one of your foolproof meals, not to experiment with not-yet-tried-out dishes. One way to save money in the dining room is not to waste time and foodstuffs by cooking up an elaborate failure; stick to the tried-and-true that you have already mastered, and no one will be tempted to leave any on the plate. If it doesn't *look* just the way you think it ought to, turn out the dining room lights and go with candlelight. Not only will every person and every viand look better, but you will be saving money on electricity as well. If you've stowed your company candles in the freezer, they will burn slower and last longer. Don't forget to turn out all the lights in the other rooms too: it's not true what you've heard all these years about using up more electricity switching on and off than in leaving your lamps burning for a couple of hours. Don't neglect the stove either—be sure it is turned off, too. Your well-insulated oven will keep things warm for second helpings. If you can douse the oil or electric heat in the dining area, too, and perhaps light a fire in the fireplace, you are ready to sit down to a meal that will cost very little in utility bills.

A well-cooked dinner served simply but elegantly, accompanied by easy talk with good friends, is *still* the best form of entertainment going, whether it takes place in the dining room, the kitchen, off laps in the living room, on the terrace, or out-of-doors. And it needn't cost you an arm, a leg, or your reputation as one of the greatest party-givers ever. Read on.

3

THE PRACTICE
OF FOODMANSHIP

Getting decent meals on the table without going broke continues to be a stimulating challenge to most of my compatriots. Since prices of everything show no signs of diminishing, while incomes doggedly observe the status quo (if indeed they don't shrink, or disappear entirely), pity is not too strong an emotion to direct toward the unfortunate on whom rests the major responsibility for the nutritional life of a home. Beset on every side by admonitions against every sort of "bargain" food, the dangerous high-cholesterol nature of the typical American diet, and the tendency of convenience foods to poison, we find ourselves spending week by week a larger and larger proportion of the family income on a smaller and smaller amount of groceries. By now we know that a balanced diet with the emphasis on high protein is the secret of health and happiness; but how to balance the diet and the budget, too, is often beyond our imagination and capabilities. If, like me, you can remember a time (during the Great Depression) when a family of four could be fed adequately on three dollars a week, well, you're in luck—and can borrow some tricks from your penny-pinching mother. But like as not you grew up in the fat fifties, when no culinary alchemy had to be practiced, which means that saving money in the kitchen is just a great big maddening frustration, an impossibility.

Nonsense. I'm here to prove that the food life of a

home need not cause anyone to declare bankruptcy or suffer malnutrition or a nervous breakdown. Even in these days of spiraling inflation it's possible to serve a beautiful, nourishing, well-cooked dinner every evening and have enough left over from your household allowance to pay the utility bills too.

Having kept a record of all my food purchases over the last six months of high-priced 1975–76, I can announce with pride and satisfaction that the total bill was $206.70, or an average of $7.95 a week. Admittedly my "family" in this time consisted of two adults and one aged cat, but we did have company to meals often—and no complaints. Part of my secret, I have to confess, has been to live in the country, surrounded by good, misguided amateur farmers who failed to stagger their plantings, so that at harvest time a certain amount of gorgeous produce came my way at a very low price. The city dweller can achieve an almost identical saving by seeking out the produce markets (often in ethnic neighborhoods) and learning when—what part of the day or week—the stand operator is likely to mark down the fruits and vegetables he hasn't sold yet, to make room for the next shipment. Late Saturday afternoons are often a good time in cities to take advantage of this kind of a markdown. The end of the selling period on any weekday is the right time in some localities.

I can hear you protesting, "But I am a fully employed person, I don't have time to go running around to this shop and that market to find a leftover cucumber or the lowest price on onions!" Of course you don't; but remember your friendly supermarket, the place where on the way home from work you can buy *everything*—the produce department there too has been known to overstock a fresh item and then face the prospect of having to discard much of it on Monday if it's not sold at a markdown price on Saturday afternoon. Patronize its "day-old" bins of fruits and vegetables, as well as the "reduced price" baskets of tinned or packaged groceries. These marked-down items in a chain store can often reduce your grocery bill by half. If the produce manager hasn't thought to reduce the aging squash, suggest it to him! Remind him that the condition of that slightly dried artichoke the next day will represent a total loss to him. Tell him that the fast-darkening bananas will have to be thrown out tomorrow (whereas half of them will make you a lovely dessert tonight and half go into a milkshake or a loaf of tea bread for you tomorrow). You may be able to convince him to reduce the price to one quarter of the original. A slightly bruised peach still has nine tenths of the luscious eating in it that a perfect round globe just unwrapped has, but may cost only one third the pennies of its more coveted younger sister. Produce department managers have even been known to *give* away tired fruits and vegetables to regular customers, rather than have to throw them out the next day. Try *your* fruit-and-vegetable person—who knows?

A public relations woman I know in New York City spends most of her Saturday afternoons traveling across lower Manhattan from her West Village apartment to the neighborhood on the fringes of Little Italy, where she shops for her produce for the week to come. She walks a different route each time, for exercise and amusement and sight-seeing, then busses back (for economy) with her packages. The funny thing is that she cooks almost entirely Chinese, believing in its charm and healthfulness, and frugality as well. Once a month or so she makes a special trip to China-town to pick up exotica like *bok choy* (the Chinese cabbage of your childhood), cloud-ear mushrooms, and the like. She is fully convinced that this weekly expedition, besides being her favorite form of leisure-time activity, saves eight to ten dollars a week on her food bill.

Other people I know swear by the Ninth Avenue markets near Forty-Second Street as the place they most like to spend a strolling Saturday afternoon, returning to their Upper West Side abodes with the week's supply of meats and produce ten to twelve dollars richer than they would be if they marketed only at the local chain store. And having seen how life is lived in Hell's Kitchen or Little Greece as well. *Your* city includes some areas of bargain markets, too—find out where they are.

Another advantage to spending Saturday afternoons this way is that you have already eaten breakfast or brunch, and you are shopping for food at a time when you're not starving. Shopping hungry, as we all know, is one certain path to exceeding the food budget—buying tempting items you don't really need and that don't appear on your marketing list. (You can fall prey to this tendency in ethnic neighborhoods just as well as in the on-the-way-home-from-work anonymous supermarket.) Make a stringent list—and don't overspill its bounds!

The next *sine qua non* for the crafty money-saver is comparison shopping. If you have the time, the mobility, and your name on the right mailing lists, you will know where the best food buys are each week; which market is having "specials" in dairy foods; who is underselling whom in the butchery; what chain store is offering twelve eight-ounce cans of frozen juice for the price of six. If for whatever reason it's impractical for you to do more than your one weekly marketing binge at your handy supermarket, you can still comparison-shop. Why pay thirteen cents more for a bottle, can, or jar of some name brand viand highly touted on TV? It's that advertising in the media that *boosts* the price. Look for the equivalent product behind some more modest label—very often, though not always, the "house brand" of your supermarket is the very best buy. Improvements in consumer law in the past few years have made it mandatory for the price and volume or weight to be clearly posted near the product you're searching for; check them, and keep the store honest.

Specials are often advertised by means of window poster, mailbox stuffer, or store ad in the local newspaper. If it's a good bargain and the store is out of the item by the time you get there on your way home after work, don't forget to collect the rain check that allows you to take advantage of that sale price as soon as the item is back in stock. A way to save the store from the charge of fraudulent advertising.

In the same area, it is always a good notion to position yourself at the checkout counter where you can watch the ringing up of your purchase. Even if you are going through at big-city speed, this tends to promote a correspondence between the prices on the various items and the numbers that are punched out on the machine. A recent survey, by the way, reported that an enormous percentage of cashier tapes displayed erroneous totals from grocery purchases, so checking your totals when you get home, even if you have been spun through too fast to check each item as it's recorded, is not a fool's errand. Machines have been known to make mistakes, and human error is legendary.

Become an avid label-reader. Again, your federal, state, and local consumer legislation has done some very good things for you in the last few years; one of them is what the packager is required to put on his label. Not only must all ingredients be listed, but so must any preservatives, artificial colorings, and other food additives. (Don't be afraid of those additives—some of them can save your life. "Additive" is not *per se* a dirty word.) The supermarket itself does some of the labeling, of meat and poultry products, for instance, and they sometimes make simple mistakes in your favor. The law says that once a ten-pound turkey has been stuck with a label that reads "fowl, 3 pounds, $1.50," it has to be sold to you for that. This may be wishful thinking, in fact it is; but a story I heard on the radio yesterday, reported by the consumer affairs editor of a local station, told of a canny shopper who found in the meat counter of a chain store a package of veal neck mislabeled veal shoulder at $1.59 a pound. I don't know how this detection of an error in labeling benefitted the customer but the store was fined fifty dollars for erring (and someone in the meat department probably lost his job).

Don't neglect to cut out those 10¢-off-the-next-purchase coupons either. Or the ones that tempt you to try a different product by offering you a reduction in its retail price. Just don't get carried away, as a friend of mine always does, and buy the couponed box of cake mix at a price that *with the coupon reduction* is still ten or twelve cents higher than that of the good old reliable house brand she's been happy with for years.

On the coupon subject, look for them everywhere. They come in the mail sometimes, in flotillas or singly. Popular magazines carry them, as do advertisements in your local newspaper or in a store's own leaflets. They can be found even in the "good, gray" *New York Times*. Never throw out these gold mines before you've gone through them to see what product *that you use regularly* can be procured this week for twelve cents less. Some kitchen economists save a lot of money this way—are even able to persuade the market of their choice to accept pennies-off coupons issued by another store. (I have never been able to do this, but perhaps only because I don't use the right technique of persuasion.) One large chain market is currently advertising on television that it will give you one-and-a-half times the amount printed on the coupon; in some cases the store will give you two of the items, at the reduced price, for one coupon.

Read the labels. And if, in the case of products sold by weight, it seems to you implausible that the three bell peppers in your hand could weigh four pounds, reweigh them (or ask the attendant to do so in front of you). It may be that the dishonest shopper before you switched labels and got away with four pounds of peppers for the price that had been affixed to *your* twelve ounces!

Paw around on the shelf and find the one bottle of lemon juice that has the original 49¢ stamping on it, left over from the time before the price went up another ten cents. The store must sell it to you at the price stamped.

It's surprising how many times this oversight occurs—and one reason my food bill is so low.

The law also says you may examine any fresh fruit or vegetable before you buy it to see if there are any spoiled specimens on the bottom. Don't be intimidated by all that glassine or plastic wrapping. If you suspect foul play, unwrap the strawberries, pour them into a bag, discard the spoiled ones, reweigh, and pay only for those you approve. If you are in too much of a hurry for that, and you discover spoilage only after you've got your evening's purchase home, take the rotten members of the collection back the next day and demand restitution. Often you can avoid this necessity by smelling the fruits as you buy them, submitting them to the nose as well as the eye test. Don't ever take home a package that smells bad to you—of anything: meat, fish, poultry, vegetables, fruit, nuts, dairy products, whatever.

Of course this assumes you know how something is *supposed* to smell. If you can't tell the difference between attar of Limburger cheese and essence of mint or basil, well, perhaps you should think about quitting smoking.

On the label, too, is where you can find out if a product has enjoyed a longer shelf life than it should have: some items, such as yeast, bread, and dairy products, are stamped with the day of their distribution, or the date before which they should be sold or used up. If the period is past, you can sometimes get the product at a markdown. In most cases it is fresh enough for comfort and/or safety, since these dates are overcautious. With milk and cream and such, the nose test is again an efficacious one. In the case of bread, how often do you use up a loaf on the day it's packaged and sold anyway? Recently I purchased (out of the half-price bin) a three-packet ribbon of dry yeast that was supposed to have been used no later than nine months ago. (It must have been retrieved that day from behind some cheese box or other where it had fallen and lain for months.) I took it home as an experiment, believing that after I had kneaded my dough, it would just lie there limply, the yeast cells deactivated forever. But lo and behold, the bread rose bloomingly, even better than the previous week's batch; and I had my home-baked bread pennies cheaper this week than last.

Whether to buy fresh, in bulk, canned or bottled, or frozen, is an interesting problem, not as simple as "Fresh is always cheaper" or "Canned has lost most of its vitamins" or "Frozen is a luxury." It's a very iffy proposition, but here are some guidelines. Just as in buying a T-bone steak you are paying for something you won't eat (the bone), in buying most fresh produce, there will be something you're paying for that you won't consume: the stem and skins of many fruits, the stems, ribs, peelings of some vegetables, the pits or seeds of others (see Chapter 10 for how not to waste *anything*). On the other hand, in buying tinned, bottled, or packaged goods you are paying for the tin, glass, cardboard, or plastic that you are *certainly* not going to eat when you try to get around this ripoff. And when you buy a package of frozen lima beans, you are paying for someone to have shelled the beans, blanched and frozen them, packaged and advertised and distributed them. So it's usually very hard to say which is the better value. One rough way to approach it is to think how much discard there is in the fresh product before it gets to the condition of the canned or frozen item. A second is to think about how much time you have for food preparation and how highly you value the time you will spend in bringing the fresh, raw product to the state of the "convenience" form. You will probably decide that a six-ounce can of concentrated grape juice is cheap at the price, when you consider gathering the grapes in season, cleaning them, skinning them, pushing the pulp through a sieve, coloring it, then evaporating it to the concentrated form, packing it into a small container, and freezing it. This is perhaps an exaggeration of the problem: let's take a simpler one. Go back to the frozen lima beans, an example of a product that is relatively inexpensive in frozen form. If you bought the beans in their shells, fresh-picked yesterday, they would run you about sixty-nine cents a pound if you could find them at all, as against thirty-nine for ten ounces frozen, or forty-nine cents (baby) or sixty-four cents (large) for a pound dried. Are those few cents difference worth it to you when you think of shelling, cooking longer, possibly drying, coming out with fewer beans than the all-edible package of house-brand frozen? (Can you even do the mathematics to find out whether there is any saving?)

Shop in a cut-rate chainstore; avoid name brands; and don't buy combinations of processed foods, such as frozen peas and carrots in butter sauce. But, alas, it isn't that un-complicated. Frozen is supposed to be cheaper, but it isn't always—so many factors enter in. You've heard that canned is always cheaper than bottled, but that isn't necessarily so either. Neither is it possible to warn you off all "conveni-ence" foods like spaghetti-meatballs-tomato-sauce in cans (the *taste* of this number should rule it out for you). Or yolkless powdered eggs, whose low-cholesterol property can't be denied. Or skillet main-dish products, as prohib-itively expensive; some actually cost less per serving than the same meal starting from scratch. Dehydrated mashed potatoes, for example, cost nearly two cents less per serving than homemade mashed potatoes; but convenience scalloped potatoes cost more. In a recent study of convenience foods by the U. S. Department of Agriculture, it was found that more than fifty percent of convenience foods had a cost-per-serving equal to, or less than, their home-prepared or fresh counterparts. So it would seem to resolve itself into a ques-tion of taste, rather than dependable saving. Your taste buds, as well as your esthetic appetite for things cooked and seasoned and served well, must be your guide in this moot affair.

Buying in bulk is another way to save many dollars a year on groceries. If you have room to keep a side of beef for the several months it will take you to cook and eat it all, you've licked the high-price-of-beef problem. Should your home boast a cold cellar with just the right temperature and humidity for the storage of potatoes, acquiring a half ton of Idahos will hardly dent your weekly paycheck. Fifty bushels of apples in September will keep you in cider, applesauce, and wine, for at least two years. Most of us, lacking the requisite amount and quality of storage space, can't do that kind of quantity purchasing; but we can occasionally take advantage of the two-for-the-price-of-one sale without having to move out of our cottages or apartments. We ought to bear in mind that when we once-a-year decide to make something in great number—a flotilla of fruitcakes, for instance, to solve our Christmas gift-giving problem—we will be buying certain things in wholesale amounts and can save by purchasing at a local wholesaling establishment. We can persuade the friendly supermarket-man that he ought to quote us a wholesale price just that once, if he wants to keep our trade year-round.

Even the hardened city grocer can sometimes be induced to pass on to you his profit (you being a steady customer he doesn't want to alienate) by allowing you to buy a *case* of this or that canned product—something you use in vast enough quantity that it pays you to "lay in" your season's supply at the bottom of your kitchen broom closet. Cans of baked beans, for instance, or other winter legumes. Wintertime canned tomatoes. (Don't, by the way, be misled and exploited into buying Stewed Tomatoes, which have undergone one more process and hence one more price-hike.) How about cans of pet food? A dog-breeder neighbor of mine saves all her stud-fee money this way.

The manufacturers of expensive canned pet food want you to believe that their products are the best diet for your dog or cat, but "it ain't necessarily so." The very best food is dry kibble (or dry cat food) blended with egg yolk and just a bit of canned food for added fat and for palatability. This, with an occasional treat of table scraps (leftover unspiced foods), will keep any cat or dog contented. Please remember to keep fresh water available to your pet at all times.

Baby food in those little individual jars is a needless extravagance. You really shouldn't buy it, because you can save dollars weekly by making your own. It's just cooked and puréed food, which you can achieve very easily, in no time at all, if you have a stove and a blender in your kitchen. If some week the little jars look like an important time-saver to you, at least save yourself some pesetas by avoiding the mixed combinations and getting the one-food jars. If baby is addicted, for example, to peas and carrots or liver and turnips, buy them pure and separate, and mix them yourself.

Speaking of pure, as this is being written, a major producer of these tiny jars of baby food is being sued for false and misleading advertising. Have you read somewhere that your infant is subject to all sorts of diseases of the digestive tract if you *don't* buy and use these products? Arrant nonsense, besides being crooked. And in processed baby foods, you are also buying water, sugar, and extra starch.

When you procure certain items is, of course, equally as important as *where* you buy them. Obviously, a papaya in the Northeast in January is a luxury purchase. On the other hand, many a bushel basket of rich, ripe, juicy, red tomatoes has gone rotten in the city supermarket in September from lack of foresight. You should have picked it up for pennies, eaten gloriously of fresh salad tomatoes the first night, stewed them the next day or added them to a *ratatouille,* then made your winter's supply of tomato sauce or purée for the freezer. If you find some not-yet-ripe tomatoes at the bottom of the basket, you can sauté them to go with tomorrow's scrambled eggs or pasta, then make a splendid green tomato soup (see p. 221).

Even as I write this, a neighbor of mine has just

delivered to me about fifteen pounds of ripe tomatoes from his bountiful vines. The idea is for me to turn them tomorrow into tomato sauce and give him back one pint of it. That will be fifty-fifty sharecropping, as that amount of this kind of tomato will produce a little less than a quart of sauce.

Soon it will be pumpkin time, and I imagine that in return for one or two pumpkin pies, I shall be rewarded with my winter's supply of pumpkin meat, for which I'm reserving a small space in the lefthand back corner of my freezing compartment. I won't fill it before I've made that squadron of pumpkin pies, pumpkin cookies (see page 209), and dried a batch of pumpkin to store in the cupboard. I'll bet that you, dear reader, don't even cook and eat that pumpkin you cut a Halloween face in and left in your window with a candle inside for a week or so in November (see pages 207–208).

Gardening works only if you have a patch of soil to work with, but if you are so blessed, and have, as I do, a plot only about two-by-fifteen feet, it will make sense for you to grow one kind of vegetable to barter with your neighbors whose soil, lifestyles, inclinations, or sun conditions are more appropriate to another sort of crop. My outdoor vegetable this year was beans; fortunately my neighbors ran to excellent backyard harvests of everything *but* beans—so we bartered. I traded beans for fresh sweet corn, succulent tomatoes, nutritious beets and beet greens, handsome, proteinous eggplant, and crookneck squash. Everyone was happy. Look around to see what you can barter with whom before you plant your next year's little kitchen door plot.

If your kitchen door is only a separation between the living room and the combined stove-refrigerator in a tiny city flat, you still may be able to work this neat kind of exchange. Does your apartment have a sunny window? Are there any plants in it? Are they earning their room and board? That is, are those plants purely decorative or can

38

you eat them? I'm not recommending iceberg lettuce (which is a tricky grower in the first place) in your window box; but even a studio apartment is a good place to grow any number of herbs: chives, parsley, mint, basil, tarragon—in flowerpots. Move your philodendron or dracaena to a darker spot, where it will do just as well, and cultivate your favorite herb, which will be handsomely decorative *and* save you money. Now persuade your best friend to concentrate on dwarf fruits and vegetables like cherry tomatoes—then you can trade when your respective crops are at their peak. If sunlight is a sometime thing in your apartment, look into the proposition of growing things under artificial light.

You may be able to barter in other than kind: perhaps you can trade your labor in your weekending neighbor's backyard plot (weeding, watering, separating) for a certain amount of *his* specialty when it is at its peak.

Even more exotic systems of barter have been worked out by friends and neighbors of mine, to save on the food bill. A couple of examples: a teen-aged boy in high school cooks dinner for an aged couple down the road two nights a week, eats with them, and spends the evening playing cards with them; in exchange for this, he not only gets his principal meal of the day (and if you have ever observed the appetites of teen-age boys you know that this is *some* saving for his parents), but he is also allowed to pick salad from the garden for his family. A middle-aged woman friend who raises little long-haired dogs of an Asian breed barters their combings (and they must be brushed and combed daily or they are in trouble) with a neighbor for her weekly ration of fresh raw milk. What does the cow owner want with the silky hairs, you may ask? She is also a home weaver and spinner, and she works them into the wool she spins. This may sound to you like backwoods pioneer stuff, but it all takes place in what is essentially a suburban community—or a scant ten miles beyond suburbia.

Another perfect trade: a cattle and horse breeder I

know pastures some of his stock in the fields of a retired gallery-owner down the road, in return for which the art dealer gets all his snowplowing and shoveling done all winter by the grateful rancher. Grazing land is exchanged for manure to fertilize the garden, and for getting dug out of snowdrifts.

With a little looking around and canvassing, you can doubtless think of some form of barter that you can put into effect to save on the food bill. What do you like to do or raise or cook or prepare that your neighbor doesn't or can't? Trading evenings of baby-sitting is not the only way to save a penny. Think cooperatively.

It is only a short skip and a jump from here to starting your own food co-op: organizing a small group of families to buy groceries together at wholesale prices. You can save thirty to fifty percent on your food bill this way. It is very much worth doing if you have the time to devote to its establishment and operation. Check your local library for a guidebook. A very useful new one is *The Food Co-op Handbook*. A free guide can be obtained from the Department of Consumer Education, 80 Lafayette Street, New York, New York 10003. There is doubtless such a bureau in your area.

Do you know the places in your locale where you can get berries and fruits and vegetables at a very low price by picking them yourself? These "bargain counters" are a very valuable addition to your money-saving sources. They are open, of course, when the crop is at its peak, and you can save from one half to three quarters of the market price by performing this hardly arduous labor yourself. It's a pleasant way, too, to spend a sunny summer or early fall afternoon. Seek out the "pick-them-yourself" spots as a way of entertaining weekend guests. Or keeping the kids out of trouble.

You can be a really great success as a host or hostess by leading your guests around to all the spots where the picking is *free*! I was overrun last summer with blackberries

40

(have you priced them in the city markets?), raspberries, blueberries, grapes, and apples, all growing wild along the sides of country roads, in the woods behind my house, or in fields and open, unposted land. I think of this windfall as a kind of barter: my ingenuity in seeking it out plus my effort in picking, traded for a summer's worth of dessert and wine fruits. I also trade, with a farmer, a loaf of fresh-baked homemade bread each week for the pick of that day's mature squash. This presupposes having a day a week to stay at home and bake bread—plus a squash-growing neighbor. On weeks when I don't have the day-at-home to bake bread, I get my *own* loaf free by barter: the day-old bread shop in the next town gives me a loaf in exchange for twenty-five paper bags (those large brown sacks from the supermarket that you may have been throwing away).

Even if you are, like me, not really a farmer, you can go a long way toward living off the land if you have a little land of your own to work with. But don't commit your limited patch of garden soil blindly. Read the seed catalogs, read the directions on the seed packets themselves if you're buying them in a store, and then read a good beginner's book, something like Bill Kaysing's *First-Time Farmer's Guide*, a treasury of good advice in a small package. There are dozens of others available, and more coming along all the time. More Americans than ever before are vegetable gardening, and free literature is available from your state or federal department of agriculture to help you plunge into the soil in the wisest and most economical way.

Starting with one kind of vegetable is a good way to begin: try some kind of squash, for instance. Pumpkin (which belongs in this family) is one of the easiest crops to grow, and in most soil, moisture, and sun conditions, yields a satisfying harvest with little work involved. The meat is nutritious, the seeds even more so, and you'll have a good barterable growth in mid-autumn when lots of people will want some for Hallowe'en and Harvest-time decorations. Having succeeded with pumpkins the first season, you might want to add ornamental gourds the next. Chard or spinach would be another good beginner's crop, and will provide you with a complementary vegetable for several months during the summer and fall.

There are vegetables that grow best in full sunlight and sandy soil, others that prosper only in acid-treated earth with plenty of moisture that can drain properly; some green leafies require a longer growing season than northern Maine and New York provide, while their cousins will perform satisfactorily in any state in the Union. Some you can start early indoors, in boxes, transferring seedlings outside later; others must sprout in the ground. Don't try corn unless you have room to plant two rows a foot or so apart (corn needs to cross-pollinate); and avoid peanuts unless they will have lots of room for their roots. Some vegetables will need poles or trellises or wire mesh to climb on; some will have to be protected from consumption by small varmints, or bugs. See what your neighbors have done well with or failed with, and learn from them. Amateur gardeners, you'll find, are always only too happy to show off their knowledge of local conditions.

For your quick reference, here is a list of the twenty-one vegetables that are the most popular with backyard gardeners the country over—presumably because of ease of growing, versatility of use, and adaptability to various geographical conditions—in no order other than alphabetical: Asparagus, Beets, Broccoli, Brussels Sprouts, Cabbage, Carrots, Cauliflower, Chard, Corn, Cucumbers, Eggplant, Lettuce, Onions, Peas, Peppers, Potatoes, Beans (Snap), Spinach, Squash, Tomatoes, and Turnips. Choose among them for your initial venture into truck gardening, and you can hardly go wrong. But learn first whether the place you want to plant them is known to be friendly to their progress.

Keeping livestock on a budget is another way of beating inflation. But everything I've said above about venturing into raising vegetables can be repeated, in spades, even for such economical types as chickens and pigs. Don't go into it blindly, for you can lose your entire investment overnight raising animals or poultry—they eat a lot and are subject to a bewildering number of ills.

The average adult human being eats ten times his weight in a year's time, I read somewhere recently, and this remarkable statement gave me considerable pause. It should you, too. If it doesn't, put it together with another statistic and see how you feel: the average American woman is 5′ 3″ tall, and she weighs—hold onto your hat—145 pounds! Now a 145-pound female of five-and-a-quarter feet in length has too much breadth; in short, she's too fat. (The male averages, which I don't remember, were equally appalling.) I don't want to hear any of that jargon about heavy bones and glandular conditions or water retention—the truth is she eats too much! (And so does he.) Most of that over-consumption does not build muscle tissue, stimulate the vital secretions, or improve the skin tone; it gets laid away in fatty tissue, which we need like a hole in the head. We as a people really do eat too much, too much of everything, and it costs us money!

Diamond Jim Brady may have had more of it than he knew what to do with (money, that is) but that was no excuse. He would sit down at the table with his stomach a measured four inches away from the edge, and start eating. Four dozen oysters followed by a couple dozen clams were an appetizer. Then he would progress to the *real* eating: fish and game birds and ham and beef, often at the same meal, and—well, it makes me a bit ill to think of it. Suffice it to say that the orgy would go on for hours, and not until his belly was pressing *hard* against the table would he consider bringing the meal to a conclusion. The fact that he died at the age of sixty-one of something probably diagnosed as apoplexy would have been a foregone conclusion to any nutrition-wise observer of today.

Five small meals a day, rather than three big ones, may be the proper procedure for hypoglycemiacs; three modest ones, the conventional practice fitting most people's lives

43

better, are preferable for most average, healthy adults. This also represents one way to start saving a lot of money on food. Almost too simple, you say? Consider this: look at your shopping basket the next time you go to the supermarket. While you're waiting in the checkout line, count the items in your basket that are "junk food": things like potato chips, pretzels, and other nibbles or between-meal snacks and drinks. Throw out all the crackers, white bread, and other products made from bleached white flour. Now get rid of all the items for dessert that are not natural sweets such as fruits. Delete all the high-sugar beverages intended more to satisfy a craving than to fill your liquid requirements. Put back on the shelves all the candied-up, sugar-coated cereals—any breakfast cereal that is not whole-grain and unsweetened doesn't deserve one penny of your hard-earned pay. Shun the candy, cookies, cupcakes, and their cousins that you've been accustomed to satisfying your sweet tooth with—or shoving at your poor little kids between meals. It was always an object lesson to me, when visiting my wholesome older sister, to hear her toddlers dash in from outdoor play and ask for a carrot or a fresh scallion!

Now look at your new total: it doesn't take an economist to see that all the junk foods you eat are responsible for too large a proportion of your burgeoning grocery bill. You don't have to be a dietitian to realize that a low-animal-fat, low-sugar, high-protein supply of a week's provisions is not only going to save you cash, but keep you and your family healthier. And skinnier.

You don't need all that fatty meat to fill your daily protein requirement. The traditional well-marbled steak is not only prohibitively expensive today, but sunflower seeds, the truly nearly perfect food, though by no means cheap, are still a better buy and a superior source of protein, pound for pound, than steak. The historical American appetite for bacon, a low-protein meat in any case, can be satisfied nicely with a low-cost soybean equivalent. Beans (the entire legume family, in fact) are not only a balanced accompaniment to

44

rice but a cheaper source of protein than eggs, without the cholesterol problem. Children's between-meals crunching needs can be answered, both at lower cost and far more healthfully, with carrot and celery sticks, indeed any raw vegetable or fruit, rather than with sugary sweets or white-flour starchy tidbits. And their teeth will not decay so readily, thus adding a dental-bill saving to what you put away by not stocking junk foods.

Last summer I bought only two chickens, and one of them was the principal dish of a dinner party. My fish requirement was taken care of for the season by one fresh turbot, a shrimp splurge in a restaurant, and four cans (a "special," blessedly cheap) of tuna fish.

Save your gooey, calorie-filled dessert serving for a once-in-a-while treat, rather than the everyday thing it now is in too many households. You will save not only your teeth, heart, pancreas, and liver, but several dollars a week that have been going to Sara Lee and her relatives. Substitute domestic cottage or farmer cheese for the imported Danish blue or French Brie or Greek feta, and you will keep your arteries from clogging and your purse from emptying. Make your own yogurt at home (once a week, while the bread is rising) and you have not only provided yourself with a batch of binder cheaper than eggs or lecithin, a topping better for you and less costly than whipped cream or its convenience equivalents, and a dessert-dish base superior to ice cream—but you have also saved all the kopecks you need for your weekly fish or poultry purchase.

A shameful amount of food is wasted in this country today, still—in spite of inflation, recession, unemployment, and whatnot. Restaurants remain archfelons in this matter of squandering of our natural resources. You may imagine that when you don't finish your meal in an eatery, the kitchen staff takes it home. But you're wrong: into the garbage can it goes. A very important way to save money in your own kitchen—one that should not be overlooked—is to bring home to it at night the uneaten vittles from your table in the restaurant at noon. You've paid for it—or if you're an expense-account diner, your company has paid for it—don't *waste* it. There are rolls and crackers in the breadbasket that will just go stale if you don't tote them; there may be three good lunches' worth of waste on your entree dish and that of your companion—don't leave it behind. Ask to have it put into a doggie bag to take with you; the half a steak your friend or business associate was too busy impressing you to eat can form the basis of a delectable casserole when combined with the over-generous serving of vegetables that you didn't finish. Baking will do away with any possible germs. (Far too much is made of the fear of catching someone's disease through cooked food, a most unlikely contingency. A half hour in a 350° oven spells doom to most bacteria. Botulism may be the one exception to this rule, but your chances of buying a can of tuna fish contaminated with botulism are now about one in umpteenzillion, fortunately.) If the bistro treats your request with anything other than utmost courtesy, never patronize it again. (Some establishments, indeed, have made up their own doggie bags—often bags, boxes, or containers with the words "People Bag" and their own business name on them—just so you *can* take away your unfinished meal, without embarrassment. It's smart advertising.)

Follow just one third of all the advice in this chapter and you'll be able to afford the occasional frivolous splurge: plover's eggs on the thinnest venison steak, with a truffle sauce over. Do *everything* recommended above—and you will qualify to join the Exalted Society of Parsimonious Chic.

4

THE CHICKEN
OR THE EGG

Which came first? is a philosophical question. Whether poultry or eggs enjoy first place in your marketing economy depends, or should, on how prices are going this week. If eggs are at their all-time low, get more than one dozen and store them. Under simple refrigeration eggs, if they are no more than a day or so old when you buy them, will keep for quite a long time. If you grease their shells completely, they will store in a cool place (not the refrigerator) for weeks. If you separate the yolks, you can freeze the whites—one each to an individual ice-cube cup is a good way. And once whole eggs (or parts) are cooked into a many-egg cake or brunch dish, you can freeze the dessert or entree for eating in the future.

If there is an appreciable variance in the price of different sizes of eggs, never buy the largest, sometimes called "jumbo." They don't give you that much more nourishment. They may not even be that much larger than the medium eggs, as the sizing is usually determined by the weight, rather than the girth, of the egg. Moreover, most cookbooks speak about large, medium, or small (hardly ever extra large) eggs. We all know by now, too, don't we, that the color of the shell has nothing to do with the taste or other qualities of the egg inside; so if you find brown eggs cheaper than white of the same size, by all means grab them. (In some areas they are *more* expensive—it all depends, I think, on local prej-

47

udices.) No matter what you may have heard on TV or in your health-food shop, fertilized eggs, or eggs from "free-range" chickens, are not superior to eggs from factory-type, non-pregnant hens; don't be trapped into paying exaggerated prices for fancy "natural" eggs. They will give you exactly the same amount of protein, and an equal infusion of cholesterol, as the supermarket eggs.

If your market ever features Grade B eggs (mine never seems to stock them) and they're very low-priced, get a dozen or two. All Grade B means is that the whites are somewhat thinner and the yellow less dense—or possibly that they are a bit less fresh than Grade A. You can use the B's for cooking, while reserving the A's for those you will eat raw (as in a milkshake or eggnog) or *as eggs*.

Not long ago, at the height of the new cholesterol-consciousness, I asked a fellow food writer who had just acquired a flock of hens what she was doing about the suspicion that we may all have been overeating eggs. "Pretty much ignoring it," was her answer, "because we like them so much, in so many forms, and now we can go out in the back yard and *pick* them, so to speak." This last remark is one powerful argument for a many-egg diet; another is that even if you don't have your own flock, eggs are cheaper than meat and an equally good source of protein. A high-protein diet is necessary to everyone, rich or poor, young or old; and the good part of this is that we don't have to go broke keeping our protein intake high if we eat eggs and poultry. In fact, if we occasionally get a piece of chicken, once or twice a week some fish, and vary this with egg dishes on other evenings, we need never have any bloody red meat at all. We can achieve a high-protein diet through judicious filling in with a variety of grains, cereals, and vegetables. Eating a couple of fried eggs for breakfast, then several more cooked into the breads, desserts, pastas, sauces, or cooked dishes we enjoy the rest of the day—every day—is probably overdoing it. We ought to take into account the "hidden" eggs we eat daily before we make them part of every breakfast. But the egg has been maligned of late, and we ought not to do it injustice.

Not so many years back, no one had ever heard of cholesterol; hence we didn't have the fear of it that we do now. Cholesterol is a necessary substance that is manufactured in the body of every animal, including *homo sapiens*. It is only when extraordinary amounts of it are laid down inside our circulatory systems that it is troublesome to us, causing high blood pressure and a number of conditions that ultimately affect the heart. There is no way of telling in advance how your particular body is going to handle the substances that you take in during meals—this remains one of the physiological processes we are still very much in the dark about—and how much of the animal-product cholesterol you ingest will find its way into the lining of your veins and arteries. Since research seems to *point to* a relationship between massive eating of high-cholesterol foods and early heart disease, it may pay us not to overdo fatty meats, high-fat dairy products, and the *yolks* of eggs. Alas, it's in the yolks that the cholesterol lies, as well as the sulphur and other trace minerals; the white of an egg contains most of its protein. So if your object in dealing with eggs is to reduce your cholesterol intake, it would seem you have it made if you eat only the whites (or those egg substitutes now on the market that take advantage of the cholesterol scare—and still cost far too much). But then what would you do with the yolks—feed them to the dog, or perhaps make gobs and tons of hollandaise sauce? For whom to eat? The better part of wisdom in this matter is simply to start counting the number of eggs in any week, both plain and used in cooking, and substitute here and there a high-protein, low-cholesterol product or food. Just so long as we don't put in the egg's place an empty-caloried carbohydrate (sugar or starch), we'll be ahead of the game both nutritionally and economically.

In cooking, whole eggs perform the function of binding or emulsifying. The eggs you add to a cake mix, or put into pancakes or some other form of bread, or stabilize your home-made mayonnaise with, count as eggs too. You may prefer to substitute whole milk in your sauce or gravy, hold your meats and vegetables together in a casserole with a margarine, flour, and stock sauce, make your frothed-up drinks with yogurt. Reserve the three eggs a week you have decided on for once-a-week binges of things that are frankly eggs in your favorite forms: soufflés or omelets, or plain honest old fried eggs—or poached or shirred or hard-cooked. If your doctor has put you on a low-cholesterol diet, you can eat all the meringue you want, as it is beaten egg *whites* only.

Always store uncoated eggs under refrigeration, but let them come to room temperature before cooking them—unless you're separating them, which is more easily done when they're cold. When you break them open, don't throw away one quarter of the white; carefully scrape the inside of the shell empty with a spoon, a rubber spatula—or your finger. And then save your eggshells. For how they will come in handy, see Chapters 9 and 10.

A surfeit of eggs is an easier notion to take in than too much poultry. My husband says he could eat chicken every night for dinner—and there have been weeks when this has almost been the case—as long as it is cooked differently each time. Our Thanksgiving turkey has not been a turkey for years. Who can afford that truly native American bird at the jacked-up prices that appear around the time of that truly native American holiday? Once it was duck, gift of a game-shooting friend, and once when a vegetarian friend was visiting, it was meatless lasagne; but usually it is chicken (the price of this fowl goes *down* at Thanksgiving time), roasted with a beautiful stuffing (see pages 54–55), and surrounded with all the traditional, seasonal vegetables and fruits.

If for reasons of family tradition you *must* cook a turkey for Thanksgiving or some other holiday dinner, watch for a *pre*holiday turkey sale, and keep it frozen until the day before you are to cook it. Don't buy a prestuffed one, and don't fall for the prebasted nonsense. In the case of pre-stuffing, you will be paying turkey prices for old bread (mainly), and the weight of the dressing can be as high as one third of the total poundage. Prebasted turkeys, of course, come a few cents higher the pound too.

The bigger the bird, naturally, the longer it will take to thaw. Be sure to give it enough time to defrost completely before you start roasting. Turkeys and other big birds have a way of thawing unevenly, which gives them time to develop decay in the smaller parts and outside while the rest is slowly coming to room temperature. One way to guard against this is to take your bird out of the freezer at least twenty-four hours before cooking, and seal it into a large paper bag. Turn it over two or three times during the thawing so that the air around the turkey has a chance to get to all surfaces.

Cautionary note: the price of turkey in the fall of 1975 was ten cents higher than in 1974! How does *this* year's gobbler compare with last year's? Check pre- and post-holidays for a surprise.

Rock Cornish game hens are fun, but they are almost as costly as goose. And squab is just a fancy name for pigeon (which, unless you can shoot or trap some on your own property, comes at a fancy price, too). Guinea hen is a rare special treat but so prohibitively expensive, unless you raise them yourself, that it has become a sort of joke ("guinea hen under glass, please"). You are more likely to come by a pheasant, partridge, wild duck, or other game bird from a hunting friend than a guinea hen; for this reason I've provided some good ways to prepare these birds. For the most part, however, poultry to the economical cook means chicken. Thus this chapter will concentrate on methods of stretching out those two chickens you bought on the weekend to provide many meals—not just one—of good eating.

First some tips on buying chicken. The days are pretty much gone—or the places few and far between—when and where you could purchase your bird on the hoof, so to speak, and take it home alive to do your own killing, plucking, etc.

The next best procedure is to buy a whole chicken, or rather two whole chickens. It is a waste of time and fuel to roast only one bird in the oven, and that's always what you should do *first* with a good chicken. For my money, nothing is more soul-satisfying than a good, roasted, stuffed chicken. Few feasts are higher in protein, lower in cost. Never buy parts of chicken because, unless you favor backs (with very little flesh adhering), you will pay more for less. So-called fryers or broilers are usually quite a few cents cheaper than roasters, and I've never been able to see that the latter are in any way superior for roasting. Always leave some chicken-space available in your freezing compartment, as then you will be able to shop the special chicken sales, whether you plan to roast birds in the next few days or not. Remove the giblets, neck, etc., from inside the birds and pop them into the freezer until you're ready to cook them. Chicken sales occur at times other than when turkey is the traditional bill of fare—don't be caught unawares. Fowl, so-called—actually a bird that is somewhat older than he or she should be for tenderness—can almost always be bought cheaper than those fit for roasting. Fowl should always be moist-cooked or stewed, else you will have a very tough proposition indeed. Read on for ways to deal with bargain fowls. Select well-fleshed, roundish birds with flexible breastbones and a good color to the skin. The larger the bird, the less of the weight in the bones, so try not to buy ones that are too tiny. If you have bought them at an inconvenient time and then frozen them, be sure to defrost them slowly (in the refrigerator for a few hours, then at room temperature for the last few hours).

How to Roast Chickens
to Get the Most Out of Them

It's surprising how many cooks (city folks mostly) don't know how to roast a chicken. It may have something to do with those already-cooked chickens you can buy in delicatessens; they are very expensive, so forget about them. I don't know how many times I have recited what follows to urban young women or men who have just set up housekeeping.

Let's assume you have bought drawn, plucked, and cleaned chickens from the supermarket. First remove the neck and giblets from inside, and wash your two birds inside and out under cold water; let them dry a bit; while they are drying you can prepare your stuffing (see pp. 54–55). Now tear off the lump of fat that may be adhering to the cavity opening: you can render the fat in an ovenproof cup or dish in the oven while the birds are roasting, and keep it in the refrigerator for those recipes that call for chicken fat. Rub the cavities of your birds with salt. (Some people rub the outside with salt, too, but unless you set great store by tough, crisp chicken skin, that is a waste of salt.)

Now stuff the birds—not too full, as the stuffing will expand in cooking—and arrange them so the dressing will not fall out. Some people sew them up, others close the opening with skewers and string; I usually just close them by wedging the necks into the apertures and, with one skewer or two, fold the skin around the necks. Oil the birds all over the outside very sparely with a light vegetable oil, fold their wings under, and lay them in the roasting pan breast side up, on a rack or not as you choose. If your roasting pan has a cover, use it for half or three quarters of the cooking time, then finish them uncovered (when you turn the heat up toward the end). If your "cover" is a used piece of foil, the timing is the same. You can use the juices that have run out of the chickens to baste them with once or twice during cooking if you want—or you can reserve all that run-off for the basis of gravy. *Don't throw it away:* even if you are not the gravy type, it will be delicious cooking fat for the sautéing of any number of dishes over the next few days, or as the basis for an experimental sauce.

The oven temperature should not be over 350°, and if you can keep it to 325°, that's better still for all but the last half hour or so. Two hours at 325°, then a half hour turned up to 375° is generally sufficient for the 2½-to-3-pound chickens that are my usual load. Two smaller birds will, of course, be done sooner than one large, so if you have a big roaster, cooking by weight may be a more reliable gauge. Fifty minutes per pound of weight, at 325°, should do it, with higher heat toward the end.

If it's the first time you've roasted stuffed chicken, try to leave the dinner hour a bit flexible, for despite all the schedules in the world, and the weight-per-minute guidelines, some birds just resist finishing on time. They are cooked through when the juices run out colorless, rather than pink, when you prick the *leg* with a fork (white meat may be done sooner). If it runs pinkish, give the birds a little longer in the oven at the higher temperature. You can use this time to make the gravy, if you want it, with a little pour-off from under the chickens. Tuck this into your bonnet for those times when you're in a hurry: if your birds are not stuffed, they will roast a bit more quickly.

Four delicious chicken stuffings follow; they are all for one three- to four-pound bird. For two birds, double amounts.

BASIC GIBLET STUFFING

¼ lb. (1 stick) margarine

gizzard and heart from 1 chicken (the chicken liver
should be tossed into your "Livers" frozen-food
container in the freezer)

1 small onion

1 stalk of celery, plus leaves

salt, pepper, to taste

1 tablespoon dried sage, or a few leaves fresh*

* On occasion I have been known to use seasoned crumbs that come in a cellophane bag from the grocery store—but only when they have been found in the "Reduced for Quick Sale" cart. I find that I still want to add some sage to the crumbs for a really tasty stuffing.

1 egg
½ cup skim milk or water
¾ cup bread crumbs or cubes (or pieces of old bread, torn up)

Melt the margarine over medium heat in a saucepan while you are cutting the giblets up small (cut the casing off the the gizzard and feed it to the cat or dog). Put the giblets into the fat while you are chopping up the onion and celery; then add the vegetables to the giblet pot with the seasonings and herb. While they are sautéing slowly, beat the egg and liquid lightly and pour it over the bread crumbs. Allow the mixture on the fire to cool slightly, combine it with the bread mixture, and mix evenly. Spoon the stuffing into the bird, leaving some space for expansion. If it is more than enough for the cavity, you can grease a small covered baking dish and have a bonus "outside-the-bird" serving: put it in the oven halfway through the roasting of the bird.

APPLE-POTATO STUFFING

Any number of fruits may of course, be substituted for the apples: try pear or peach if you have a crop waiting to be picked off the grass underneath the trees. There is something very satisfying, though, about using up some of those apples which your neighbor told you to take from under his trees and which you consider inedible fresh.

2 small apples (or 1 large)
1 small onion
½ cup (½ stick) margarine or ½ cup light vegetable oil
salt, pepper
pinch cinnamon or nutmeg

½ to ¾ cup yesterday's mashed potatoes
a couple of dried prunes or apricots, cut up
skim milk, water, or yogurt, if needed

Peel and cut up the apples. Chop the onion. Melt the
vegetable fat over medium heat and brown the onion
in it. If the apple is very hard, let it brown a little in
the oil too. Cool, add seasonings and spices. Add the
mashed potatoes, broken into chunks if they are cold
from the refrigerator, and the dried fruit. If the mashed
potatoes are recently warmed and not in lumps, distribute the fruits and vegetables throughout. If the stuffing
seems too dry, add a bit of skim milk or water or yogurt
to moisten it, and stuff cavity loosely.

NUT STUFFING

*Turkey with chestnut or walnut stuffing is ambrosia; but
chicken with peanut stuffing may be more in keeping
with the lean pocketbook, depending on what nuts you
can gather from under your own trees, or those of gen-
erous neighbors. If you have some forthcoming hazel,
hickory, or chestnut trees in the back yard, by all means
take advantage of them. If not, peanuts are still finan-
cially within reach—or were at this writing—especially
if you have the time (and the thumbs) to buy them in
the shells and shell them.*

½ cup shelled, skinned nutmeats (a mixture would be
nice)
½ cup mushrooms
¼ cup shortening
½ to ¾ cup cooked brown or white rice (or oatmeal or
wheat cereal)
salt, pepper, or your favorite seasoning

If the nut you've selected is a particularly hard one, like a brazil nut, it should probably be roasted or boiled for half an hour first; if your peanuts are raw, they certainly should be roasted first. Just put them, shell and all, in a 350° oven for a half to three quarters of an hour. Brown the mushrooms, either cut up or whole, in the shortening. Then chop up the nuts or leave them whole, depending on their size and your inclination. Combine the rest of the ingredients with the nuts and mushrooms, distributing chunks evenly. If the stuffing is still too dry, moisten with some liquid, and stuff cavity loosely.

MIXED VEGETABLE STUFFING

Of course what vegetables you use in this stuffing will depend on what vegetables you have to use up before they loose all their pizazz—and also what vegetables you plan to serve with the roast chicken. Here is a combination that nicely uses up those cracker crumbs you've been saving from the bottoms of your cracker boxes, and lends vegetable juices to the mixture and flavoring.

1 small (or half a large) bell pepper
1 small onion
½ cup margarine or oil
2 garlic cloves, minced
½ cup cubed zucchini (or other squash)
1 small fresh tomato, quartered
½ cup or so crumbs from any kind of crackers

Core, seed and de-white the bell pepper. Chop the pepper and the onion and brown both in the oil, adding the minced garlic later. Throw in the squash and tomato and soften them a little. Then after the mixture has cooled a bit, add it to the crumbs. Stuff cavity loosely and tie the chicken up a little more securely than usually. Some people would add to this stuffing a couple of shelled hard-boiled eggs; I can always think of so many better uses for eggs than stuffing them whole back inside their parents. Besides which, poultry *and* eggs (more than one) at the same meal is gilding the lily animal-proteinwise.

Some of these stuffings, or your variations on them, will go just as well inside birds other than chickens. Just use your imagination on the combination of tastes: wild rice isn't the only possible complement to duck, for example, or the least expensive. Try stuffing a roast duck with cooked sauerkraut, caraway seeds, and bacon or bacon substitute. Remember to roast the excess dressing on the side, along with the white or sweet potatoes, or squash, that have been baked during the longish oven-on time.

Gravy and Sauces

Since gravy is a kind of sauce, this may be the place to make a few remarks about both. A sauce, basically, is a liquid with a flavoring, sometimes thickened, sometimes not, frequently with a base of some kind of fat or grease. Don't be afraid of making your own sauces, and of experimenting with developing new sauces to go with various dishes. Inexpensive cuts of meat, unexceptional sorts of fish, or blandish vegetables can be infinitely improved with the addition of a sauce of your invention. Only in posh restaurants do we expect sauces that have taken days to make. The juices that cook out of a food, or that food is cooked in, should never be discarded— they are part of future sauces. If you haven't originated a sauce on the spot when cooking, say, a roast of venison, or half a dozen carrots, or a baked apple, just put the juice into a container and freeze it (labeled) until the time when you feel like devising a sauce.

Gravy is by definition a sauce that contains some fat, usually the fat and juices that drip from cooking poultry or meat. You can thicken it or not as you choose. Your thickener need not be white wheat flour—it can be whole-wheat or rye flour, or cornstarch, or arrowroot, or potato or rice flour, any number of things. (I made a particularly good one the other day with sesame flour.) The drippings in the pan around the nearly-cooked chicken make a scrumptious gravy. Just put a half cup of drippings over a medium fire in a saucepan. Now, using a whisk, whip your thickening agent (whether flour, starch, or whatever) into milk in the ratio of two tablespoons of flour to a cup of milk. Add this mixture a little at a time to the drippings, whisking continually until the gravy thickens. You may season it to taste if it seems bland. And add things to it like sautéed chopped onions, chives, or shallots—or sautéed chicken giblets if you didn't put them into the stuffing. If the gravy gets away from you and overthickens, just thin it by adding a little warm water. If overthinned, stir in a little more thickening. And *voilà*, foolproof gravy.

All right, now that you've got all the mileage out of a dinner of roast stuffed chicken with gravy, you can do one of three things: if there's a whole cooked bird left, and you don't want to repeat a poultry meal within a few days, freeze the bird whole, stuffing scooped out and frozen separately. Or you can cut the chickens up into serving-size pieces and make one of the recipes that follow; they are designed for variety and economy in stretching out pieces of second-day chicken. (Your bird will be much easier to render into sections now that it's been cooked than when it was raw. You may not even have to borrow the wire cutters from the workbench, or a cleaver from a butchering neighbor.) Or you can skin the chicken, cut the meat from the bones, and use it in one of the second group of poultry-stretching recipes that follow.

If you decide on the last course, don't you dare feed the bones to the dog or the garbage can. Put both bones and skin into a heavy plastic bag (the double kind that birdseed and some hardware items come in is good for this) and then into your freezing compartment. This is the genesis of your soup bag, for a discussion of which see page 310.

Poultry-Stretching Recipes
(Cooked serving pieces, skin on)

CHICKEN ORANGE
4 to 6 servings

2 tablespoons butter or margarine
2 tablespoons flour, or other thickener
¼ teaspoon cinnamon or powdered ginger
1 teaspoon salt
1½ cups orange juice
sections from 1 orange or tangerine
about 2 lbs. cooked chicken or duck in serving pieces

Melt the butter or margarine in a saucepan over a low flame, then stir in the flour, spices, and seasoning. Add the orange juice, little by little, stirring constantly until the sauce thickens a bit. Now add the orange sections and the chicken pieces to the saucepan, cover, and cook over medium heat, just long enough for the chicken to be heated through, about 20 minutes.

Serve with rice or mashed potatoes.

CHICKEN IN BEER
4 to 6 servings

This is an agreeable way to use up that old flat beer in your refrigerator. Plus some leftover boiled potatoes.

2 cups flat beer

1 cup tomato juice or ½ cup tomato sauce

salt and pepper to taste

flour or other thickener if desired

1 cup or more small white onions

1 cup or more small white new potatoes, or chunks of
larger potato, partially cooked

1½ to 2 lbs. cooked chicken in serving pieces

Combine the beer, tomato sauce, and seasonings, and heat in a large saucepan. (You may want to thicken this sauce a little—if so, whisk in some thickening, over medium heat.) Add the little onions and potatoes and the pieces of chicken. Cover (if the sauce is thickened) or leave uncovered (if the sauce is unthickened) and simmer over medium heat until the poultry is heated through, about 15 to 20 minutes.

SWEET AND SOUR CHICKEN
4 to 6 servings

2 tablespoons margarine

1½ to 2 lbs. cooked chicken in serving pieces

2 tablespoons brown sugar

2 tablespoons vinegar

⅛ cup soy sauce

1 tablespoon cornstarch

1 9-oz. can pineapple chunks, plus juice

1 medium-sized sweet pepper, red or green

Melt the margarine in a skillet, and brown the chicken pieces in it. Cover and keep it hot. Now in a saucepan mix the sugar, vinegar, soy sauce, and cornstarch, and stir over low heat until it thickens a little. Add the pineapple chunks with the juice from the can, and simmer about 5 minutes. Cut up the pepper (after removing seeds and white part) into strips or squares and add it to the sauce. Cook another 10 minutes or so. Pour the sauce over the chicken and serve hot.

CRANBERRY TURKEY
4 to 6 servings

In the American sensibility, cranberry sauce is so firmly connected with turkey that it's ridiculous: look at how this recipe title just naturally swam out of my typewriter. This could, of course, be just as tasty a stretching dish with chicken or duck meat.

3 tablespoons margarine
½ cup flour or other thickener
salt and pepper to taste
1 cup red wine
1-lb. can whole-berry cranberry sauce
1½ to 2 lbs. cooked poultry in serving pieces

Melt margarine in saucepan over low heat, then add flour and seasonings. Stir or whisk in wine and cranberry sauce. Add pieces of chicken or turkey or duck; turn heat up to medium. Cover and simmer until heated through, about 20 minutes.

Serve with corn muffins, rice, or—better still—halves of baked sweet potatoes.

MUSHROOM CHICKEN
4 servings

½ lb. fresh mushrooms
3 tablespoons margarine or oil

1 10-oz. box frozen green beans, defrosted
1 cup chicken gravy (see page 58)
1½ lbs. cooked chicken in serving pieces

Cut large mushrooms into quarters or smaller; small ones may be left whole. Heat the margarine or oil in a skillet and brown both mushrooms and beans. Then add the gravy to the skillet and combine it with the vegetables. Put the chicken parts in and heat, covered, until poultry is heated through, about 15 minutes.

Serve hot with noodles or baking powder biscuits.

SOUR CREAM CHICKEN
4 servings

½ to ¾ cup sour cream
2 tablespoons each chopped chives and parsley
1 to 1½ lbs. cooked chicken in serving pieces
½ cup grated Pecorino or Parmesan cheese
½ cup bread crumbs or cubes

Preheat oven to 375°. Mix sour cream with chopped herbs, then add it to a greased baking dish into which you have put the chicken pieces. Bake, uncovered, in a 375° oven for a half hour. Mix cheese and bread crumbs and sprinkle over the chicken-in-sour-cream. Let the dish sit under the broiler for approximately 5 minutes until the cheese has melted and bread crumbs are a nice, toasty brown. Serve hot in its baking dish.

Cooked asparagus, beets, or carrots—or all three—would be a pleasing accompaniment.

Poultry-Stretching Recipes
(Boned, skinned and cut into pieces)

CHICKEN DIVAN
3 or 4 servings
½ lb. slender spaghetti

1½ to 2 cups cooked chicken meat in bite-size pieces

1 10-oz. package frozen broccoli (or equal volume fresh)

2 tablespoons butter or margarine

2 tablespoons flour or arrowroot

1 cup skim milk

salt and pepper to taste

½ teaspoon paprika or powdered mustard

½ cup shredded Cheddar or grated hard cheese

Preheat oven to 375°. Boil the spaghetti *al dente* in salted water, and drain. Put it into the bottom of a greased baking dish. The next layer is the chicken pieces, distributed evenly. Then the broccoli (if frozen, simmer in a half cup of water for a few minutes first; if fresh, chop up and cook *al dente* before adding). Now make a white sauce of margarine, flour, and milk, whisking it over medium heat until thickened. Season with salt, pepper, and paprika or mustard. Stir in the cheese after turning the heat off. Pour this sauce evenly over the assembled dish and heat in a 375° oven for 30 to 40 minutes.

TURKEY SUCCOTASH
4 servings

1½ to 2 cups cooked turkey or other poultry meat in bite-size pieces

1 1-lb. can creamed corn

1 10-oz. package frozen lima beans, defrosted, or similar
amount fresh-cooked beans
salt and pepper to taste
1 teaspoon curry powder

Preheat oven to 350°. Combine all ingredients in a buttered baking dish and bake in the oven for 30 to 40
minutes.

This is a highly nutritious chicken-stretcher, full of
protein and including some roughage as well. The seasonings aren't necessary if you're on a bland diet. If
you're not, a lovely accompaniment would be lightly
fried, sliced green tomatoes.

CAULIFLOWER CHICKEN
4 servings

1½ cups cooked chicken meat
1 10-oz. package frozen cauliflower, defrosted
¾ cup chicken gravy or white sauce (see Chicken
Divan)
1 teaspoon mustard
½ cup chopped peanuts or walnuts

Preheat oven to 350°. Combine first four ingredients in
a greased baking dish and bake for a half hour or so.
Sprinkle nuts on top just before serving.

With the "given" a cup or so of cooked chicken (or
duck, squab, turkey) meat, the number of casserole dishes
you can think up is astronomical, the combinations suggested
by what else you have in the refrigerator, freezer, or cupboard. Sometimes the colors of the vegetables will help you
decide what will make an attractive creation. Here is a very

simple-minded dish for baking that could be blah in tone if not for the *green* noodles.

GREEN-NOODLE CHICKEN
4 to 6 servings

½ lb. green noodles
½ lb. fresh mushrooms
margarine or oil
1½ to 2 cups cooked chicken meat in bite-size pieces
1 cup chicken gravy or white sauce

Preheat oven to 350°. Cook the noodles in boiling salted water until almost tender. Slice the mushrooms, and sauté them in oil until light brown. Drain the noodles and put them in the bottom of a greased baking dish. Combine the chicken, mushrooms, and sauce, and spoon the mixture over the noodles. Or mix the chicken-mushroom sauce in with the noodles, rather than layering them. Cover, and bake 25 or 30 minutes.

Leftover chicken can be combined with so many things that you are limited only by your imagination. I've always thought patties or croquettes some sort of a desecration of the fine taste of chicken, but not so chicken hash, for some reason.

CHICKEN HASH
4 servings

2 tablespoons butter or margarine
½ cup chopped celery

¼ cup chopped onion or scallions
2 cups chicken stock or broth
salt and pepper to taste
1 cup cooked chicken meat in bite-size pieces

Melt the butter or margarine in a skillet; sauté the celery
and onion in it. Stir in the chicken stock or broth, then
the seasonings and the cooked chicken pieces. Simmer
for 5 or 10 minutes, then serve hot. If it seems too
"loose" for hash, you could add some cooked rice or
potatoes (in pieces) to soak up some of the liquid.

For warm weather even the cliché of chicken salad is
dandy, especially if you make up a novel new salad. Here
are two different kinds to get you started. Either would go
nicely on a bed of fresh, crisp, raw greens.

CHICKEN SALAD I
4 servings

1 cup cooked chicken meat
(or other poultry), diced

2 hard-cooked eggs, sliced

½ cup dice-sized blocks of semi-hard cheese
(Fontina or Emmenthal?)

1 cup white seedless grapes

½ cup red radishes,
cut into lengthwise quarters

2 cups elbow macaroni, cooked

½ cup mayonnaise,
perhaps thinned with a little juice
from a can of olives or jar of pickles

Combine all ingredients and mix for even distribution.
Serve chilled.

CHICKEN SALAD II
4 servings

1 cup cooked chicken meat, diced or in strips
½ cup dark raisins
½ cup chopped fresh celery, stalk and leaves
1 cup sweet or tart apples, sliced or diced, skin on
½ cup shredded raw carrot
½ cup sunflower seeds
¼ cup nutmeats of your choice
½ cup dressing, half mayonnaise, half sour cream

Ditto.

In case your budget doesn't have room for store-boughten mayonnaise, here are a couple of recipes that will save you some money. The first one will even save you some cholesterol, being made with nary an egg or other form of saturated fat.

HEALTHY MAYONNAISE
about a pint

¾ cup water
½ cup vinegar
1 cup powdered milk
1 teaspoon honey
¼ teaspoon powdered mustard
1½ cups or so vegetable oil (safflower, peanut, or some such)

Combine all but the last ingredient in a blender. Whiz for a minute or so, then turn blender to its lowest speed. Add the oil a drop or two at a time. As soon as the consistency pleases you, discontinue adding the oil. Of course, lacking a binder, this mayonnaise tends to separate after a few days into its component parts. A few flicks of the wrist and whisk will bring it back to its original consistency.

CHOLESTEROL MAYONNAISE
about a half pint

3 egg yolks
½ teaspoon salt
pinch white pepper
½ teaspoon powdered mustard
2 teaspoons lemon juice
1 cup olive oil (or cut it with some lighter oil)

In a warm and perfectly dry bowl, whisk the egg yolks, salt, pepper and mustard, and half the lemon juice. Now start adding the oil, drop by drop, whisking all the time, until you have used up half the oil. Continue whisking while you add half the remaining lemon juice, then the remaining oil, still a drop at a time. Finish the lemon juice and blend thoroughly.

Mayonnaise brings up the question of other kinds of salad dressings that much lucre can be wasted on: Russian dressing, Thousand Island, tartare sauce, and the like, which are terribly costly in view of the fact that all the manufacturer had to do was to stir a couple of other ingredients into mayonnaise to make them. You can do the same thing, and then blow the price of the salad dressing on some far-out greens like rugola or endive for your next salad.

To turn mayonnaise into Thousand Island dressing, all

you need add is a little chili sauce and some finely chopped red and green peppers. Chopped green olives and pimientos can be added as well, for a variation. Russian dressing has become synonymous with Thousand Island in this country, although what made it Russian originally was the addition of some caviar.

Tartare sauce, the *sine qua non* for many a fried-fish fancier, can be made by adding to mayonnaise some chopped green pepper, olives, green pickle, and grated onion. According to some cooks, a little extra vinegar is necessary too.

If we wanted to get a good deal more fancy (or French), we could turn mayonnaise into *sauce rémoulade* by adding anchovy paste and capers, pickles and herbs (usually parsley, tarragon, and chervil).

For other salad dressings, see 230.

Now we come to the pages where you deal with the really least expensive kind of poultry—the fowl or "stewing chicken." This, as we noted before, is the vendor's quaint way of telling you that what you have bought is a middle-aged hen (or rooster) whose flesh is not so young and soft as it once was. You'd better cook it in some tenderizing manner, and slow-cooking in some liquid or other is probably best. Here are a number of ways to get the most out of your bargain in poultry. You don't have to stick to just plain old chicken-in-the-pot, simmered for hours in water with some vegetables thrown in willy-nilly the last half hour for good measure.

CHICKEN CACCIATORE
for 6

This is how I stretched out one of my two poultry purchases of last summer. It fed one of my two dinner parties easily. (Two of the guests even had a second helping of chicken.)

3 tablespoons olive oil

2 tablespoons corn oil (or other vegetable oil)

1 fowl, cut into serving pieces (gizzard and heart included)

1 clove garlic, minced

2 cups tomato sauce

salt and pepper to taste

1 teaspoon oregano or basil

Combine the oils (all olive oil would be too costly, and too rich) in a saucepan and heat. Sauté the chicken pieces very quickly, turning them on all sides, just to brown the skin. Remove the chicken and add the garlic, browning it in the oil. Now add the tomato sauce, the chicken pieces (which should be at room temperature or warmer), seasonings and herb. Cover the saucepan, turn the heat down low, and let simmer for 1½ to 2 hours. Serve hot with rice, a vegetable, and/or a fresh green salad.

The acid of tomatoes has a very salubrious effect on a tough old bird. But it isn't the only juice that can turn a "stewer" into a delectable morsel. How about apples?

APPLE CHICKEN
for 5 or 6

4 tablespoons margarine

1 fowl, cut into serving pieces (with or without skin)

6 to 8 tart cooking apples

brown sugar

salt and pepper to taste

1½ to 2 cups apple juice or cider

Preheat oven to 300°. Heat the margarine in a skillet and sauté the chicken pieces in it, turning them on all sides to brown. Peel and slice the apples, then dip the slices in the sugar to coat. Arrange the chicken pieces and the apple slices in a well-buttered casserole dish. Sprinkle with salt and pepper. Add the cider or juice to the still-warm skillet, stir a bit with a wooden spoon, and scoop all the stuff in the pan, along with the cider, into the baking dish. Bake covered at 300° for 2½ to 3 hours—or until the chicken is tender to the fork.

Coq au Vin literally translated is a rooster cooked in wine. We don't imagine that when you have some good wine, however, you will want to use up that much of it cooking an old bird. If you're anything like us, you'll prefer to drink the wine *with* the cooked chicken. But did you ever wonder how plain old skim milk might do the job? Remarkably well. Try the next recipe when you have plenty of time.

MILK-FED CHICKEN
(Coq au Lait)
for 5 or 6

1 stewing chicken, cut into pieces, skinned or not
1 medium onion, sliced
1 large stalk celery, diced, plus leaves
1 tablespoon paprika
dash cinnamon or nutmeg
bay leaf or few sprigs of fresh thyme
1½ pints to 1 quart milk, skim or whole

Note that you don't brown the chicken first this time, but let the milk work its magic instead. Preheat oven to 275°. Place the chicken pieces in a large baking dish, together with the cut-up vegetables. Sprinkle with the seasonings and herbs. Then pour in the milk so the chicken meat is entirely covered with it. Bake, covered, in a 275° oven for 2½ to 3 hours, or until the milk is all absorbed and reduced to solids. Then the chicken will be tender and very subtly flavored as well. Remove the bay leaf (if used). Serve hot with cooked carrots and peas. Or serve it cold with a tossed salad and good, crusty bread.

The other way to handle an inexpensive older bird, and some kinds of game birds as well, is to marinate it, cold, for rather a long period, thus reducing your cooking time. The marinade does the job of tenderizing that the long, slow cooking might have done. The pieces of chicken should be rather small, the skin off, and the marinade some order of acid. Wines are effective; so is soy sauce; and a combination of soy sauce, vinegar, and fruit juice makes a good marinade. Citrus juices, particularly, combine well with poultry: orange, lemon, grapefruit juices, singly or in combination, are excellent for marinating chicken or goose or duck. Lime is thought of less frequently, but if you have some limes left over from an anticipated summer vodka-and-tonic party that never materialized, try the following recipe.

LIME CHICKEN
for 4 to 6

4 or 5 limes
salt and pepper
that same old bird, cut in small serving pieces, skinless
1 tablespoon margarine
½ cup chicken stock or bouillon
1 tablespoon cornstarch or arrowroot
½ cup nutmeats (optional)

Squeeze the limes, extracting every bit of juice you can. Soaking the whole fruits first in warm water will help. Salt and pepper the chicken segments and cover them with the lime juice. Let them sit in it for 12 hours or so, possibly overnight, in refrigerator or a cool place. The next day remove the meat from the marinade. Reserve the marinade. Heat the margarine in a saucepan, add the stock, then stir in the thickener over medium heat. When it has thickened a bit, add the chicken pieces and some of the marinade, cover the pan, and simmer the chicken in the lime sauce for 1 to 1½ hours. It will be a new flavor experience. Sprinkle with nutmeats, serve it hot, accompanied by white or sweet potatoes, baked or boiled.

As may be obvious by now, I do not belong to a game-hunting family. My neck of the woods, however, abounds in prosperous-looking wild gamebirds. For a while I lived in a house whose backyard was rich every autumn and winter with "partridge in a pear tree." Literally. Because I couldn't bear to shoot them, even with bow and arrow, it wasn't until a handsome, fat woodcock came to a violent end by flying straight into the glass of my greenhouse that I was able to make the following dish. I don't actually know the bird's proper name, but I think it was a partridge—at least it had recently eaten its fill of partridge-berries. This is how I turned it into a Lucullan feast.

WOODCOCK CHASSEUR AU VIN
for 2

1 fresh gamebird suicide
2 cups or so aged Burgundy wine

2 cups thin-sliced hard vegetables: carrot, turnip,
parsnip, celery

3 tablespoons margarine

½ cup stock

3 tablespoons flour or arrowroot

pepper or paprika

2 tablespoons dried herbs: parsley, tarragon, dill

Pluck and draw the bird, then separate the several pieces
of meat from the bones—there isn't very much, even in
a well-fed wild bird, but enough for a meal for two.
Marinate it overnight in the red wine, in a cool place,
being sure that you use enough wine to submerge the
meat in (add a little vinegar or citrus juice to it if you
wish). If you are insomniac, turn the meat over once or
twice while it's marinating.

The next day, drain off and reserve the marinade. Put
the pieces of meat into a lightly greased baking dish and
into a warm oven. Bring a saucepan of water to a
boil and add the hard vegetables, simmering all together until they are partially cooked. Drain and add
them to the baking dish. Melt the margarine in a skillet,
and rub the flour into it. Heat the marinade and stock
together, and add them to the skillet, a little at a time,
whisking until the sauce thickens a little. Season the
sauce, add the herbs. Pour the sauce over the meat and
vegetables. Bake, covered, in a 350° oven for an hour
and a half.

Serve with wild rice, samp, or bulghur for a delectable new taste experience.

Eggs

Now we return to the age-old question of which comes first,
by dealing with eggs, as eggs, second.

In my childhood, fried eggs were a lot of fun when located in the middle of a slice of good bread, any sort that can be sliced. Not poached eggs slid onto a whole piece of toast (a meal that always filled me with dismay when I saw people ordering it), but cooked as follows. Try it on the fried-egg devotee in your household. To my editor, Barbara Burn, who claims it is her favorite breakfast, I am indebted for the title of the recipe.

EGG THING
for 1

1 slice of bread, white or whole-grain
1 tablespoon or so butter or margarine
1 fresh egg

Cut a circle two inches or less in diameter out of the center of the slice of bread. Place a frypan over high heat, add the butter, and when it is sizzling, put the bread in. Now drop the whole egg from its opened shell right into the empty circular hole, and fry for a few minutes, two or three at the most. Then flip the whole thing over, and fry on the other side. Breaking the yolk facilitates this process, but an unbroken yolk, for those who fancy them, can be managed with a little care. Don't forget to fry the little circle of bread alongside the egg slice, flipping it over, too, for a minute or so on the other side. (I suspect the "cookie" was the part I liked best in the days before I learned more elaborate ways to fix eggs!)

The next—not so fancy—recipe is a concoction I delighted in making for myself as a child. A version of milk toast, it was a good rainy-weather lunch. I suspect it was the *name* I liked in this case.

EGGS À LA GOLDENROD
1 serving

1 hard-boiled egg
warm whole milk
1 slice of toast

Separate the yolk from the white of the egg. Pour the milk over the toast, then press the yolk through a fine sieve onto the milktoast.

Of course, a more sophisticated dish would result if, instead of the milk, you used a flavored white sauce; you could even chop up the cooked egg white in it, plus some capers, olives, and whatnot, and give it a French name.

Since everyone knows how to scramble or fry or poach eggs properly (even my tiny English grandson, who stands on a chair at the stove to "do" himself an egg), we go on now to one of the most delightful, and easiest, uses of egg: The Omelet. A plain omelet is dull—you may as well scramble or fry or poach; but an omelet used as an envelop for something else is jolly, and an excellent way to use up small amounts of leftovers. It can be a means of getting some vegetables into a recalcitrant member of your family, or just varying the way you eat your weekly allowance of eggs. *Frittata, pipérade, foo yung,* or omelet, it matters not what you call it, combining eggs with something else in a frypan is a good way to be imaginative and creative at the stove.

Just for starters, here are several of my favorites, cooked in a plain old blackened skillet.

ONION-CHEESE OMELET
for 2

1 medium onion
1 tablespoon oil
3 medium eggs
½ cup whole milk (or cream)
salt and pepper
1½ tablespoons margarine or butter
½ cup sharp cheese, shredded or fine diced (I use
Cheddar usually, but any sharp cheese will do)

While you peel, slice, and then cut up the onion, heat
the oil to quite hot in a skillet. Brown the onion in the
oil, then remove it to a warm plate. Turn the heat
down to low. Beat up the eggs in a bowl with the milk
and seasonings. Add the butter to the skillet, and let
it melt. Pour the eggs into the melted butter and cook
until they semi-solidify, pulling the cooking egg away
from the edges of the pan and letting the runny egg
spread onto the pan. Scatter the cheese onto half the
surface of the egg, then add the cooked onion, distributing it evenly over the same half. Now fold the
"empty" half of the omelet over the filled half. Cut
the semicircle in half, and serve hot on warmed plates.

TOMATO-PEPPER OMELET
for 2

1 sweet green pepper
1 tablespoon cooking oil
1 medium-sized red (or yellow) tomato
3 medium eggs
½ cup milk or yogurt
1½ tablespoons margarine or butter

Remove seeds and white part from the pepper, and slice or dice it. Heat the oil in a skillet, and cook the pepper until almost soft. Meanwhile, slice up the tomato, and add it for the last few minutes of the pepper's cooking. Put the vegetables aside, keeping them warm. Turn the heat down to low. Now beat the eggs, mixed with the milk or yogurt. Then follow the omelet-making directions above.

TUNA-CELERY OMELET
for 2

1 stalk celery plus leaves
2 teaspoons oil
½ cup flaked tuna fish
2 or 3 eggs
½ cup milk (or half milk, half sour cream)
1 tablespoon margarine
1 tablespoon chopped chives or whole capers

Destring and chop up the celery stalk and leaves. Heat the oil in a skillet, and soften the celery in it. Add the tuna, and keep the mixture warm. Now proceed as with other omelets, except that the chives or capers should be sprinkled over the finished product for color and visual interest.

Naturally, the fish in the last recipe doesn't have to be tuna; you could use any other fish that you happen to have found at a good bargain, or that you have a leftover bit of. This reintroduces the notion that the omelet is a fine vehicle for using up small amounts of leftover anything: meats, fish, cheese, fruits, vegetables—not enough for a healthy serving but too much to consign to the garbage pail or soup bag. Look in your refrigerator, and see what needs accommodating. One day I made a dandy omelet by enveloping in egg one little saucerful of the remains of an eggplant *parmigiana*.

Here are some suggestions for things that might be taken care of by adding them to an omelet:

Bean sprouts, chestnuts, diced veal or pork (in other words, the end of a Chinese meal)

Chopped spinach and crumbled bacon

Mushrooms and apple slices

Anchovies, tomato sauce, and cheese scraped off the top of that last slice of pizza with the dead crust

Chopped zucchini, shallots, and sesame seeds

Bits of cooked poultry, with olives and pimiento

Minced clams and baked beans

Sliced peaches or nectarines with chopped mint

A collection of mixed, chopped greens and herbs— lettuce, parsley, thyme, and basil, for example, or tarragon, oregano, dill, and watercress

The possibilities are endless. Just be sure that the cooked leftover bits are chopped small (if not already in bite-size pieces) and are warm when they are added to the eggs. Accompanied by a salad and some good whole-grain bread, such a leftover omelet will make a good brunch for family or guests.

If it's a company dinner you want to do with eggs, your best bet is a soufflé. Don't be shy about substituting eggs for meat—your guests probably eat too much meat anyway for their own good. If you've been scared off soufflés by a chic-chef friend who wants to corner the market, forget it: a soufflé is one of the simplest dishes in the world to entertain with. It will never "fail" if you observe two easy rules: Don't overbeat the egg whites; and see that the soufflé is eaten when it comes out of the oven and is not allowed to sit around while your guests finish that last cocktail or predinner story. If you use more egg whites than yolks, you will be guaranteed a lighter soufflé (and the gratitude of your limit-the-cholesterol company), but an equal number of yolks and whites makes just as splendid a dish.

Soufflés, like omelets, can clothe any number of foods. You can add bits of chopped-up this and that, for using-up or for novel flavor, just so the pieces are small and light enough not to sink like stones to the bottom of the soufflé. Fancy-schmancy things like lark's tongues, artichoke leaves, or pickled walnuts get into the soufflé act. But the plain egg soufflé, or the one-step-further cheese soufflé, besides being relatively inexpensive to make, has always struck me as just right for the "meat" course of a company dinner. Hence, those are the two soufflés I'm providing recipes for, urging their accompaniment by complementary vegetables. Followed by fruit desserts, they make delicious, nutritious, balanced meals.

EGGS SOUFFLÉ

First butter a round baking dish (or a soufflé dish if you chance to have one), and have it ready. Next, separate the egg yolks, whole if possible, from the whites, straight out of the refrigerator, and have them ready.

6 to 8 servings

6 tablespoons margarine
6 tablespoons flour
1½ cups milk
½ teaspoon salt
1 tablespoon Worcestershire sauce
6 or 7 eggs, separated

Preheat oven to 425°. Melt the margarine in a saucepan, then stir in the flour. In a separate pot, heat the milk to the boiling point, and add it to the saucepan. Whisk until the mixture thickens and is smooth. Stir in the salt and Worcestershire. Remove the mixture from the heat, let it cool a little, then add the egg yolks, one at a time, stirring them in well. Now beat the egg whites until rather stiff *but not dry*. *Fold* them into the yolk mixture. Now turn the mixture into the baking dish, being careful not to restir it or mess it around too much. Bake 30 to 40 minutes, or until the top has a golden brown color.

Serve immediately by putting the dish onto the dining table, and ask your favorite diner to make six or eight equal portions, cutting it like a pie.

CHEESE SOUFFLÉ

The same firsts *as for the plain soufflé. Preheat oven to 425°.*

6 to 8 servings

5 tablespoons margarine
4 tablespoons flour
1½ cups milk or cream
½ teaspoon salt
pinches black and cayenne pepper
½ lb. (or 2 cups) grated Cheddar, Swiss, or Parmesan cheese
6 or 7 eggs, separated

Heat a saucepan, melt the margarine in it, then blend in the flour. Bring the milk to a boil, and pour it into the saucepan. Whisk until you get a smooth, thickened texture. Add the seasonings, and let it cool for about 2 minutes. Then stir in the cheese until it combines with the mixture. Cool a bit longer, then stir the egg yolks into the mixture, one by one. Beat egg whites until stiff but *still moist,* and fold them in. Turn the soufflé into the baking dish, and bake for at least 40 minutes. When the top is slightly browned, serve immediately, as with the plain soufflé.

You may notice that margarine, rather than butter, is indicated. Some purists would quarrel with that, but in my lights, soufflés are not among the dishes that absolutely require butter. That may be because I think such preparations are few and far between. Margarine, a low-cholesterol, unsaturated vegetable fat, tastes so good today and is substitutable in almost every place we formerly would have used butter. In fact, I can think of only two spots where I still sometimes use butter: in hollandaise sauce (though a creditable one can be made with margarine) and in some especially light, crisp cookies.

Hard-cooked eggs make so many good salad or appetizer dishes, or garnishes for the tops of baked casseroles, or pocket lunches, sandwich spreads, etc., that it's hard to know where to head in with them. I'm therefore skipping my own personal favorites and including instead a hard-boiled-egg dish thought up by one of the best cooks I ever knew, Maurice Brockway. Maurice used it in his splendid book, *Come Cook with Me,* and I resurrect it now in tribute to his memory. The reason for the recipe's name is that Maurice created it for the opening of a restaurant with a Mexican motif. Make it for a summer luncheon, first or salad course, when you have just talked your greengrocer into letting you have that softening avocado for fifteen cents.

EGGS SAN DIEGO
for 8

1 avocado, peeled and cut up
2 cloves garlic, peeled
½ cucumber, peeled
1 teaspoon salt
1 teaspoon chili powder
juice of 2 lemons
Tabasco
1 cup finely minced clams
few leaves lettuce, chopped
8 eggs, hard-boiled
few teaspoons chives, chopped
8 ripe olives, pitted

Make a *guacamole* by placing in a blender the avocado, garlic, cucumber, salt, chili powder, lemon juice, and a few drops of Tabasco. Blend on high speed. Remove from blender and stir in clams. Chill for three or four hours.

For each serving: on a bed of chopped lettuce in a stemmed sherbet glass, place 1 sliced hard-boiled egg.* Cover with the sauce, sprinkle with chopped chives, and in the center place a pitted ripe olive.

* If you don't have one of those harp-like gadgets that slices an egg neatly all at once, do it with a knife—it will go more easily if you have wet the knife first with cold water.

Quiches, those named *Lorraine* or by any other title, are such fun that I should include one. They use a lot of eggs, plus something like bacon, and classically are baked in a pastry crust. But they are in everyone's book. So I'm going to provide instead, as a grand finale to the eggs section, a very inexpensive though posh hot hors d'oeuvre that is something

like a *quiche.* It stretches one egg to feed twenty-four people
—that's one (1). The catch is you have to have twenty-four
shrimps. Or it serves eight people three times. Here's the
second use for those multi-cup muffin tins that I gave away
—but which you may still own.

SHRIMP QUICHE
24 appetizers

24 small soft rolls
24 uncooked, shelled small shrimp
1 medium or large egg
½ cup evaporated milk or light cream
salt, pepper, cayenne, nutmeg, to taste
about 2 ounces cheese (Swiss, Gruyère, Münster)

Preheat oven to 375°. Grease 24 cups of your muffin
tins. Press a roll into each cup, forming a shell. Put
one shrimp into each shell. Beat up the egg, and add it
to the milk and seasonings, blending well. Now cut 24
thin rounds from the cheese. Pour the egg mixture
over the shrimps, about two teaspoons to each shrimp.
Add a slice of cheese to each cup, and pop them into
the oven. Bake for 15 to 20 minutes—until the tops
look slightly browned.

These hors d'oeuvres can be frozen right in the
muffin tins should your party be postponed. When you
reschedule it, they can go right from the freezer into
a preheated 400° oven, which will bring them to bubbling hot in about 15 minutes.

5

A BEAUTIFUL ROAST

Perhaps it is our heritage from carnivorous forebears—or maybe the job that the public-relations people for the meat-packing industries have done on our consciousness—but the epitome of satisfying dining for most Americans has for too long been a juicy steak or a beautiful roast of beef. Is it some racial memory of fresh-killed meat sizzling over an open fire or a noble animal turning on a spit over the coals in a great fireplace at the end of a baronial hall that so turns us on? Whatever its origins, we can't lay the urge to kill and eat our fellow mammals to the pressing need of our bodies for daily protein intake. This nutritional requirement does exist, but it can be satisfied in multifarious ways far more interestingly than with a slab of beef. And far more cheaply too.

Quite aside from the flesh of fish or poultry, there are so many kinds of meat available to us besides the flesh of steers that it's a wonder any herds of beef cattle still exist. There has been much in the national news in the past few years to indicate that the cost of raising cattle for the food market has discouraged a good many cattlemen, who have turned to other sorts of crops instead; one of the reasons for this is the doubling and tripling of grain prices, and unfortunately a good beef animal can't be achieved without feeding him well on grain. We are a heroic grain-producing nation, but if the "have" part of our population continues to insist on consuming beef in such unwieldy (and unhealthy) quantity, we'll be unable to feed our large grain production to people. The human animal is starving for want of it, both abroad and at home (the "have-not" portion of the nation). It's a vicious circle and a tense drama.

Now enter centerstage a curious character, the beefalo. Although cases can be made for switching our principal table meat to buffalo, zebra, rabbit, opossum, or snake, these beasts are either difficult to come by in any quantity or just as expensive to "beef up" as cattle. Not so the beefalo, which is a cross between a cow and the American bison, the latter a creature we've nearly—but not quite—succeeded in rendering extinct. Like his progenitors, the beefalo is a grass eater, not requiring any of that valuable grain to be brought to an edible state; its flesh, very similar in taste to that of steers, is far better nourishment (higher in protein, lower in cholesterol) than the traditional well-marbled sirloin. Whether or not the beefalo supplants the cow or steer as the principal supplier of meat for the table of America depends on a number of factors, one of the most important being a public demand for this change to take place.

So start agitating. Talk to your congressman. See what your state department of agriculture is doing in this realm of crossbreeding of food animals.

Meanwhile, until such time as prime roast of beefalo is as commonplace as hamburger now is, start shrinking your meat bill by boycotting the more costly cuts of beef. Watch the market ads with an eagle eye; if your life will be a shabby thing without that gorgeous red-meat roast once a season, you can get it for the price of chopped chuck if you catch the market with a glut of the stuff, which does happen from time to time. Unless you are lucky enough to have grown your own steer and had him slaughtered and packed away in your own frozen-food locker—or have a close personal relationship with your neighborhood butcher—what you're watching for is "Beef Sales." When you attend one, don't take anything for granted: make sure that the meat cut is correctly labeled and if possible have it weighed before your eyes. (The best simple course in the identification of meat cuts, by the way, is in the inexpensive and colorful *Better Homes and Gardens Meat Cook Book, 1969.*)

Don't worry about the amount of cancer-producing growth hormone the meat you've bought contains (actually it's a good deal less than in one birth control or menopause-easing pill)—carry it home as if it were gold, and don't waste a bit of it! Rest easy in the knowledge that you have purchased the core of any number of great dinners, and perhaps the flavoring for a host of lunches as well. Bones from unboned roasts (unless your pet pooch has first choice of them) should be thrown into your freezer-compartment bone bag, against the time when you make your next home-grown soup. The fat that drips out under the rack on which you roast your rolled loin is the basis of gravy. If gravy isn't in your plans, pour it into a Fat Can, store it in the back of your refrigerator, and you will have it handy to cook some-thing else in soon. The hard or gristly parts that your guests leave on their plates do *not* go into the garbage—they either go into the bone bag too or are added to your dog's or cat's supper dish. (If you opt for bone-bag and thence freezer, don't lie awake fretting about the possible disease germs that may be adhering to them; when you boil the soup you'll destroy any possible contamination.) So buy the larg-est roast you can afford.

Don't overcook it. In the first place you'll use up an extravagant number of kilowatts by running your oven higher than 350°; in the second, if you're interested in flavor, you'll taste more beef (or veal or lamb or whatever) if it is under-done than if it's nearly burned. Government inspection has obviated the risk of trichinae and other dangerous organisms in your pork. Always use a rack of some kind when roasting any fatty meat, so that you can collect the fat that runs off and also prevent the underneath part from recooking in the gathering grease and getting very tough. Decisions about searing first or not, pricking or scoring the fat, dredging first in flour or salting, drying or rubbing with some juice, inserting slivers of garlic, selecting the exact heat and roasting time will vary according to your type of roast. Some specific recipes for specific cuts follow soon.

Whether you serve the annual beautiful roast to guests or hoard your gold for the family depends a lot on how you feel about your guests. If you decide in their favor, treat them to a feast for all the senses by carving at the dining table, a splashy performance full of entertainment value if your guests (and your carving!) are anything like mine. The danger is that second helpings will be accepted and there won't be leftovers for the next night's family dinner, and the one after that; but that chance can be taken once a year. Carving in the kitchen and offering only one serving of meat is inhospitable; seconds on vegetables and other accompaniments as a substitute somehow don't earn you the reputation of a great host. With luck (and a minimum of gourmand guests) you will have, after the dinner party, some extenders for the rest of the week without having paid an extra price to the butcher for making the flesh into stew meat, ground meat, steaks, or what have you.

If you have found a beautiful roast on sale but don't want to cook it that very day, keep it under refrigeration for several days. In fact, many taste specialists claim its flavor will improve in direct ratio to the number of days you keep it before you cook it. And of course it will keep for weeks or even months if you freeze it. Whichever you do, remember to anticipate and defrost it (allowing it ample time to come to room temperature all the way through) before you start to cook it; you'll save yourself cooking time and hence energy expense. Also, don't open your oven again if you can help it once you've started roasting—you can lose a lot of heat that way. That's why some modern oven doors are equipped with a little window: so you can peek through it at your meat thermometer (if that's your method of gauging doneness) without opening the door and losing twenty percent of the heat. With a well-insulated oven, basting isn't necessary for most meats to achieve a finely browned outside, even in slow-roasting.

Rib or Rolled Rump Roast

Besides being alliterative, this is the kind of roast that has always been considered eating high off the animal. Boned and rolled or standing (which means still attached to the bones), it makes a showy dish. (As does tenderloin or sirloin tip, but these two cuts are usually so expensive that I'm not going to deal with them at all.) Ribs and rump are top-grade meat that can on rare occasions be purchased without your throwing in your own arm and leg; it would be a waste and a shame to do anything but roast it, uncovered, on a rack in the oven, fat side up, seasoned lightly with salt and/or pepper. Some cooks say no salt, because it tends to draw the juices out of the meat and you want them to stay in; some say if you salt only the fatty surfaces, you don't need to worry about that.

You can seal the roast by searing it in a very hot oven (500°) for about 20 minutes, or in a little hot fat in a frypan, turning it quickly to all sides; or forget this and just roast it at 300°, 20 to 30 minutes to the pound, depending on how much of it you want to be well done (the middle of the roast will be medium or rare in most large cuts if you don't exceed this heat and timing). If you sear in the oven, turn the heat down to 300° for the rest of the cooking time. If you don't sear first, put your roast into an oven preheated to 300°.

Since you're stuck with that oven heat for a fairly long time, take advantage of it: bake some large, hard vegetables at the same time. White or yellow potatoes in their skins, or some kind of squash in theirs, or other root vegetables, whole. Or the rice or buckwheat you will serve with the roast. Anything that doesn't require a higher temperature, just so you don't waste that space around the roast. (You can even finish drying some recently washed clothing that hasn't yet dried out in your damp bathroom or cellar while it's raining!)

If you want your finished roast Britishly accompanied by good old traditional Yorkshire pudding, you will have to make that separately. Since it's a reasonably inexpensive and easy way to make an impression, why not make it for the next roast with some of the drippings from this one? That way you don't have to disturb *this* roast's cooking to get the drippings, then raise the heat of the oven, etc. Of course if you have two ovens, then you've got it made and can serve it with *this* roast.

YORKSHIRE PUDDING
4 to 6 servings

1 cup flour
½ teaspoon salt
½ cup milk (whole if possible)
2 eggs, beaten until fluffy
¼ cup water
½ cup hot beef-roast drippings (or melted shortening)

In a bowl, sift the flour and salt together. Combine the milk, eggs and water, and add the liquid to the dry ingredients, mixing well until bubbles form. Pour this batter onto the top of the hot drippings (or melted butter or margarine) in a baking dish. Bake for ½ hour with the oven at 400° for the first 15 minutes, then at 300° for the last 15 minutes.

With a serving of this next to a thick juicy slice of roast beef, only the real trenchermen will ask for seconds!

The question of gravy, which we met head-on in the previous chapter, now arises again. The very best sort of gravy for the roast just described is its own. (*Au jus* on a menu means just that—in its own juice.) Take the drippings from the bottom of the roasting pan, and while the roast is cooling enough for you to carve it, skim off excess fat if there is any, then add a little water (or wine if you prefer), simmer the *jus* for a few minutes and serve it hot in a pouring vessel on the table. Some people would strain it; others would not, keeping all the little bits of substance that can be scraped off the roasting pan.

For an elaborated beef gravy, you can add to it any one or a combination of the following:

Chopped sautéed onions or shallots or leeks

Fresh green chopped chives or watercress

Sliced or chopped mushrooms, raw or sautéed

Chopped parsley and capers

A little wine or cider or even beer

Chopped celery (with leaves) or green pepper, sautéed

Mustard or horseradish (for a gravy with a bite)

Thickened gravy, in my opinion, doesn't belong with this sort of roast. But of course you can use the drippings as the liquid part of a sauce for another dish. You would proceed as for chicken gravy, and then use your imagination for ways to enhance the flavor with herbs and seasonings. Here, for the record, is a recipe for making a thickened gravy from drippings. Naturally, if you lack the drippings, some shortening may be substituted.

BASIC (THICKENED) MEAT GRAVY
about 1¾ cups

½ cup roast drippings
2 tablespoons flour or cornstarch

1 cup meat bouillon or stock
herbs and/or seasonings
Kitchen Bouquet or Maggi or caramel coloring
(see next recipe)

Blend first two ingredients in a saucepan. Heat the stock in a separate pan and add it a little at a time, whisking, over medium heat, until it thickens. If it thickens too much, add a little more liquid. Season to taste, and color to taste.

HOME-MADE
CARAMEL COLORING

The trouble with caramel coloring is that it not only colors but sweetens a sauce as well. Even so, if you want to have a supply on hand, all you have to do is burn some sugar. Start with granulated sugar. Heat a small saucepan and stir the sugar in it over medium heat until it melts and turns brown; let it burn on a little, then scrape it away from the pan, using a wooden spoon. Add a very little water to make it into a syrup, and store it in a warm place to keep it from crystallizing.

The cuts of beef that most of us are content to buy are those that are more properly pot-roasted, or braised. Notably the top or bottom round, shoulder or chuck roast, or brisket. A pot roast of this kind will obligingly make its own gravy for you as it cooks. You may "improve" the gravy when the roast is finished by adding some red wine, some soy sauce or Worcestershire sauce, or some Kitchen Bouquet, Bovril, or caramel coloring.

POT ROAST OCCIDENTAL

For a 3- or 4-lb. roast you will need:

½ cup flour
salt, pepper
2 to 3 tablespoons oil or margarine
1 small onion
1 garlic clove
2 cups vegetable stock or bouillon

Wipe the roast with a damp cloth. Dredge it in the flour, to which you have added salt and pepper. Heat the oil to nearly smoking in a skillet. Now sear the roast all over, turning it from side to side and end to end until its surface is very brown. Chop the onion and garlic, and add them to the stock. Bring the stock to a boil, then pour it over the roast in a pot with a tight cover. Cover tightly, and put it on a low fire so the liquid simmers, never boils, for 2½ to 3 hours. If for some reason you prefer oven-cooking, preheat oven to 300°, and leave closely covered pot in for at least 3 hours.

POT ROAST ORIENTAL

For the same 3- or 4-lb. roast you will need:

2 tablespoons flour
1 tablespoon curry powder
1 teaspoon salt
¼ teaspoon black pepper
2 tablespoons vegetable oil
1 cup equal parts honey, soy sauce, sherry, and water
2 tablespoons fresh ginger, minced

Combine the flour, curry powder, salt, and pepper. Wipe the roast with a damp cloth, then dredge it in the seasoned flour. Heat the oil quite hot in a skillet, and sear the roast all over, turning it to brown all surfaces. Add the ginger to the honey-soy mixture, and bring it just to a boil. Now proceed exactly as in the recipe above.

As with poultry, a tougher sort of meat can be tenderized by marinating it for a number of hours in some acid liquid: wine or beer or cider or even fruit juice of some kind. You can save money by buying the less expensive cut of meat, but you must pay for it in time. The marinade performs double service by going on to become the liquid for the moist-cooking. Get flank steak, for example—not the kind called London broil but a less costly variety—and soak it overnight in cranberry or cranberry-grapefruit juice. Then pot-roast it, substituting the fruit marinade for the stock. Add half-cooked vegetables (potatoes, carrots, and turnips, for example) to the pot for the last half hour of roasting. And serve slices of the roast with the vegetables and a fresh green salad.

Some of the best pot roasts imaginable can be cooked with fruit—not just vegetables. The following is a beautiful dish, not costly to make. Don't ask me whether its flavor is Eastern or Western—try it yourself and see.

PRUNE-APRICOT POT ROAST
6 to 8 servings

2 tablespoons margarine
3 to 4 lbs. pot roast
1 small onion, chopped fine
salt and pepper, to taste

½ cup red wine
1½ cups dried prunes and apricots
3 tablespoons flour or arrowroot

Heat the margarine in a skillet, and sear the roast in it, browning on all sides. Put the meat into a pot with a cover, and add the onion, salt, pepper, and wine. Cover tightly, and simmer for 2 hours. Meanwhile, freshen the dried fruit by letting it soak for an hour or so in a cup of hot water. Reserving the soaking liquid, remove the fruit to the top of the roast, then re-cover and cook another hour. Now use the reserved soaking liquid to make a sauce, combining it with one cup of juice from the pot roast, and thickening it with the flour or arrowroot.

One of the great things about having cooked a roast of beef, pot or not, is that you're bound to have some meat left for next-day or next-week combined dishes. Such as stews and casseroles of all sorts, which you creatively dream up according to what else you have left over. Or perhaps you have found a bargain in stew-beef rather than acquiring it on the second carving from a roast. Either way, you can perhaps use a recipe for beef stew, an all-time favorite, a good meat-stretcher, and a hearty one-dish meal.

EVERYBODY'S BEEF STEW
5 or 6 servings

1½ lbs. stew meat
2 tablespoons flour
salt and pepper

2 to 3 tablespoons oil or margarine

2 cups tomato sauce

1 cup beef or vegetable stock

2 large onions, quartered

¼ cup chopped parsley

1 bay leaf

4 medium-sized potatoes

6 or 8 carrots

2 stalks celery, plus leaves

Dredge the meat, cut in cubes, in flour that has been seasoned with salt and pepper. Heat the oil, and brown the meat cubes in it, turning them to brown on all sides quickly. Combine the tomato sauce and stock, and heat; pour this liquid over the meat cubes in a heavy pot or Dutch oven. Throw in the onions, parsley, and bay leaf; cover, and simmer for 2½ hours. Meanwhile, quarter the potatoes, halve the carrots, and cut the celery up into one-inch lengths. Boil the vegetables (together) until almost tender, then add them to the stew to cook for the last half hour. Remove bay leaf before serving.

Stews, you've heard until it's coming out your ears, are much better the second time around, when the flavors have had time to "marry" and the textures may suit you better. Another advantage of the second-day beef (or lamb or veal or squirrel) stew is that you can change its nature by the addition of different vegetables. It seems to me that the stew above is crying for some green peas the second day; or stir in some baked beans of one stripe or another. Mushrooms, too, could be added handily, or Brussels sprouts. Try combining it with some leftover rice or pasta shells, and a different herb or spice to change the flavor.

I know a woman, living very frugally alone on small earnings, whose habit it is to buy a beef, lamb, or pork roast on the weekend and serve it for Sunday dinner (at which she usually has one to three guests), then use the roast for the rest of the week as flavoring for her largely vegetarian weekday life. This is another way of saying that with the leftover bones and adhering meat scraps from a luxurious roast, you can make a *stock* that will be the basis of many future dishes. And save money on those packaged cubes that are so costly, like most "convenience" products in which a lot of work has been done for you.

Speaking of flavoring, chili is one of the all-time greats, in my estimation, for a one-dish meal that uses up leftover meat and provides you with a balanced, high-protein feast at the same time. You may think, unless you live in the Southwest, from whence this delight migrated, that chili is too hot a dish for your taste. And when made with fresh *chileños* (chili beans) it can be—but it needn't. The secret is all in the amount of chili powder you use. My recipe for non-tongue-burning chili follows. (Real chili aficionados, Southwestern style, would quarrel with the use of tomatoes —and even possibly of beans—so I guess you'll have to consider this an effete Easterner's dish far removed from its origins.)

COOL CHILI CON CARNE
about 10 servings

4 or 5 large onions, sliced
3 or 4 green bell peppers, cored, sliced
oil or margarine
3 garlic cloves, peeled, minced
1 lb. leftover beef, cut in chunks
2 16-oz. cans red kidney beans with liquid
2 16-oz. cans peeled tomatoes with liquid

98

salt and pepper, to taste
2 to 3 tablespoons chili powder

Sauté the onions and peppers until softened, in a little oil, adding the garlic at the end of frying. Then mix with everything else and simmer, covered, on top of the stove for an hour or so; the longer you simmer, the more the flavors will blend and the softer the meat and vegetables will be. Naturally if you have fresh tomatoes and recently picked beans, you will want to use them instead of the canned items; and in that case you will need to add water or tomato juice or beef or vegetable stock to moisten—and cook longer to soften the beans.

This is a nourishing, low-cholesterol dish. If cholesterol isn't one of your worries, you may want to add half a cup or so of bacon bits, which produce an even more interesting flavor. In that case, you can brown the bacon first, and sauté the onions, peppers, and garlic in the bacon fat instead of oil or margarine. And there's no law that says you can't add a handful of leftover pieces of chicken or other poultry. Either way it will be an inexpensive, filling dish. Just increase the chili powder a little if you have a "hot" tooth.

VARIATION: Add one cup corn kernels, and it becomes Chili Corn Carne.

Another good and easy employment for that second-day beef is of Chinese origin: stir-fried meat and vegetables. Only let's not have a bowl of gluey, overcooked, stuck-to-gether white rice on the side, as we so often find in otherwise good Chinese restaurants. Let's instead stir-fry the rice (brown *or* white) into the other ingredients, which then add up to a more attractive one-dish meal. If you have a wok, use it; but if you don't, use your skillet. And be not intimidated by the unfamiliar terms. Stir-fry simply means what it says: you stir and fry at the same time, in a small quantity of oil. You save heat by doing it quickly with vegetables and meat precut into small pieces.

STIR-FRIED BEEF AND VEGETABLES
2 to 4 servings

1 cup brown or white rice
½ to ¾ cup vegetable oil
2 large bell peppers (if one green and one red, so much
the better for color), diced
1 large onion, diced
¼ cup thin-sliced bamboo shoots (optional)
1 cup snow peas or stringbeans, cut in 1-inch pieces
salt and pepper, to taste (or a dab of sesame or curry
paste)
1 cup second-day beef, cut in ½-inch cubes

Cook rice (if not a cooked leftover) *al dente*. Heat the oil to smoking-hot, then throw in the vegetables in the order of their hardness (hardest first), stir-frying a little before you add the next one. Stir in the seasonings. Add the cooked rice after the other vegetables, and the meat last, so it won't have a chance to over-cook. Leave it all on the fire, covered, a minute or two before serving.

Leftover chunks of beef go nicely into casseroles, combined with a variety of vegetables, plus something to hold them together either firmly or loosely—and some seasoning or flavoring to spruce them up. (See that your vegetables are not all high-starch ones.) Here is a particularly good casserole that combines beef with eggplant.

BEEF-EGGPLANT CASSEROLE
6 to 8 servings

2 8-oz. cans tomato sauce
1 teaspoon each dried oregano and basil
1 eggplant (about 1 lb.)
2 or more tablespoons vegetable oil
2 medium eggs
1 lb. leftover cooked beef, cubed
½ cup bread crumbs
1 cup grated cheese (Parmesan or Romano)
1 8-oz. knob mozzarella cheese

Preheat oven to 350°. Heat the tomato sauce, add the herbs, let simmer for about 10 minutes. Meanwhile wash the eggplant (don't peel), and slice it into ¼-inch rounds, then cube it. Heat the oil until almost smoking, and sauté the eggplant cubes in it until they turn translucent. Beat the eggs slightly and combine them with the tomato sauce. Now add the beef and eggplant to this sauce. Combine the bread crumbs and grated cheese. Lightly grease a baking dish, and pour in one third of the beef mixture; on top of this, sprinkle one half the cheese-crumbs. Repeat this sequence, with the last third of the beef-and-sauce on top. Cover the top with a layer of mozzarella, cut in slices and overlapped. Bake, uncovered, for 30 to 45 minutes at about 350°.

VARIATION: For the eggplant, substitute summer squash or zucchini, or any kind of squash. Or whatever vegetables you want to use up.

For some additional dandy ways to use up leftover beef (or other meat or poultry) see Chapter 7—just add chunks of meat to the vegetable casseroles.

If there's anything about beef that all Americans know well, it's hamburg. The classic hamburger. Salisbury steak. Meat patties. Chopped beef (usually made from chuck, frequently a "bargain" meat). We know how to s-t-r-e-t-c-h it out before cooking it in hamburgers or meatballs or a meat loaf: with egg and milk; bread crumbs or bits of leftover crusts; oatmeal or other cooked or dry cereal; chopped onions, peppers, or celery; ketchup or soy sauce. All this does help to extend the meat and cut down on the amount of saturated fat you take in at one meal. There are all sorts of lovely combinations, too, of hamburg and pasta, or rice and/or other vegetables. We sometimes forget, however, that certain classic dishes calling for whole pieces of beef can equally well be put together with hamburg, at considerably less expense. Here are a couple of examples.

HAMBURGER STROGANOFF
5 or 6 servings

1½ lbs. chopped beef
salt and pepper, to taste
2 tablespoons margarine
1½ cups chopped onion
½ lb. fresh mushrooms, sliced or chopped
2 tablespoons flour or arrowroot
2 tablespoons lemon juice
1 tablespoon Worcestershire sauce
½ cup meat or vegetable stock
1 cup sour cream

Season the meat, and form it into small balls (marble size). Heat margarine in skillet, and brown meatballs in it; remove them and keep them warm. Add onion and mushrooms to melted margarine, and brown them; remove vegetables, and add them to meatballs. Add a bit of margarine to the skillet if necessary, and stir in the thickening, then the juices and stock, everything but the sour cream. Whisk over medium heat until thickened. Return the meatballs and vegetables to the sauce, cover, and simmer about 15 minutes. Stir in the sour cream just before serving, and blend well. Serve hot, accompanied by noodles or rice or mashed potatoes or barley.

If you don't finish the Stroganoff on first serving, then combine it with the noodles (or whatever accompaniment) in a casserole for the next night. Change its character and extend its life by stirring in some different vegetables you happen to have on hand (thin-sliced carrots, say, or some cooked spinach or chard or beet greens). And break up that little end of blue cheese or Gorgonzola on top before you put the dish into the oven for 20 or 25 minutes at 350°.

HAMBURGER BOURGUIGNONNE
6 to 8 servings

¼ cup margarine
1½ lbs. lean hamburg
2 tablespoons dry sherry
salt and pepper, to taste
2 dozen small white onions
¼ cup flour or cornstarch
1 tablespoon tomato paste
1 bay leaf
1 teaspoon mixed thyme and marjoram
2 cups hearty Burgundy
chopped parsley

Preheat oven to 325°. Melt margarine in large skillet; break up hamburg and brown it in the margarine. Lightly grease a casserole dish and put meat in it.

Sprinkle meat with sherry, salt, and pepper. Brown onions, kept whole, in the margarine in the frypan, then add onions to the hamburg. Add flour, tomato paste, herbs, and Burgundy to the frypan, and whisk over medium heat until thickened. Pour this sauce into the casserole dish, then cover and bake for 1½ hours. Garnish with chopped parsley before serving, hot, with crusty homemade bread or bulghur.

Penny-pinching is hard to do these days if you vary your beef-eating with baked sugar-cured ham, pork chops, or saddle of veal. But a few farthings can still be saved this side of the South Pacific by switching to lamb. Not chops, but good roasting cuts are sometimes offered at thrifty prices. If you must buy a rather large hunk of lamb to take advantage of the sale, don't hesitate; it can be the center of four or five meals in various guises.

An international tradition says that the perfect accompaniment to a leg of lamb is mint jelly or mint sauce. And that is a good taste combination, but so old hat that you might want to try roasting your lamb in one of the following ways instead. The less tender (and hence usually cheaper) cuts are very good for stewing and braising, while the favorite roasters in this country are the legs. A friend of mine recently served at a dinner party a large, boneless, rolled roast of lamb that had been pre-sliced. She seemed to think this a very big deal, but she had paid dearly for this extra service on the part of the butcher; if she had sliced it herself after roasting, she'd have saved more than a few sous.

The British (and other Europeans) prefer lamb cooked pink, whereas most Americans don't feel lamb is done until it has lost all its rosiness. White, brown, or pink, lamb is another meat that can benefit from cooking with fruits. A few suggestions to stimulate your imagination come next.

PLUMBED LAMB
8 to 10 servings

4- or 5-lb. leg of lamb
1 clove garlic
salt and pepper, to taste
1 16-oz. can purple plums
2 tablespoons lemon juice
1 tablespoon soy sauce
1 teaspoon Worcestershire or A-1 sauce
1 teaspoon fresh basil, minced, or ½ teaspoon dried

Preheat oven to 325°. Wipe the lamb with a damp cloth. Peel and sliver the garlic and push it into slits cut into the meat here and there. Then season the meat and place it, fat side up, on a rack in a roasting pan. Roast for 3 hours. Meanwhile, drain the plums, reserving the liquid from the can. Pit the plums, and push them through a coarse sieve. Combine them with ¼ cup of the reserved liquid, the lemon juice, sauces, and basil. During the last hour of its roasting, baste the lamb with this sauce, heated. At the end of the roasting time, take the leg of lamb out of the oven, and let it cool a bit before serving. Gather all the sauce and drippings from under the roast, and cool enough to bring the fat to the top. Skim off the fat, bring the remaining sauce to a boil, and serve it in a gravy boat with the roast.

IBERIAN LAMB
6 to 8 servings

4- or 5-lb. leg of lamb
1 cup dried apricots
½ cup orange juice

1 tablespoon powdered ginger (optional)
2 cloves garlic
salt and pepper
1 teaspoon fresh tarragon, chopped,
or ½ teaspoon dried
1 cup Madeira

Preheat oven to 350°. Trim excess fat from leg of lamb, and wipe it with a damp cloth. Cover apricots with water in a saucepan, and simmer them until softened. Add the orange juice and ginger to the saucepan, and continue to cook until the liquid thickens. Now strain the fruit sauce, and set it aside. Peel and sliver the garlic cloves and insert the slivers here and there in the leg of lamb. Season it all over with salt and pepper, and set it on a rack in a roasting pan. Add the tarragon to half the Madeira, and pour it over the meat. Add ½ cup of water to the roasting pan. Cook for 1 hour at 350°. Heat the reserved fruit sauce, and baste the lamb with it through the next 2 hours or so, until done to your taste. While the lamb roast is cooling, skim the fat from the top of the roasting pan. Add the other half cup of Madeira to this liquid, and simmer it for 10 minutes or so, whisking. Serve the fruit sauce in a gravy boat with the lamb.

Cold sliced lamb the next day is an entree that should not be slighted. (I personally prefer cold lamb to hot, but that may be a peculiarity.) Cold lamb invites embellishment by any number of sauces or relishes, piquant or bland, hot or cold. So this seems as good a place as any to put in some sauces. (For relishes, see Chapter 7.)

The first three of these sauces are very good with fish or egg dishes too.

MUSTARD SAUCE

Prepare a standard white sauce and stir into it as it thickens either 1 tablespoon prepared paste mustard or 1 teaspoon powdered mustard. Taste for hotness.

SORREL SAUCE

Pick about a quart of sorrel (sour grass), soften it in butter or margarine, and add it to a white sauce made of margarine, flour (or cornstarch), and milk or cream, thickened over medium heat. Season with salt and pepper, and stir in slowly a whole raw egg.

SAUCE VERTE

Put 1 egg yolk in a bowl and start whisking. Salt and pepper to taste, and add 3 tablespoons wine vinegar, whisking all the while. Then add, a drop at a time, a cup of oil (half olive oil and half something lighter). Then stir in 2 cups of mixed, fresh minced chives, scallion blades (omit the white bulb), parsley, and tarragon.

PIQUANT BROWN SAUCE

Mince a little onion, and brown it in butter or margarine. Add an equal amount each of flour and of lemon juice, and whisk over medium heat. Add hot

meat or vegetable stock, a little at a time, until the
mixture thickens, whisking slowly. Season with salt
and pepper and strain. Color with Kitchen Bouquet
or your own caramel coloring (see p. 93 for recipe).
Add to the sauce 1 tablespoon each chopped sour
cucumber or dill pickles and capers.

JUNIPER LAMB
4 to 6 servings

If you have some juniper bushes, wild or cultivated,
around your home, and a little ginger ale that has gone
flat in the refrigerator, you are nicely set up for
braising that lamb shoulder (or even more economical
cut) that you found at thrift-shop price in the spring.

1 cup juniper berries
3 or 4 lbs. boned lamb
salt and pepper
1 cup ginger ale

Preheat oven to 325°. Crush the berries a little with the
flat of a stout knife. Salt and pepper the lamb all
over, and put it into a baking dish (one that has a
secure cover) that is not much larger than the volume
of the lamb. Add the ginger ale and berries to the
baking dish, cover tightly, and bake for 3 or 4 hours.
Turn the meat over once during that time. Can you
imagine gin-flavored lamb? That's how it will taste—
surprisingly good.

It would be lovely and appropriate (and economical)
to serve this lamb with some wild weeds called lamb's

quarters (another name for this green is pigweed, but never mind that). Very tasty, something like spinach, lamb's quarters grow practically everywhere. Washed and then softened in a little melted butter or margarine, they would be the perfect accompaniment. The only hitch is that these little leaves soften to a fraction of their slender bulk, so you will have to gather a great deal to make anything like a "serving" for even one. Perhaps, on second thought, you should instead add the lamb's quarters to your spinach, chard, and/or beet greens, softening them all up together in a little margarine or oil.

Then the next day, when it is cold, this lamb could be served with Sauce Béarnaise (which you can hardly open a cookbook without finding a recipe for). The sauce won't curdle if you don't let it get too hot; keep it warm in a hot bowl. A nifty sauce it is, too, for poultry, meat, or fish dishes.

Another post-roast meal, using the pieces you cut off the bone, would be a hearty shepherd's pie.

SHEPHERD'S PIE
6 to 8 servings

4 cups white baking potatoes, peeled and cubed
8 tablespoons butter or margarine
½ cup whole milk or cream
salt, pepper
1 large onion, chopped
1 garlic clove, minced
3 tablespoons flour or cornstarch
1½ cups lamb drippings or meat stock
1 teaspoon tomato paste
1 tablespoon wine vinegar or cider vinegar
2 to 2½ cups small pieces cooked lean lamb
1 tablespoon parsley, chopped

¼ cup grated cheese (Parmesan, Fontina or other hard
variety)
½ cup bread crumbs

Boil potatoes in salted water until tender. Drain them,
and then shake them in a dry skillet over medium
heat until they are dry. Mash the potatoes with half
the butter, the milk, salt, and pepper, and keep them
warm. Preheat oven to 400°. Melt 3 tablespoons of
the butter in the skillet, and sauté the onion until
golden, adding the garlic toward the end. Turn the
heat low, and stir in flour or cornstarch. Pour in the
lamb drippings or stock little by little, whisking over
medium heat until you have a smooth gravy. Add
tomato paste and vinegar, and continue whisking over
medium heat for 2 or 3 minutes. Mix in the lamb
chunks, and cook another 3 minutes. Taste, and correct
the seasoning if desired. Lightly butter a casserole or
baking dish, and spread half the mashed potatoes on the
bottom. Add the lamb in gravy, and sprinkle it with the
parsley. Cover the gravy with the rest of the mashed
potatoes, spreading evenly to make a top crust. Sprinkle
cheese, crumbs, and remaining butter (in dots) over the
top. Bake at 400° for 20 to 30 minutes, or until the top
of the dish is browned.

Don't forget to put the bare bones into your freezer
bone bag. They will lend flavor to the next batch of
meat stock you boil up.

Another way to use your second-day lamb is in a
marvelous stew that is customarily made with chicken or
squirrel. If you happen to have a freshly killed squirrel on
hand, braise the meat first, then add it. But to my way of
thinking, lamb does best with these concomitants.

BRUNSWICK STEW
4 to 6 servings

2 or 3 cups cooked lean lamb, cut into small pieces
1 quart tomatoes, peeled and chopped
1 pint lima beans
6 small potatoes, sliced
1 large onion, chopped
raw kernels from 4 or 5 ears of corn, cut off the cob
¼ lb. bacon, fried and crumbled, plus the bacon grease
(or soybean substitute, with some melted butter)
salt and pepper, to taste
2 quarts meat or vegetable stock
1 cup red wine

Put everything but the wine together in a stewpot with a cover, stir up to blend, cover, and let it cook very slowly, for 2 to 2½ hours over low heat. Uncover and stir once or twice while the stew is simmering. Then add the wine, give it another stir or two, and let it simmer for 15 minutes longer, uncovered. A splendid one-dish meal.

Mutton, the meat of the grownup sheep, is so unpopular in this country that in most localities you are hard put to find any in the markets. (Those few sheep that are allowed to attain maturity here seem to be the donors of their wool, not their flesh, to the American industrial machine.) When you can get mutton (if, for example, you slaughter your own sheep), don't scorn it: it bears the same relationship to lamb as beef does to veal. Much of the "bully beef," in fact, that U. S. soldiers ate in the Pacific in World War II was mutton. Because it's from a more mature creature, the meat is tougher and gamier than lamb; so one treats it like some of the less succulent cuts of beef and stews it, marinates it, or braises it. Nineteenth-century Americans roasted mutton (saddles, haunches, shoulders) after "hanging" it for a few days to age, and served it with fine brown sauces made from port and other wines. They often made stews of the leg or neck meat, or boiled it within an inch of its life and ate it with pickles and capers in butter sauce, with dumplings alongside.

If you *do* find a leg of mutton next time you go to the butchery, here is a peachy way to cook it.

OYSTER-STUFFED MUTTON
serves 8 to 10

2 dozen oysters
½ cup chopped parsley
¾ cup minced onion
2 tablespoons basil or thyme, minced
3 hard-boiled eggs (yolks only), crumbled
1 4- or 5-lb. leg of mutton

Preheat oven to 325°. Parboil the oysters, then remove the beards and hard parts, reserving the cooking water. Chop them, and mix them with the parsley, onion, basil or thyme, egg yolks, and a bit of the oyster-cooking liquid. Trim the leg of mutton and wipe with a damp cloth. Cut five or six holes in the fleshy part of the mutton leg and stuff this oyster mixture in. Now put the leg into a baking dish, cover it tightly, and leave it in the oven for 3 hours. Serve the leg of mutton with a pungent brown sauce (see p. 107).

Both lamb and mutton are cooked everywhere in the Middle East, often in combination with vegetables. To cite only one of the vegetables so used, the marriages of eggplant and lamb in one-dish meals are legion. The varieties of moussaka (which combines these two good-tasting staples) know no end. So great a dish is it that it seems a fitting conclusion to a discussion of lamb and mutton. Plus being a good way to use up third-day bits of this meat, and a quick lesson in making béchamel sauce, which is only a simple white sauce with egg yolk added.

ONE KIND OF MOUSSAKA
6 to 8 servings

1 large or 2 small eggplants
salt, pepper, allspice
olive or vegetable oil
2 large onions, chopped
4 tablespoons parsley or cilantro, chopped (or celery
leaves will do in substitution)
1 small can peeled tomatoes in sauce*
3 cups leftover lamb or mutton, chopped fine
3 tablespoons margarine
3 tablespoons wheat or rice flour
1¼ cups whole milk
nutmeg or cinnamon
yolk of 1 egg
½ lb. Gruyère or Jack cheese

Wash eggplant, leave skin on, and cut into half-inch slices crosswise. Salt the slices, and leave them to drain for 20 to 30 minutes. Rinse in cold water and dry. Heat olive oil (or lighter vegetable oil), and sauté the slices of eggplant until translucent. Remove from

---

* Just because I, in the Northeast, believe I can't get a decent fresh tomato from November through May (and seem always to be making moussaka in that period) is no reason you shouldn't use good, fresh, juicy, peeled tomatoes, in equal volume.

frypan, and keep them warm. Add more oil if necessary, and sauté the onions until golden, salting them and adding pepper and allspice (to taste). Now throw in the parsley and tomatoes in sauce; cook over low heat 10 or 12 minutes, stirring in the meat when you take it off the heat.

Now you are ready to make the sauce. Melt the margarine in a saucepan, and rub in the flour. Warm the milk separately, and add it little by little to the saucepan over low heat, whisking until it thickens. Season to taste with salt, pepper, and nutmeg or cinnamon. Turn off the heat, and whisk in the egg yolk, blending well.

Cube or shred the cheese. Lightly grease a baking dish, and start assembling the moussaka, in alternating layers of eggplant slices and tomato-lamb mixture. Pour the sauce over, top with the cheese. Bake uncovered for 40 to 50 minutes in a 375° oven—or until the top is brown and crusty.

NOTE: This delectable dish can be made just as well from ground raw lamb or beef—just be sure you brown the chopped meat first before baking, and proceed otherwise as above. Moussaka is not difficult, only a little time-consuming; the resulting feast, served perhaps with a fresh green salad, is well worth it.

If you're willing to cut short the life of a wee little lambie for your own nutrition, how about a goat? We spoiled Americans would find goat's meat unattractive, but kid (baby goat) is delicious. It has to be slaughtered before it's weaned, but milk-fed kid is a feast supreme. Talk a local goat-farmer out of his next-born kid, and cook it in one of the following ways.

VERMONT ROAST KID
serves 6 to 8

The kid, if you're lucky, will come to you skinned and drawn, with the legs and head removed. Wash it well inside and out, wipe it dry. Stuff the body cavity with a dressing made of bread crumbs, butter, sweet herbs, pepper, salt, nutmeg, grated lemon peel, and beaten egg. Sew it up or skewer it together, oil it lightly all over, and put it on a rack in a roasting pan. Let it roast at 350° for about three hours, during which time you should baste it from time to time with either cream or salted water; then, when it has dripped sufficiently, with its own drippings. Use this dripping to form the basis of your gravy (thickened with flour and a little margarine). Garnish the roasted kid with lumps of currant jelly or with roasted chestnuts.

Hare or rabbit may be cooked in the same way.

RHODE ISLAND ROAST KID

An even more Lucullan stuffing (for after all, how often in your life will you eat stuffed kid?) could be made of rice, raisins, chestnuts or pistachios, onion, cloves, powdered ginger, salt, and pepper. Then follow otherwise the directions above.

BEIRUT BANQUET ROAST KID

Rinse the kid inside and out, and dry it well. Rub the cavity with a mixture of coriander, ground ginger, salt and pepper, and the juice of 2 onions. Stuff the kid with a dressing made of rice, saffron, chopped onion, olive oil, chopped almonds and walnuts, salt, and pepper. Stuff the kid, skewer or sew it up. Put it on a rack in a roasting pan, cover it securely, and roast in an oven preheated to 450° for 10 minutes. Then reduce the heat to 325°, and roast for 2 hours. Uncover the kid, turn the heat up to 375°, turn it over, and roast it for another half hour.

Garnish the cooked kid with hard-boiled eggs and parsley, and serve it with rice prepared the same way as the stuffing.

You've heard that every part of the pig but the whistle is useful to man? That's no lie (and the reason a neighbor of mine quickly named his new-bought piglet Lorraine—so its cute, cuddly pinkness wouldn't obscure from his doting children the beast's ultimate destiny as the bottom layer of a quiche); it's also true that the flesh of the hog is one of the highest in saturated fat. So if the cholesterol spectre looms in your household, you will want to keep a check on your consumption of bacon, pork, ham, and sausage. Parsimony, too, dictates only an occasional ham purchase. A hint: for roasts, fresh pork shoulder (sometimes called picnic ham) is usually the best buy, aside from the almost entirely fat cuts. You can simply roast it (about ¾ to 1 hour to the pound). Smeared with mustard and stuck with cloves, it will masquerade as a more patrician kind of ham. Then eat from it for several meals, refrigerating in between. Or you can get about a 5-pound picnic, and do the following two meals for eight with it. Have it boned—but *don't leave the bone behind;* take it with you, for soup. Cut off a 1-pound slice before cooking the first meal, and save it for pork-dish number two.

PORK SHOULDER
PRUNELLA
8 or so servings

4 or 5 prunes

3 medium-sized apples

½ cup dark bread crumbs
(pumpernickel or dark rye)

1 tablespoon sugar

¼ teaspoon cinnamon

salt and pepper, to taste

4-lb. pork shoulder (with pocket where the bone
came out)

Preheat oven to 325°. Pit and chop the prunes; peel,
core, and chop the apples. Combine bread crumbs and
fruit with sugar and seasonings, and stuff the pocket in
the ham with this mixture. Skewer the ham closed
and put it on a rack in a roasting pan. Roast for 3½
to 4 hours. At this heat you won't lose much when
you open the oven door for a few seconds, so it
might be a good idea to baste the shoulder from time
to time with wine or, better still, the syrup from
canned fruits. Serve it with sweet or white potatoes
and some greens, either tossed raw in a salad or
softened in margarine.

The second meal is a *cassoulet* that uses no duck or
goose or poultry at all, but is thrifty and chic to make and
utterly delicious. It is one of the best dishes I can think of
for that slice you cut off the pork shoulder for the previous
recipe. All it takes is a little time, and a bit of sausage. Or
this would be a good place to use the bacon scraps that some
butchers part with for practically nothing.

BIRD-LOVER'S
CASSOULET
8 or so servings

1 lb. dried white beans

1 large onion,
sliced or chopped

salt and pepper

½ lb. smoked sausage,
of your choice

1 lb. fresh pork shoulder

2 cups peeled, chopped tomatoes
(and their juice if canned)

½ cup white wine or cider

2 garlic cloves,
pressed or minced

1 teaspoon parsley, minced

Cover beans with cold water, and soak them a few hours, or overnight. Drain beans and combine them with the onion and a bit of salt and pepper. Cover again with water, and simmer the pot, covered, for 2 hours. Preheat oven to 350°. Cut the sausage in thin slices, and brown them in a skillet. Remove. Cut the pork in cubes and brown them in the sausage fat. Now pour off the fat into your Fat Can (for future sautéeing).

Drain the beans and onions, and combine them with the meat and all the rest of the ingredients. If you have a *cassoulet* (or bean) pot, use that, but a covered baking dish will do. Put the combined ingredients into pot or dish, and bake, covered, in a 350° oven for 1½ to 2 hours. Presto—*cassoulet!*

Here's one lovely, easy soup to make with that bone you brought home from the butcher's.

BONE-BEAN SOUP
4 to 6 servings

1 lb. dried black (turtle) beans
1 pork shoulder bone
3 cups chopped onion
¼ teaspoon powdered clove
½ cup chopped celery
½ cup dry red wine
1 hard-boiled egg yolk (optional)

You don't have to soak these black beans, because you'll soften them in the cooking.

Put them with the bone, onion, clove, and celery into a soup pot, pour in a quart of water, and bring to a boil. Then turn down the heat, and simmer for 2 to 3 hours. Then strain the soup; or remove the bone, put the rest into your blender, and purée it. Add the red wine when you reheat it. Serve it hot for a nourishing lunch. (The egg yolk is to press through a strainer onto the top of each cup of soup—pretty but unnecessary.)

While we're utilizing some of the bones of the no-waste-parts pig, we might as well have a little fun with pork spare ribs. To avoid the traditional (and, let's face it, a bit boring) Spare Ribs with Barbecue Sauce, we'll flavor them in a Hawaiian manner.

WAIKIKI SPARE RIBS, SWEET-AND-SOUR
for 4 to 6

4-lb. rack of spare ribs
salt and pepper

119

2 10-oz. cans pineapple chunks
1 sweet green pepper
1 stalk celery (with leaves)
2 tablespoons margarine
2 tablespoons cornstarch
1 clove garlic
¼ cup vinegar
2 tablespoons soy sauce
1 tablespoon brown sugar
½ teaspoon ground ginger (optional)

Preheat oven to 450°. Cut ribs into serving pieces, and season with salt and pepper. Place in a roasting pan, and roast for ½ hour. Drain off fat, and roast for another hour at 350°. Drain pineapple, reserving liquid. Core and seed the pepper, and cut it in small pieces. Chop the celery. Heat the margarine in a saucepan, and brown the pepper and celery in it. Whisk the cornstarch in the (cold) reserved pineapple liquid. Add this to the saucepan, whisking over medium heat until mixture thickens. Mince the garlic and add to the sauce, together with pineapple chunks, vinegar, soy sauce, sugar (you may need more than 1 tablespoon if the pineapple wasn't packed in heavy syrup), and ginger. Pour this mixture over the ribs, and roast them another half hour, spooning the sauce over them from time to time.

The lean meat of the hog is lower in cholesterol content than butter, eggs, organ meats, and many seafoods. It's also likely to be considerably higher in price. So it behooves us to slice our ham paper-thin. Here's a dandy dish to make with thin-sliced ham, in which it combines particularly well with endive. If you can't find or afford the endive, roll up some other salad greens of your choice. A sumptuous quick lunch.

HAM ROULADES
for 2

4 paper-thin slices smoked ham
4 Belgian endives
2 tablespoons mayonnaise
1 teaspoon vinegar or lemon juice
2 hard-cooked eggs, chopped
2 teaspoons mustard
1 teaspoon sweet relish
1 teaspoon fine-minced raw onion

Preheat oven to 375°. Roll a slice of ham around each endive, and secure it with a toothpick. Put the ham-endives in a small baking dish. Now blend all the other ingredients into a sauce, pour it over the *roulades*, and bake for 15 minutes, or until heated through.

Pork sausage, about which we can never say that it's low in cholesterol, should be eaten occasionally just because it tastes so good. Why not keep it to a minimum by considering it more a flavoring than a basic meat? As, for example, in the following one-dish meal which features eggplant (or one of its relatives).

SAUSAGE EGGPLANT CASSEROLE
serves 8 to 10

½ cup vegetable oil
½ lb. pork sausage
2 cloves garlic
1 cup chopped onion

2 medium-sized eggplants, unpeeled (or equal volume
of zucchini, summer squash, or other squash)

1 lb. macaroni

salt and paprika, to taste

½ teaspoon oregano

2 cups tomato sauce

1-lb. knob mozzarella cheese

1 lb. ricotta cheese

Preheat oven to 350°. Heat the oil in a skillet, and
brown the sausage in it, breaking it up into pieces.
Peel and mince the garlic, peel and chop the onion,
and add them to the oil and brown them. Cut up
the eggplant or squash into cubes, add it to the skillet,
and cook it until softened. Cook the macaroni in
boiling salted water about 10 minutes, then drain it
and add it to the skillet. In another pan, add the
seasonings and oregano to the tomato sauce and bring
to a simmer. Put half the eggplant and macaroni mixture into the bottom of a baking dish; pour in half
the tomato sauce. Cut the mozzarella into 1-inch cubes,
and add half of them, then spoon in half the ricotta.
Repeat the layers and bake for half an hour. Serve hot.

The price of veal, you may be convinced, is so astronomical as to preclude your cooking it at home until after
your spaceship comes in. This is certainly true of all the
roasts, chops, and other luxury cuts of veal. A pity, because
veal ranks next to chicken in the high-protein, low-fat scale,
an excellent meat for those who must watch their caloric
or cholesterol intake. But again, even Ms. Pinchpenny can
invest in an occasional piece of veal if she goes for the
lesser cuts, which moist-cook very nicely. This means reserving the cutlets for fantasy, or that very special once-in-a-
lifetime meal designed to do more for its partakers than

fill the gut. Something spiritual will be built up to over the next few pages.

The first veal recipe, however, shows what can be done with veal shoulder (a modest-priced cut) and neck (even more so) and a little imagination. Operating on a shoe-string budget, my daughter-in-law fed me with such brilliance recently that she deserves credit and notice. The kohlrabi had gone a bit limp in the refrigerator. The veal was begged from a SoHo (Manhattan) butcher at a reduced price. And the flavor combination was marvelous. (Some other greens, I imagine, would do just as well, depending on your taste—*and* your refrigerator.)

JUDY'S VEAL AND KOHLRABI
5 or 6 servings

1 medium-sized onion
½ lb. kohlrabi
2 tablespoons vegetable oil
1 lb. veal shoulder and neck, with bones, cut in chunks
1 lb. flat noodles (or bow-ties)
⅔ cup chopped fresh dill
1 teaspoon dried thyme

Preheat oven to 300°. Peel and chop the onion. Refresh the kohlrabi in ice water for a few minutes. Heat the oil in a skillet, and brown the onion and meat in it at a low heat. Remove the meat, and keep it warm. Cut up the kohlrabi, and soften it in the same skillet and oil. Meanwhile, boil enough salt water to accommodate the noodles, and cook them for only about 5 minutes in it. Drain and rinse the noodles. Combine all these ingredients, plus the dill and thyme, in a small casserole dish, with just a little bit of water added. Bake, covered, for 1½ hours.

The next recipe celebrates the fact that a very few gold-plated cutlets of veal can be stretched to justify themselves if you stuff them, and accompany them with extenders of a complementary nature. This dish will make a middling impression on five guests you have to treat medium-warm.

VEAL BIRDS IN BROWN SAUCE
6 servings

6 thin veal cutlets, about 6 inches long
peel of 1 orange
3 tablespoons margarine
¾ cup chopped scallions
½ cup seasoned bread crumbs
½ teaspoon dried oregano
Marsala or similar wine
¼ cup chopped nuts (of your choice)
salt and pepper
6 thin slices prosciutto
2 tablespoons vegetable oil
5 cups brown sauce

Pound the cutlets even thinner than they are. Slice off strips of the orange part of the peel with a vegetable peeler, then mince them. Heat half the margarine in a skillet, and brown the scallions in it. In a bowl combine the bread crumbs with oregano and scallions. Moisten the bread with a tablespoon or two of wine, and add the nuts, chopped. Put the orange peel in, and mix this stuffing well. Salt and pepper it if the crumbs weren't seasoned enough for your taste. Divide the stuffing up into six equal parts, and spoon onto the veal slices. Top each one with a slice of prosciutto, and squeeze the "sandwiches" together. Now roll each sandwich up lengthwise into a cylinder, veal-side-out, and secure each one with toothpick, skewers, or string.

Combine the rest of the margarine with the vegetable oil in a skillet, heat it, and brown each veal "bird" in it, turning each package on all sides. Remove the birds, and keep them warm. Add 2 or 3 tablespoons of wine to the skillet, and heat it while scraping the bits of meat stuck to the pan. Combine the brown sauce (see page 107) with this wine sauce, and blend them, whisking over medium heat for a few minutes. Put the birds in a baking dish, pour the sauce over them, cover tightly, and simmer them about an hour and a half, until the meat is tender. Serve hot, accompanied by brown or white rice, and a fresh green salad.

VEAL FANTASTIQUE

This is the veal dish you dream about, made of the most costly meat in the market, the flavor so delicate and so good that you don't want to glop it up with any strongly competing tastes. The tenderest veal scallops or cutlets are such a pleasure in themselves that a little lemon sauce is the only distraction that should be allowed.

for 2, no more

½ lb. veal scallops, very thin
white flour
6 tablespoons butter or margarine
3 tablespoons very light white wine
11 tablespoons lemon juice
salt and pepper (if you must)

Dust the veal slices with flour (or dredge them in it) so they have a thin covering all over. Over medium

125

heat, melt half the butter or margarine in a skillet to quite hot. Sauté the slices in the butter quickly (they are thin and will cook rapidly), turning them once. Keep them warm. Add the rest of the butter or margarine to the skillet, leaving the heat on medium. Stir in the wine and lemon juice (and salt and pepper if you insist), and let it come just to a simmer. Strain the sauce if you wish (I wouldn't bother, even in fantasy), and serve it poured over the veal.

Accompany the scallops with some tiny green peas and one small boiled potato on each plate—and serve them in soft candlelight.

Variety meats or specialty meats. These are the white-wash terms we have evolved for what used, simply, to be called "offal." Sometimes "innards," or "organ meats." So brainwashed are some contemporary Americans by former terminology (or possibly the fake gentility of their parents or mentors) that they go through life *never* eating any "variety meats." A pity. If you're going to be a meat-eater at all, you would do well to pay more attention to "organ meats"—they are the highest in iron, minerals, and proteins, very good for you, and as a rule far less expensive than the muscle cuts (roasts, steaks, chops) you've been eating all your life. Specialty meats are probably principally responsible for the survival of many an American black in slavery: the masters felt this fare was garbage, so they threw it to the servants, while they themselves feasted on the far less nutritious roasts of pork and beef, filling their veins up with cholesterol while the sinews of the fieldhands prospered.

When many of us think of these meats at all, our inner voice says "liver" (usually calves' liver) and lets it go at that. Calves' liver is a superb meat for anyone who is anemic, we've always heard. And so it is, but beef liver is a whole lot cheaper. At this writing, I can get beef liver locally for forty-nine cents a pound. What other high-protein meat is that accessible? Of course, the liver of the mature bovine is not always perfect if just broiled quickly a few minutes on each side, as calves' liver is, so don't take chances preparing it that familiar way. The following two recipes are foolproof, and they will stretch liver into several more servings than just broiling would do.

BEEF LIVER IN BEER
4 to 6 servings

1 lb. beef liver
6 tablespoons flour or cornstarch
salt and pepper, to taste
2 tablespoons vegetable oil
3 large onions, sliced
2 or 3 garlic cloves, minced or pressed
2 to 3 tablespoons margarine
1 cup beer (flat will do)
½ cup meat or vegetable stock
1 tablespoon cooking sherry (optional)

Cut up liver with scissors into 1-inch pieces. Season 3 tablespoons of the flour or cornstarch with salt and pepper, and dredge the liver chunks in it. Heat the oil in a skillet, and sauté the onions in it until golden, adding the garlic toward the end of this process. Remove onions, and keep them warm. Now turn heat up to high, and sauté the liver pieces quickly, turning them to brown all sides. Remove the liver, and keep it warm with the onions. Add the margarine to the skillet and, when it is melted, the other 3 tablespoons of flour. Pour in the beer and stock, and whisk over medium heat until thickened. Add the (optional) sherry now, whisking it in. Pour this sauce over the liver and onions, and serve the dish hot, with rice, noodles, or potatoes. A bit of chopped parsley or watercress sprinkled over the dish for color would not be amiss.

If this stretches out to another meal, it will taste even better the second day. See Chapter 10 for the curious career of one such recipe.

SCALLOPED BEEF LIVER
serves 4 to 6

½ lb. beef liver, sliced very thin

2 cups bread crumbs

½ cup scallions, tops and stems

1 tablespoon dried sage

salt and pepper, to taste

¼ cup butter or margarine

2 cups canned tomatoes (see footnote under Moussaka p. 113)

The only way to slice liver very thin is to do it when the meat is half frozen. So freeze the liver first, then thaw it out a bit before you try slicing.

Preheat oven to 350°. Spread one third of the bread crumbs in the bottom of a lightly greased baking dish. On top of these place half the liver slices, half the scallions, and half the sage. Salt and pepper this layer, dot it with butter, then put on half the canned tomatoes. Now another third of the crumbs and the other half of the liver, scallions, and sage. Salt and pepper and butter again, and cover with the other half of the tomatoes. Top with the remainder of the bread crumbs. Bake dish, uncovered, for 30 to 40 minutes.

Try a meatloaf by grinding up the liver in your meat-grinder after boiling it for 5 to 7 minutes. Add all the things you would add to a meatloaf made with hamburg. Or do this with the liver and onions you have left over from Beef Liver in Beer. And moisten with a little flat ginger ale if you have any, to "lighten" the taste of the liver.

Foie gras is not the only kind of pâté in the world, though I have to admit that its snob value is immense. Chicken livers can be turned into a creditable pâté. Take out of the freezer those livers you packed in there every time you bought a duck, chicken, or turkey over the last six months. All kinds of poultry livers can be combined (and subsumed under the generic term chicken livers) in a tasty pâté that you will be pleased to have in your refrigerator for a few days. Use it for hors d'oeuvres, to spread on crackers, for a hearty sandwich lunch, or in a neatly rounded mound as one feature of a cold-plate dinner. Even without the donation from a cruelly, mechanically fattened goose (*foie gras*), or some truffles imported from France or Italy at highway-robbery prices, your pâté will be a treat.

GOOSELESS PÂTÉ
makes about a pint

¼ lb. margarine (1 stick)
¾ of a pint-size freezer container's worth of poultry livers, thawed
2 medium-sized onions, peeled and quartered, or chopped
2 medium eggs, hard-boiled, halved
salt and pepper

Melt the margarine over medium heat, and sauté the livers. Turn them quickly as soon as they've browned on one side, and do the other side, saving the margarine. My own taste says turn off the heat and don't sauté the onion, but grind it into the livers raw; some other people at this point would leave the heat on, and sauté the onion until golden. Now set up your grinder (or blender), and feed the chicken livers, egg halves, and onion into it in rotation. Hand-blend the melted margarine, salt, and pepper into the pâté after it comes out of the grinder, and chill it until serving time.

(Stirring in a little sherry, or a little dried thyme, before chilling is desirable, but not necessary.)

This is for when you have bought livers from the market, fresh, and economically. Lamb kidneys could be substituted in this; but better still, cook them as per recipe on page 132.

CURRIED CHICKEN LIVERS
4 servings

cooking oil (about 3 tablespoons)
1 lb. fresh chicken livers
¼ lb. fresh mushrooms
2 tablespoons chopped bell pepper
1 tablespoon chopped parsley or cilantro
1 clove garlic, minced
1 teaspoon to 1 tablespoon curry powder (depending on how "hot" you like it)
½ cup water or chicken or vegetable stock
1 cup yogurt or sour cream

Heat the oil in a skillet, and sauté the livers and vegetables in it until lightly browned. Now stir in the curry powder, add the water or stock, cover the skillet, and simmer the mixture for 15 to 20 minutes. Just before serving (on rice or other starchy vegetable), stir in the yogurt or sour cream.

Beef kidney has for too long been deemed appropriate fare only for American furry pets. Perhaps when you price it at the supermarket next time, you will promote it to people treat. If you find to go with it a bit of dry red wine in the bottom of a bottle opened long ago—you've got it made.

BEEF KIDNEY FOR PEOPLE
3 or 4 servings

1 beef kidney (about 1 lb. usually)

2 cups meat stock or beef bouillon

2 cups chopped hard vegetables: carrots, celery, red or white radishes, for example, singly or mixed

salt and pepper

1 bay leaf

2 tablespoons red wine

2 tablespoons flour or cornstarch

Trim the kidney, removing all hard white parts, and slice it rather fine. Put the meat, stock, chopped vegetables, seasoning, and bay leaf into a saucepan; bring to a simmer, cover, and cook about an hour and a quarter. Without turning off the heat, take about 2 tablespoons of the liquid out, and cool it by adding it to the wine in a skillet. Whisk the flour into this, and continue to whisk over medium heat until it thickens, while the kidneys continue cooking another 15 minutes. Now remove the bay leaf, stir the wine-sauce into the meat and vegetables, and serve it hot.

You will wonder how the cat and dog got so lucky!

How well I remember some of the Sunday breakfasts of my childhood: baked beans, brown bread, and sautéed lamb kidneys! Sometimes this breakfast was quite simply leftover Saturday-night supper, with the kidneys added at the last moment, fried very quickly, so as not to toughen them (and not to be late for church). If you don't think this combination sounds like the best thing since sliced bread, how about the following? (There seems to be a natural affinity between kidneys and mushrooms, although if you lack mushrooms, try substituting some small flowerets of cauliflower or broccoli.)

LAMB KIDNEYS SUPREME
serves 5 or 6

12 lamb kidneys
3 tablespoons margarine
1 small onion (or equal volume shallots)
½ lb. fresh mushrooms, sliced
salt and pepper, to taste
1 cup vegetable stock
2 egg yolks (uncooked)
4 tablespoons heavy cream or sour cream

Clean the kidneys by removing membrane and fat, then halve them. Heat the margarine in a skillet, and sauté the halves, very quickly, on each side; remove, and keep them warm. Add the vegetables and seasoning to the skillet, and sauté them to golden. Now add the stock, and bring it to a boil, letting it cook for 20 minutes. Combine the egg yolks and cream, stirring them together briefly. Turn heat down to low under the stock and vegetables, and stir in the egg-cream mixture, then the kidneys. Allow them to heat through and serve hot, perhaps with buttered noodles, and garnished with chopped fresh greens of some kind.

Naturally you can do the same dish with veal kidneys, if you can find them, and if you can afford them when you do find them.

So far we've been on relatively familiar ground with organs. Now we'll get down to the nitty-gritty, the true innards or offal. Let's plunge right into the heart of the matter.

BRAISED STUFFED BEEF HEART
serves 4

1 beef heart
2 tablespoons margarine or vegetable oil
2 tablespoons chopped onion or scallion
1 stalk celery, plus leaves, chopped
1 cup bread crumbs or cubes
salt and pepper, to taste
1 large bell pepper
½ cup meat or vegetable stock
3 or 4 whole cloves

Preheat oven to 350°. Cut the heart in half lengthwise. Heat the shortening, and brown the onion and celery in it. (If you had some pine nuts left over from stuffed grape leaves or *caponata,* this would be a good place to throw them in—don't buy them especially for this, though, because that will turn a modest dish into a platinum-plated one.) Add bread crumbs and seasoning to complete the stuffing. Push the stuffing into the cavities of the heart, working it into all the crannies. Tie or skewer the two stuffed halves together. Cut off any of the stem that would keep the pepper from sitting flat when turned upside down. Now cut the non-stem end off the pepper, and clean the white and seeds out of the inside. Insert the heart into the pepper, then use the severed end of the pepper for a cap to hold the stuffing in the heart. Tuck the edges of the pepper cap inside the top edges of the heart. Put the whole assemblage into a small baking dish with a tight cover, add the stock and cloves. Cover and bake for 2 hours. To serve, simply cut the heart lengthwise in four sections.

CHICKEN-HEARTED PASTA

Just as likely to supply your protein needs, and lower in cholesterol, is this hearty dish. Again, it depends on your being able to get together all these tiny organs at once. Some markets sell them in collections; some don't.

4 servings

1 lb. chicken hearts
cooking oil or margarine (about 5 tablespoons)
4 or 5 shallots, chopped
½ cup tomato sauce or water
2 tablespoons fresh basil (or 1 tablespoon dried)
salt and pepper
1 lb. spaghetti or macaroni

Wash the chicken hearts, but leave them whole. Heat the shortening, and brown the shallots in it. Add the hearts, and let them brown. Stir in the tomato sauce or water, basil, and seasonings; cover the pan, and simmer the whole thing for about 15 minutes. Serve the hearts on top of mounds of hot pasta that you have just cooked in boiling salted water, *al dente*.

This is an interesting textural experience, besides being good-tasting and good for you.

After heart, the next most logical step is brains. Though it's high in cholesterol, a more nutritious dish than the gray matter of a baby beef is hard to find. The brains of any smaller animal are too hard to find to make it worth the trouble, though there's no reason why you can't dine on lamb's or pig's brains, too, if you choose to. In some parts of the Middle East (and the West Side of Manhattan) the whole head of a sheep is considered a great delicacy, and everything inside is eaten with pleasure. (Just don't go looking for chicken brains!)

BLACK-BUTTERED
BRAINS
for 4

1 double calf's brain (two halves)
salt and pepper
¼ cup wine vinegar or
cider vinegar, plus a few drops
1 large carrot, cut up and parboiled
a sprig of fresh thyme
(or dried equivalent)
1 bay leaf
¼ cup butter (1 stick), *not* margarine
1 tablespoon chopped parsley

Soak the brain halves in cold water for an hour, then peel off the membranes. Wash the skinned brain, drain, and cover it in a saucepan with fresh water. Add salt and pepper, ¼ cup vinegar, carrot, thyme, and bay leaf. Boil, uncovered, for 10 minutes, then drain well and cut each brain half in two, and keep warm.

Heat the butter in a hot frypan until it turns brown. Add the parsley and few drops of vinegar and cook until the brown deepens, or turns black. Pour over the brains, and serve hot. (A good accompaniment is green peas and small boiled white potatoes.)

Brains in that form still look like brains, and hence may offend your tender sensibilities. Though the title may addle you, the recipe below disguises the brains and makes an interesting combination of texture and taste.

SCRAMBLED BRAINS
3 or 4 servings

½ lb. calves' brains
2 teaspoons vinegar
salt
2 tablespoons margarine
4 medium eggs, beaten lightly
2 tablespoons milk or cream

Soak brains in cold water and vinegar for ½ hour, then remove membranes. Put brains into fresh salted water to cover, and simmer uncovered for 20 minutes. Drain, rinse in fresh cold water, and chop brains into small pieces. Brown them over medium heat in the margarine. Combine eggs and milk (and seasonings if you want). Turn heat to low, and pour the beaten eggs and milk into the saucepan or skillet containing the brains. Now proceed as for scrambled eggs, or let the eggs cook as an omelet, in which case you rename the dish Brainy Omelet.

Capers (or pickled nasturtium seeds) scattered over the top of each serving would be nice.

Here is the way a Frenchman (or -woman) would probably do it.

GALLIC BRAIN SAUTÉ
4 to 6 servings

about 1 lb. calves' brains
2 tablespoons wine vinegar
peppercorns and salt, to taste
1 bay leaf
pinch fresh thyme
3 tablespoons flour
3 tablespoons butter
3 tablespoons vegetable oil
3 tablespoons lemon juice
2 tablespoons dill, chopped fine
½ teaspoon oregano
1 tablespoon capers

Cover brains with cold water, and let soak several hours, changing the water from time to time. Drain and remove membranes. Now bring about 1 quart of fresh water to boil, add the vinegar, seasonings, and herbs. Drop the brains in, then simmer for a very few minutes (3 to 5). Drain the brains again, and chill them under cold running water. Now dredge the brains in the flour (seasoned if you wish). Heat the butter in a frypan. Slice the (cooled) brains about ¼-inch thick, and brown them in the butter, turning each slice over once. The rest of the ingredients are for a sauce—combine them in a saucepan, and simmer for a few minutes. Serve the brains hot with the sauce poured over.

It's but a short leap from brains to sweetbreads, which are actually the thymus gland of a lamb or calf, one of the most "organic" of the organ meats. They are often available at surprisingly low prices at certain times of the year in some markets. Like brains, they are highly nutritious high-protein meats. Two recipes, one presenting a still-recognizable gland and one disguising it, follow.

BROILED
SWEETBREADS
for 4

2 pairs sweetbreads
2 tablespoons lemon juice
2 stalks celery, with leaves
1 small onion, chopped
salt and pepper
paprika
flour
bacon
butter or margarine
lemon juice

Soak the sweetbreads in cold water for half an hour. Drain them, and put them in a saucepan, adding fresh water to cover. Add the 2 tablespoons lemon juice, celery, onion, salt, and pepper, and simmer for half an hour. Drain sweetbreads again, and remove skin. (Save the cooking liquid for beef stock.) Break the sweetbreads into several large pieces, dredge them in paprika and flour, and wrap a slice of bacon around each piece, securing with toothpicks. Dot with butter or margarine, and broil under a high flame until they are browned. Serve them hot, with their drippings, improved with a bit of lemon juice, poured over them.

SWEETBREAD "STEAKS"
for 4

2 pairs sweetbreads
2 tablespoons lemon juice
2 stalks celery, with leaves
1 small onion, chopped
salt, pepper
flour
1 large egg, beaten
2 tablespoons milk
1 cup (or more)
seasoned fine bread crumbs
cooking oil or margarine

Soak the sweetbreads, simmer with the next four ingredients as in the recipe above, drain and skin them. Now wrap the sweetbreads in foil or plastic, and put them in the refrigerator with weights on them. When they are chilled and firm, slice them about ½-inch thick. Dredge the slices in flour, dip them in the egg and milk (combined), then into the bread crumbs to coat. Sauté them in the oil or margarine, heated first, over medium to high heat. Or, if you prefer, bake them 20 minutes at 375°, and serve them with tomato sauce or white or brown sauce.

When I was a child, I once tasted tripe; I never again could abide it until it was cooked properly for me in adulthood. It wasn't the idea of a cow's stomach lining that was so disagreeable, it was a failure to prepare it cleverly. Very high in protein, tripe is reasonable in price and not to be overlooked when we strive for some variety in the beef products we cook. Honeycomb tripe can be a most attractive dish, and a tasty one if you have the patience to cook it long enough. Here is one way:

MUSTARD TRIPE
for 6 to 8

2 lbs. tripe

water, or vegetable or meat stock (with 1 cup dry white wine added, optional)

butter or margarine

2 cups mustard sauce (see page 107)

Put the tripe in a heavy saucepan or Dutch oven, and add the water or stock, cold, to cover. Turn heat on to medium, and boil the meat until it is tender—it may take 5 hours. (Don't include any vinegar in the cooking liquid; I think that's where my sainted mother went wrong—the finished meat had too acid a taste.) When it is tender, you might bread and sauté it, but broiling is preferable. When the slabs of meat have cooled, cut them in strips, brush them with melted butter, and broil them under high heat for a few minutes on each side. Then serve them with hot mustard sauce, accompanied with baked sweet potatoes and creamed spinach, for example.

Another way to prepare tripe is by very long baking (overnight usually), as part of a *daube* or *cassoulet*. But that's a more complicated story, which we won't go into here. What we *will* go into is how tripe is sometimes prepared in the southern or southwestern United States. It's also a means of rendering a basically unattractive foodstuff

very colorful and toothsome. This dish has a hot "bite"—
so watch out.

TRIPE SAN ANTONIO
10 to 12 servings

4 lbs. tripe

salt to taste

2 tablespoons vegetable oil

½ cup salt pork or fatback

2 cloves garlic

2 small or 1 medium onion

2 cups flat beer or vegetable stock

1 dried *chileño* (omit if you don't like Mexican-style
flavoring)

3 to 5 fresh tomatoes

3 tablespoons minced fresh herbs (parsley and/or
rosemary, for example)

hard cheese, grated

Cover the tripe with salted water in a large pot, and
simmer for three quarters of an hour. Drain, cool, and
cut the tripe into bite-sized pieces. Put vegetable oil
and fatback together in a baking dish. Peel and chop
the garlic and onion. Heat the oil, and sauté the garlic
and onion in it until golden. Add the tripe pieces, and
stir-fry them until browned. Now add the beer and
red pepper, and continue stirring. Put the tomatoes and
herbs in last, turn the heat down, and simmer this
mixture for 2½ to 3 hours, stirring from time to time.
Sprinkle with grated cheese before serving, hot. Or let
your guests add their own cheese.

Tripe was also cooked in the early days of this country
by fashioning ten- or twelve-inch squares of it into bags

tied together by the four corners, stuffed with beef and seasonings, and boiled practically forever, then stored for some months in a pickling fluid. This, I suppose, is not unrelated to the Scottish dish haggis (innards, oatmeal, and spices tied inside the larger stomach of a sheep and boiled for hours on end—the Scottish terrain being inhospitable to cattle but not to sheep).

At many times and places, the lungs (sometimes called "lights") of the lamb or calf have been eaten, in fact have been considered a great delicacy. So passé, however, is the taste for the breathing apparatus that I doubt you can find them for sale in most markets in the United States today. If you have your own specialty butcher, ask him to save you a pair of lungs, and cook them as follows.

LUSCIOUS LIGHTS
for 2

vegetable oil or margarine
4 large onions, sliced
2 carrots, sliced
1 tablespoon fresh tarragon, or 1½ teaspoons dried
salt and pepper
½ cup dry red wine or cider
1 pair calf's lungs

Preheat oven to 350°. Heat a small amount of oil in a skillet, and brown the onions and carrots in it. Grease a baking dish, and put the vegetables on the bottom, along with the tarragon, salt and pepper, and the wine or cider. Lay the lungs atop the vegetables, dot them with margarine or oil. Bake, uncovered, for 1 hour, checking from time to time to see if the moisture is depleted and adding a tablespoon or so of water or stock if it is.

Don't ask your butcher for intestines, though, if you get carried away by an organic enthusiasm, unless you plan to make sausage in one of its many variations. You *can* find intestines—many wholesale and some retail butcheries stock them—sold by the "hank," very inexpensively. And good fun it is, too, to make sausages, or salami, or liverwurst, or stuffed derma. You certainly don't need a sausage-stuffing machine, but you do require a number of kinds of meat and seasonings. (Most good home preserving books have a section on sausage-making.)

Lamb or beef tongue (both cheaper than calf's) should occasionally appear on the table of the penny-pinching adventurer into the realms of variety meats. Again, the secret here is sufficiently long cooking. Boil the tongue until tender with some robust vegetables and herbs thrown in (for example: carrots, celery, onions, parsnip, thyme, fresh parsley, and peppercorns). Slice it diagonally across the grain, and serve it with some kind of piquant sauce. And once more you've beaten the High Cost of Beef Roast.

And now, fittingly, we conclude the meat chapter with a dandy dish that utilizes all those lambs' and calves' tails you have lying around. Quite seriously, in many parts of the world oxtail stew is considered splendid fare; and anywhere that sheep are bred professionally, they have been docked of their tails at an early age. The meat that adheres to the bones of the tails, though sparse, is very succulent and tasty (as is, for a reminder, that of veal shanks—otherwise there'd be no *osso bucco*). Combined with appropriate vegetables and a good stock, it makes a savory stew. The trick, of course, is locating a butcher who will stock tails for you—unless you are your own butcher. If you succeed in this quest, you could do a lot worse than the following concoction.

TAIL-END RAGOUT
6 to 8 servings

7 or 8 lbs. tails (lamb and/or beef)
½ lb. margarine
salt and pepper
flour
3 medium-sized onions, sliced or chopped
3 garlic cloves, minced
½ lb. turnip, cubed
2 stalks celery, plus leaves, chopped
1 bay leaf
½ teaspoon dried rosemary
½ teaspoon dried thyme
2 cups rich meat stock
1 cup dry red wine

Wash and dry the jointed tails. Grease them all over with about half the margarine, then salt and pepper them. Brown them under the broiler, turning them over to brown on all sides. Cool the tails, and then dredge them in flour. Now melt the rest of the margarine in saucepan or stewpot. Add the onions and garlic, and sauté them until golden. Add the tails to the saucepan, then the turnip, celery, herbs, and stock. Cover, bring to a boil, then skim off foam. Simmer the stew, covered, for about 2½ hours, or until the meat is tender. Add the wine, and simmer a bit longer, uncovered, about 15 minutes. Cool and refrigerate the ragout, and when the fat rises to the top, remove it. Reheat the dish slowly before serving it hot.

6

JEWELS FROM THE SEA

Not pearl earrings and coral necklaces—but the whole world of seafood, a rich and varied one, and fish from other waters as well. Even completely landbound Americans should (and can now, thanks to modern methods of preservation and distribution) include a certain amount of fish in their diet. Many varieties provide a less expensive way of maintaining high protein (and necessary vitamins and minerals) than does constant ingesting of meat and/or eggs. Unless prepared in huge amounts of saturated fat, most fish is quite low in cholesterol, too. Fish twice a week is the average at my house, but if I lived near a source of fresh, home-grown finny creatures, this figure would rise considerably. Lucky the cook who can catch trout or bass or mullet or perch in a nearby pond or stream; fortunate the seaside dweller who can take mackerel from the tides, or mollusks from the rocks and sand from which the tides have momentarily receded.

For most of us, however, a seafood dinner means a trip to the local fishmonger or seafood department of the supermarket. There the choice is rather limited—unless you have just come from the bank, where you withdrew your entire account. The only fish I have been able to afford in the last year or so is something called Japanese turbot. Hence we have eaten a good deal of this turbot, which is a most adaptable fish, lending itself well to breading and quick-frying, to chowders and stews, to broiling with lemon butter, to baking with various vegetables. Even the lowly mackerel, which used in my youth to be considered the poor person's fish (or fare for cats), has risen in price so that it's on the "no" list. Chunks of red snapper, frozen, sometimes are within reach. And of course there is still occasionally a sale on canned tuna, clams, bonito, or sardines, which we *always* take advantage of: the cans are so small that they present no storage problem.

As for the nice big plump striped bass, pompano, salmon, or some such, which you buy fresh and whole and take home to stuff and bake—forget it for the time being. As soon as things change behind fish counters, and all sorts and varieties of seafood are again available to the average pocketbook, well, three cheers will go up from many quarters, this one in the vanguard. In the meantime, pinching pennies in the kitchen is not synonymous with investing in lobster, salmon, sturgeon, even sole or flounder. You'll find no recipes in these pages for such species—unless it's a way to make some other fish *look like* one of these. You will find some methods of stretching out the fish you can buy, some clever substitutions you can make, and a number of things to do with good old standby codfish—and, naturally, with turbot.

Some seafood enthusiasts claim that if you have to eat frozen fish, you may as well not bother, so diminished is the flavor, so altered the texture. My position is: better frozen (or canned) fish than none at all. Should you come into a windfall of fish too copious for you to cook on the same day—as from a neighbor's catch larger than his family can handle—you had *better* freeze it. Fish and shellfish don't keep well at all unless they're dried or otherwise preserved. On the other hand, they freeze well and lose very little of their food value if deep-frozen promptly and then thawed and eaten within a few weeks. The texture won't suffer much transformation if you anticipate your use of the fish and defrost it slowly, putting it first into the refrigerator and then, after a few hours, allowing it to finish thawing at room temperature. *Don't* rush things by holding your frozen fish package under running hot water; and *never* plunge it into a pan of hot water, or let it finish thawing in the cooking.

As with poultry and meat, you won't want to waste a bit of your precious fish purchases. If you do manage to get some large fish fresh and whole, and have to gut them yourself, the insides can be fed to your pet dog or cat. Don't—please don't—throw away the bones after you've baked and picked them clean, or the bones you remove before cooking. Bones, and also fins, heads, skin, tails, can go into your fish-bag (another double plastic one is best) in the freezing compartment, for that day soon when you have the time to convert them into fish stock, an invaluable homemade staple no economy-minded cook should be without. Very good for cooking fresh-water fish, or others without a strong, distinctive flavor. Use your fish stock over and over again, once a fish has been cooked in it, keeping it frozen between uses. Here is a good way to make it.

FISH STOCK
about 1 quart

1 or 2 lbs. fish bones, heads, skin, etc.
1 medium onion, chopped
1 stalk celery, plus leaves, chopped
1 tablespoon parsley
a few whole cloves
dashes of salt and pepper
3 tablespoons lemon juice or vinegar

Boil all the ingredients for 30 to 40 minutes in 1½ quarts of water, skimming the surface from time to time. Strain through a fine sieve, and cool as quickly as possible.

If you have a French grandmother, you can really make an impression on her by saving money and coming up with a really great *bouillabaisse* at the same time. This is ironic, because *bouillabaisse* (actually only a fish chowder despite the *haute cuisine* title) probably originated in the Middle East, not in La Belle France, where its ingredients are the subject of endless controversy. Since it *is* a stew or chowder or ragout, you should combine several fish, but their precise identities need not be of the utmost importance. As long as they are lean and fresh (or freshly thawed), and flavorsome, you will have a good fish chowder.

Julia Child, in *The French Chef Cookbook,* suggests you choose your combination of fish from this assortment: "bass, cod, conger or sea eel, cusk, flounder, grouper, grunt, haddock, hake or whiting, halibut, perch, pollock, rockfish or sculpin, snapper, spot, sea trout or weakfish, wolf fish. Shellfish—crab, lobster, mussels, clams, scallops." But any reasonably firm-fleshed fish will do nicely.

If saffron is beyond your pocketbook, or geography, use mustard (dried) in its place. Likewise a bit of cayenne (red) pepper or Tabasco instead of dried crushed red peppers.

BOUILLABAISSE
4 to 6 servings

4 lbs. various fish (of light, firm flesh)

8 or 10 clams (or other shellfish)

4 garlic cloves

1 teaspoon allspice

1 teaspoon salt

½ teaspoon pepper

3 tablespoons vegetable oil or margarine

2 medium onions, minced

2 medium carrots, sliced thin

1 cup peeled tomatoes (plus juice)

4 pinches ground saffron
2 pinches dried crushed red pepper
6 cups fish stock (see page 147)
1 cup cleaned shrimp or crabmeat
juice of 1 lemon

Clean the fish, reserving heads, skins, fins, etc., for your next batch of fish stock. Open the clams but leave the meat attached to the shells. Mash 2 of the garlic cloves together with the allspice, salt, and pepper; rub the firm-fleshed fish with this mixture, cover, and refrigerate for an hour or two. In a large skillet, melt the oil, and sauté the onions, carrots, and other 2 garlic cloves (minced) in it. Add the firm-fleshed fish to the skillet, then the tomatoes, saffron, red pepper, and stock. Simmer, covered, for 20 minutes, then add the clams and shrimp or crabmeat plus the lemon juice. Simmer, covered, for another 10 minutes. Serve hot.

If you are blessed not with a French *grand-mère* but a Jewish mother-in-law (or better still father-in-law), you can win points and save fishmonger pennies, too, by making your own *gefilte fish*. As with *bouillabaisse*, many and passionate are the debates over just which fish are musts for this delicacy; but, again, by the time the dish is completed, no one is really going to be able to pick out the three distinct fish fleshes, and face you with the exposure of a deception. Some tradition has it that the combination should be whitefish, carp, and pike; but if you were to substitute bluefish, shad, and pickerel, I doubt any but the most fiercely discerning father-in-law could tell the difference.

(By the way, did you know that herring are canned as sardines when they're young? That a sardine, if it were left alone, would grow up to be a herring? And that a middle-aged shad is not a herring, but only looks like one? If anyone should offer you a mature shad on the East Coast in May, and it comes with eggs inside, grab it; two of the most delicious fish dishes you can possible eat are shad and shad roe.)

While we're on the subject of finny relationships, do you know what Boston scrod is? It's not a variety of fish at all, but a term that is applied to any one of several species, including cod and haddock. Invented by the Boston Parker House, the designation came about because they had to print their menus before the fishing boats came in and wanted to be sure their special of the day was the freshest variety, the last fish the boat happened to catch—and that no one could predict. Take a tip from the Parker House: tell your guests you're serving scrod, whatever the fish; your dinner will sound more elegant.

GEFILTE FISH
1 or 2 quarts

3 medium-sized light-fleshed fish (carp, pike, and whitefish, or other combination)

eggs

salt and pepper, to taste

pinch sugar

3 or 4 carrots

3 medium-sized onions

Clean and fillet the fish, reserving the fins, skins, heads, bones, for the cooking. Grind or blend the raw fish fine; if using a grinder and different varieties of fish, put each through in several pieces, alternating kinds of fish. Add one raw egg for each pound of fish, and mix well. Mix in the salt, pepper, and sugar. Shape the mixture into balls or ovoid patties.

Slice the carrots in thin rounds, the onions in rings. Put carrots, onions, and fish trimmings into a deep pot and add enough water to cover well. Bring to a boil, and boil hard for 15 to 20 minutes, replenishing water if necessary. Then add the fish balls or patties, lower the heat, and simmer for 45 minutes. Now pack the fish balls into hot sterilized jars, and fill the jars up with the cooking liquid (minus the fish fins, etc.— you can still get some mileage out of the fish trimmings, though, for making fish stock. Throw them now into your fish-stock bag, heads and all, in the freezer.)

If you are going to eat this *gefilte fish* within a few days, you must put it when cooled into the refrigerator. But if not, you should process the jars in a pressure canner (½ hour for pint jars, 40 minutes for quarts).

If (once in a blue moon) you do come into possession of a large bake-whole fish—say a sea bass, a white Alaskan salmon (not all salmon has orange flesh), or something of the same proportions—a really festive dish can be made by stuffing it with a handsome and tasty filling. This method is obvious when a deep-sea-fishing friend has presented you with a big, firm-fleshed, nonscaly fish, but few people think of it in connection with a differently shaped fish. Here are recipes for some lush, large, stuffable fish—and for the lowly squid as well.

STUFFED LAKE TROUT
serves 3 or 4

1 lake trout, about 5 lbs.
1½ cups bread crumbs or cubes
1 medium onion, minced
1 stalk celery, plus leaves, chopped fine
½ cup raisins, black or white
1 medium egg

½ cup melted margarine
salt and pepper, to taste
1 teaspoon combined dried herbs (sage, thyme, parsley,
tarragon, for instance)
6 to 8 slices bacon (optional)

Preheat oven to 300°. Clean the fish, and wipe it dry. Combine all the rest of the ingredients except the bacon, for stuffing. Fill the fish's cavity with the stuffing, and lay the bacon slices diagonally across the stuffed fish. Put on a well-greased rack in a baking pan. Fill bottom of pan with water a half inch deep. Bake for 1¼ hours. Baste with the drippings two or three times during the cooking.

You could substitute rice for the bread cubes if you wished, and add vegetables other than onion and celery to the stuffing. Choose for color and shape, so that the spilling-out stuffing makes a good-looking platter for your table.

Here is a stuffed fish with a Pacific flavor.

STUFFED SEA BASS
for 2 or 3

½ cup dried mushrooms
1 sea bass (or similar fish), about 2 lbs.
salt
3 or 4 scallions or shallots, chopped
1 4-oz. can shredded bamboo shoots
4 slices ginger root, shredded
¼ cup slivered almonds
½ cup sherry or dry white wine
¼ cup soy sauce

Preheat oven to 300°. Refresh the mushrooms by soaking them in half a cup of soda water or plain water for ½ hour. Slice or chop mushrooms, reserving the soaking water. Clean fish, dry it, and rub inside and out with salt. Mix vegetables, ginger, and almonds together, and stuff the fish with them, securing it with toothpicks (or lay the flesh out flat and pile the vegetables on top). Place the fish on a well-greased rack in a baking dish. Bake for 50 minutes to 1 hour, basting from time to time with a sauce made of the mushroom-soaking liquid, wine, and soy sauce.

STUFFED SQUID
6 servings

½ dozen squid
½ cup bread or cracker crumbs (or cooked rice)
2 tablespoons parsley or fresh dill, minced
6 garlic cloves
1 medium egg (or ½ cup plain yogurt)
2 tablespoons grated hard cheese
5 tablespoons olive or other vegetable oil
salt and pepper, to taste
¾ cup peeled tomatoes, in sauce
½ cup white wine or vegetable stock

Clean squid and chop off tentacles. Mince the tentacles, and combine them with crumbs (or rice), herbs, and 2 of the garlic cloves, minced. Beat the egg slightly, and stir into the mixture, together with the cheese and 1 tablespoon of oil. Mix in salt and pepper, and divide the stuffing into six parts. Stuff each squid, and skewer or sew up the openings. Heat the remaining oil in a skillet; cut up the remaining garlic cloves in 4 or 5 pieces each, and brown them in the oil. Remove the garlic, and then brown the squid in the oil, turning them from side to side. Add the removed garlic, the tomatoes with their liquid, plus the wine or stock. Cover the skillet, and simmer for half an hour. Serve hot in the sauce.

A lovely accompaniment would be cauliflower and green beans.

CAROLINA SHAD
for 5 or 6

3-lb. shad
salt and pepper
2 cups dry bread crumbs or cubes
⅓ cup melted butter or margarine
2 tablespoons lemon juice
¼ cup chopped onion or scallion
2 tablespoons chopped parsley
1 teaspoon salt
dash pepper
¼ cup sweet pickle or relish of your choice

Preheat oven to 350°. Clean, wash, and dry the shad; sprinkle it inside with salt and pepper. Place the fish on a well-greased pan or a baking dish that can go from stove to table. Combine the bread, a little melted butter, lemon juice, onion, parsley, salt, pepper, and pickle or relish, and stuff the fish loosely. Brush the outside of the fish with the rest of the melted butter, and bake for 45 minutes, or until the fish is tender.

This recipe is not radically different from the Stuffed Lake Trout; we include it because it came from a friend in North Carolina, and because of the novel addition of pickle to the stuffing. (This would work fine with any number of slightly oily fish.)

PERCH VÉRONIQUE

This is a lush dish usually made from fillet of sole. Perch, which can sometimes be afforded (unlike sole these days), serves just as well. What makes it "véronique" is the grapes.

3 or 4 servings

1½ lbs. perch fillets
3 cups fish stock
½ lb. white seedless grapes, separated from stems
2 tablespoons flour
2 tablespoons butter or margarine
½ cup heavy cream
salt and pepper, to taste
2 tablespoons minced parsley or cress
brandy (optional)

Preheat oven to 350°. Place fish in baking dish. Pour stock over, and leave in oven 20 minutes, then keep fish warm on a serving dish. On top of the stove, cook the liquid in the baking dish until it has been reduced to about a cup and a half. Meanwhile, plunge grapes into boiling fresh water for 3 minutes. Add them to the fish.

Rub the flour and butter together, then add this roux by teaspoonfuls to the fish stock, stirring over low heat until it is all combined and thickened. Then stir in the cream, all at once, and simmer some more, stirring, until it attains the consistency you like. Do not boil. Correct seasoning. Then pour the sauce over the fish and grapes, and sprinkle the minced greenery on top. Stir a bit of brandy into the sauce after the cream for a *haute cuisine* taste.

Here's another fish chowder you can do with easy-to-get fish. Though it has nothing to do with *bouillabaisse* (see p. 148), it is far more elegant than it may sound. And can be cooked *inside* the stove.

UNFRENCH FISH CHOWDER
6 to 8 servings

2 lbs. fillets "ordinary" fish (cod, haddock, mackerel, pollock, for examples)

3 medium onions, sliced or chopped

4 medium potatoes, sliced or diced

1 clove garlic, minced

salt and pepper

1 stalk celery, plus leaves, chopped fine

¼ lb. margarine, in "pats"

1 bay leaf

¼ teaspoon dill seed, powdered

½ cup white wine

1½ cups light cream or whole milk (or half-and-half)

Preheat oven to 375°. Put all but last two ingredients in a casserole dish. Add hot water enough to cover, about 2 cups or so. Cover the casserole, and leave it in the oven for an hour. Then combine the wine and cream or milk, and heat slowly to just under boiling. Add it to the chowder and remove the bay leaf. Serve hot for a hearty one-dish meal.

AFRICAN FISH STEW

This is really steamed fish over a vegetable melange. (When I first started making it, having found it in an African cookbook, I also added some shredded coconut meat to the stewing vegetables.) The second time

around, with the fillets in pieces, mixed into the vege-
tables, it's even better. On serving number two, you can
also add some cooked rice, or croutons, to stretch it out.

3 or 4 servings

about 4 tablespoons cooking oil

2 medium onions, chopped

2 medium sweet peppers, chopped

3 medium tomatoes, chopped

3 tablespoons soy sauce, Worcestershire, or Sauce
Diablo

salt, to taste

1 lb. turbot fillets (or others of your choice),
washed, dried

1 tablespoon margarine

1 tablespoon tarragon

Heat the oil in a skillet, then soften the onions and peppers in it. Add the tomatoes when the other vegetables are rather soft. Then when the tomatoes have cooked a little, stir in the piquant sauce and salt. Leave the heat on, and lay the whole fillets right on top of the vegetables. Or grease a rack that fits into your skillet, and lay the fish on the rack; then put the rack on top of the vegetables. Dot the fillets with the margarine and sprinkle with tarragon. Cover the skillet, and let the fish cook about 20 minutes. If you've used the rack, you now have a tricky maneuver to accomplish: transfer the fillets—without breaking any of them—onto the top of the stew, so that you can serve it right out of the skillet. If you didn't use the rack, you're now one step ahead of the game. It is a pretty dish.

Someone is always throwing a can of tuna fish into a casserole dish, along with cream-of-mushroom (or -celery) soup plus some corn flakes, and calling it tuna casserole. Which I guess it indisputably is. With the addition of a little creative imagination, some lovely and still very inexpensive things can be done with tuna, aside from making a salad, a sandwich, or a gelatine mold of it. Here are a couple of suggestions. Salmon could of course be substituted for the tuna—if you can afford it. Or bonito, if the special is 3 cans for 89¢ that week.

TUNA LOAF
4 to 6 servings

1 1-lb. can (or 2 smaller cans) tuna fish, plus its juice
¼ cup lemon juice (or dry wine)
½ cup scallions, white and green parts, minced
1¼ cups bread crumbs, soft
¼ cup vegetable oil
½ cup milk
2 small eggs, beaten
1 1-lb. can (or more smaller cans) sliced peaches or apricots, drained

Preheat oven to 350°. Flake the tuna. Combine it and the juice from the can with the lemon juice, scallions, crumbs, oil, and milk. Beat the eggs lightly, and stir them into the tuna mixture. Reserve half the fruit, and chop the rest smaller. Stir the chopped fruit into the tuna mixture. Line a loaf pan with paper that has been well greased. Spoon the fish mixture into the pan, and leave in oven for an hour. Cool for 10 minutes before turning out the loaf upside down on a platter. Peel the paper off, and press the other half of the fruit on top of the loaf—it's the fruit that makes the difference.

Tuna—or similar canned "convenience" fish—can combine well with vegetables other than mushrooms, too. The following recipe is another pretty dish made from fish, this time with asparagus.

TUNA-ASPARAGUS CASSEROLE
3 or 4 servings

1 lb. fresh thin asparagus
1 7-oz. can tuna, plus liquid
¼ cup flour or arrowroot
salt and pepper, to taste
2 cups milk
½ cup cheese: grated Parmesan or shredded sharp
Cheddar
1 tablespoon lemon or orange juice
3 tablespoons pimiento, in strings or dice

Preheat oven to 350°. Trim the toughest part off the ends of the asparagus, and boil it until it is tender. Put it into a greased baking dish. Remove tuna from can and flake it; distribute over the asparagus. Pour the tuna liquid into a saucepan, and add the flour and seasoning. Stir this mixture over medium heat, adding the milk gradually, until it thickens. Remove saucepan from heat, and stir in cheese and fruit juice. Pour the sauce over the tuna and asparagus. Bake, uncovered, for half an hour. Serve hot, with the pimiento slices or dice arranged on top in an interesting design.

An undistinguished fish, say mullet or halibut, can of course be lent a degree of nobility by the judicious use of seasonings and herbs. One of the ways to accomplish this transformation is by wrapping in foil a whole, cleaned fish (or a steak or fillet) sprinkled with your favorite combination of herbs and seasonings, and just baking it, wrapped securely, for a half hour to an hour, depending on size. Include a bit of butter or lemon juice, or both. Experiment with the herbs and seasonings until you get what seems to you the perfect fish pickup.

Many is the hurried end-of-a-workday supper that I've made into a more restorative experience by pulling a one-pound package of frozen fish out of the freezer in the morning, leaving it in the refrigerator all day, and then just baking it quickly on a greased pan at night for 20 minutes at 350°, or poaching it in a close-fitting covered dish for slightly longer at the same heat, adding a little wine or cider to the bottom of the dish, and slathering it halfway through cooking with a sauce stirred up out of whatever seems to be handy on the condiments shelf.

The following two recipes are a couple of my more successful minute sauces.

FISH SAUCE I

½ cup melted margarine
1 tablespoon Worcestershire sauce
1 tablespoon ketchup
1 tablespoon dried bread crumbs
1 tablespoon mustard
½ teaspoon salt
⅛ teaspoon pepper

FISH SAUCE II

½ cup sour cream (or half yogurt, half sour cream)
2 tablespoons mushroom pieces
1 tablespoon piccalilli
¼ teaspoon cayenne pepper
¼ cup black olives, chopped fine

Despite the true existence of fish named grayling (a variety of whitefish), the only reason I have used it in this recipe title is for alliteration. You can do this dish with any number of frozen fillets from the supermarket—perhaps ocean perch.

GRAPEFRUIT GRAYLING
4 servings

1-lb. package perch fillets

juice of 1 lime

1 16-oz. can unsweetened grapefruit sections (sometimes marked *way* down in the dented-cans basket in the market), plus juice

salt and pepper, to taste

1 bay leaf

dry white wine

¼ oz. plain gelatin

2 teaspoons cornstarch

Preheat oven to 375°. Skin the fillets, and sprinkle them with the lime juice. Drain the grapefruit sections, reserving the juice from the can. Put half the fillets in a lightly greased small baking dish. Arrange the grapefruit sections on top of the fish, then cover with the rest of the fillets. Salt and pepper the top of the fish, and add the bay leaf. Pour the juice from the can into the baking dish. Cover the dish, and bake for half an hour, then cool to room temperature. Pour off the cooking liquid, and strain it. If there is a cup, put it aside; if not, add enough white wine to make a cup. Arrange the fillets and grapefruit sections on a serving platter, and chill the whole dish. Meanwhile, heat the liquid in a saucepan; stir in the gelatin and cornstarch over low heat until the mixture just comes to a boil. Turn off heat, and let it cool a little. Then coat the fillets on the

161

platter with this gelatin. Put the dish back in refrigerator to set. A lovely, refreshing warm-weather dish.

Sometimes you can get fresh-water trout in frozen packages at the supermarket. Better still, from fresh water. Either way, cook it as soon as possible after it has been brought to the room temperature of your kitchen. Some trout can be induced to turn blue by cooking in an acid: lemon juice or vinegar. So try the following recipe, and if it works, you can rename the dish *Truite au Bleu,* which sounds a good deal more elegant than Poached Trout.

POACHED TROUT
3 or 4 servings

6 medium-sized carrots

3 small onions

3 or 4 8-oz. trout,
cleaned but not skinned

½ cup fresh parsley, chopped

1 tablespoon dried thyme

salt and pepper

1½ cups vinegar
(wine or cider)

Slice carrots rather thin; chop onions coarsely. Arrange these vegetables in a saucepan or skillet with a cover. Place the trout on top of the vegetables. Sprinkle them with the parsley, thyme, salt, and pepper. Pour the vinegar into the side of the pan so that it doesn't float the herbs and seasonings off the fish. Cover the saucepan or skillet, and put it on low heat. Let the fish cook for one hour. Serve them hot, spooning a fish and some of the vegetables and liquid onto each individual plate.

The sweetness and texture and shape of flounder make it one of my favorite fish, alas too seldom within reach in the supermarket. Naturally you can substitute for the elusive flounder any reasonably firm fillets.

FROZEN FLOUNDER BAKE
4 servings

4 flat fish fillets
3 tablespoons margarine
12 slender white radishes
¼ lb. fresh mushrooms
1 cup fresh green peas
salt and pepper, to taste
2 tablespoons cornstarch
¾ cup dry white wine

Preheat oven to 375°. Wash and dry the fillets. Melt the margarine in a skillet, and roll the radishes in it over a low heat for a few minutes, just to give them a golden color without softening them too much. Slice the mushrooms and brown them in the margarine from which you have removed the radishes. Wrap each flounder fillet around three radishes, and secure each package with a toothpick or skewer. Grease a small baking dish, and stand the four fish rolls in it, close together. Scatter the green peas and mushrooms over and around them, and salt and pepper to taste. Now rub the cornstarch into the margarine in the skillet, and turn the heat under it to medium. Pour in the wine, and whisk this combination into a sauce; when it has thickened a little, pour it over the fish and vegetables. Bake for half an hour or a bit longer.

This sophisticated fish dish would combine well with the native American Indian samp (see page 184)—it would be a good marriage of proteins, tastes, textures, colors—and cultures.

You will have noticed in this book so far an egregious lack of sole recipes, Dover or otherwise. That's because sole from below the white cliffs of England or the gray ones of New England have entered the aristocracy, in price anyway. *My* Dover is a town in New Hampshire where the Great Bay wanders in from the Atlantic, mixing salt water with fresh as it narrows down to a river. *My* sole, poached from those waters some years ago, were smelts, which are available, frozen, at frugal prices, in supermarkets. Braised in this way the plebeian fish takes on nobility.

DOVER SOLE
5 or 6 servings

2 lbs. smelt fillets
4 tablespoons margarine
4 tablespoons chopped shallots
¼ cup almonds
½ cup fish stock (or less—just enough to slightly soak the fish in the dish)
6 dates
3 tablespoons chopped fresh parsley

Preheat oven to 350°. Clean, wash, and dry the fillets. Melt the margarine in a skillet, and quickly brown the shallots. Sliver the almonds, and brown them a little, too. Put the "sole" fillets in a small baking dish, greased, with a cover. Heat the fish stock, and pour it over the fillets. Now pour the melted margarine with the shallots and almonds over the fish. Cut up the dates, and sprinkle them on top, along with the parsley. Cover and leave in oven for 50 minutes to an hour. Serve hot, with some millet or semolina to accompany.

Salt-preserved fish is still a bargain in some parts of the country, indeed in many parts of the world. The secret is to soak and rinse the salt fish long enough. Where I have lived much of my life, it's the cod that gets salted the most, though mackerel probably runs it a close second. It's in Bermuda, however, that the most delicious salt-cod dish I know originates. If you don't live in Bermuda (or some other tropical land) where you can pick avocados off the trees in your backyard, perhaps with the centavos you save on the salt fish, you can afford to buy one perfect fresh avocado.

AVOCADO COD
serves 5 or 6

2 lbs. salt cod
8 small white potatoes, peeled
¼ cup butter or margarine
½ teaspoon Tabasco
½ teaspoon mustard
1 large egg, hard-boiled and minced
1 avocado, peeled and sliced
2 bananas, peeled and sliced
2 tablespoons watercress, chopped

Put salt cod in saucepan, cover well with water, and simmer for 2 hours. Drain fish (but save the salty water for your fish stock) and put it, together with the potatoes, in fresh water to cover. Boil about 30 minutes. Drain fish and potatoes, and keep warm. In a small saucepan, melt the butter or margarine. Stir in the Tabasco, mustard, and egg, over medium heat. Arrange the avocado and banana on top of the potatoes and fish. Pour the sauce over, and sprinkle the cress on top.

Salting is one way to preserve fish for a long time or a lengthy journey. Smoking is another. Where I grew up, finnan haddie (made of haddock) was the big bargain, though you may find other smoked fish at something less than exorbitant prices. Finnan haddie was a New England specialty (actually Scottish in origin), that usually found itself being scrambled up with eggs and a little cream. Or going into a fish chowder after being soaked in cold water for a half hour or so.

If you're willing to go all out in the preparation, you can make a most luxurious summer dish from simple smoked haddock. As follows:

FINNAN HADDIE MOUSSE
8 or 10 servings

1 lb. finnan haddie (smoked haddock)
1 tablespoon butter
1 egg white
3 tablespoons lemon juice
1 medium onion, sliced or chopped
1 cup clam broth or clam juice
¼ oz. plain gelatin
1 cup mayonnaise (see pp. 68–69)
1 cup heavy cream

Soak the finnan haddie in cold water for ½ hour. Add the butter to 1½ cups of water, and bring it to a simmer. Add the fish to the butter-water, and simmer for 10 minutes. In another pan, combine egg white, lemon juice, onion, and clam broth, and simmer for 10 minutes. Let cool for 15 minutes, then strain through cheesecloth. Soften gelatin in 2 tablespoons cold water in a measuring cup. Set the measuring cup into a pan of hot water; let the water come to a simmer while you stir the gelatin until dissolved. Stir the gelatin into the clam broth. Coat the bottom of a soufflé dish or fancy (fish-shaped?) mold with this aspic (you will have some

166

left over) and put the dish in the refrigerator. Also chill the rest of the aspic. Flake the finnan haddie; mix it with the mayonnaise and the remaining aspic. Whip the cream until stiff, then fold into the fish mixture. When the aspic at the bottom of the mold is firm, spoon the fish mixture into the mold and chill until firm. Turn out onto a platter and serve cold.

The eel is an oily fish and, possibly for this reason, in some areas a very inexpensive one to buy. It bears no relationship to a snake, so if you don't find the eel pleasing, try thinking of it as a fish, not a snake—you may make out better. Though it wins no beauty contests, it's a really good-tasting fish, considered a delicacy in many countries of the world. One good way to cook it is to sauté it and then marinate it, as in the following recipe. The reason for the title is that this is the traditional Christmas-Eve dish in parts of Italy. Start it five days before Christmas.

NOELLINE EEL
5 or 6 servings

1 2-lb. eel
2 tablespoons olive (or other vegetable) oil
4 bay leaves
salt and pepper
2 cups red wine or red-wine vinegar
2 cloves garlic
1 sprig rosemary
4 whole cloves

Scrub the eel with hot water and a brush; don't skin it. Put the head and tip of the tail into your fish-stock bag, then cut the fish across into 5 or 6 pieces. Remove the insides by washing again under running water. Dry the fish. Heat olive oil in a skillet, and sauté the fish sections, browning them on all sides. Let them drain, and put them in a pan that will just hold them in one layer.

Boil together all the rest of the ingredients for less than a minute, then pour over the eel pieces so that they are immersed in the marinade. Cover the pan, and let the eel marinate in a cool place for four days and nights, turning the pieces over twice a day. Serve either hot or cold.

Clams, mussels, quahogs, and such are great in many ways: eaten raw with a little lemon or lime juice squeezed on them; in cream sauces, just plain steamed, in milky chowders, etc. Here is a way to get some mileage out of a very few of these versatile bivalves.

SHELL APPETIZERS
12 hors d'oeuvres

1 cup cracker or bread crumbs
8 clams (or mussels or quahogs), minced
2 teaspoons butter or margarine, softened
½ teaspoon Tabasco
salt and pepper, to taste
1 small onion, grated
½ cup sharp cheese, grated
2 tablespoons melted butter
2 tablespoons minced parsley
1 teaspoon paprika

Moisten the crumbs with warm water (about ¼ cup—enough to dampen them), then blend them with the minced clams, butter, Tabasco, seasoning, grated onion, and cheese. Now, from the top shelf get down those clam or scallop shells you picked up at the seashore, and divide the glop evenly into 12 of them. You can freeze them shells and all, if you don't want to use these appetizers immediately. When you are ready to serve them, take them out of the freezer an hour or so in advance, sprinkle the tops with the melted butter, parsley, and paprika, and pop them in the oven for 20 minutes at 350°. *Voilà!* a delightful seafood appetizer in a most appropriate serving dish.

Scallops—either sea or bay—are obliging little mollusks with a distinctive taste and interesting texture. They are happily and quickly cooked in various liquids and liquors. Here is a recipe that uses up the ¾ cup of vermouth or leftover white wine you were wondering what to do with.

TIPSY SCALLOPS
5 or 6 servings

5 or 6 slices partially cooked bacon or prosciutto ham
¾ cup dry vermouth or leftover white wine
1¼ lbs. scallops
2 tablespoons butter or margarine
2½ tablespoons flour
⅔ cup Clamato juice
salt and pepper
½ cup toasted bread or cracker crumbs
¼ cup sharp cheese, grated
paprika or nutmeg

Preheat oven to 350°. Very lightly grease a baking dish, and then line it with the bacon or ham. Bring the vermouth to a boil in a saucepan, pop the scallops into the wine, turn down heat and leave to simmer for 4 minutes. Drain the scallops, reserving the wine, and distribute them over the bacon. Melt the butter or margarine in a skillet, and rub the flour into it. Then, over medium heat, add the wine in which you cooked the scallops, slowly, whisking continually. Now whisk in the Clamato juice until the sauce thickens. Season to your taste with salt and pepper, and pour the sauce over the scallops. Sprinkle with crumbs and cheese, and bake for about 20 minutes. Sprinkle with paprika or nutmeg just before you serve it, hot.

Crabs are either a costly indulgence or practically free for the taking, depending on where you live. If the latter, you hardly need advice on how to cook them to get the most out of them, since they've doubtless been your substitute for lobster, lo, these many years. Therefore, the reason for the following recipe, one of my favorites, is that after it you can serve rice and beans for a main course, and your family or guests will think they've been to a royal feast.

CRAB SOUP
3 or 4 servings

10 or 12 ounces crabmeat, fresh or canned
4 hard-boiled eggs, yolks only
1 cup cream
4 cups whole milk
½ cup sherry
2 tablespoons grated lemon rind
1 tablespoon chopped basil buds and leaves (optional)

Shred the crabmeat. (If you don't know what to do with the whites of the cooked eggs, you might save them and add them, chopped fine, to your next tossed salad.) Combine the cream and milk in the top of a double boiler, and rub in the egg yolks. Add the shredded crabmeat, and heat to just under a boil. If using canned crabmeat, add its liquid to the soup. Stir in the sherry just before removing from heat, and serve garnished with the lemon rind and (optional) basil.

Tiny shrimp are out of sight in every way you can think of in my neck of the woods; but not so the big fellows, which sometimes can be purchased without first going to the bank. Two of them can make a splendid seafood meal if you fool around with them a little. One of the ways I devised is to substitute them for the ham and eggs in Eggs Benedict, a popular favorite with weekend guests who tend to eat brunch rather than breakfast and lunch.

BUTTERFLY BENEDICT
for 6

12 large shrimp
½ lb. fresh mushrooms, caps intact
2 tablespoons butter or margarine
6 English muffins (untoasted)
2½ cups hollandaise sauce (béarnaise will work if you are timid about hollandaise)

Preheat oven to 350°. Clean and peel the shrimp. Steam them over boiling water until they become opaque. Then slice them in half not quite through the middle, leaving a section of back intact. Open them up butterfly fashion, and keep them warm. Separate the caps from the stems of the mushrooms; melt the butter or margarine in a skillet, and brown the mushrooms in it. Halve the English muffins and put two halves on each of six ovenproof plates. Place one butterfly shrimp on each muffin half, then divide the mushrooms into six servings, and add them. Pour the sauce over each dish, and leave them in the oven for 5 or 10 minutes while you get your five guests assembled at the brunch table.

A while back I averred that anyone dedicated to saving money in the kitchen would be unlikely to have much truck with lobster; and unless some miracle in the briny deep results in the lowering of the price of these noble crustaceans, that statement still stands. Therefore, lobster gets my vote for the seafood that Ms. Pinchpenny eats only (for fiduciary reasons) in her imagination, where its subtly delicious flesh is at its best in the dream recipe that concludes this chapter. In the meantime, here is a deception you may want to practice any day of the week. The tail portion of a large white fish from which the fishmonger has cut off the steaks is what you're after—and you can get it cheap.

POOR MAN'S LOBSTER
for 3 or 4

Tail portion of a large, firm, white-fleshed fish (about 2 lbs.)

4 cloves garlic, pressed or fine-minced

2 tablespoons olive oil

2 to 3 tablespoons paprika

3 large carrots, sliced in thin rounds

Preheat oven to 375°. Skin and bone the fishtail, trying to keep the section of meat intact, or as close to in one

piece as you possibly can. Then tie several pieces of
string around it. Wash and dry the fish. Combine the
garlic with the olive oil, and rub it all over the outside
of the fish. Now roll the fish in the paprika. Put it into
a covered baking dish that will just barely accommodate it. Add the sliced carrots to the dish, and cover it.
Leave the dish in the oven for about half an hour, or
until the fish is cooked through. Remove the string, and
leave the fish on a platter in a warm place while you
put the cooked carrots and accumulated liquid through
a strainer. Serve this sauce hot with the fish, which will
look quite a bit like lobster, its surface pink with white
marks on it where the string was.

RICH WOMAN'S LOBSTER
for 1 wealthy person

1 1-lb. lobster
lots of melted butter

Buy the lobster alive, plunge it into a large kettle of
rapidly boiling water, and let it boil for about 8 minutes.
Split the lobster in half lengthwise, and clean it (remove
head, stomach, and intestinal vein). Twist off the claws,
but don't discard them; save the liver and coral, too.
Now brush the flesh side of each lobster half with
melted butter, and put both halves plus the claws under
the broiler for just a few minutes, no more than 5, or
until the flesh just barely turns opaque. Sit down, and
eat the lobster immediately, picking the flesh out of the
shell and claws with a nutpick, dipping it into the rest
of the melted butter on its way to your mouth. (The
only other thing you should require for the perfection
of this experience is, perhaps, a lemon wedge to squeeze
a drop of juice on every other bite of lobster.)

Despite the fact that the method above—or simply boiling in salted water—is the best way to appreciate the delicate flavor of lobster, people sometimes insist on gussying it up in dishes like Lobster Newburg, Lobster Thermidor, Lobster *Ceviche,* or Seafood Bisque. My advice is: if you don't feel you're cooking unless you make combined repasts of that kind, substitute crab, shrimp, or crayfish for the lobster. There's no law against crayfish soup, shrimp *ceviche,* crab thermidor, or prawn Newburg. The flavors of these stand-ins aren't so likely to be overwhelmed by the cheese, vegetables, seasonings, and sauces that these concoctions embrace. Queen Lobster, for which you've paid a king's ransom, deserves all the undivided attention she can get.

7

ALL THINGS BRIGHT
AND VEGETATIVE

The case for a modified vegetarianism can be argued on both moral and medical grounds—can be and is, persuasively, by convincing authority. What concerns us here is its economical aspects. Look at your last week's grocery bill; subtract all the flesh and meat by-products from it, and see what happens. Now take out the eggs, and notice again how it shrinks. (Some vegetarians draw the line at anything that ever has been *or could be* animal life. Among other pursuits, this lets them out of making cheeses that require rennin (or rennet) in their manufacture. Which seems a shame.) The important point is that you can maintain a beautifully balanced diet, high in protein and all the necessary vitamins and trace minerals, without ever going near the meat counter of the supermarket, where so large a proportion of your marketing dollar is often laid down. You won't do it by steady ingestion of French fried potatoes, or even macrobiotically by eating nothing but whole-grain brown rice. But why not experiment with the bounteous family of legumes: peas and beans from goober to soy? These vegetables can be the "meaty" basis for a number of one-dish dinners, five out of seven nights a week. A pasta dish need not have ground beef as one of its components to be filling and nutritious. The spectrum of grains grown abundantly in this country and available to us at reasonable prices is almost overwhelming—it certainly is not limited to polished wheat and cracked rye.

"Rice and beans" may represent the nadir of alimentary life to many a Latin American who has now come on better times; but actually rice and beans contain a good balance of vitamins and constitute a very nourishing meal. Not long ago, an impoverished Puerto Rican family in New York City was pictured on television having a supper of rice-and-beans and pigs' feet. We weren't shown the composition of the rice dish, and so couldn't tell if it was cooked with a few onions, some brown stock, etc. But if it was, it wasn't basically different from what some of their fellow Manhattanites were eating at an expense-account restaurant: say, *osso bucco* (calves' knees instead of pigs' feet), white rice, and green peas. And not inferior nutrition. In fact, if the poor-people rice happened to be unpolished (brown), the pigs'-feet meal may even have been superior in nourishment value.

This brings up a principle to keep in mind: any time you can substitute a whole grain for a polished one, do it. There is a lot more protein in brown rice than in white, so if you can get whoever eats at your table to accept it, by all means substitute brown for white. (Only remember that it has to be cooked somewhat longer than white rice.) I have found that the white-rice devotees around me will usually not balk at a rice dish that is half brown and half white. The same goes for wheat. Brown rice and other whole grains, such as barley or bulghur, are far more easily sneaked in when combined with vegetables in a casserole than when served plain. Whole-wheat or rye flour with some white flour added makes a bread that is more acceptable to the white-bread lovers than a completely dark-grain one (it rises more easily too).

I have to confess that I'm not so successful in foisting on them the whole-wheat pastas, though. Thus I try to use white-flour spaghetti and macaroni and their relatives sparingly, substituting other whole grains fairly often for their "white" counterparts, and seeing that a variety of vegetables accompany the white-flour products when they do appear. Boston baked beans, another "poor people's dish," is really a most efficacious substitute for meat or fish; it has doubtless been responsible for many an indigent Yankee's survival through a long, cold winter. When accompanied by Boston brown bread (sometimes called Indian bread), it makes another very balanced, high-protein meal, particularly if the beans have been cooked in tomato sauce and onions, as they frequently are.

A large collection of recipes will follow that should prove (if it's not by now a straw man to be knocked down) that a vegetarian diet needn't be a dull, routine, uninteresting regime. It's quite obvious, I think, that it is a money-saving one. If only nuts and seeds weren't so expensive! They are, of course, the kernels of life, sources of highly concentrated protein and a number of necessary vitamins and poly-unsaturated fats. In my neck of the woods, however, most seeds are as costly as sirloin, being largely the province of the ripoff health-food shops. The only nut you can touch with a low-budget finger is the peanut (which isn't, properly speaking, a nut at all, but nearer in genealogy to the pea—thus the name goober peas). If you have a patch of dry, sunny soil that won't support much by way of peanuts or green leafy vegetables, one of the crops you'd be well advised to cultivate is sunflowers. Besides being tasty—and a must for homemade granola—the sunflower seed is one of the most nearly perfect high-protein foods you can come by. I heard a news story the other day to the effect that the sales of meat and sugar to Americans during 1975 were far lower than in 1974, while the figures on fruits and vegetables were far higher. The report failed to say whether a new awareness of nutrition or the rise in prices was responsible.

If you're luckily placed, you have growing around you some nut trees. Chestnuts (they come in several varieties, so watch out that yours are edible), hickories, pecans, and a number of others obligingly produce year after year for

Americans, sometimes free for the gathering. I made my first batch of hickory nut cookies from my own trees this year; it was worth all the laborious drying, cracking, and picking out of the shells (hickory nuts, though their taste is similar, aren't as cooperative as walnuts). And so were the *marrons glacés* that I made from a gift of Chinese chestnuts from a chestnut-tree-owning friend.

If you're city-bound, and have growing children besides, peanut butter is doubtless one of your staples. Next time you're marketing for it, compare the prices of a three-pound jar and four pounds of peanuts in the shell. You may decide that instead of knitting or smoking or nibbling fattening *and* costly finger foods while watching the tube, you'll pass around the peanuts in shells for cracking. Then make your own peanut butter by popping all the shelled peanuts into your blender, adding just a bit of vegetable oil, and salting to taste. This way you can control the amount and nature of additives and acquire a better-tasting, less health-threatening product than some of the ready-made peanut butters on the market. Hold out a few peanuts for adding to vegetable casserole dishes. And stop worrying about whether Johnnie is getting a nourishing enough school lunch if what he invariably takes is a peanut butter sandwich. If it's on whole-wheat bread, he's better proteined than if he were dining in a restaurant on a slice of roast beef and French fries. Stop turning up your nose, too, at splendid African-inspired dishes like ground-nut stew (groundnut being one of the peanut's other names), and peanut-baked chicken.

Another practice in vegetable shopping that will save you more than a few pfennigs, and also introduce you to a whole new world of taste, is to stop looking for the biggest potatoes, the huge carrots, the mammoth (or whatever is now the utmost gradation) olives. Bigger is *not* better in the case of many vegetables—in fact, the smaller varieties are often, aside from coming cheaper, superior in flavor. It's the American obsession with largeness that has led you astray.

Unless several very small vegetables mean a greater proportion of nonedible parts, you are better off skipping the gargantuan. If the large vegetable includes seeds, the seeds will more likely be inedible; the skin or shell will also be less tender and require longer cooking. So unless they come higher in price (which can happen, as, for example, with baby carrots), always go for the more diminutive vegetables when there's a choice. It is perhaps worth repeating that the closer to the time of picking your vegetables are bought and cooked (or tossed raw in a salad), the more nutritive value you will get out of them.

Many vegetables have already been mentioned in this book; always previously they have been accompaniments, not the central point of the dish being discussed. All the recipes appearing in this chapter will be vegetarian in their essence, though of course there's nothing to prevent you from cooking them in conjunction with meat, fish, poultry, or egg dishes.

With a few exceptions, I'm omitting directions for cooking single vegetables, such as the best way to boil potatoes or braise spinach, since that's the sort of information I think everybody has. Instead, I shall concentrate on combination dishes—they are the most fun for the economy-minded cook looking for ways to put things together in a new and different mode.

One of the greatest of all combined vegetable dishes is *ratatouille,* a French word for a meal that is no more exclusively French than is *bouillabaisse.* It is a mellifluous name for a lovely, versatile process that adapts itself beautifully to whichever soft and semi-hard vegetables you have on hand that combine well, lending flavor to each other. Since the vegetables used soon give over their liquids for cooking, a saving in oil is also involved. It's therefore an economical dish to make, whether you bake or sauté, and to serve as main dish or side dish. So *allons* . . . I'm providing a top-of-the-stove recipe, principally because that gives a saving in time as well: you can peel and chop as you go along.

RATATOUILLE
for a crowd

cooking oil, 3 tablespoons or more
4 medium-sized onions
4 medium-sized bell peppers
1 medium or 2 small eggplants
1 medium summer squash or zucchini
salt and pepper, to taste
herbs of your choice
4 medium-sized fresh tomatoes

Heat the oil in a large skillet with a cover. While it is heating, peel and slice the onions; core and seed the peppers, and slice them. Put these vegetables into the hot oil, and let them sauté over medium heat while you peel and cube the eggplant. Add the eggplant, and stir it around to soak up some of the oil and onion and pepper juices. When the eggplant has absorbed some of the liquid, see if you need to add a bit more oil. Meanwhile, you can be slicing or cubing the zucchini. Add it, plus the seasonings and herbs, cover, turn heat down low, and proceed to cut up the tomatoes. Stir the tomatoes in last, re-cover the skillet, and let the *ratatouille* cook another 10 minutes or so. Or until you're ready to serve it—nothing terrible will happen to the vegetables if they continue to cook slowly to accommodate your meal-timing. Stir occasionally to prevent sticking. Serve hot.

If you consumed all the *ratatouille* on the first serving, who can blame you? If you didn't, let it demonstrate its versatility in the leftover field. Try combining it the next night with some cooked rice (brown, of course—the vegetables will make it palatable) or pasta or potatoes. Or serve it with some cracked wheat (also known as bulghur) cooked to semisoftness. On second heating up, add a bit of garlic and chopped celery to change the flavor and texture, and thicken it with some shredded cheese. Or add it to baked beans.

The *ratatouille* recipe above presumes that you are making it at a time when fresh vegetables are readily available; there is, of course, no reason why canned or frozen can't be substituted for some of them—tomatoes, for instance.

There's also no reason why I shouldn't provide a short list of which vegetables are *better* canned or frozen than some versions of fresh-bought. Pricing, as already discussed, is dicey and changeable; but there are some vegetables whose qualities of taste, texture, and general pleasingness can be actually improved by processing. Here they are.

PREFERRED METHOD OF PROCESSING
VEGETABLES IF YOU CAN'T GET THEM FRESH

Asparagus Canned or frozen

Beans (pods) Canned or frozen

Beans (podless) Dried or frozen

Beets Canned

Broccoli and *Cauliflower* Frozen

Brussels Sprouts Frozen

Carrots Canned

Celery Canned

Chickpeas Canned

Corn Canned kernels

Eggplant Canned

Lentils Dried

Mushrooms Dried or canned

Onions Canned

Peas Frozen

Peppers Canned

Potatoes Canned

Spinach and *Other Greens* Frozen or canned

Squashes (of all kinds) Frozen

Tomatoes Canned (not stewed)

Turnips Canned or frozen

The varieties of legumes (peas, beans, lentils, etc.) available to most American marketers are nearly limitless. They are cheap to buy and packed with protein, so it is worth your while to investigate a bit beyond the standard can of pea beans packed in tomato sauce that comes to mind when the word "beans" is mentioned. To discuss all the kinds of legumes that are cultivated in the Western hemisphere— with their comparative virtues—would use up all the rest of this chapter. So instead, I'll list the major groups and encourage you to poke around on the shelves of your super-market to see how many you can find offered to you. The various entries in this list will appear in the recipes that follow.

PEAS

Green peas are pretty straightforward: there's the kind where you eat the seed, and the kind where you eat the pod (with seeds inside), called Snow peas, Chinese Peas, or sometimes Sugar Peas.

Then there are Goober Peas, which are not peas at all but peanuts.

And Black-Eyed Peas, which are not peas at all, but technically beans. Sometimes called Cowpeas.

Pigeon Peas *are* members of the pea family; other-wise known as No-Eye Peas, Congo Peas (or Congo Beans), or Hoary Peas.

Chick Peas are peas, too. Also known as Garbanzos.

BEANS

The kind where you eat the pod divide roughly into two groups by color:

Yellow, also called Wax Beans, Butter Beans, Snap Beans.

Green, also called Snap Beans, String Beans.

BEANS*

The kind where you eat the seed only, are wonder-fully multifarious. Here are some:

Kidney Beans, white or red.

Lima Beans, pale green, large and small.

Navy Beans, white (sometimes called Haricots or Marrow Beans).

---

* In the recipes that include dried beans, there is some vagueness about how long to presoak them. It's impossible to be precise, because there are so many variables: how dry the beans are when you acquire them, how tender you want them to be, their innate denseness, the permeability of their skins, etc. Overnight is sometimes necessary, at other times a few hours will do—you will have to work it out for yourself.

Pea Beans, white or red.

Pinto Beans, speckled, tawny (*frijoles*).

Mung Beans, golden or green.

Black Beans (sometimes called Mungo, but not the same as Mung Beans).

Soy Beans, white (sometimes called Broad Beans, Soya Beans, Fava Beans, Butter Beans).

BEAN SPROUTS

A most nutritious form in which to eat beans. Most beans can be persuaded to sprout by leaving them in water and warmth for a while. The most popular beansprouts in America are grown from Mung Beans.

LENTILS

Golden, brown, red, or green.

The reason lentils don't appear under either peas or beans is that most classifiers don't know which they are. A play often performed in schools during my childhood, entitled "Six Who Pass While the Lentils Boil," dramatized this confusion. In the prologue of this drama, a "plant" in the audience called out, "But what *is* a lentil?" Whereupon the response from the stage came: "Neither a pea nor a bean but akin to both."

I've already made some arguments against using polished white rice, so while we're listing high-protein foodstuffs, here is a list of grains that are substitutes superior in nutrition:

BROWN RICE: Complete with its "germ," where most of the protein lies

WILD RICE: An edible grain unrelated to the usual kind of rice, white or brown

MILLET: Infrequently grown in the Western Hemisphere; handle the same as brown rice

OATS: Oatmeal can be used for more than breakfast; try combining it with sharp-flavored vegetables

BARLEY: A cereal grain believed by our forefathers to have great medicinal value; very good in soups

BUCKWHEAT: A different plant from regular wheat; groats of buckwheat are sometimes called kasha

SEMOLINA: The hard part of wheat left after the white flour is milled off; use as you would brown rice

BULGHUR: Cracked (slightly processed) wheat, a bit more edible than the whole-wheat berry

SAMP: Another debt to the American Indian, tasty when cooked like cornmeal mush. Doesn't really belong in this list, as it is a *combination* of wheat and coarse cornmeal but too good and too nutritious to be omitted. If your natural-foods shop doesn't stock it, make your own by combining equal parts of coarse cornmeal and bulghur.

Now, to get back to the subject of legumes, here are two ways to achieve that durable and hearty New England classic bean dish.

BEANHOLE BEANS
2 quarts
(it's not worth going through this for less)

8 cups dried beans: pea, kidney, or pinto

½ teaspoon baking soda

2 tablespoons minced onion

salt pork or bacon (optional; if you have principles against it, just substitute a little vegetable oil)

salt and pepper

pinch powdered mustard

½ cup molasses or brown sugar

Find a traditional bean pot, or a sturdy kettle with a fasten-down cover and a stout wire handle. Soak the beans in the pot until softened somewhat. Drain, then re-cover the beans with water to which the baking soda has been added, and simmer them for an hour.

Now dig a hole in the ground big enough to accommodate some stones plus your bean pot with space left over; burn out this hole by filling it first with stones and then with hard wood, setting the wood afire, and letting it burn for 6 to 10 hours. When good hot coals have resulted, you are ready to bake the beans.

Add all ingredients to the bean pot, together with some fresh boiling water, cover the pot securely, attach a stiff wire to its handle, and leave this wire upright. Now remove all stones plus hot coals from the hole. Lower the beanpot into the hole and return the coals and the hot rocks, surrounding the pot on all sides. Fill the hole up with earth, packing it solidly around and over the pot. Stamp the soil down firmly, leaving the wire protruding from the ground to mark the spot. Leave all this in place for 24 hours, then dig the soil off, and remove the bean pot by the wire.

EASY BOSTON BAKED BEANS
2 quarts

8 cups dried beans: pea, pinto, or kidney
salt and pepper, to taste
pinch dry mustard or ginger
1½ cups tomato purée
¼ cup vegetable oil

Soak beans in cold water until softened somewhat. Drain, re-cover with water, and simmer for an hour, or until skins break. Preheat oven to 300°. Drain beans again, and mix them with all the other ingredients in a bean pot (see recipe above). Cover bean mixture with boiling water, then cover the pot securely, and put it in the oven. Bake for 6 to 8 hours, checking from time to time to see if you need to replenish water to cover beans (if you do, use boiling water). Uncover the pot when beans are cooked to your taste, and leave them in the oven for another half hour or so, to brown and dry a bit.

If you don't add these beans to the leftover *rata-touille*, serve them alone, accompanied with Boston brown bread and a tossed green salad, for a cheap and nourishing complete meal.

COLOMBIAN BAKED BEANS
4 to 6 servings

2 cups dried kidney beans
½ teaspoon dried thyme leaves
1 bay leaf
⅛ teaspoon cayenne pepper
1 teaspoon salt
1 small yellow onion, peeled
1 1-inch square salt pork
1 pound cherry or plum tomatoes (or canned tomatoes)

GARNISH:
cherry tomatoes
1 green bell pepper, chopped
fresh chives
Italian parsley
1 avocado, very ripe

Rinse the beans in cold water, then put them into a heavy casserole (an earthenware pot) and cover with water. Bring to a slow boil, reduce heat. Add the thyme, bay leaf, cayenne, salt, the whole onion, and the salt pork. Cook, uncovered, for 3 hours, stirring occasionally and adding more boiling water when necessary, to cover beans. Add the tomatoes whole, and cook for 2 or more hours, until the beans are soft. Taste for seasoning. Serve the beans garnished with the fresh tomatoes, green pepper, chives, parsley, and avocado, peeled, stoned, and sliced.

MACARONI AND BEANS
6 to 8 servings

1½ cups dried navy or pea beans
½ lb. macaroni (shell or bow-tie type, for visual
interest)
2 medium onions
3 tablespoons margarine or oil
1 cup thin-sliced carrots
2 cups peeled tomatoes, cut up
2 teaspoons mixed herbs: sage and oregano, for instance
salt and pepper, to taste
grated hard cheese

Soak the beans, then drain them, cover again with fresh water, and simmer until not quite tender. Drain again, but reserve the liquid. Boil the macaroni in salted water* for 2 or 3 minutes. Peel and chop the onions. Heat the oil, and sauté the onion and carrots, covered, about 15 minutes. Add to the skillet the tomatoes, herbs, salt, and pepper. Re-cover, and cook another 15 minutes.

---

* Salted water comes to a boil sooner than unsalted—thus saving you utility pennies; remember: if you are going to salt a food, you may as well do it in the cooking water first.

Transfer this mixture to a large saucepan or flame-proof casserole dish, and add the beans and macaroni. Add also 1 cup of the bean-cooking liquid. Simmer, covered, for another 30 or 40 minutes, stirring from time to time, and adding more of the bean liquid if necessary. Correct seasoning, and serve hot, sprinkled with the grated cheese.

LENTIL CASSEROLE
serves 4 to 6

2 tablespoons vegetable oil
2 medium onions
1 garlic clove
2 stalks celery, plus leaves
3 medium carrots
1 lb. dried lentils
salt and pepper, to taste
½ teaspoon marjoram or thyme
1 bay leaf

Don't soak the lentils—they will soften more quickly than most beans. Preheat oven to 325°. In a skillet heat the oil. Peel and slice or chop the onions. Peel and mince the garlic. Chop the celery, and slice the carrots (don't skin or scrape the carrots first—you'll be reducing their nutritive value by about half if you do). Sauté the vegetables for about 5 minutes in the hot oil. Then combine them, plus the oil, with the lentils in a casserole dish, adding the seasonings and herbs together with enough hot water to cover the lentils well. Now cover the casserole dish, and bake for about 2 hours. The lentils will be quite chewy. (If you prefer them mushy, simmer them for about 10 minutes *before* you bake them.) Remove the bay leaf before serving.

Here's a clever lentil dish that gets a number of other good vegetables into the act as well.

MEATLESS "CHOPPED LIVER"
4 to 6 servings

7 or 8 small hard-cooked eggs
½ lb. dried lentils
2 medium onions, chopped
3 tablespoons vegetable oil
1 tablespoon peanut butter
salt and pepper, to taste
a few leaves of lettuce
2 medium tomatoes, sliced
white or red horseradish

Hard-cook the eggs and shell them. Simmer the lentils long enough to make them mashable, and mash them. Peel and chop the onions. Chop the eggs fine, and mix with half the chopped onions, raw. The remaining half of the chopped onions should be browned in the vegetable oil. Now blend well the lentils, cooked onions, eggs-and-onions, peanut butter, salt, and pepper. Make a bed of lettuce leaves, and mound the "chopped liver" onto it, arranging the tomato slices around it. Add horseradish to your taste—or let your family or guests add their own, to *their* taste. The latter may be preferable, horseradish not being everyone's cup of tea.

SEVERAL-BEAN MEDLEY
6 to 8 servings

1 cup each 4 or 5 kinds of beans (suggested combination: pinto, baby lima, black, and green string)

1 medium-sized Bermuda onion
2 medium carrots
1 cup fresh mushrooms
1 garlic clove
¼ cup vegetable oil
3 tablespoons soy sauce
salt to taste
1 teaspoon mixed dried herbs (suggested combination: dill and oregano)

If using any dried beans, soak them as necessary to soften somewhat. Cut the green string beans in strips lengthwise. Peel and chop the onion (the Bermuda onion is for color; white or yellow onion will do as well). Slice the carrots in very thin rounds and the mushrooms any way you want to. Peel and mince the garlic. Heat the oil in a skillet, and sauté the onion and garlic until softened. Then add the beans, carrots, mushrooms, soy sauce, seasonings, and herbs, and sauté (or stir-fry) them for a few minutes. Serve very hot.

This is not only a very nourishing meat-substitute dish, but it is very handsome too, combining colors, shapes, and textures in an interesting way.

M & M & M DISH
for 4 to 6

1 cup mung beans
1 cup marrow beans
½ cup macadamia nut meats
1 medium leek (or onion)
2 eggs
1 cup milk or yogurt
½ cup shredded sharp Cheddar (or similar cheese)

Since macadamia nuts (those lovely round nuts from the subtropics and tropics) are quite expensive, you can substitute peanuts if you don't mind messing up the alliteration.

Soak the beans as necessary, then simmer them. When they are nearly soft, drain and crush them. Preheat oven to 375°; chop (or blenderize) the nutmeats and the onion or leek. Beat the eggs, and combine them with the milk or yogurt. Then mix all ingredients together thoroughly. Grease a baking dish, spoon the mixture in, and bake it, uncovered, for half an hour.

An international favorite is the four-bean salad. In a hot climate, or on a summer day, it offers refreshment without sacrificing nourishment. You can make this from leftover cooked beans or canned beans.

FOUR-BEAN SALAD
6 to 8 servings

1 lb. red kidney beans, cooked
1 lb. cut green beans, cooked
1 lb. yellow wax beans, cooked
1 lb. lima or white beans, cooked
1 small red onion
5 tablespoons lemon juice
½ cup vegetable oil
salt and pepper, to taste
½ teaspoon mixed dried herbs: basil, thyme, tarragon,
for example

Some other combination of beans may be used—variety in shape and color is the principle.

Cut the onion into very thin rings, and mix with the beans. Combine all the rest of the ingredients, shaking them up together in a dressing bottle or jar, and pour over the beans and onions. Serve very cold.

SOYA "LOAF"

The reason for the quotation marks is that the first time I made this it didn't hang together. Not enough binder, I guess. Rather than add more egg (and cholesterol) or lecithin or yogurt or something like that, I let it hang loose and called it thereafter a baked dish.

4 to 6 servings

2 cups dried soy beans

2 eggs

½ cup tomato sauce (or ketchup)

2 tablespoons vegetable oil

½ cup diced sweet pepper

½ cup sunflower seeds

3 tablespoons wheat germ

½ cup bread crumbs
½ cup grated cheese (Parmesan or Romano)

Soak the beans for several hours, then simmer them until nearly soft. Preheat oven to 375°. Beat the eggs, and combine them with the tomato sauce and the vegetable oil. Drain the beans, and mash them; then combine the mash with the rest of the ingredients, including the liquids. Shape the mixture into a loaf, or if it doesn't so shape, just spoon it into a baking dish, and bake for 40 minutes.

Delicious and very high-protein.

BLACK-EYED PEAS AND BUCKWHEAT
for 4 to 6

2 cups dried black-eyed peas
2 cups buckwheat groats
2 small onions or several scallions
1 tablespoon butter or margarine
1 cup Bacos or Krisp*
1 tablespoon chili powder
3 tablespoons parsley or watercress
½ cup bread crumbs

Soak the black-eyed peas for a few hours, then simmer them in fresh water until almost tender. Drain, reserving the liquid. Meanwhile, boil the buckwheat, separately, for a half hour, and drain. Preheat oven to 350°. Now chop the onions or scallions quite fine. Melt the butter, and brown them quickly in it. Mix together the onions in their butter, the peas, and the buckwheat. Stir in Bacos and chili powder, and add about a cup of the pea-simmering liquid. Grease a baking dish, and put the mixture into it. Top with the mixed parsley and crumbs and bake, uncovered, for half an hour.

CHICK PEAS AND RICE
serves 8 to 10

Chick peas, or garbanzos, come in several colors; but in this country you are most likely to find only the white (or light yellowish) ones. Thus the red and green ingredients, to cheer up this dish.

---

* Bacos and Krisp are soybean products that reproduce the flavor of bacon without adding to your cholesterol problem. There are a number of meat substitutes made from soybeans, some more tasty and more accurate reproductions than others. Look into them.

3 cups dried chick peas

2 cloves garlic

1 stalk celery, plus leaves

2 tablespoons margarine

2 cups peeled tomatoes in sauce (or equal volume fresh
tomatoes plus tomato paste)

2 teaspoons curry powder

1 teaspoon cayenne pepper (optional)

1 cup cooked rice (or other grain)

1 small onion

mint leaves

Soak the chick peas for some hours. Drain, and then simmer in fresh water until almost tender, and drain again. Peel and mince the garlic. Chop the celery. Heat the margarine in a skillet and brown the garlic and celery in it. Add the tomatoes in sauce to the skillet, together with the spices and rice; mix them around over high heat. Now turn the heat down, add the chickpeas, and allow the whole thing to simmer about a half hour. When the dish is ready to be served slice the onion in very thin rings, and sprinkle them on top with some whole mint leaves for decoration.

Chick peas are an excellent meat substitute, more nourishing than a pork chop. They are eaten in all kinds of ways: in soups, salted and roasted and nibbled like nuts, added cold to salads. Here is a cold chick-pea dish that is a favorite in my house—as an hors d'oeuvre, a sandwich spread, or just by itself, a scoopful on a leaf of lettuce.

GARBANZO MASH
about 1 pint

1 1-lb. can chick peas

2 medium onions

2 tablespoons minced parsley or chives
3 tablespoons margarine or vegetable oil
20 to 24 pine nuts
1 teaspoon lemon juice
½ teaspoon Tabasco (or other hot sauce)
4 tablespoons sesame seeds

Canned chick peas have already soaked for a long time, so they are softened enough to go directly into the blender, grinder, or mortar. Drain off the liquid, and rinse the peas well under cold running water. Then blend, grind, or mortar-and-pestle them to a purée consistency. Peel and chop the onions; mince the parsley or chives. Heat the margarine in a skillet, and brown the onion. Then blend all the ingredients except 1 tablespoon of sesame seeds together, mixing well. Press into a bowl and cool. Put the remaining sesame seeds onto a cookie sheet or metal dish, and heat them briefly in a 300° oven to brown; then sprinkle them on top of the mash.

BLACK-EYED PEAS AND BANANAS

Actually this dish is basically a combined vegetable dish; the addition of the bananas and fish is what makes the difference. A delicious, hearty, and (depending on the tariff on bananas that week) inexpensive one-pot meal.

5 or 6 servings

2 cups dried black-eyed peas
1 sweet green pepper
1 cup chopped fresh tomato or 1 cup canned peeled
tomatoes or 1 cup tomato sauce with tomato pieces in it
1 teaspoon crushed hot red peppers or 1 tablespoon
Tabasco

¼ teaspoon oregano

about 14 oz. canned tuna plus its liquid (or fresh
fish of your choice)

3 or 4 bananas, not overripe

salt

2 to 3 tablespoons light vegetable oil

Soak the peas for a few hours, then drain, and simmer
them in fresh water for an hour or until nearly tender.
Meanwhile, seed and cut up the green pepper. Add it,
the tomatoes, and red pepper to the cooked peas; cook,
covered, over medium heat for an additional 20 minutes. Now add the oregano and fish plus its liquid, stirring to distribute, and cook, covered, for another 10
or 15 minutes. While this is going on, peel and slice the
bananas; salt them liberally. Heat the oil, and fry the
banana slices until golden. Drain them, and arrange
them on top of the bean mixture. Serve hot. (Don't
throw away the banana skins: see page 328.)

LIMAS AND PEARS

*Before we abandon the subject of legumes cooked with
fruits, here is an unlikely-sounding but tasty combination. You may, of course, use frozen, canned, or fresh
lima beans for this dish, and fresh or canned pears.*

4 servings

3 cups cooked lima beans

1 stalk celery, plus leaves, chopped

2 tablespoons margarine or butter

2 pears, peeled, sliced lengthwise

1 tablespoon brown sugar (optional)

1 tablespoon chopped nuts (optional)

Preheat oven to 375°. Grease lightly a casserole or baking dish, and put the drained beans in it. Brown the celery in the (melted) margarine, and add the celery to the beans. Then lay the slices of pear on top and pour over them any of the margarine left in the skillet. Sprinkle with the optional brown sugar and/or nuts. Heat for 20 to 30 minutes.

There is something so satisfying to the American palate about a baking potato (the mealy-fleshed varieties) done to a turn, opened up with a pat of butter melting into it, or topped with some sour cream and chopped chives. Heaven! And the potato is a vegetable that has been much maligned. It is a good source of protein and a number of vitamins— not just starch. Don't neglect to eat the skin of that lovely baked Idaho or Maine potato when you've sated yourself with the insides. The skins of other varieties should be eaten, too—the firm-fleshed types that are so delightful boiled or roasted and accompanying meat or fish or poultry. If esthetics dictate your peeling them, be sure to add the skins to your soup bag, or eat them later according to the recipe on page 201. *Don't* throw them away.

There are also a couple of uses for raw potatoes that should not be overlooked. In the first place, you can cut a largish one across its middle, and use the flat cut surface for a block print. Just cut your design into the surface of the potato, then dip it in ink, and print with it. In the second place, should you have accidentally and irretrievably oversalted some soup or stew, you can reduce the startling effect by adding some grated raw potato to the dish.

The second day of cooked potato is just as exciting, for then we can combine it with any number of other vegetables in a casserole or stew or chowder—or even make potato salad of it. Or a shepherd's pie. Pan-fry it with onions chopped fine, in a dish that's found on every continent in the world, a dish that's called, in the Massachusetts offshore islands, "Scootin' Along the Shore." Scootin' Along the Shore, if it doesn't get eaten up at the first serving, can be combined with those leftover beets in a hash that deserves a better name.

RED FLANNEL HASH
(BAKED STYLE)
4 or 5 servings

2 tablespoons chicken fat or margarine
2 cups leftover cooked potatoes and onions
2 cups leftover cooked beets
salt and pepper
1½ cups milk

Preheat oven to 350°. Butter a baking dish. Melt the fat. Combine it with all ingredients. Bake for half an hour, uncovered.

Sweet potatoes or yams (which, just by the way, are not at all related to white potatoes except by name in English) have such a distinctive taste that we usually just bake them and eat them with a little margarine or sour cream on top, and who can blame us? They are indeed so "sweet" that it always seems to me that candying them or gucking them up with marshmallows or honey is really gilding the lily. On the other hand, substituting them for white potatoes in many of the places we don't expect to meet them produces novel and taste-teasing results. So does combining them with white potatoes. Here are some examples of both. First in a soup, from South America.

SWEET POTATO SOUP
about 6 servings

4 medium-sized sweet potatoes
1 medium-sized onion
7 tablespoons margarine
¼ cup cooked spinach or chard
salt and pepper
1 quart water
½ teaspoon chopped orange peel
pinch mace or nutmeg
2 tablespoons cornstarch or arrowroot
3 cups milk
½ cup peanuts

Peel and cut the sweet potatoes in half-inch cubes. Peel and slice the onion. Melt 3 tablespoons of margarine in a large saucepan, and add the onions and potatoes. Chop the green vegetable fine, and add to the saucepan with the salt and pepper and the quart of water. Cover and simmer until potatoes are tender. Now mash the vegetables, and leave them on the heat, adding all the rest of the ingredients except the peanuts. Stir constantly over medium heat for about 15 minutes, while you get someone else to chop the peanuts for you. Serve very hot, with the chopped nuts sprinkled on top of each bowlful.

THREE-TONED SCALLOPED POTATOES
4 to 6 servings

2 medium-sized white potatoes
3 medium-sized sweet potatoes
1 small onion

¼ cup chopped green olives
1 cup grated Cheddar cheese
dash pepper or paprika
4 tablespoons margarine
1 cup milk

Preheat oven to 375°. Peel both white and yellow potatoes, and slice them *very* thin. Ditto the onion. In a buttered baking dish, arrange the potatoes, onions, olives, cheese, and seasonings in layers, dotting the margarine around each layer. Taking care not to dislodge and float all the olives into one place, pour the milk over the whole thing. Bake, covered, for 1 hour. Now remove cover, and leave under the broiler for 5 minutes or so to brown the top.

NOTE: For the white potatoes, you can substitute rutabagas, turnips, or parsnips without anything dreadful happening.

If those Three-Toned Scalloped Potatoes aren't entirely consumed on the first serving, retread them the next evening the following way.

RETREAD SCALLOPED POTATOES
4 to 6 servings

half the recipe for Three-Toned Scalloped Potatoes
½ cup cooked green peas or peapods
1 cup peeled tomatoes in sauce
½ cup cooked wax beans
¼ cup brown gravy or white sauce
½ cup whole-grain bread crumbs

Preheat oven to 375°. Butter a baking dish. Stir together all ingredients except crumbs, and turn them into the baking dish. Top with the bread crumbs, and bake for half an hour, uncovered.

You haven't done anything with those potato peelings, have you, but add them to your soup bag? Both kinds of potato peelings go there, white and sweet.

If through all this talk of potatoes you have been dreaming unreconstructed guilty dreams of French Fries, your waiting is over. We have come, at last, to the recipe, courtesy of Glenn Andrews, that was promised way back in the front of the book. It seems a fitting conclusion to this potato section.

FRENCH FRIED POTATO SKINS

And I quote:

"Use thin skins if possible, ones you've shaved from washed potatoes with a potato peeler. They can be large or small; it doesn't matter. Heat about ¼ inch of bacon or sausage fat in a frying pan. Add the pieces of potato skin and stir until they are brown and crisp. Drain on paper towels. Sprinkle with salt."

Or simply spread margarine on the skins, and then broil them. Marvelous!

Here's one way to achieve that leftover portion of red beets that lent color to the Red Flannel Hash. And nice to know that beets in season are usually satisfyingly cheap from local gardens.

ORANGE BEETS
4 to 6 servings

2 lbs. whole fresh beets, with stems
¼ cup margarine
½ cup orange juice
1 teaspoon orange or lemon rind, grated
½ teaspoon powdered clove

Leave the tail and about 1½ inches of the stems on the beets (so they won't bleed to death in cooking). Now boil the beets for 40 minutes to 1 hour, depending on their size. (Don't throw away the leaves—put them into your greens bag in the refrigerator.) When the beets are cool, peel and slice or cube them. Heat the margarine in a skillet, and add the orange juice, rind, and clove. Now put the beet slices in, and simmer them for a few minutes until heated through.

This method can be applied to any of the paler root vegetables with equally good results. You can make a root-vegetable medley: parsnips, turnips, rutabagas, salsify (if you grow it in your area) all combine well with beets. Sprinkle buttered crumbs on top, and run them under the broiler for a few minutes before serving.

Some people think there is nothing more delicious than plain Brussels sprouts simmered until tender, with a bit of crisp bacon sprinkled on them. And some like the experience of cooked-until-soft barley; but the combination below enhances both, in my opinion, and nourishes inexpensively too.

BRUSSELS SPROUTS AND BARLEY
5 or 6 servings

2 cups dried barley
1 quart Brussels sprouts

3 tablespoons light vegetable oil or margarine
½ cup small white onions, sliced
¼ cup chopped mushrooms
salt and pepper, to taste
½ cup grated cheese (hard Swiss or semisharp Cheddar,
for example)

Soak the barley for a few hours, then drain, and cover with fresh water. Simmer barley until it is almost the texture you like. Drain, and keep warm. If the sprouts are large, halve or quarter them; if small, leave them whole; boil them 10 minutes in water to cover. Reserve the cooking liquid. Preheat oven to 375°. Heat the oil, and sauté onions and mushrooms in it until the onions are golden. Combine sprouts with onions, mushrooms, and oil in a baking dish. Add salt and pepper. Stir the cheese into the warm barley, and add the mixture to the vegetables in the baking dish. Add a bit of the sprouts-cooking liquid to the dish, and bake it, uncovered, for about half an hour, or until everything is heated through and the cheese nicely melted.

If you don't use up all the barley you have on hand with the dish above, you can combine it with that little bit of left-over white rice, and your brown-rice-refusing relatives will be delighted. Or use it for the grain part of stuffed cabbage, stuffed bell peppers, stuffed tomatoes, or stuffed grape leaves.

Stuffing these convenient receptacles, by the way, allows you to combine vegetables with a difference, provide a little visual interest on the dinner plate, and sneak all manner of leftovers inside. Bits of meat or fish (don't imagine that hamburg is the only possible meat component for stuffed peppers), small hunks of beginning-to-go-hard cheese, hand-fuls of currants or raisins, a few nuts, small pieces of fruit—all bake or braise together, safely contained in these natural, edible packages.

You can use up the less attractive outer leaves of the cabbage in this way, or the not-so-firm-as-they-once-were bell peppers. The grape leaves needn't be bought all done up in brine from the Middle Eastern specialty shop; they can be picked off vines in your backyard or down the road at the edge of the field where the wild grape grows. Then you can put them up in your own jars of brine (salt and water), or use them within days, before they need storing in salt water. I live in an area full of such woods and fields, and so every spring I pick great bunches of wild grape leaves and bring them to city friends who don't enjoy this option but love to make *dolma,* or stuffed grape leaves.

While we're dallying with the engrossing subject of vegetables that serve as receptacles, we must not forget all the receptacle squashes. The squash family is such a large and versatile one that it's hard to think of all their numbers at once. Dividing them up into summer and winter squashes doesn't quite fill the bill. Let's, for our present purposes, categorize them handily as soft-skinned or hard-skinned. Into the latter group go winter squash, acorn squash, Hubbard squash, turban squash; into the former go zucchini, butternut, summer crooknecks, scallops, and pattypan, with pumpkins falling somewhere in between.

Obviously the hard-shelled squashes are the ones to use as holders for other vegetable combinations—even fruits. But the soft-shells can be stuffed too, with slightly different effect. Be inventive in making stuffing combinations. Most squashes have subtle enough flavor that they combine well with all manner of other foods. If you prefer, the vegetables can be softened a bit first in water or oil, then stuffed into a half squash for baking.

The first time you serve such squash halves, the diners can eat the stuffing and part of the squash meat; then you can refill them with a different vegetable (and pasta) mélange, and rebake them the next night. Even after the very skin has been scraped clean, you still haven't finished getting

the most out of your squash—the skin goes into your vegetable soup bag in the freezer.

Just to get you started thinking "stuffed squash," a
couple of suggestions follow.

STUFFED ACORNS, FIRST TIME
for 4

2 medium-sized acorn squashes
butter or margarine
2 small raw carrots
1 cup leftover baked beans
4 tablespoons sunflower seeds
salt, pepper, nutmeg

Preheat oven to 375°. Cut the squashes in half (I find
the most efficient tool for this purpose is a hatchet).
Scoop out the seeds and strings. Now score the squash
meat with slashes lengthwise and crosswise, being careful not to go through to the skin with your knife. (The
unimaginative would now simply butter and salt and
pepper and possibly sweeten a little with brown sugar
and put into the oven to bake.) Butter or margarine
the inside surface of the squash. Shred the carrots, and
mix with the beans and sunflower seeds. Divide this mixture into four, and mound it in the cavities of the acorn
squash halves. Sprinkle tops with salt, pepper, nutmeg,
to taste. Bake for an hour and a half. Serve with a dish
of mixed greens and some noodles, for a nicely balanced vegetarian meal.

Here's how you use up those bits of leftover spinach and
yellow squash.

SECOND-TIME ACORN SQUASH
for the same 4

1 medium onion
2 tablespoons vegetable oil
1 cup leftover cooked spinach
½ cup leftover squash meat
½ cup cooked pasta (small shells, for instance)
salt, pepper, curry powder
4 half-eaten-out acorn squash halves
¼ cup shredded cheese of your choice

Preheat oven to 375°. Peel and chop the onion. Heat the oil, and sauté the onion in it. Cut the spinach and squash meat small, and add that to the skillet. Then stir the pasta into the skillet. Add seasonings. Heap these vegetables, in four equal parts, into the four acorn-squash containers. Sprinkle the shredded cheese over the tops. Bake until heated through, about half an hour.

Your accompaniment this time might be hot buttered beets and corn bread. A very pretty meal.

For this dish you sauce the cranberries with sugar to combat their excessive tartness; then the slightly shocking piquancy of the berries makes a pleasant contrast with the blandness of the squash and cauliflower. Also, the colors are very handsome.

BUTTERNUT SQUASH AND CRANBERRIES
for 4

2 medium-sized butternut squashes
3 cups cranberries
2 cups sugar
2 cups cooked cauliflower

Preheat oven to 350°. Cut the squashes in half length-wise, and discard the seeds if they are well developed. If they are young and tender, combine the seeds with the cranberries. Wash and pick over cranberries, combine them with the sugar in a saucepan, and cook over medium heat until skins have popped and they have softened somewhat. Cut up the cauliflower, and combine it with the cranberries. Score the squashes length-wise and crosswise, being careful not to let your knife blade reach to the skin. Scoop cranberry-cauliflower mixture into the cavities of the squashes. Bake for an hour or so.

Buttered snap green beans would go well with this dish, especially at Yuletide.

Here's where you find out what to do with the Jack-o-Lantern you cut a face into at Hallowe'en time. It's threatening to collapse now that Thanksgiving has come and gone; let it fall over into a soup, rather than the garbage can.

JACK-O-LANTERN SOUP
3 or 4 servings

1 small, tired, cut-out pumpkin
2 cloves garlic or 1 bulb fennel
1 cup peeled chopped tomatoes
1 pinch coriander
salt and pepper, to taste
1 cup vegetable stock or dry white wine

Remove the candle from your jack-o-lantern, and then cut him into large pieces. Peel or cut the orange outer skin off the pieces, then scrape off any of the strands that may be left on the concave sides of the hunks.

Now chop what is left of your pumpkin into smaller pieces. Peel and mince the garlic or fennel. Combine all the ingredients in a saucepan, and simmer them for 15 to 20 minutes. Then pour the mixture into your blender, and run it at medium speed for a minute or so. Serve hot or cold.

PUMPKIN PUDDING
4 to 6 servings

The same tired old jack-o-lantern
3 medium eggs, separated
½ cup honey
1 teaspoon cinammon
½ teaspoon nutmeg or allspice
½ cup orange juice
1 cup yogurt
2 tablespoons sherry or cognac (optional)
1 teaspoon grated orange or lemon rind

Preheat oven to 375°. Do the same things to your jack-o-lantern as in the recipe above, until you have turned him into pumpkin meat. Then steam or simmer the pumpkin meat over, or in, water until tender. Strain through a sieve if you like very smooth texture; if you want it a bit chunky, forget the sieve. Drain pumpkin meat if simmered. Separate the eggs, and add the yolks to the pumpkin meat, along with the honey, spices, and orange juice. Stir in the yogurt and (optional) liquor. Beat together to blend well. Now beat the egg whites until stiff; fold them into the mixture. Bake for 45 minutes, or until the custard is set. Sprinkle grated rind on top of the pudding.

This can be used for a pie filling: just bake the pudding in a partially pre-baked pie crust.

When I first saw a recipe for pumpkin cookies, I didn't believe it—or rather I thought that that was carrying things too far. Then I made them, and they were beautiful; so I experimented with making some dessert-type things with all kinds of squashes. One of my favorites turned out to be a most unlikely-sounding confection. I pass it along to you for amazement—and the delight of your sweet-toothed beneficiaries.

ZUCCHINI COOKIES
12 large or 18 smaller

½ cup sugar
¼ cup margarine (this is not the sort of cookie that insists on butter)
1 small egg
¾ cup grated raw zucchini
½ teaspoon baking soda
1 cup whole-wheat flour
½ teaspoon each cinnamon, cloves, salt

Preheat oven to 375°. Cream the sugar and margarine; stir in the egg. Add this mixture to the zucchini and baking soda, stirring to distribute. Sift the flour with the spices, and combine this with the first mixture. Blend well, and drop by spoonfuls onto a greased cookie sheet. Bake the cookies 12 to 15 minutes, or until they have begun to brown on top.

The addition of raisins, chopped dates, and/or chopped nuts to the cookie batter at the last moment would make an even more luxurious cookie—and you might in that case reduce the amount of sugar.

A few recipes back we used up some leftover cooked spinach. If you often have such leftovers, don't despair:

cooked spinach can be chopped fine and go into practically any meat or vegetable soup you care to mention—or combine with any number of other vegetables in a casserole. Spinach reminds me of one of my recent discoveries: Swiss chard. A noble vegetable, with which, for some reason, I had negative associations (probably stemming from another childhood experience). It grows easily and has a long season, even benefits from a touch of frost. In case you aren't situated so that you can have a row or two of chard in the backyard, you'll find it reasonably priced in the markets. It can be eaten raw, torn up in a green salad, and it combines well with such other greens as spinach, lettuce, endive, turnip tops, escarole. It is even better when cooked just slightly along with some beet tops and—if you happen to live in that part of the country—collard greens.

A MESS OF GREENS
4 servings

About a gallon of fresh-picked greens: Swiss chard
alone, or others mixed
4 tablespoons margarine or vegetable oil
salt and pepper, to taste
1 teaspoon lemon juice (optional)

Wash the greens under running cold water, and, in the case of chard, separate by tearing the ribs from the leaves. Chop up the ribs; tear the leaves into smallish pieces. Now heat the margarine or oil in a large skillet, throw in the chard rib pieces, and sauté them a little. Then add the rest of the greens with the water still adhering to them, cover, and wilt them a bit. Serve before they have softened too much, seasoned to taste.

Cooked greens the next day also go into a lovely lasagne, that broad-noodle concoction that usually features tomato sauce, some kind of ground meat, and several kinds of cheese. Let's say that the greens you have on hand are mostly spinach with a touch of beet greens and/or chard, and make the following handsome dish.

SPINACH LASAGNE
3 or 4 hearty servings

½ lb. broad noodles
2 tablespoons margarine
2 tablespoons flour
2 cloves garlic
salt and pepper, to taste
¼ teaspoon nutmeg
1 teaspoon powdered mustard
3 cups milk
3 egg yolks
about 10 oz. of greens, cooked
5 medium-sized ripe tomatoes, cut up
½ lb. cooked meat, in small cubes (optional)

Boil the noodles in salted water until they are cooked *al dente*. Drain, then cover with cold water so they don't stick to one another. Preheat oven to 350°. In a saucepan, melt the margarine and stir in the flour. Peel and mince the garlic, and add it to the flour and margarine; then add the seasoning and spices, stirring over medium heat. Bring the milk separately to a boil, then add it, a little at a time, stirring until the sauce thickens. Now remove the pan from the heat, cool it a little, and stir in the egg yolks. Grease a casserole or large flat baking dish. Make a bottom layer with one third of the noodles, removed from their cold bath. Now layers of half the mixed spinach and tomatoes, one third the sauce, and half the meat cubes, if you're using them. Now a second layer of noodles, and repeat, finishing with a top layer of noodles, and pouring the last third of the sauce over. Bake for 30 to 40 minutes, long enough for everything to be heated through and bubbling.

I once made this variation on the classic lasagne when I was caught cheeseless. It worked fine.

One day when I cooked up a mess of greens, I added to the dish a few inky-top mushrooms I had just found where they had sprung up between the flagstones on a neighbor's terrace. Sheer heaven! (Don't emulate except under the direction of an experienced mycologist, because the identification of wild mushrooms is nothing to fool around with.)

Chard, which cooks down like spinach to a mere suggestion of its fresh volume, also combines well with a number of other vegetables—tomatoes and/or potatoes, for instance —or with meat and fish. Or rice and pasta. It's also good with various dairy foods. Try the following soufflé.

CHARD-CHEESE SOUFFLÉ
5 or 6 servings

2 cups cooked chard
3 medium eggs
1 cup cottage cheese
¼ cup grated Parmesan or Romano cheese
1 cup cream or sour cream
salt, pepper, nutmeg, to taste

Preheat oven to 375°. Chop the chard quite fine. Beat the eggs slightly, but don't separate them—this is a fast version of soufflé. Then mix all the ingredients together, put into a greased baking dish, and bake for half an hour. A teaspoon or so of fresh-grated horseradish sprinkled over this when you serve it wouldn't be bad.

SWEET-AND-SOUR CABBAGE
6 or 7 servings

1 medium onion
core and inner leaves of a red or green cabbage
2 medium-sized carrots (or 4 small)
3 tablespoons vegetable oil or margarine
¼ cup raisins or currants
3 tablespoons vinegar
1 cup water
3 tablespoons brown sugar
salt and pepper, to taste

Peel and chop the onion. Shred the cabbage leaves coarsely; chop the core and ribs fine. Shred the carrots. Heat oil or margarine in a skillet, and sauté the onion in it until golden. Add cabbage, cover, and cook over medium heat 10 minutes or more. Mix the raisins, vinegar, water, sugar, and seasonings together in a bowl, then add this mixture to the skillet. Stir it around a few more minutes on the heat, until everything has had a chance to heat through, and serve.

If this dish is made with red cabbage, it is spectacularly colored; if green, you may want to throw in a few slices of pimiento or a few chopped red radishes, along with the raisins.

Cabbage is often the best bargain in the supermarket vegetable bins; it's a pity the kitchen economist doesn't think of it more often as her "green leafy" for the day—rather than the usually more costly iceberg or bibb lettuce. A welcome change from green is the beautiful red cabbage, which is just as fine for soups, for stuffing, and for any number of other dishes both cheap and healthful.

What you should do first to get the most out of your

two-penny cabbage, red or green, is to remove the outermost leaves if tattered, and put them immediately into your soup bag in the freezer. Then carefully peel off whole the next largest, cup-shaped leaves for making your stuffed cabbage, cutting them away from the core as you go. The now-smaller head and core can be shredded and boiled with small, peeled potatoes. Or cooked on top of the stove in the following way.

POMME DE CABBAGE
4 or 5 servings

core and inner leaves of a cabbage
1 celery stalk, plus leaves
3 tablespoons vegetable oil
2 medium-sized apples
salt to taste
1 tablespoon caraway or sesame seeds

Shred the cabbage leaves in not too small pieces; dice the core and ribs quite fine. Chop celery in ½-inch pieces. Heat the oil in a skillet, and sauté the cabbage and celery in it, over medium heat, for 5 to 10 minutes, according to your taste for firmness. Peel, core, and slice the apples. Reduce heat, add apple slices to the skillet, together with the salt and seeds. Cook, covered, about 15 minutes longer. Serve hot.

Sweet corn, which grows in a startling number of varieties in this country, is one of the many debts we owe to the American Indian. Fresh from the field, boiled for 7 or 8 minutes within as short a time as possible of its picking, then slathered with butter and salt, it is an incomparable treat. Nothing to compare with it can be found in the British Isles or Central Europe, where the corn is nothing like our native

American maize. Something to do with meteorological differences, no doubt. Besides being an important source of one of the B vitamins, corn kernels are, like all grains, a good fiber food (we used to call it roughage). So even if you can't enjoy fresh sweet corn-on-the-cob, you should include corn in some other form in your diet. Besides, in the canned-kernels form, it is one of the most frequent bargains in your supermarket. Here are some combinations utilizing corn, which lends an interesting color, form, and texture.

CORN COMBO
4 servings

½ lb. broccoli
3 tablespoons cooking oil
2 cups eggplant cubes
3 cups cooked corn kernels
salt and pepper
1 cup sour cream or white sauce
paprika

Boil the broccoli standing (stalk down, flowerets up) in a small saucepan or coffeepot, until the stalk is nearly tender. Then cut it into pieces. Preheat oven to 375°. Heat the oil, and sauté the eggplant cubes in it until translucent. Then combine the corn, other vegetables, salt and pepper, and the sauce or sour cream in a baking dish. Sprinkle top with paprika, and bake uncovered for half an hour.

Some interesting things to make with leftover cooked corn (or cans of kernels) are corn chowder, corn muffins made with whole kernels dropped into the cornmeal, and corn fritters or pancakes. Another is a sort of soufflé, familiarly called Corn Pudding.

CORN PUDDING
about 4 servings

½ sweet green or red pepper
2 tablespoons margarine
2 cups corn kernels
salt and pepper, to taste
4 medium eggs
½ cup milk
½ cup cream
½ teaspoon sugar

Preheat oven to 375°. Chop the half pepper quite fine; heat the margarine, and sauté the pepper until somewhat browned. Add corn kernels, salt, and pepper to skillet, heat through, and keep the vegetables warm. Separate 2 of the eggs, and beat the 2 egg yolks together with the other 2 whole eggs in a bowl. Then stir the milk, cream, and sugar into the bowl. Remove skillet from heat, and stir egg mixture into the vegetables, a little at a time. Beat the remaining egg whites until stiff but not dry; then fold them into the soufflé. Turn it all into a greased baking dish, and bake for 45 minutes.

Where would the world be without hominy grits? I used to think that this corn product was forbidden by law to migrate above the Mason-Dixon line. I had only encountered it while traveling in the Southland, where you couldn't turn around without finding grits on the menu: breakfast, lunch, or dinner. But lo and behold, the other day I found on my very own Yankee supermarket shelf a product labeled "Instant Grits"! Very costly, of course, like most convenience foods. Hominy grits (for the uninitiated) are dried kernels of white corn, coarsely ground, which, when boiled in water, make a cereal-like substance not unlike Cream of Wheat. If grits are part of your larder, you may want to make the following northern version of a southern dish with them.

YANKEE HOMINY
6 to 8 servings

1 pint dried white beans
1 quart dried white corn
1 lb. pickled pork
1 cup tomato sauce

Pre-soak beans for an hour or so. Wash the corn, drain it, then cover it in fresh water. Bring to a boil, cover, and boil for 4 hours, replenishing the water from time to time. After 4 hours, add the white beans, pork, and tomato sauce. Cover again and simmer another hour or so, until the texture pleases you. Taste for saltiness, too, and correct seasoning if you wish. Serve hot or cold.

NEXT-DAY YANKEE HOMINY
4 servings

Half the above dish, if it's leftover, can be nicely transformed in the following way.

1 medium-sized onion
2 tablespoons margarine
1 medium egg
½ cup bread crumbs
½ cup sunflower seeds
pinch of your favorite dried herb
½ the recipe above

Peel and chop the onion. Melt the margarine in a skillet, and brown the onion in it. Turn off the heat, and remove the onions to a mixing bowl, keeping the margarine in the skillet. Beat the egg lightly, and add it to the onions, together with the bread crumbs, sunflower seeds, herb, and the leftover cold hominy. With your hands mix this well, and form it into flat patties. Reheat the margarine to quite hot, and fry the patties, turning them onto both sides, until brown and crusty. Serve hot.

Mushrooms have sneaked, in one form or another, into a number of dishes previously mentioned, so far in a subsidiary way. They combine so well with so many other viands that we sometimes forget how savory a vegetable they are in themselves. Entire books have been devoted to their "stalking," their cultivation, and their cooking; don't imagine that you can just go out into your woods and pluck the first ones you come to, sauté them in a little butter, and that's it. If you want to save money on mushrooms—and what kitchen can function for long without them?—your first, best bet is getting a mushroom-fancier among your friends to give you for your next birthday a mushroom-growing set (which you can put to work in a cool, damp, dark place, like for instance a cellar). Failing that, buy mushrooms fresh at the produce counter when they're in season. When they're not, canned mushroom "pieces" or "stems and pieces" are your most economical buy. In that form, you sacrifice nothing but the sight of a whole mushroom with stem and cap intact, which, in nine cases out of ten, you proceed to slice or cut up anyway before adding it to a dish. Fresh, raw, and crisp mushrooms are awfully nice sliced in a salad; or stewed a few minutes in meat or vegetable stock, then eaten by themselves. And here are some combinations you may not have thought of.

CUCUMBER MUSHROOMS
3 or 4 servings

½ lb. mushrooms
4 tablespoons margarine
1 small onion, chopped
1 medium-sized cucumber
2 tablespoons whole-wheat or rye flour
1½ cups milk
¾ cup grated Swiss or Jack cheese
salt and pepper
¼ cup sunflower seeds
¼ cup bread or cracker crumbs

Preheat oven to 350°. Clean and slice or chop the mushrooms, if fresh. If canned, drain and save the liquid for stock. Heat 2 tablespoons of the margarine, and sauté onion and mushrooms together until the onion is golden. Peel and slice the cucumber. Melt the other 2 tablespoons of margarine in another skillet, rub in the flour, then add the milk a little at a time, whisking over medium heat until the sauce begins to thicken. Remove skillet from heat, and add cheese and seasoning, stirring until cheese melts in. Now mix in the mushrooms, onion, and cucumber, and turn the mixture into a buttered baking dish. Mix the seeds and crumbs together (seeds whole or ground, as you choose) and sprinkle this mixture over the top of the dish. Bake for half an hour, or until heated through, and serve hot.

Millet is another grain that you may not think of very often; it has nurtured many an Asian and African for years, but is rather new to this country as a dietary mainstay. One hears that those legendary Hunzas live to over a hundred years in perfect health largely on millet and yogurt. You could do worse than to combine mushrooms with millet in a lovely pilaf. (Pilaf is usually made with rice, but there's no law against using millet in it.)

MILLET-MUSHROOM PILAF
4 to 6 servings

2 cups millet
2 cups mushrooms
1 small onion or several scallions (white and green parts)
¼ cup light vegetable oil
1 tablespoon fresh parsley
4 cups meat or vegetable stock
salt and pepper, to taste
1 bay leaf

Soak the millet for a few hours, and drain. Preheat oven to 250°. Dice or slice the mushrooms. Peel and chop the onion, or chop scallions. Sauté onion and mushrooms in the oil. Now mix all ingredients except the bay leaf in a casserole. Put bay leaf on top, cover, and bake for an hour or until liquid has been absorbed. Remove bay leaf, and serve hot.

Another sneaky vegetable which, in various colors, shapes, and conditions, has already been discussed is the tomato. When you can get it fresh and just-ripe, the tomato is the king and queen of vegetables, and eating it raw an incomparable treat. But the green tomato, which you may find you're still swimming in at the end of the tomato season, is a prince or princess. Don't leave it on the vine for the frost to nip: gather it green, and turn it into pickles and relishes (which follow). That's one good way to solve the problem of plenty-all-at-once. But not before you've had at least one tureen of this wonderful soup.

GREEN TOMATO SOUP
about 4 servings

3 to 5 large green tomatoes
1 teaspoon baking soda
1 cup milk
2 tablespoons flour or arrowroot
2 tablespoons butter or margarine
salt to taste
pinch thyme or tarragon

Chop tomatoes not too fine. Add soda to a quart of water, and bring to a boil. Drop tomatoes in, and let them cook 5 minutes. Drain the tomato pieces, then put them in 2 pints of fresh boiling water, and boil another 5 minutes Turn heat low. Blend milk and thickening with a whisk, and add it gradually to the green tomatoes and water, stirring continually over low heat until the mixture comes to a boil. Add the butter or margarine, and let it melt and blend into the soup. Remove from heat, add the salt and herb, and serve warm.

GREEN TOMATO PICKLE

½ peck green tomatoes
12 medium-sized onions
5 tablespoons salt
1 quart vinegar
2 tablespoons chopped fresh dill
2 tablespoons celery seed
1 tablespoon mustard seed
pepper to taste

Leave the smaller tomatoes whole; halve or quarter the larger ones. Peel and chop the onions. Sprinkle tomatoes and onions with salt, and leave them overnight. The next day drain off the accumulated liquid. Add the vinegar, dill, seeds, and pepper to the tomatoes in a large saucepan, bring to a boil, then simmer for 20 minutes. Pour into sterilized jars, and cover tightly. This is a very sour (or sour-dill) pickle. Should you prefer a sweeter one, add sugar before you cook.

Or make the relish that follows instead.

SWEET TOMATO RELISH

1 peck green tomatoes
12 medium-sized onions, peeled
8 sweet peppers, red or green, chopped and seeded
1 cup salt
2 quarts vinegar
4 lbs. brown sugar
2 lbs. white sugar
¼ lb. mustard seed
¼ lb. celery seed
1 tablespoon each cinnamon and allspice
1 teaspoon each dry mustard and black pepper

Put the tomatoes, onions, and sweet peppers through a food grinder. Add the salt, and let stand in a crock overnight. In the morning drain the vegetables, put them into a large saucepan or kettle, and add all the rest of the ingredients. Bring to a boil, then turn the heat down to a simmer. Cook for 5 or 6 hours, until the mixture turns a rich, dark-brown color.

This sweet relish is a favorite in my family—has been for generations.

While we're on the subject of pickling, it's time for me to fill in the pickled watermelon rind promised earlier; it's a kind of chutney. If you want a plainer watermelon pickle, just omit the apples, raisins, and ginger.

WATERMELON CHUTNEY

the rind (white part) of 1 watermelon
1 teaspoon powdered alum
6 tablespoons salt
1 lb. apples (or pears)
3 medium-sized onions
vinegar
1 tablespoon celery seed
2 tablespoons mustard seed
3 cloves garlic
1 lb. raisins
1 cup preserved ginger
2 cups sugar
1 sliced lemon
juice of 2 more lemons
2 teaspoons each: cinnamon, allspice, ground pepper, ground clove

Pare off the green part and cut the white watermelon rind into small pieces. Add the alum and 4 tablespoons of salt to enough water to cover the rind; boil for 15 minutes, and drain. Peel, core, and cut up the apples or pears; peel and chop the onions. Cover apples and onions with vinegar, then add the rest of the salt and the softened rind. Let stand 3 hours, then drain, reserving the vinegar. Mash the celery seed, mustard seed, and garlic. Add this mash to the reserved vinegar. Add the raisins, ginger, sugar, lemon and juice, and spices, and bring to a boil. Stir well, and add the watermelon mixture. Turn heat low, and simmer until texture

223

becomes syrupy and rind is transparent. Cool, and let stand 8 or 9 hours. Bring to a boil again, pour into sterilized jars, and seal.

One of the things to do with your excess harvest of *red* tomatoes is to make your year's supply of ketchup. Here's one way.

TOMATO KETCHUP
about 2 quarts

1 gallon ripe, red tomatoes
4 tablespoons salt
4 tablespoons black pepper
2 teaspoons allspice
8 chili peppers (or equivalent of hot red pepper powder)
2 quarts vinegar
2 garlic cloves

Plunge each tomato into hot water for a minute to facilitate peeling. Chop them fine, and put them into a large saucepan or kettle. Stir in the salt, black pepper, and allspice. Mince the hot peppers, and add them. Pour in 1 quart of the vinegar, bring the mixture to a boil, then turn it down to a simmer, and let cook for about 3½ hours, adding the rest of the vinegar from time to time as it cooks. When the consistency looks right to you, cool the mixture, and strain it through a fine sieve. Peel the garlic cloves, and press them; stir their juice into the ketchup. Store it in sterilized jars. Or if you've saved them, you can use the ketchup bottles left over from when you used to *buy* it.

If this ketchup isn't quite as *red* as the old commercial preparation (because it's not treated with red dyes

#2 and #40), be thankful. The acid of the tomatoes and the vinegar will preserve it for quite a while, but if you don't anticipate getting to half of it for months, perhaps you'd better freeze it.

I know that I'm flying in the face of tradition when I suggest that there is any way to eat asparagus but cooked to a turn and treated with hot hollandaise sauce. That surely is one of the vegetable kingdom's great combinations, but it almost certainly requires fresh spring asparagus to be at its best. What follows is a dish that makes a thing of beauty (and nutrition) of canned asparagus.

ASPARAGUS NONPAREIL
3 or 4 servings

1 16-oz. can asparagus (tips or whole)
juice of 1 lemon
¾ cup buckwheat groats
grated rind of 2 oranges
4 scallions, chopped fine
salt and pepper
¾ cup white sauce
½ cup toasted bread crumbs

Drain the canned asparagus (reserving the liquid for stock), sprinkle it with the lemon juice, and let stand. Meanwhile, boil the groats in salted water for half an hour and drain. Preheat oven to 350°. Butter a baking dish, and lay the asparagus in it. Add the groats, the orange rind, chopped scallions, salt, and pepper. Pour the white sauce over, and top with the toasted bread crumbs. Bake for half an hour or so, and serve hot.

Turnips were among my least favorite root vegetables until I discovered that they function, along with carrots, cauliflower, celery, and others, nicely as *crudités*. Sliced paper-thin with a swivel peeler, they add immeasurably to a tossed green salad. They also combine well with cheeses and cooked greens, as in the dish that follows.

TURNIP FROMAGE
serves 4 to 6

1 medium-sized turnip, about 1 lb.
1 knob of mozzarella, or equal amount similar soft cheese
2 cups cooked escarole or Chinese cabbage, chopped
1 cup cottage cheese
1 cup bread crumbs
½ cup grated hard cheese
3 cups tomato sauce

Preheat oven to 375°. Cut the turnip up into 1-inch cubes; simmer in water to cover until nearly soft. Cube the mozzarella somewhat smaller. Lightly grease a baking dish, and put half the turnip cubes in. Scatter in half the chopped greens. Now spoon the cottage cheese around in teaspoonfuls; spread half the mozzarella cubes on, then half the bread crumbs and grated cheese. Pour on half the tomato sauce. Then repeat all this in a second layer. Bake, uncovered, for half an hour, or until the cheeses are nicely melted and the dish heated through.

So many and various are the shapes that pasta is made in here in the good old U.S. of A, that it's a wonder anyone ever buys plain tubular macaroni, or plain straws of spaghetti. One of my favorite forms is the little round one that looks like a cross section of okra or a wheel for a tiny wagon. It has lent visual and textural interest to many a casserole at my house. Here is one you may want to try.

CONESTOGA CASSEROLE
6 to 8 servings

1 lb. wagon-wheel pasta
1 tablespoon margarine
3 medium-sized carrots
3 scallions, white and green parts
2 tablespoons light vegetable oil
2 cups pattypan squash cubes
2 cups beansprouts
salt and pepper

Cook the pasta in boiling salted water for about 13 minutes, until it is almost soft. Meanwhile, put the casserole dish with the margarine in it in a warm oven. Cut the carrots in quite thin diagonal slices. Chop up the scallions. When the pasta has cooked and drained, add it to the casserole dish, cover, and turn the heat up in the oven to 375°. Heat the vegetable oil in a wok or skillet to almost smoking. Then stir-fry the squash cubes, carrot slices, scallions, and beansprouts in it, adding them in that order and stir-frying a minute or two with each addition. Salt and pepper the vegetables, and pour them onto the wheels in the casserole dish. Serve hot.

Rigatoni is another shape of pasta—a sort of ridged cylinder—that is popular at my house. The large ones get stuffed with all manner of cheese, meat, vegetables, grains. The small ones just get thrown into a combined vegetable dish. An accidental combination recently turned out so satisfactorily that I have to include it—the play of colors, forms, textures, and tastes was superb.

RIGATONI TINTORETTO
7 or 8 servings

1 small onion
½ green bell pepper
¼ lb. cooked (small) rigatoni
6 whole fresh mushrooms
½ cup cooked carrots, diced
½ cup cooked sliced zucchini
½ cup cooked corn niblets
¾ cup sour cream
¼ cup soy sauce

Preheat oven to 375°. Peel and chop the onion; core and seed the half pepper, and slice it thin. Then just stir everything up together, trying to distribute all the various colors and shapes evenly. Put the mixture into a greased baking dish, and bake for about 40 minutes, to be sure it is hot all the way through. Serve hot, and marvel at the oil painting effect.

Artichokes are a vegetable I never *saw* until I was twenty-one years old. In the many years that have ensued I've made up for lost time, often by picking artichokes up for practically nothing when they've started to brown and shrivel in the supermarket. The best way to prepare them when they have attained that reverend age, I find, is as follows.

REJUVENATED ARTICHOKES
for 2

2 aging artichokes
¼ cup lemon juice
1 large stalk celery, plus leaves
1 small onion
salt and pepper
¼ lb. (1 stick) margarine or butter
1 garlic clove

Cover the artichokes, stems still on, in cold water and keep them submerged by means of a small board or some such weight for an hour. Drain, and cover the artichokes anew with hot water, to which you have added the lemon juice. Simmer them for an hour, adding to the pot the stalk of celery, coarsely cut up, plus the onion, chopped, and some salt and pepper. Toward the end of the hour of simmering, melt the margarine. Peel the garlic, then press or mince it, and add it to the melted margarine. When the artichokes have cooked for an hour, serve them, hot, cutting off their stems so they can sit up on either side of the small bowl of warm garlic-butter, which is used as a dip. Peel the artichoke leaves off one by one, dip the bottom meaty part of each leaf into the margarine, and eat it, discarding the top of the leaf. When you get down to the papery leaves or "choke," discard, but cut up the heart into bite-sized pieces, with which you soak up what's left of the garlic-butter.

People who aren't as crazy about artichokes as I am feel that different sauces are necessary for dipping, such as hollandaise, Mornay, or even vinaigrette. I agree with the last if you've let the cooked artichoke go cold, when a salad dressing is the thing to use—even mayonnaise (see p. 68). This gives me a chance to disabuse you of the notion that there's anything exotic about vinaigrette, which is simply an oil-and-vinegar salad dressing with a French accent. Three parts vegetable oil to one part vinegar (or lemon juice if you prefer) plus some herbs and spices: what you've been doing all along for your green salads. Its variations are almost limitless; here are a couple of suggestions to get you started.

SAUCE VINAIGRETTE I
1 cup

¾ cup olive oil
¼ cup lemon juice
2 cloves garlic, quartered or minced
pinch mustard
pinch salt
tiny pinch pepper

Shake well, and pour on your salad to toss just before serving.

SAUCE VINAIGRETTE II
1 cup

¾ cup peanut oil
¼ cup vinegar
pinch curry powder
pinch tarragon
pinch basil
a few capers or nasturtium seeds

If your artichokes are the fresh, young, plump, tender, *expensive* ones, there still is no better way to prepare them than as above. But you may want to vary your method by stuffing and baking them, a popular way in many parts of Europe and Asia. Here's a really lush way to embellish an artichoke.

ARTICHOKES ALBANIA
for 4

4 fresh artichokes
1 small onion
½ lb. chopped meat (or meat substitute like Bacos)
salt and pepper
¼ cup uncooked bulghur or kasha
4 tablespoons chopped mint and/or parsley
¼ teaspoon paprika
¼ cup pine nuts or chopped walnuts
1 cup chopped hard vegetables: carrots, celery, turnips, peppers
1 bay leaf
4 teaspoons margarine
1 cup stock or bouillon

Trim the artichokes of the bottom outside leaves, the stems, and the hard tips (if any) of the larger leaves. Now cover the artichokes with boiling water, and let them simmer, submerged, for 15 minutes. Drain, cool a bit, and open up the centers to get at the chokes. Remove them, being careful not to disturb the meaty heart of the artichokes. Peel and chop the onion fine. Combine it with the chopped meat, salt, and pepper. Soak the bulghur or kasha for about 15 minutes, in enough cold water to cover, then drain.

Preheat oven to 350°. Add the grain to the meat, together with the chopped mint or parsley, the paprika, and the nuts. Knead this mixture with your hands, or stir it with a spoon until combined well. Divide the mixture into four, and stuff the artichokes with it.

Spread the chopped hard vegetables and the bay leaf on the bottom of a greased baking dish, and set the artichokes on the vegetables. Add a teaspoon of margarine to the top of each artichoke. Bring the stock or bouillon to a boil, and pour it into the baking dish. Bake 1 hour or longer (until the artichokes are tender).

A sauce with these stuffed artichokes might strike you as excessive, but some people would "pass" one. A tomato-based sauce would be interestingly colorful, as would a hollandaise or other yellow one. Either would make a truly splendid dish of this conclusion to the vegetable chapter.

8

THE GARDEN
OF EARTHLY DELIGHTS

Since the Garden of Eden, the fruits of the earth have been both the temptation of man and the salvation, if not of his soul, then of his alimentary canal, his inner person. Besides providing a number of nutritive elements essential to health, fruits have, since the dawn of history, delighted our palates and elevated our spirits. Why, out of the panoply of taste sensations, the "sweets" group should be associated with light and joy is not for delving into here: it has not been true in all cultures in all times, but among contemporary Americans it is very much the case.

The principal, in fact almost ubiquitous, sweetener—whether hidden, as in commercial food products, or blatantly apparent, as in desserts and picker-uppers we treat ourselves to all the time—is sugar. It used to be one of the all-time bargains in the market (can you still remember nine cents a pound?), but it is no longer. There has been some pretty persuasive research besides, accusing sugar of being an important contributing factor in all sorts of maladies from tooth decay to coronaries. An excessive use of sugar, that is. And the ailments seem not to distinguish between brown and the more refined white sugars. These studies are not absolutely conclusive—very little about what goes on inside the body is—but indications are that we consume far more sugar than is good for us.

That being the case—and the prices of sugar and candy and all the junk foods being what they are today—we can definitely save some wear and tear on our systems *and* some money by substituting fruits as our main source of sweets, and by trying to promote this habit in our children. The saccharinity of fruits and berries, in all their infinite variety, should be enough to satisfy any sweet tooth in any head, young or old, if we hadn't been indoctrinated early into the notion that the refined product of the sugar cane (or sugar beet) is the only way to Happiness. Also, natural sweets, un-like sugar, can provide us with some of the all-important fiber that is another vital aspect of diet.

Even if it means allocating some of our previous meat budget, we should all make a point of eating at least two different kinds of fruit a day. The best way to afford this, of course, is to stroll out in the garden or field and pick your own apples, oranges, bananas, strawberries, peaches, and what-have-you. What-you-have is seldom a combination like that in the last sentence, for meteorological reasons alone. How many of us are even so fortunately situated that our backyards boast even one tree laden with ripening cherries or pears? We must rely on the gifts of friends, or, failing this, the largesse of the supermarket.

I don't know about your supermarket, but mine is not in the largesse business, particularly when it comes to lus-cious, fresh ripe fruits, in or out of season. Not *this* year. Nor are the roadside stands in my neck of the woods. As mentioned earlier, though, my marauding into neighboring woods and fields in quest of berries was very productive. I also picked up a summer-long supply of apples from under the trees that didn't seem to belong to anyone in particular—or if they did, the owners were content to leave the windfalls for the deer or other smaller apple-fanciers.

Somewhere in between these two poles of cost lies the good old American convention of selling fruit to passersby at a much lower price than they would pay in the market, if they will come into the orchard, field, or garden and pick their own. If you can possibly take advantage of these seasonal offers, by all means do. Sometimes you can even get bonuses of "free" fruits or berries—culls or groundlings that will otherwise just go to waste—at the same time. Pick a bushel of perfect apples from the trees, for your fresh eating pleasure, and gather off the ground another bushel for cooking with. Pluck the high-up grapes for your Perch Véronique (see page 155) or table-decoration-into-dessert: grab the less than perfect bunches and those discards lying underneath the vines for your wine-making. Take the peaches displaying their handsome red and yellow coloring for your pocket lunches; and bring home the slightly wizened ones to put up in preserving jars.

If you're city-bound and not privileged to go a-berrying in this way, then your best bet is to learn what fruits are indigenous to your area, and buy them fresh in season. Obviously you will pay less for a pound of plums that have only traveled a couple of miles down the road in August than you will for a pound of nectarines that have flown coast-to-coast in January to reach your doorstep. The only time this rule breaks down is when the grocer has overstocked on some fruit in the belief that his audience for it was larger than it was. Watch for such bargains, which often occur late on Saturdays—when it looks as if the fruit in question will not last in its pristine condition through the long weekend—or early on Monday morning, when it *hasn't*. Despite its somewhat shop-worn appearance, it still promises gorgeous taste —possibly even sweeter than when it first arrived.

Pay attention also to the radio advertising and "consumer advisors" for stores in your area—they frequently tell you what the best buys in fruit are that month, week, or even day. Fruit juices, either canned (whole or concentrate) or frozen (concentrate), often are on special, usually in numbers inconvenient for the tiny city-apartment storage facility, but sometimes in amounts you can cope with. With frozen concentrated citrus juices, you invariably save money over buying whole fresh limes, oranges, grapefruit, or lemons, at no sacrifice of health-giving properties. With noncitrus fruits and berries, your economy is usually greater the fewer processes the fruit has endured before it gets to market. Fresh is usually cheaper than dried, canned, or frozen; whole (seeds or pits in) is less costly than pitted, seeded, peeled, cored, cut up, sliced, halved. But not always, and comparison shopping is recommended with fruits and berries. Read the price-weight or price-volume signs carefully in the supermarket. And again, don't be seduced by "name brand" labels; go for the house brands, or the ones you have *not* seen constantly advertised on television. You won't be poisoned by a jar or tin of cherries packed by something less than the number one national advertiser; and you may even get a smaller infusion of unnecessary added sugar in the package. Look in the dented-cans basket; if the slight crushing has not resulted in an oozing of juice from a break, there is no danger.

We have already cooked with fruits in some of the earlier chapters, but in those instances another kind of food was the focus of the recipe. Now we'll deal with the principal American fruits (alphabetically, as that takes us first into the Garden of Eden, where it all began) with the fruit itself being the *raison d'être*. I've omitted a list of the fruits that benefit from going into cans, jars, or frozen-food packages, because their taste and texture is never enhanced by these sometimes necessary processes. In fact, if you are on a sugar-free diet, you sometimes have to let a frozen strawberry packed sugarless sit around for a while after thawing to get back some of its taste. And if you are reduced to buying frozen melon balls, you may as well forget about texture. Canned peaches, pears, pineapple, etc., are simply *not* the same fruit as fresh, and it's up to you which you prefer.

The dishes that follow will be *low* on sugar, concentrating on the taste of the fruit itself for flavoring. Many of have omitted sugar entirely. Our American palates are so saturated with the taste of sugar that we've forgotten how to savor the myriad marvelous flavors of our rich heritage of fruits. Is there anything quite as pleasing as the taste of a sun-ripened pear? Not canned or frozen or pickled pears, though all these products have a place in our repertory. It's time we recovered our taste for real fruits and berries.

Apples

Possibly the most versatile American fruit, apples grow not in hundreds, but in thousands of varieties all over the United States. Your lifelong companion may feel (as mine does) that the only one really worth eating is the McIntosh. There are, however, a number of others equally sweet, which make that lovely crunch and ooze juice when you bite into them. Cortlands, for instance, or Jonathans, Pippins, Gravensteins, Winesaps, or even the somewhat over-rated Delicious. These mostly red varieties make splendid fresh eating and preserve well too. Of the yellow apples, the Golden Delicious is probably the best eating, while the other yellow (or partly yellow) apples, such as Northern Spy, Yellow Transparent, Lodi, and York Imperial, do better for combined desserts and cooking, being as a rule more mealy. The apple known as Greening (or Rhode Island Greening) is thought by some Yankees to be the best apple alive for both pies and eating fresh; its unripe appearance is misleading.

These varieties, while they are probably the most common in my part of the country, don't begin to scratch the surface of appledom, nor do I doubt that your own favorite species has as much to recommend it. *All* apples are good for you, and if you have the proper storage space, you should come by them when they are in season in as large a quantity as you can accommodate. "An apple a day keeps the doctor away" is not archaic superstition. For dessert, for school or work lunchboxes, as between-meal snacks, take out of the bushel basket the apples most nearly perfect in color and

237

shape. Wash and polish them, and use them for a fresh table decoration or centerpiece for your next dinner party. Serve each diner a wedge of some domestic cheese as accompaniment—it's a great combination!

Apples when just picked are, by themselves, an incomparable delight. More venerable fruits can be turned into all manner of splendid dishes, hardly limited to old standby apple pie or applesauce. A few suggestions follow.

APPLE SLUMP OR PANDOWDY
4 servings

5 medium-sized apples
sugar or honey (optional)
cinnamon, nutmeg, powdered clove, to taste
1 cup flour
2 teaspoons baking powder
4 tablespoons margarine
½ cup milk

Preheat oven to 425°. Peel or quarter or slice the apples, leaving skin on. Put them in a greased baking dish. If your apples are not an especially sweet variety, you may want to add a little sugar or honey. Season them with the spices. In a bowl, sift together the flour and baking powder. Work 3 tablespoons of the margarine into this mixture with your fingers; add the milk, stirring up the dough. Take tablespoonfuls of the dough, and arrange it atop the apples. Dot with the remaining tablespoon of margarine, and bake for half an hour.

This dish can serve equally well as a luncheon dish or a dessert. I've even known people to eat it for breakfast.

There is something basic, simple, and at the same time elegant, about plain baked apple for dessert. The meanest looking "seconds" or non-red apples can turn into a very special treat when cored, with their cavities stuffed with raisins or prune bits, or nuts and a little peel from a citrus fruit, plus a little butter or margarine. Bake them about 1 hour at no more than 350° and serve them with or without cream, sour cream, ice cream, or sherbet.

You can add apples to a salad bound with mayonnaise. Here is an atypical twist on the hackneyed Waldorf Salad.

SKID ROW SALAD
4 servings

4 medium-sized apples,
not in the bloom of youth

lemon juice

a few sprigs of parsley
(left on someone's plate)

a handful of peanuts

2 stalks of celery

4 red radishes

mayonnaise

Peel and dice the apples. (Stow the peels and cores in your fruit freezer-bag.) If you treat the apples with lemon juice, they won't turn brown while you go foraging for the parsley and peanuts, which you can then chop up at your leisure. String and cut up the celery. Cut up the radishes small, leaving a spot of the red on each piece, for the touch of color you'll miss by peeling the apples. Mix all together in a bowl, and add dollops of mayonnaise until you get the consistency you like. Serve cold, in or out of a cup formed by a leaf of lettuce or some other leafy green.

APPLE MERINGUE PUDDING
6 servings

2 lbs. not-necessarily-fresh apples
4 tablespoons margarine
spices of your option
4 egg whites
2 teaspoons cornstarch
½ teaspoon vanilla
½ cup chopped nuts (optional)

Peel the apples, and cut them up. Melt the margarine in a skillet, and add the apple pieces to it. Cover the pan, and simmer the mixture until fruit is very soft. Put it through a strainer or sieve, or purée in a blender, and season with spices. Preheat oven to 250°. Spread the purée in a shallow baking dish. Now beat the egg whites until they are stiff, adding the cornstarch and vanilla while they are whipping. Spread the stiff meringue on top of the apple purée, either sticking the optional nuts into the meringue or reserving them for scattering on top of the finished dish. Bake for 1 hour or more, until the meringue has browned well at its edges. Serve hot.

Now from India, for fun, an archaic, imperial sort of thing to do with your older apples. If you lack saffron and rose water, make substitutions. The dish won't be an exotically fragrant as this one, but you may invent something new in the process.

IMPERIAL APPLESAUCE
4 servings

¼ cup raisins
¼ teaspoon saffron threads

2 tablespoons rose water
5 medium-sized apples of a tart variety
1 teaspoon lemon juice.
½ cup margarine
½ cup half-and-half or light cream
¼ cup slivered almonds

Cover the raisins with fresh water, and let soak for an hour or so. Crumble the saffron threads, and add them to the rose water. Peel, halve, and seed the apples. Cover them with cold water into which you have mixed the lemon juice. Heat the margarine until foaming, then remove from heat. Grate the apples into the margarine pan. Put the pan back over low heat, and cook, stirring, until liquid is nearly all gone. (Don't blenderize this—it ruins the texture.) Drain raisins, and add them, with the saffron-rose water, to the apple pan. Add the cream and the almonds, and continue to cook until consistency is quite thick. Serve hot.

If you don't feel like making an elaborate apple dish, why not slice them up in plain yogurt, along with any other aging fruits you may have on hand, for a quick, easy, healthful dessert or luncheon for one?

The whole exciting adventure of cold fruit soups originated in Scandinavia. Here's a delicious one, of which the core is apples.

APPLE SOUP
4 or 5 servings

about 1 lb. overripe apples
2 tablespoons lemon juice, or 1 tablespoon grated lemon
peel

2 whole cloves
1 tablespoon honey (optional)
dash cinnamon
½ cup dry white wine or cider
2 cups yogurt

Peel and core the apples, and cut them into chunks.
Add lemon juice or peel, cloves, honey, cinnamon,
and enough water to cover. Simmer until fruit is tender;
then spoon out the apple pieces, and press them
through a strainer or purée them in your blender.
Remove the cloves from the cooking liquid, and return the apple purée to it. Cool the mixture, and add
the wine and yogurt, stirring in well. Serve chilled.
A lovely first course for a warm-weather luncheon.

(You will find other things to do with your apples
as they age, or with the peelings and cores, in the last
two chapters.)

Apricots

As a deprived citizen of the northeastern United States, I
seldom see a fresh apricot, to say nothing of eating one. But
dried apricots, despite their pungent taste, are wonderful
additions to cereals, puddings, salads—even to meat and fish
dishes. They are a good source of trace elements and vitamins and so should not be omitted entirely from the diet,
regardless of where you live. Cook them, chopped fine, in
your rice one day, or make the following tasty dessert. (It's
also a good way to use up some aged bread.)

APRICOT PUDDING-CAKE
about 8 servings

8 slices of bread you've let go stale
6 dried apricots

¼ cup other fruit, in small pieces (apple, fruit salad, or
your choice)
1 tablespoon minced citrus peel
1 medium egg
¼ cup light vegetable oil
1 teaspoon cinnamon

Break the bread up into smallish pieces, cover with water and soak for ½ hour. Soak the apricots for an hour, then drain them. Preheat oven to 350°. Cut the apricots up quite fine, and add to the other fruit and citrus peel. Strain the bread, and squeeze it in a cloth. Lightly beat the egg, and mix it with the bread, fruits, vegetable oil, and cinnamon. Butter a cake tin or baking dish, and spoon the apricot mixture into it. Bake for an hour or so—test for doneness as you would a cake. Serve hot or cold.

Avocado

This delectable fruit (another viand I had never laid eyes on until I reached voting age) is usually so expensive in northern markets that it sometimes seems worth moving to the South for. A really mind-bending experience was picking them off a tree in the yard of California friends I once visited.

If you don't find avocados growing in your own private orchard, and you don't feel like spending the sixty-nine cents and up that just one of these fruits usually brings in New York or Boston when perfectly ripe, one thing you can do is to keep an eye on the shipment in your supermarket. Avocados don't sell so fast, and some Saturday night soon you are going to be able to pick them up for about ten cents apiece. I have often spent a whole quarter for two avocados with enough ripe (but not rotten) meat on them to enhance a tossed green salad for four or spread on crackers for cocktail snacks. In some localities avocados can be bought cheaper when unripe. If you fall into such a bonanza, bring them home and simply leave them in a dark cupboard or drawer until they ripen.

Aside from the usual green salad, here are some hints as to how to eat avocados.

AVOCADO DIP I
about 1 cup

1 avocado, overripe is okay
2 teaspoons lemon juice
dash Worcestershire sauce
1 teaspoon garlic salt
half a 3-oz. package cream cheese

Peel and stone the avocado. Mash all ingredients together, mixing well. Keep cold until ready to serve, with cocktail crackers or as a sandwich spread.

AVOCADO DIP II
about 1 cup

1 overripe avocado
1 overripe tomato
1 small onion
salt and pepper
dollop sour cream

Peel and stone the avocado. Peel the tomato. Mince the onion. Then mix everything up together, blending well. Keep cold.

Or just sprinkle really overripe avocado flesh with lime juice, add some seeds (sesame, sunflower, pumpkin) or nuts, or both, and a few of your favorite herbs, either dried or fresh. And enjoy. There are lots of calories in avocados, but oversweetness is not one of its problems. Try to think of other vegetables (aside from the recipes including avocado in Chapter 7) that you can combine it with, too.

The overripe avocado is also a good thickener for soups, either hot or cold. It would be a fine combination with the Apple Soup on page 241. All you have to do is think on whether avocado flavor "goes with" the soup you've already made from vegetables, meat stock, or whatever, and cook some of it in.

Bananas

Though they don't grow in the continental United States, bananas are so much a part of the American scene that we have to consider them an American fruit. Eating them plain, peeling the skin as they go, most American children have grown up with bananas. Cut up on morning cereal, they are another institution, and whipped up in a milkshake, they improve the flavor immeasurably. Contrary to early twentieth-century opinion, they are good mashed for very young babies.

At my house, they are eaten fresh nearly every other day—in one of the ways above, stirred into yogurt with other fruits, or combined with vegetables in a casserole. Then, when they have started on the overripe course, I cook them in other ways: adding them to pancake, bread, or cake batter (see p. 253), or letting their sweetness contribute to a pie of tart apples or apricots. Also, overripe banana mashed up with a little blue cheese makes a dandy cracker spread or sandwich filling.

Or I just bake them for dessert. Here are two ways that have been successful.

BAKED BANANA HALVES
for 2 to 4

2 overripe bananas
1 tablespoon butter or margarine, soft
1 tablespoon red or white wine (optional)
2 tablespoons shredded coconut

Preheat oven to 350°. Peel and cut the bananas in half lengthwise. Don't bother to cut out the brown spots. Spread each flat side with butter or margarine, sprinkle with wine, if using, then with coconut. Bake in a buttered dish for about 15 minutes.

CURRIED BANANAS
for 2 or 4

2 overripe bananas
½ cup orange or grapefruit juice
2 tablespoons lime juice
2 tablespoons yogurt or sour cream
½ teaspoon curry powder

Preheat oven to 300°. Peel bananas, and slice lengthwise. Place in a buttered baking dish. Combine in a bowl the citrus juices, yogurt or sour cream, and curry powder; blend well. Pour this liquid mixture over the bananas, and bake for 20 to 25 minutes. This dish could be either a dessert or an accompaniment to a dish of meat, poultry, or fish.

Blackberries

I gathered these wonderfully succulent little fruits and ate them daily all summer from my own and beside-the-road bushes (very brambly, so watch out and use gloves). They are so sweet and delicious all by themselves that only when I couldn't keep up with the supply, and they began to ferment slightly, did I turn them into something other than what they were. See Chapter 9 for something to turn them into, or make this frozen dessert.

BLACKBERRY ICE
4 to 6 servings

about a quart of sweet blackberries, picked over and washed
1 pint of whole milk
1 tablespoon lemon juice

Froth the berries and milk up together in your blender, or mash the berries first, and stir them into the milk. Add lemon juice, and put the mixture into freezer trays or, lacking trays, plastic refrigerator dishes that will fit into your freezing compartment. Freeze for a couple of hours. Be sure to remove from freezer and let loosen up a bit before serving.

Blueberries

This native American berry (not to be confused with huckleberry, though people often consider them synonymous) is often to be had for the picking. New England cookbooks, among others, are full of recipes for its use. Try to find blueberries in the wild, or for the low-cost picking on some-one else's land.

Canned or frozen blueberries work very well in pies or other kinds of desserts or breads. One of the advantages of the large plastic bags of frozen berries is that you can take out just a few at a time to toss into whatever dish you're making at the moment. I did this last with pancakes, which were a triumph; the berries naturally defrosted while the griddle cakes were cooking.

One of the most sumptuous blueberry-season desserts imaginable is effected when you pile berries into the cavity of a half cantaloupe melon. The tastes and textures complement each other nicely. A few fresh blueberries can be spilled onto your raspberry sherbet or tapioca for a nice touch. When they are a little older than that day's picking, a number of lip-smacking concoctions can be made of them, too. The first is hot bread that can serve as a breakfast, lunch, or dinner food—first, middle, or last course. Use up some of your beginning-to-age blueberries on it.

BLUEBERRY HOT BREAD
for an 8-inch cake

1½ tablespoons margarine
1 egg
2 cups flour
1½ to 2 cups blueberries
3 teaspoons baking powder
1 teaspoon salt
½ teaspoon nutmeg
¾ cup milk

Preheat oven to 400°. Cream the margarine. Beat in the egg. Remove a tablespoon of flour from the two cups and roll the blueberries in it. Sift the rest of the flour with the baking powder, salt, and nutmeg. Add these dry ingredients to the egg and margarine, then stir in the milk. Add the berries last, each one covered with flour to keep it from breaking and streaking. Butter a cake pan, pour in the batter, and bake for about 50 minutes, or until top is nicely browned and cake tests for doneness.

Blueberry dishes, like those made with apples, come in as many funny names as you can think up—in New England anyway. Pandowdy, slump, grunt, crisp, buckle, and so on. Here is a blueberry dessert that lets the sweetness of the overripe berries themselves provide the taste-teasing, and evades the cliché of blueberry pie.

BLUEBERRY TOAST
for 6

6 slices of bread
(any kind that toast well)

2 cups blueberries,
fresh, frozen, or canned

1 egg

¾ cup milk

pinch salt

¾ tablespoon margarine

½ teaspoon cinnamon

1 cup cream (optional)

Trim the crusts from the bread. In a saucepan, bring the berries to a boil (in a bit of water if they don't seem juicy enough). Cook about 10 minutes, stirring so they don't get gummy. Put them into a greased, large, flat baking dish. Beat the egg lightly, then stir the milk and salt into it. Heat the margarine in a skillet. Dip the bread into the egg-milk mixture to coat both sides of all slices. Fry the bread in the margarine, both sides, until golden brown. Place the bread on top of the blueberries, covering them completely. Sprinkle the top of the toast with cinnamon, then put the whole dish under the broiler for 5 to 7 minutes, or until toast is browned. Serve hot, possibly with cream poured on each one-slice serving.

Cherries

Can anything be more charming than a sweet cherry tree in the side yard? If you have one, you know how hard it is to get ahead of the birds when the splendid, juicy, round berries are red and ripe; if you manage to beat the feathered folk to them, there is no taste better or sweeter than a plain bowl of cherries—finger food *par excellence*. When your cherries are a little past their prime, you can spark up a dinner party by making this dessert to top it off.

CHERRIES IN RED WINE
4 to 6 servings

2 cups tired sweet cherries

2 cups claret, or other red wine

2 teaspoons cinnamon

1 teaspoon arrowroot

1 tablespoon currant jelly (optional)

1 cup yogurt or sour cream

Stem the cherries, and pit them or not, as you choose. Pour the wine over the cherries, add the cinnamon, and cook over low heat for ten minutes. Let cool, and remove the cherries. To the liquid add the arrowroot (and the optional jelly) and cook, stirring over medium heat until it thickens a little. Let cool, stir in the yogurt, and pour syrup over the cherries. Serve cold.

If, by the way, you chance on an overstock-sale of canned cherries in your supermarket, grab them. The sour cherries combine beautifully with the more fatty meats that you sometimes have on hand. For instance, an easy and delicious casserole of sour cherries, uncooked rice, and pork chops, plus the liquid from the cherry can, is a once-a-year *must*. The sweet cherries can be used, among other ways, in the following dish.

MOLDED CHERRY SALAD
about 6 servings

1 1-lb. can sweet black or red (not maraschino) cherries
1 13½-oz. can crushed pineapple (often on special sale)
¼ oz. plain gelatin
½ cup chopped celery
½ cup chopped nuts or seeds

Drain both cherries and pineapple, but combine and save their liquid. Bring 1 cup water to a boil, remove from heat, and stir in the gelatin. Then combine ½ cup of the fruit liquids with ¼ cup of cold water, and stir into the gelatin. Stir in the whole cherries and pineapple, and pour the whole mix into a glass bowl or salad mold. Chill in refrigerator until firm, which will take 2 to 4 hours. Unmold onto lettuce or other leafy green if you want it to be a salad, and sprinkle the chopped celery and nuts or seeds (or nuts *and* seeds) on top. If you want it for a dessert, unmold onto a chilled plate (and you could, if you were so inclined, pour a bit of cream over it when you serve).

Cranberries

These bright red berries, which grow in profusion in some bogs in the northern United States, are related to the blueberry. Their taste, when fresh and ripe, is acid and tart, so that people almost invariably combine them with lots of sugar to make them palatable, in the form of sauce, jelly, other sweet gooeys, and condiments. People seldom think of baking them in bread, which is a very good thing to do if you have a seasonal excess of cranberries. The jaunty touches of red add an unexpected note to a dark bread, and the piquancy of their taste is somewhat ameliorated by the surprising surroundings they find themselves in.

CRANBERRY BREAD
2 loaves

1 cup cranberries
3 cups milk
3 tablespoons margarine
2 tablespoons salt
1 envelope powdered yeast
3 cups rye flour
3½ cups whole-wheat flour

Quarter the cranberries, or cut them even smaller if you have the patience. Now scald the milk, and pour it onto the margarine and salt in a large mixing bowl. When it has cooled to room temperature, scatter the yeast on top, and leave it until it begins to foam. Now mix the two kinds of flour together, and begin stirring it into the liquid, cupful by cupful. Add a little more of any kind of flour if this mixture cannot be kneaded, then knead it on a floured board for 5 minutes or so. Cover with a dampened cloth, and let rise in a warm place until doubled in volume. Punch down, knead a bit more, and add the cranberries to the dough. Grease two loaf pans or baking dishes, divide the dough in two, and put it in the pans. Let rise again in the same warm place. When it has again doubled in bulk, bake in a 350° oven for 50 minutes.

Dates and Figs

Along with apricots, dates and figs are often found dried rather than fresh in most markets. Canned figs are possible, but they are horrendously expensive, so we buy them rarely. The dried fruits when soaked are excellent in combination with other fruits or added to meat, fish, or vegetable dishes for a touch of sweetness. They can also be made part of a steamed pudding, or muffins, or sugarless bread, which then becomes more of a cake. May I suggest this classic, to spice up a blandish sort of luncheon or supper and to use up some of those old bananas you were going to throw away?

CLASSIC BANANA-BREAD-INTO-CAKE
1 loaf

½ cup butter or margarine
a few grains of sugar, optional
2 medium or small eggs, beaten
2 or 3 bananas, going bad
1 teaspoon lemon juice
2 cups flour
3 teaspoons baking powder
½ teaspoon salt
3 dried figs
6 dried dates

Preheat oven to 350°. Cream the butter. (The few grains of sugar I use just to have something to push against while creaming the butter.) Add the beaten eggs. Mash the tired old bananas, and combine them with lemon juice. Sift the flour, baking powder, and salt together, and stir these dry ingredients into the moist mixture, a half cupful at a time. Stir in the bananas. Cut up the figs and dates quite small, and stir them into the batter to distribute them evenly.

Bake for 50 minutes to 1 hour. Test for doneness with a straw.

Grapes

Leave the less beautiful bunches for wine (see Chapter 9), in which you will actually benefit by mixing the unripe with the overripe and just-ripe. Decorate your dining table with the perfect bunches before you combine them with other fresh fruits in a dessert fruit cup, or let your diners pick them from the centerpiece for dessert. American grapes come in patriotic colors: red, white, and blue. (Of course the white tend to be greenish, and the blue are more purple, but . . .) The red and white ones go nicely into mayonnaise-bound salads; the purples make good jelly. Here, just for fun, is a dessert dish you can make from the purple grapes, the sweeter the variety the better.

GRAPE SHERBET
about 3 pints

enough sweet purple grapes (10 to 15 pounds) to yield
1 quart of juice

2 cups orange juice

1 egg white

2 teaspoons powdered sugar

Let the grapes sit in the sun for a day or two after you've picked them or brought them home from the market. Then simmer them in a saucepan until the skins break (you can help them along by squashing them with a potato masher or something) and the juice has started to run. Now put them through a sieve that will catch all the little stems, skins, seeds, and squeeze out as much thick juice as you can. To this juice add the orange juice, and mix well. Put into the freezer, and let it stand until almost frozen. Meanwhile, beat the egg white until nearly stiff, add the powdered sugar, and fold into the fruit-juice mixture. Return to the freezer, and let it stand for several hours.

Grapefruit

If you have been reading the same diet books over the years that I have, you will be sick and tired of the old "half-grapefruit" dessert suggestion. Actually, some kind of citrus fruit should be part of your every day. If you habitually start your day with orange or grapefruit juice, then you can forget about the half grapefruit at lunch or dinner time. But who wants to forget it completely? Just for sheer taste excitement, is there anything so lovely as the sweet pink or white pulp of this vitamin-packed food? With or without a maraschino cherry in the center, or a bit of brandy or sherry spilled in, cold or heated momentarily under the broiler, grapefruit is a wonderfully cleansing finish to a dinner that may have been just a bit too heavy (after a cheese, tomato, and pasta dish, for example).

Canned grapefruit sections, which, unaccountably, seem to turn up in the marked-down-from-age-or-denting basket in the markets more frequently than other canned fruits, are great added to slices of banana, peach, and apple as a homemade fruit compote with a satisfying meld of flavors and textures.

Combine grapefruit sections, either canned (and drained) or from a fresh, whole grapefruit, with other foods more or less shaped like them for a novel sort of appetizer. Alternate the sections around a plate with cooked shrimps, for example, or raw oysters, or roasted brazil nuts, or slices of avocado.

Here's a cold dessert dish that uses both the juice and the sections of one of those five-for-eighty-nine-cents grapefruits you found on sale at the market the other day. Pick them, by the way, for thinness of skin, heaviness, and firmness, and don't worry about speckles on the skin. Store them for a few days outside the refrigerator before eating—the longer they sit, the sweeter they taste.

GRAPEFRUIT SNOW
about 6 servings

2 envelopes plain gelatin (½ oz.)
1 cup grapefruit juice
(sugar is optional, and depends on the sweetness of the grapefruit—you're on your own)
½ cup sour cream or yogurt
2 egg whites
¼ cup coconut shreds
intact grapefruit sections (about 6)

Soften the gelatin in half the grapefruit juice. Now add 1½ cups of boiling water, and stir until gelatin is completely dissolved. Sugar, if used at all, can be stirred in now. And the half cup of sour cream or yogurt. Or you can add the sour cream or yogurt to the egg whites. Whip the egg whites until nearly stiff. Then fold them into the cooled gelatin mixture. Top with the coconut, and chill in refrigerator until set, which should take from 2 to 4 hours. Just before it's completely firm, press the grapefruit sections into the top of the snow, in any pattern you fancy.

Serve for dessert in the middle of a long, hot summer.

Huckleberries

These are the little fellows* not to be confused with (though related to) blueberries—except that if you live where you can gather them freely, you are in luck. Do so whenever you can, and see how many you can get home without eating them fresh from the bushes. They may be blue, white, or black, and they can be used in just about any way the blueberry can. Use them to spruce up bread or muffins, to combine with other fruits in a compote, to scatter on sherbet or ices or custards. Or make the following pudding.

HUCKLEBERRY BREAD PUDDING
about 6 servings

2 cups huckleberries
1 tablespoon flour
½ teaspoon salt
¼ teaspoon ground cloves
1 teaspoon lemon or orange juice
thin-sliced bread, any kind (pumpernickel would be interesting)
1 cup heavy cream or other topping

Pick over and clean the berries. Mix the flour and salt, and toss the berries in it. Bring half a cup of water to a simmer in a saucepan. Put the berries in, and simmer until softened, about 5 minutes. Add cloves and fruit juice, and cool. Grease a flat baking dish, and cover the bottom with the bread, overlapping the slices. Spread the berry mixture over this. Whip the cream until stiff, and use it for topping, spreading it in a layer. Or you can spread the berries thinner, and make several layers of the bread, like a triple-decker sandwich, topped with the cream. Chill in refrigerator for several hours, and serve ice-cold.

* Also called in some localities bilberries or whortleberries.

These lovely fruits, so often employed as flavorings for all manner of provender, can hardly be eaten by themselves, plain. But the well-stocked economy kitchen should never be without one of them, either in whole or juice form. If you have run out of reconstituted lemon juice and have only lime juice (left over, perhaps, from the last time you served vodka and tonic to summertime friends), use it in some of the places where lemon juice is called for—the results will surprise and delight you. Or make a fish salad, using any easily flaked fish of which you have a pound around. This, of course, would be a non-dessert dish.

LIME-FISH MOLD
6 to 8 servings

½ cup lime juice
2 envelopes plain gelatin (½ oz.)
½ cup mayonnaise
1 pint cream-style cottage cheese
1 tablespoon horseradish
1 teaspoon grated onion
2 or 3 drops Tabasco
1 lb. fish (one kind or a combination), flaked
1 cup sour cream
¼ cup chili sauce

Add lime juice to 1½ cups boiling water, then dissolve the gelatin in it. Add a cup of cold water, and chill until slightly thickened. Blend the mayonnaise, cottage cheese, horseradish, onion, and Tabasco until you achieve a rather smooth mixture. Stir this into the gelatin, then stir in the fish flakes. Turn into a refrigerator bowl or mold, and chill until firmly set. Combine the sour cream and chili sauce. Turn the mold, when jelled, onto green leaves or a cold plate, and serve cold with the sour-cream-chili-sauce spooned over it.

Then there's a very nice, reliable, foolproof pudding that can actually be made with any kind of fruit juice, not necessarily citrus—try cranberry juice, for instance. But for fun, why not see what happens if you do it with a combination of lemon and lime juices? The honey is optional, the eggs are not.

LEMON AND LIME RAISIN PUDDING
4 to 6 servings

2 tablespoons flour
½ teaspoon nutmeg
1 tablespoon margarine
2 medium eggs
¼ cup honey (optional)
2 teaspoons grated rind (lemon and lime)
½ cup raisins
¼ cup lemon juice
½ cup lime juice
1 cup milk

Preheat oven to 350°. Mix the flour and nutmeg in a baking dish or casserole. Soften the margarine, and blend it into the flour. Separate the eggs. Add the egg yolks (whole) and the honey (if any), and beat the mixture until it is smooth. Add lemon and lime rind, raisins, both juices, and the milk. Stir well to blend in. Beat egg whites until stiff, and fold them in. Now set the baking dish in a pan of hot water, and put the whole assemblage on the lowest rack of the oven. Bake for 45 minutes.

I have had little direct experience with mangoes, though I once ate one fresh—again from a Southwestern friend's tree. Good authority, however, tells me that a mango behaves much like a melon and can be served in some of the same ways. Melons—whether cantaloupe (sometimes called muskmelon), honeydew (sometimes called casaba), or watermelon—I *do* know something about. The first thing I want to share with you is that these melons aren't as difficult to grow in your truck garden as you may have feared. Watermelons, like many a vegetable, need not be mammoth to be sweet and successful. In fact, they should not be so huge, and there is a small variety that grows just as well in the summer of cold northern climes as it does in the deep South. Try some in the row next to the kale and the snap beans, and be surprised with the results. What dessert could be sweeter than a slice of fresh-picked, home-grown watermelon?

Juicy cantaloupe and honeydew melons go well with salty cured meats and fishes, as appetizers or main dishes, sliced, or merely cut in half and their cavities mounded with the accompaniment. They provide both container and basic foodstuff for a cool summer fruit salad. Many people think there is no lunch so lovely (and so slimming) as a half melon filled with cottage cheese and sprinkled with a bit of grated lemon or orange peel. Chunks or slices of varicolored melons (you really don't need one of those little scoops that form the melon into balls), combined perhaps with chunks of pineapple and sprinkled with a few raspberries or blueberries, make a festive and delectable dessert, full of taste-tingling zest.

If you have come by a large quantity of melons in season (the only time you can afford them), and, unaccountably, they have sat around in your kitchen or refrigerator getting sweeter (and riper) until they aren't the fresh, firm delights they once were—I'll bet you haven't thought of making cold drinks of the still succulent flesh. One of the most delicious, cooling, and beautiful-to-behold drinks I ever frothed up was the one made from watermelon, as below. I don't see why the same sort of libation can't be done with the slightly tired flesh of cantaloupe or honeydew.

WATERMELON FROTH
dessert for 2

2 cups of pink watermelon flesh, in chunks
1 cup yogurt
the bottom of a container (about ¼ cup) of raspberry
sherbet
1 tablespoon shaved ice

Tumble everything into the blender, and run it at medium speed for about 30 seconds. It makes a gorgeous big bubbly pink drink. And why not serve a cool, frosty dessert that you can drink?

The white part of the watermelon flesh—everything between the pink part of the pulp and the actual green skin—you save in your fruit-leavings freezer bag until you have enough gathered, and enough time, to turn it into a pickle (see p. 223). Or if pickling isn't your bag, combine this white rind with crabmeat in an exquisite stir-fried dish.

WATERMELON AND CRABMEAT
4 to 6 servings

½ cup vegetable oil
8 cups white watermelon chunks
2 cups sliced mushrooms
4 or 5 scallions, with tops, cut in 1-inch lengths
2 cups cooked crabmeat
2 tablespoons soy sauce

Heat the oil in a wok or flat skillet, and add all the fruit, vegetables, and crabmeat at once. Over a very high flame, stir-fry until melon is just barely tender. Pour in the soy sauce at the last minute before serving, hot, over white rice. This is one dish that enhances rather than overwhelms the taste of crabmeat, which is so horrendously expensive in my neighborhood that one wants to get every ounce of flavor out of it on the rare occasions when it is in the larder.

Oranges and Their Relatives

The closest relatives of the orange in terms of use, it seems to me, are temple oranges and tangerines. Tangerines are so easy to peel, section, and eat with the fingers that I don't see why anyone would want to do anything else with them, aside from combining them with other fruits in a compote, or possibly slipping a few into gelatin desserts occasionally.

Orange juice in the morning is so much a part of my life that I doubt a day could be successfully begun without it. But oranges combine well with poultry, fish, and vegetable dishes, as we have already seen, and some incomparably fine desserts a bit more complicated than just halving an orange —navel, temple, Seville, or plain. Then it's usually the juice or the rind, or both, that is employed, rather than the sections of pulp. Here are a couple of such desserts, the first employing all three aspects of the orange.

ORANGE DELIGHT
7 or 8 servings

2 envelopes plain gelatin (½ oz.)
2 tablespoons lemon juice

½ cup orange juice
2 tablespoons grated orange rind
1 cup heavy cream
8 or 10 orange sections

Boil 2 cups water, and dissolve the gelatin in it. Add the lemon juice, orange juice, and orange rind, and chill in refrigerator until slightly thickened but not firmly set. Meanwhile, whip the cream until stiff, and fold into the orange mixture, turning it into a mold or refrigerator dish. Let partly thicken again, and press orange sections into the top. When it has become very firm, turn out onto a cold plate, and serve chilled, with orange sections on bottom. Or serve right from refrigerator dish with orange sections on top.

The name of this dessert I learned when I first experienced it in Puerto Rico, although it goes by other names in any number of Latin American countries, restaurants, and cookbooks. Barbara Norman's *Spanish Cookbook* calls it, with crystalline logic, Orange Cream Custard. She makes it as follows.

NATILLA
about 4 servings

2 cups milk
⅔ cups sugar*
peel of 1 orange, grated
2 egg yolks
6 egg whites
intact peel of ½ orange
slivered almonds (optional)

* I have had fine results omitting the sugar and substituting for it ½ cup frozen orange-juice concentrate.

263

Beat the milk, sugar, grated orange peel, egg yolks, and whites together until foamy and stiff. Strain into the upper part of a double boiler. Add the intact peel, and cook over hot (not boiling) water for 20 minutes, stirring from time to time to prevent lumps. When the custard is thick and smooth and creamy, remove the peel, pour into individual dessert cups or dishes, and chill. Serve cold. A few slivered almonds sprinkled on top wouldn't hurt.

Papayas

It's surprising how many parts of the United States grow this fruit, which some northerners persist in regarding as strictly tropical. Not so, and you may even be able to find local ones for reasonable prices in your supermarket. The papaya, or pawpaw, is a versatile fruit that can serve as a dessert, appetizer, or breakfast fruit, eaten as you would a melon. It can go into salads, and it makes good jellies, jams, preserves, and the like. Don't throw away the seeds of the papaya. Grind them up, and rub them on the surface of tough cuts of meat. They make a very good tenderizer, as does the juice of the papaya.

Here is a rather clever way to make a dessert of papaya; it is really simpler than it may sound.

CHERRY PAPAYA
4 or 5 servings

1 ripe papaya
¼ oz. plain gelatin
1 cup sherry or brandy
1 tablespoon crème de menthe
½ cup stoned cherries, or seedless grapes, or both

Slice the top fourth off the papaya. Remove seeds (but save them). Heat a cup of water to boiling, remove pan from heat, and dissolve gelatin in it. Add sherry or brandy and creme de menthe to the gelatin, and put in the refrigerator to firm partially. Then stir in the cherries and/or grapes, and distribute them evenly throughout the gelatin.

Now pour the gelatin into the cavity of the papaya right up to the top, and replace the "cap." If you have any gelatin that didn't fit inside the papaya, pour it into a glass bowl, and set the papaya into it, so that the jelly will hold the papaya upright when it sets. Put papaya and gelatin into the refrigerator. When the gelatin has set firmly, in 3 to 4 hours, cut the papaya into slices, and serve cold. An interesting play of colors and textures.

Peaches

In the front line of American fruits in popularity and widespread growth, the peach has long been synonymous with virtue, beauty, and tastiness. And rightly so. Succulent and delicious and raised everywhere, the peach in season is a bargain at the supermarket and roadside stand; it is often on sale, canned, the rest of the year. When it is fresh and just-ripe, there is nothing quite like a plain peach for dessert; and when it has attained a little maturity (and possibly a few brown spots), there are hundreds of things you can do with it, aside from combining it with other fruits in a fruit cup or salad, or cooking some main-course meat or vegetable dish with it. The peach even dries well.

Here are just a few tasty dishes that depend on the natural sweetness of peaches, rather than on sugar, for their appeal.

PEACH MERINGUE PUDDING
serves 4 to 6

4 medium-sized peaches
¼ oz. plain gelatin
1 pint light or heavy cream
2 egg whites
1 teaspoon cream of tartar

Peel and stone the peaches, and slice or chop them. Dissolve the gelatin in a little warm water (⅛ cup or so); then mix gelatin, cream, and peaches together. Put in refrigerator to set. When firm (in 3 or 4 hours), remove peach gelatin from refrigerator, and decorate top with meringue, which you have made by beating the egg whites together with the cream of tartar until stiff.

BAKED PEACHES
4 or 5 servings

4 or 5 medium-sized peaches
2 tablespoons margarine
½ teaspoon cinnamon
¼ teaspoon nutmeg or powdered cloves
½ cup crushed cornflakes or bran flakes
2 tablespoons nuts (peanuts, pecans, walnuts),
chopped fine

Preheat oven to 350°. Peel and pit the peaches, then halve or slice them, depending on their appearance. (If peaches have lost some of their juiciness, add a bit in the form of orange or grapefruit juice, or the juice you have saved from canned fruits.) Grease a baking dish, and arrange peaches in it. Melt the margarine and mix it with the spices, cereal flakes, and chopped nuts. Pour this sauce over the peaches, and bake for 20 minutes.

PEACH COBBLER
8 or 10 servings

6 to 8 medium-sized peaches
2 tablespoons lemon juice
1¾ cups whole-wheat flour
2½ teaspoons baking powder
½ teaspoon salt
¼ cup margarine
¾ cup milk
1 teaspoon cinnamon

Peel, stone, and slice the peaches, and put them in a saucepan. Cover them with water to which you have added the lemon juice, and simmer, covered, about 20 minutes. Preheat oven to 425°. While they are simmering, combine the flour, baking powder, and salt in a mixing bowl. Cut the margarine into the dry ingredients by wielding two knives in opposition. Stir in the milk, and knead this dough very briefly. Drain the peaches and arrange them in a buttered baking dish; sprinkle with cinnamon. Place dough on top, in one layer or in tablespoon-size balls. Bake for half an hour.

Peaches can combine with other fruits and dates and figs in and out of various kinds of dough. But I wonder—after you have eaten corn fritters, banana fritters, eggplant fritters, potato pancakes, and such until they come out your ears—if you have ever considered Peach Fritters. An interesting new approach to breakfast or brunch.

PEACH FRITTERS
serves 2

2 peaches
1 cup flour
2 teaspoons baking powder
¾ cup milk
1 teaspoon salt
1 tablespoon vegetable oil or margarine

Peel, pit, and chop up the peaches. Mix all the rest of the ingredients into a pancake batter, then stir in the peach chunks. Heat a griddle or large skillet to piping hot, grease it, and proceed to make fritters, spooning the peach batter onto the griddle by serving-spoonfuls. Let the batter cook on one side until bubbles form before you flip it over to the other side. If you're going to serve them all at once, keep the finished ones warm in a low oven until you have used up all the batter. Possibly you'll want to sprinkle them with cinnamon when serving.

Naturally everything you can do with peaches you can do with nectarines, their first cousins. You may even leave the nectarine skin on when you eat or cook with it (the only advantage, as I see it, to nectarines over peaches).

Pears

Next to apples, pears are probably the most popular non-citrus, non-berry fruit, and with good reason. They grow in almost every part of the country and are not prohibitively expensive in season. What we may forget about them is that pears can be used in practically every way that apples can (except where we're relying on the superior number of pectin or yeast cells on the skin of the apple to perform some process for us). Try substituting pears in any of the apple recipes, making allowances for the slightly juicier quality of the pears.

Once again, a handsome, shapely fresh pear, by itself, is a really exquisite dessert. Served with a wedge of cheese (blue, Camembert, Brie, or Limburger, if the budget can stand it that week), and a fruit knife with which to cut and spread, pear for dessert is very festive and very chic these days, too.

Pears don't keep as well as apples, so you may find yourself with a few pears that have seen their best days. Don't despair: there are wonderful desserts to make of middle-aged pears, without going all super-sugary and gooey. Try, for instance, cooking pears on the verge of overripeness in some wine.

PEARS IN RED WINE
for 6

6 pears
2 tablespoons lemon juice
1 cup red wine (port, claret, Burgundy)
½ teaspoon honey
1 tablespoon cinnamon
2 tablespoons orange and lemon peel, minced or grated

Peel the pears. Add lemon juice to a quart of cold water, and soak the pears in it. Add 1 cup of water to the wine, honey, cinnamon, and fruit peels. Bring it to a boil, add the pears (drained), turn heat down, and simmer for 10 minutes, or until the fruit is tender. Let cool in syrup, and serve cold.

If you have on hand two softening-beyond-the-point-of-return pears, plus one greengrocer's-reject avocado, you might try the following dessert, which is economical and very pretty besides.

PEAR MOUSSE
4 or 5 servings

In this dish you get the mousse effect by whipping the fruit, rather than by the use of gelatin, eggs, or cream. It actually works better with overripe fruits than with just-ripe ones.

1 overripe avocado
2 overripe pears
2 tablespoons lemon juice
2 tablespoons grated orange rind
2 tablespoons rum or cider
½ cup peanuts, walnuts, or hazelnuts

Peel the avocado and pears, and get rid of the stone and seeds. Cut fruits in quarters, and put them into your blender together with all the rest of the ingredients. Run blender on high speed for about a minute, then pour its contents into a bowl, and chill in refrigerator for an hour or so.

VARIATION: This easy mousse can be done with any number of fruits in substitution for the pears and avocado. Try it with plums, peaches, fresh apricots (if you're in that part of the country), raspberries, or strawberries. You can even make it without a blender, if you're willing to put in some time with a wire whisk. The new French "skinny" cooking whisks fruits endlessly to save its beneficiaries' health and to capitalize on the essence of the fruit. An enticing lily-gilding sauce for this and similar fruit custards can be made by combining equal parts chocolate sauce and crème de menthe.

Persimmons

The persimmon, originally from the Orient but now grown all over the world, is a fruit that you may be overlooking. Since it's a quick ripener that soon grows overripe in the shops, you may be able to pick up a few at bargain rates from time to time. Don't ever try to eat it until it's *fully* ripe: then you can make a dessert of it by just peeling the skin back like petals and cutting the fruit with knife and fork, sampling its distinctive sweetness. (Unripe, it has a shockingly astringent "edge" to it.) You may want, instead, to turn your bargain persimmons into an ice or a pudding.

PERSIMMON ICE
3 or 4 servings

2 ripe persimmons
¼ oz. plain gelatin
1 tablespoon lemon juice

Peel the persimmons. Simmer the flesh in a small saucepan over low heat until translucent. Cut up the flesh, and put into blender; blend at low or medium speed until puréed. Soften the gelatin in a little warm water in a cup, then stir it into the persimmon purée until dissolved. Add lemon juice, then pour into a refrigerator tray or dish, and put into freezing compartment. Freeze only until mushy, then take out, and beat in a mixing bowl until smooth. Return to freezer, and freeze until firm.

PERSIMMON PUDDING
about 4 servings

1 cup persimmon pulp
2 teaspoons baking soda

1 cup flour (not necessarily white)
½ teaspoon ginger
½ teaspoon nutmeg
½ cup chopped nuts
½ cup seedless raisins
¾ cup milk
1 tablespoon margarine
1 teaspoon vanilla

Preheat oven to 350°. Combine in a bowl the persim-mon pulp, baking soda, and flour. Then stir in the rest of the ingredients until you have a homogenous mixture. Liberally grease a baking dish or casserole. Pour the mixture into the dish, and bake it for 1 hour. Serve hot.

Pineapples

There is something about fresh pineapple that sets my teeth on edge, but to some people it is sheer ambrosia. Combined with other fresh fruits of less stringy textures I don't mind it—peaches, plums, even apples and berries marry well with fresh pineapple in a fruit cup. But generally I opt for canned pineapple, which comes in obliging forms: sliced, chunks, crushed. Since it's usually to be found in the dented-cans bin at the markets where I shop, I always have a supply in my stores. I throw pineapple often into freezes, into fruit salads, or cook fish or meat or vegetable dishes with its aid.

Slices of canned pineapple can act as the basis of amus-ing salad or dessert dishes (forming the wings of butterflies in salads, for instance, or flower or sun motifs in desserts). But this sort of whimsy in never worth, to me anyway, the extra price you pay for the sliced over the diced or crushed versions. Try substituting pineapple crush, or chunks, in some of the dishes that have come earlier in this chapter.

You can get an awful lot of drama out of a fresh pine-apple by flambéing it, as follows.

FLAMING PINEAPPLE AND BANANAS
5 or 6 servings

1 fresh, ripe pineapple
1 banana
2 tablespoons butter or margarine
1 tablespoon arrowroot or cornstarch
½ cup pineapple or grapefruit juice
2 tablespoons chopped mixed nuts and raisins
¼ cup liquor (brandy, rum, cognac, or your choice)

Peel and core the pineapple, and cut it in very thin slices. Peel and slice the banana. Heat the butter in a skillet, and brown the pineapple slices in it. Add the arrowroot to the fruit juice, and whisk it up a bit. Then add the juice to the skillet a little at a time, stirring over medium heat until it thickens a little. Add the banana, nuts, and raisins. Now heat the liquor in a separate small saucepan, set it aflame with a lighted match, and pour it over the pineapple and banana. Carry it, carefully, aflame to the table, and serve as soon as the fire goes out.

The canned variety of pineapple can be utilized in one of these harmless little desserts.

PINEAPPLE SPONGE
5 or 6 servings

½ cup pineapple juice
1 tablespoon lemon juice

273

3 tablespoons flour
1 teaspoon grated lemon rind
2 medium eggs
2 tablespoons margarine
½ cup milk
½ teaspoon salt
1½ cups pineapple chunks

Preheat oven to 350°. Combine the juices, and stir the flour and lemon rind into them. Separate the eggs, and add the yolks, stirring each in separately. Then melt the margarine, and add it and the milk. Whip the egg whites, with the salt added, until they are stiff. Fold them into the mixture. Put the pineapple into the bottom of a buttered baking dish, and pour the custard mix over. Then place the baking dish in a pan of hot water, and bake for about half an hour. Serve hot or cold.

PINEAPPLE SNOW
7 or 8 servings

¼ oz. plain gelatin
2 cups crushed (canned) pineapple
1 teaspoon almond extract
1 tablespoon shredded coconut
2 cups cream

Soften the gelatin in a little cold water (⅛ cup or so). Heat the crushed pineapple, and stir in the almond extract and shredded coconut. When this mixture begins to boil, remove from fire, and add the gelatin, stirring it in until dissolved. Put this mix into the refrigerator, and chill until beginning to set. Whip the cream until it is stiff, then fold it into the pineapple mixture. Pour the whole thing into a mold or bowl, and chill until firm. Unmold onto a plate, or serve from bowl.

Plums

Fresh plums have a bit of tartness around the skin that some people find piquantly pleasant and others can't stand. There is something rather untidy, besides, about eating a plum just plain, fresh, in the hands. Fresh plums just *look* very attractive with contrastingly colored fruits in collections or arrangements. These same plums that decorate your table center so handsomely can, when they get a little aged, be worked with wonderfully well. Sweeter now, they will provide an excellent flavor for cold or hot desserts. Here's one of each.

PLUM RICE PUDDING*
6 to 8 servings

8 cups milk
1 cup raw rice
4 tablespoons butter or margarine
2 medium eggs
3 or 4 ripe plums
1 teaspoon vanilla
cinnamon or nutmeg, to taste

Pour the milk into a heavy saucepan, along with the rice and butter. Beat the eggs slightly, and combine with the rice milk. Cook over low heat, stirring frequently, for about an hour. Peel and stone the plums,

* Baked or steamed plum pudding, by the way, classically doesn't contain any plums—the red, globular, stoned fruit we're working with here. The "plums" in that rich holiday dish are raisins, currants, nuts, sometimes citron.

cut them into small pieces, and stir them, along with the vanilla, into the rice about halfway through its cooking. Sprinkle the top of the pudding with cinnamon and nutmeg (or other seasonings of your choice), chill in refrigerator, and serve cold.

FRESH PLUM CRUMB PUDDING
5 or 6 servings

enough fresh ripe plums to make about 6 cups when cut
into quarters
1⅓ cups flour
¼ teaspoon salt
½ cup margarine

Preheat oven to 375°. Wash, pit, and cut up the plums. Don't peel them. Mix 4 tablespoons of the flour with the salt, and sprinkle it among the plums in a baking dish. Now cream the rest of the flour with the margarine until you get a crumb consistency. Sprinkle these crumbs over the top of the plums. Bake for 1 hour.

NOTE: I should think that fresh figs could be prepared in the same way, but I've never cooked a fresh fig, so don't take my word for it.

PLUM-NUT PIE
6 or so servings

about 1½ lbs. ripe plums
1 or 2 unbaked pastry crusts
½ lb. nutmeats (peanut, pecan, chestnut, or whatever)
grated rind of 1 lemon
½ cup margarine
1 medium or small egg

Preheat oven to 375°. Peel and stone the plums, and cut into slices (or halves). Lay the bottom crust on a pie plate, prick a few holes in it, and arrange the plums on top of it. Chop the nuts and sprinkle them, along with the lemon rind, among the plum pieces. Melt the margarine, and pour it over—all of it if you're making a 1-crust pie, half if a 2-crust. (The other half of the melted margarine goes on top of the top crust, which you spread over the plums, pinching the edges of the two crusts together, and pricking some air holes in the top crust. Beat the egg and brush the crust with it.) Bake for an hour if 1-crust, 10 minutes longer if 2-crust. Serve hot.

Prunes

The prunes that some varieties of plums are made into are an invaluable part of the economy gourmet's cuisine. They can be added to morning cereal, stewed and eaten as the principal waking-up fruit, combined with other fruits in a yogurt cup for lunch, and used to cook (and sweeten) many meat, fish, or vegetable dishes. The prunes I ate most recently, combined with apples and onions, came out of the cavity of a goose roasted for New Year's Eve dinner. Prune Whip is probably a pudding-category dessert you're familiar with, but here's one you may not have thought of.

PRUNE TAPIOCA
6 servings

1 cup pearl tapioca
8 or 10 dried prunes
2 tablespoons margarine, melted
½ teaspoon vanilla (optional)

Soak the tapioca overnight in a cup and a half of water. Cover the prunes with water, and simmer them for half an hour. (This creates a lovely syrup that can be used in place of regular sugar-based syrup in any number of ways.) Preheat oven to 325°. Now cut up the prunes, discarding the pits, and combine them with the tapioca and its liquid, and the margarine. If it doesn't look quite wet enough, add the optional vanilla and a bit of the prune syrup. Pour into a baking dish and bake for about 1 hour. Serve hot or cold.

Raspberries

Red or black, these seedy fruits are of such almost overpowering sweetness that it's hard to understand how anyone can *add* sugar to them, powdered or granulated. They were so costly in my part of the country last summer that, for the first time in years, I failed to serve handfuls of the fresh, hot-pink berries as a dinner finale. They are cheaper now, either frozen or canned—in your area too I trust—so that's how I recommend buying them. Remember to comparison-shop among the frozen foods; store-brand labels can sometimes make the difference of more than a few sous. So can buying frozen berries in a large plastic sack, rather than a small waxed carton. Defrosted or drained, raspberries can cheer up many a pale, bland pudding or sugarless tea bread. Raspberries can also delight in the following ways.

RASPBERRY CREAM
about 8 small servings (it's very rich)

20 oz. frozen raspberries
2 cups heavy cream
1 teaspoon ground ginger

Several hours before you want to make this confection, defrost the raspberries in a bowl, draining and reserving the syrup that accumulates. Whip the cream until it is stiff, gradually adding the ground ginger as you whip. Now fold the berries into the whipped cream, taking care not to break them up. Chill in refrigerator until ready to serve. Just before serving, dribble the reserved syrup on top.

VARIATION: Substitute loganberries, boysenberries, or strawberries. Or make a sherbet or milk ice with the berries, non-cholesteroling yourself out of the heavy cream. Or delete the cream altogether, and substitute a non-fat commercial whipped dessert topping.

Another dish that frozen, fresh, or canned raspberries go into gracefully is a version of something a friend of mine calls Danish Dessert. I have changed the locale and the dramatis personnae, having the tart properties of the fruits in mind.

FINNISH DESSERT
8 small servings

1 10-oz. package frozen raspberries
1½ cups fresh cranberries
rhubarb enough to make ⅔ cup diced
2 tablespoons cornstarch

Start the raspberries defrosting several hours before you proceed with the rest. Catch the juice that drains out. The next step is to wash and pick over the cranberries, and put them in a saucepan over medium heat, mashing them a little. Clean and cut up the rhubarb; add it to the saucepan. Whisk the cornstarch into the liquid drained from the raspberries until it is dissolved. If there's not as much raspberry liquid as you need—about ½ cup—make it up with cold water. Stir the raspberries into this liquid, crushing them a bit as you do so. Then combine this sauce with the stewing rhubarb and cranberries, and continue to cook the mélange, stirring constantly with a wooden spoon so it doesn't stick to the pan. When it begins to thicken, turn it out into a bowl, let it cool, then chill it in the refrigerator until ready to serve. A delectable dessert.

Rhubarb

Other things you can do with rhubarb stalks are to combine them with other fruits in pies—apple, notably—and sauces and puddings and such. Make the dish above, omitting the raspberries. Sweeten rhubarb if you must (most palates can't take its excessive acerbity) with the juices from sweet fruits, and simply stew it by itself. Make a superb home-grown wine with it (see p. 295). Be sure to get rid of the leaves as soon as you pick it; they're toxic to both man and beast. The only thing in the world they're good for is for polishing aluminum, and they are scarcely worth keeping around for just that purpose. Try cooking a rather fatty fish in rhubarb, or stuffing a duck with rhubarb in one of your favorite dressings. Steam it in the upper part of a double boiler in combination with prunes, plums, or pears.

The only thing *not* to do with rhubarb is just leave it moldering in the ground. It grows so valiantly in so many unlikely places (I once found some coming up between the cracks in the cement outside a gas station) that it's a shame not to take advantage of this vitamin-filled fruit.

Surely the most elegant fruit within the range of the economy-minded, strawberries can be grown in most parts of the
United States with very little trouble. If your backyard lacks
strawberry space, then just about everything said about *buying* raspberries (not to mention their sweetness) applies
equally to strawberries. If you have saved up all summer for
a box of real-fresh strawberries for the Labor Day weekend,
then you would be ill-advised to mash up the whole quart
(or even pint) to make a sauce for gilding your less interesting desserts, fruit salads, or whatnot. Stow them in the
refrigerator, and use them only a few at a time. One plump,
juicy, beautiful strawberry in the center of a half grapefruit,
or atop a custard, can make the difference between an ordinary and a festive dessert. Some would consider this taste
preference eccentric, but I've always thought that strawberry
combines particularly well with chocolate—I deem two or
three strawberries on top of a dish of cholocate ice cream
or mousse or sherbet a Lucullan feast. (Some obviously
agree with me, else we would not have in the world the
phenomenon of the chocolate-dipped strawberry.) Put one
in a glass of white wine, and use it as an aperitif before your
next dinner party.

Enough of such richness. Now for what to do with the
frozen strawberries, or those that started out fresh and have
been hanging around your kitchen a bit long.

STRAWBERRY MOUSSE
4 to 6 servings

1 10-oz. package frozen strawberries (or equal volume
    aging fresh strawberries)
¼ oz. plain gelatin
½ cup sweet cider
2 cups sour cream or yogurt

Defrost the strawberries in a bowl, reserving the liquid that gathers. Mash those berries that have remained whole. Soften the gelatin in the half cup of cider; then add a half cup of hot water, and stir until dissolved. Add ¼ cup of cold water. Combine the strawberries with yogurt or sour cream; then add this mixture to the gelatin, blending for even distribution. Spoon it into a bowl or a mold, and chill in refrigerator until firmly set. Unmold onto a cold plate, or serve from the bowl.

Here's another sort of disguise for fresh pineapple. With the strawberries helping its cause, how can it fail?

STRAWBERRY
AMBROSIA
4 to 6 servings

1 fresh pineapple
1 pint of fresh
(but not so firm any more) strawberries
1 peach or nectarine, peeled and cut up
2 to 3 tablespoons lime juice
1 cup shredded coconut

Cut the pineapple in half lengthwise, remove core, and cut the meat up in small cubes. Now you have two pineapple-half "boats" in which to serve the combined fruit. Slice the strawberries if they're still sliceable; otherwise mash. Mix them with the pineapple dice, peach or nectarine, and the lime juice. Stir in half of the cup of coconut, then spoon the fruit into the pineapple shells. Sprinkle the rest of the coconut on top, and serve chilled.

SCARLET SORBET

The term sorbet is just a slightly fancy way of saying frozen punch. Which, when you come to think of it, is just what some sherbets or ices are (sherbets usually but not always contain milk). The use of some kind of wine or liqueur in a sorbet will keep it from freezing solid.

about a pint

1 16-oz. package frozen strawberry halves (or pieces)
1 8-oz. package frozen raspberries
2 tablespoons apricot brandy or other liqueur or wine

Defrost the berries only partially, and put them into the blender. Add the liqueur, and blend on medium speed until nearly smooth. Substitute some other fruit or berry for the raspberries if you wish—nearly anything will do, except bananas. Now pour this mixture into an ice-cube tray or other freezer container, and leave it in the freezer for 2 or 3 hours. It will make a positively scrumptious finale to an otherwise nonsweet meal.

Any rather prosaic dessert dish, or cottage-cheese-mound luncheon, can be made more exciting by being treated to a fruit sauce. Make one of any combination of fruits you happen to have on hand, in whatever quantity, just mashed up together and spread or spooned on. There are very few fruits or berries whose enticing flavors fail to entice when combined; experiment with a free hand. The longer you've had the fruits, the better they will sauce up. Save yourself money on fancy dessert ingredients, and your insides possible contamination from overdoses of sugar.

Fruits and animals are so much a part of fantasy and legend that I hope you will bear with me as I conclude this chapter with a factual story about a beast made of fruit. This whimsical creature was dreamed up to win an apple-cooking contest for me, first prize for which was a microwave oven. I'm convinced that the only reason I'm still microwave-ovenless is that the day of the competition I wound up at the hospital instead of the building where the apple-dish judging was taking place. But that's another story. . . . Unimaginative concoctions like apple ketchup and apple pizza were the winners. If poorer by one fancy miracle oven, I am richer in an amusing dessert dish, guaranteed to bring a smile to the lips of the most jaded and satiated dinner guest. Back to the Garden of Eden!

APPLE TURTLES
for 4

4 large, firm apples of oval shape
2 tablespoons molasses
1 tablespoon cinnamon
4 egg whites
16 cashew nuts
4 dates
thin root tips of 4 carrots or parsnips

Cut the apples in half; core, stem, and peel them. Cut a half-inch flat slice from four of the apples halves, and set aside. Now, cut up the four less-than-halves, and cover them with water in a saucepan. Add one tablespoon of the molasses and the cinnamon, and simmer until you have a thick chunky applesauce. Meanwhile, cover the four complete apple halves with water in another pan, and simmer them for just a few minutes, perhaps 3, to just barely soften the outsides. Drain and cool; cool the applesauce. Beat the egg whites until stiff. Divide the beaten egg white in half, and fold half of it into the cooled applesauce. Put one of the reserved apple slices on each of four cold ovenproof plates, and spread eggwhite-applesauce on each one. Then top each with one of the softened complete apple halves, sandwich fashion, rounded side up. Smear these convex surfaces with the remaining molasses, which will act as an adhesive to hold the remaining beaten egg white, which you apply next. Run the plates under the broiler (at least 4 inches below) for about 5 minutes, or long enough to brown the surfaces a little. Now insert the cashews (legs), dates (heads) and root tips (tails) in the proper spots between the bottom and top "shells" of the turtles, poking one end far enough in so the beasts don't become dismembered as you bring them to the table with a flourish.

After a peanut butter sandwich, this finale should earn you points at any child's party. And set the parents back a lot less than the clichéd mountains of cake and ice cream.

9

HOMEMADE SPIRITS

Obviously you're not going to feed your family of four, or
your friends, on Sixteen Dollars a Week if a large part of
your budget goes out for wines, liqueurs, and other spirituous
beverages. You can fritter away your food money very
easily if you *buy* all of the spirits you include in your cooking and entertaining. We've all heard enough complaints
from the proprietors of eateries that have not yet acquired
their liquor licenses to know that "There is much more
profit in the predinner drinks than in the meal that follows
them." So it really behooves the kitchen economizer to
make some of the wines that will be served to company
throughout the year. Hard liquors are more difficult; perhaps the thing to do when you're bent on saving money is
to switch to a steady regime of beers, wines, or liqueurs.
And make your soft drinks at home, too.

Beers

Contrary to what you may have heard, you can make beer
at home a lot less expensively than you can buy it, whether
in cans or bottles—or draft, it goes without saying—and
of a high quality, too. Wines are easier, because they don't
require as much special equipment or ingredients. Beer must
be protected from any contact with air while it is fermenting;
this dictates the use of a fermentation lock, the only piece

286

of equipment the average household doesn't include. This device, sometimes called an air lock, can be used over and over again, for winemaking as well, so it's not really an outlandish extravagance. Making beer at home is not illegal as long as it is limited in quantity to your own use. If you try peddling it, however, you may run afoul of The Law.

Unfortunately, you will have to use a good deal of sugar—that dubious substance I cautioned against in the previous chapter—both in beer and most winemaking. Cane sugar, along with natural sugars, some moisture, and an even temperature in the high sixties or low seventies, are what work together to turn the fruits or vegetables from which beers and wines are made into spirituous beverage.

Other tools you will need are a rather large mixing pot or crock (or two), some cheesecloth or dispensable dish towels, plastic sheeting (such as that used to wrap dry-cleaned clothes in), a siphoning hose, sturdy bottles, a second large container that will fit the fermentation lock, and a long wooden or plastic spoon.

Special materials you will need for beer are malt extract (unless you have barley growing in your backyard), yeast, sugar, and hops. The flavors of beer are many and varied, as are the strength of alcoholic content and the color. For the neophyte home-brewer, the best way to achieve beers of various degrees of light and dark is to order lighter or darker malt extracts, which you can get from suppliers of beer-making equipment or perhaps from your local pharmacy. Beer yeast is practically the same as baker's yeast, so I would use that rather than add to the cost by ordering a special beer yeast. Plain granulated cane sugar will work for beer, though corn sugar will probably produce a taste somewhat closer to what you are accustomed to in commercial beer, and dextrose is used by experts. If you don't have hops growing in your fields, look for dried hops in your local health-food shop, or order hop extract from your beer-equipment supplier. You can even buy something called "hopped malt extract," thus killing two birds with one stone. Let's assume, though, that you can come by a few dried hops. (If not, you can use fresh nettles, for a different sort of beer.) Just remember that the hops are what produce the bitterness, so the more you use, the more bitter the brew.

To make two gallons (eight quarts) of a nice lager beer, you will need: two pounds of malt extract, two ounces of brewer's or baker's yeast, a pound of sugar, about a pint of dried hops, and lots of water. Here's what you do.

Moisten the yeast in a cup of lukewarm water. Bring a gallon of water to a boil, then let it cool down to room temperature, and pour it onto the malt extract in a fermentation crock or large bowl. When the malt has dissolved, add the sugar, and stir it well.

Now put the dried hops into a pint or so of water, bring it to a boil, then simmer the hops for ten minutes. Strain the liquid into the fermentation crock, and cover the hops with fresh water. Repeat this procedure two or three times. Then add to the fermentation crock enough fresh water to bring the volume up to a little more than two gallons. While the liquid is still lukewarm, add the softened yeast, stirring it into the crock.

Cover the top of the bowl or crock with plastic sheeting, secure it well by tying or taping, and put the crock in a warm dark place where it can sit undisturbed for days. If the only properly warm place is a *light* place, and the container or covering is transparent, swaddle it with a towel or blanket to keep out the light.

The two stages of fermentation are not unlike the two stages of bread rising, except in time. The first stage of beer fermentation will take from two to four days, depending on the surrounding temperature. During this time a head of foam will develop, then subside somewhat. Don't start checking for the end of this stage until at least two days have passed.

The beer should now be transferred to the receptacle that accommodates the air lock, for the second stage of fermentation. You can still joggle it at this point, so you don't need to siphon yet; pour the beer into the second container, attach the air lock, surround the container with a towel (if necessary; see two paragraphs above), and leave it alone for four days to a week. You can tell when this stage is over by watching the bubbles rise in the air lock. At first they will be fast and profuse, then slower; when they are rising only one or two a minute, you can proceed to bottle.

It's the bottling that should be done with a siphon, so as not to stir up the beer, and to leave any sediment that may have accumulated at the bottom of the fermentation crock. Into whatever bottles you have accumulated and thoroughly cleaned, siphon off the beer. (The bottles should *not* be clear, colorless glass.) Leave a little air at the top of each bottle to avert explosion should a tiny bit of fermentation still take place, and cap securely. You can drink it right away, or you can store it in a cool, dark place for one to six weeks.

Next time, you can experiment with different ratios of malt to water, hops to malt, and different sweetening agents. Honey in place of sugar will produce a sort of mead; molasses something reminiscent of porter or stout; while ale, or something like it, can be achieved with stronger infusions of hops. But the technique, as outlined above, remains the same.

Here is how to make the nettle beer I spoke of earlier: Gather nettles early, before they have had a chance to get ferocious and stinging. About two pounds of the green only (chop off the roots) will do for a little more than a gallon of beer. Wash and dry them. Then collect two lemons, a pound of sugar, an ounce of cream of tartar, and a teaspoon of powdered yeast.

Squeeze the lemons for their juice, and set the juice aside. Then put the thinly-peeled-off rind into a large saucepan, together with the nettles. Pour in a gallon (four quarts) of water, bring to a boil, and let boil for fifteen minutes. Remove the lemon peel. Put the sugar and cream of tartar into your thoroughly clean first fermentation crock, and pour the hot lemon-water on top, straining out nettles; stir until completely dissolved.

Let it cool to room temperature; add the lemon juice and then the yeast. Now cover the top of the crock with plastic sheeting and proceed as above, for regular beer.

When you get to the end, don't store for up to six weeks—don't leave nettle beer for more than a week in bottles. Drink it cold no more than a few days after you bottle it.

Wines

The making of wine at home is even easier and cheaper than the brewing of beer—if, that is, you have a free or inexpensive source of grapes. Grapes carry in their skins the yeast cells that are necessary to wine fermentation, so that most home-grown wines start with a quantity of grapes. Adding raisins to other fruits, flowers, or vegetables is another way, and some recipes will follow that don't include grapes at all. Lacking grapes, you can order special wine yeast, or employ baker's yeast, or even make some yeast of your own (see p. 315). Apples are the only other fruit that approaches grapes in yeast-cell production; more about that later.

My most successful home-grown wine was made from grapes; my parents' *pièce de resistance,* however, was from elderberries and raisins; and that of a friend and neighbor grew from baker's yeast and dandelions. Recipes for all follow, but first the basic winemaking directions. The same tools and equipment as for beer can be used, though you should be certain they have been thoroughly cleansed of any residue or odor from the beer-brewing.

Gather as many grapes as you can. If you are going to invest the time in this process, you may as well make a quantity of wine that is worth your while. Thirty pounds of grapes will yield ten to twelve quarts of wine. (Federal law says you may put up as many as two hundred bottles a year before you are subject to the antibootleggers' laws.) Most of your time will be spent in picking over the grapes. Be sure to include some green (unripe) grapes, but get rid of the really rotten ones. Pick out all the leaves, sticks, tendrils, but don't wash the grapes, and don't try to deseed them at this time. (If by chance they have been sprayed during growing with some toxic substance, *do* wash them very scrupulously.)

Now (and here's where the dancing and stamping in bare feet comes in) mash the grapes a lot with a potato masher or other similar instrument to break their skins and start the juices. Doing it in more than one crock will facilitate the process, since you can see better which skins remain to be broken, as you mash and turn the fruit over and stir it around. Let air into the mash, as this will aid fermentation, but don't add anything else at this point. Just crush the grapes thoroughly, then cover your crocks with plastic sheeting, or several layers of muslin or cheese-cloth. Leave the containers in a warm, not hot, dark place for several days. Don't fasten your covering securely, because you are going to have to get at the grapes every day (once or twice daily) to turn the fruit over and submerge the fruits that have floated to the top.

Many wine-fanciers are intimidated from making their own, in the mistaken belief that all homemade wines must perforce be sweet. If you want a dry wine—and the grapes you started with are quite juicy—this is really all you need, except some additional time, for dry wines may take a bit longer to make. You must add sugar for a sweet or semi-sweet wine; an equal volume of sugar to the (picked over, cleaned) grapes will produce a sweet wine, and the addition of a little water to the vat at the same time will make up for any lack of juiciness that you detect. (It will also dilute your wine, so avoid this step if possible, for maximum flavor.) Add half as much sugar as the volume of your uncrushed grapes for a semisweet wine.

Cover the fermentation vat, or vats, and leave them in this state for the period of tumultuous fermentation, which will last anywhere from three days to three weeks, depending on such variables as temperature, the amount of air that gets into the grapes, the amount of sugar included, etc. When the fermentation has quieted down a bit, strain out the skins, seeds, and pulp and let the wine enter the second stage. (Don't discard the pulpy remainder, called "must"; store it in your freezer in a plastic container, if you have room. You may want it later for making grape jelly, grape juice, or a "small" wine, made from a second pressing of the grapes.) Now you should use the second container, the one fitted with the air lock if you possess one. Again, you can tell when the second stage is over by the speed with which the air bubbles rise in the lock, or break through the surface in the crock. In most wines you will notice at some point between two days and two weeks that the bubbles are rising only about one or two a minute; then you know you can bottle.

You may want to clear the wine during this second stage of fermentation. A cloudy wine tastes no different from a clear one, but there is an esthetic satisfaction in holding a glass up to the light and seeing the light shine through, demonstrating its fine color and crystalline quality. Wine can clear at this stage by simply being left along long enough for all the sediment to collect on the bottom of the container, which means you have to do four things: 1) leave it unmoved long enough, 2) avoid jiggling or disturbing the vat, 3) siphon it off into bottles without stirring it up in any way, and 4) sacrifice a bit of the liquid at the bottom of the vat. Since the last is a piece of sacrilege to the kitchen economist, I recommend clearing the wine with egg shells that are completely free of any egg white. The shells can be put into the second-fermentation vat when you strain the wine into it. They won't alter the taste of your wine at all, and the shell of one egg is sufficient for a gallon. The oily look that some wines acquire, which causes the wine to cling to the side of the glass as you tip it, is produced with glycerine, which I don't recommend to the home distiller.

Now when the second fermentation is completed, or nearly so, you can siphon off into bottles, and cap. Cap loosely at first, so that if there *is* some action still going on, you won't mess up your wine cellar or bedroom closet with an explosion. When there is no longer any possibility of this disaster, you can cork the wine tightly—even wind the top with foil if you wish—lay it on its side in a cool, dark place, and let it age. Leave it from two to six months after bottling tightly.

Having mastered this basic grape wine, you can go on to experiment with making wines from all sorts of other food products. Think of your favorite flavors and what growing things you have for the picking, or can afford to buy. The taste of the fruit, vegetable, grain, or whatever will be reflected in the flavor of the wine you make from it.

GRANDFATHER'S ELDERBERRY WINE
about 3 quarts

3 qts. elderberry blossoms
2 lemons
3 cups sugar
1 cup chopped dark raisins
1 3-oz. package dry yeast
1 slice dark bread

Gather the blossoms of the elderberry bush just after apple blossom time. Don't use the stalks.

Cover the blossoms with about three quarts of water, bring to a boil, and simmer for 20 minutes. Cool to lukewarm, then remove the flowers, straining if necessary. Slice the lemons thin, and stir them, with the sugar and chopped raisins, into the liquid. Moisten the yeast in a little lukewarm water; toast the bread. Spread the yeast on the bread, and float the slice, yeast side down, on the surface of the liquid. Allow to ferment in a warm place for two or three weeks in a crock covered with cheesecloth, then strain through cheesecloth into air-lock container. Leave another few days, then siphon into bottles, corked loosely. When all fermentation has stopped, cork tightly, and store for about a year before drinking. A dark red, moderately sweet wine.

DANDELION WINE
about 3 quarts

3 qts. dandelion blossoms
2 lemons
2 oranges
½ cup chopped white raisins
4 cups sugar
1 3-oz. package dry yeast

Gather the dandelions when they are in full bloom, no later in the day than 3:00 P.M. Use only the yellow and white part of the blossom. (Stems, leaves, or even the green sepals on the blossoms will produce a bitter wine.)

As soon as possible after gathering, put the dandelions into a clean fermentation crock. Heat 3 quarts of water to boiling, and pour it over them. Cover with a cloth or plastic sheeting, and let the vat stand in a warm place for about a week, stirring occasionally. Remove the flowers, straining if necessary. Peel and slice the citrus fruit, and stir it, along with raisins and sugar, into the liquid. Sprinkle top with the yeast, and let ferment in a covered vat, in a warm place, for about 2 weeks, stirring every day. Then strain the solids out, and pour the liquid into the vat with an air lock. Leave it there 2 weeks to 1 month. Then, when all fermentation is over, siphon into bottles. Cork loosely for a few days, then tightly. Store in a cool, dark place for several months before drinking. A semi-sweet golden wine.

NOTE: You can make wine from any number of flowers: try marigolds, camomile, mayflowers, jasmine blossoms, roses, of course, or even goldenrod. Experiment.

RHUBARB WINE
about 8 quarts

10 lbs. rhubarb stalks
7 cups sugar
2 cups chopped white raisins
rinds of 2 lemons, chopped
1 3-oz. package dry yeast

Clean the rhubarb, but don't peel it, and cut it up in 1-inch pieces. Bring two gallons of water to a boil, and pour it over the rhubarb. Let stand three or four days in a warm place, stirring from time to time. Strain the liquid through cheesecloth, then add to it the sugar, raisins, and lemon rind, stirring well. Sprinkle yeast on surface, and let stand, covered, two or three weeks at room temperature. Strain again, into air-lock jug if you have one, and let stand another day or two. When all fermentation has stopped, siphon or pour into bottles, cork loosely, and let stand until you're certain no more bubbles are rising. Then cork tightly, and store for at least six months before drinking.

This is a rather tart, amber-colored wine. If you would prefer a red rhubarb wine, add beets to the rhubarb—grate them first, then boil for half an hour, and put them in the vat with the rhubarb. Use about half as many beets as rhubarb, and the flavor of the wine will not be changed much. Fewer beets will give you a rosé wine.

Incidentally, this concoction has turned despisers of the lowly weed that produces it into rhubarb lovers overnight.

PARSNIP-POTATO WINE
about 4 quarts

2 lbs. potatoes, old and mealy
2 lbs. parsnips, any age
4 cups sugar
1 cup dried prunes
1 cup raisins
2 cloves
1 package dry yeast
1 slice whole-wheat bread

Don't peel the potatoes and don't scrape the parsnips. Scrub both well to clean, then slice the potatoes thin. Grate the parsnips, and boil both vegetables in water to cover for an hour. Remove from heat, and pour into fermentation crock. Now add the sugar and let dissolve. Chop the prunes and raisins, mash the cloves, and add both. Let the liquid cool to lukewarm. Soften the yeast in a bit of warm water. Toast the bread, spread the yeast on it, and float it yeast-side down on the surface of the liquid. Leave to ferment, covered, in a warm place, for about 2 weeks, stirring every day or so. Then strain out solids and the liquid into the second-fermentation vat. Leave for 3 or 4 days, until fermentation ends. Siphon off into bottles, cork loosely for another day or two, then cork tightly, and store for a minimum of six months before drinking.

A full-bodied amber wine, this brew would be hock if it weren't for the parsnips.

Perhaps you still have some apples left from your harvest that you don't know what to do with. Especially those crabapples, which just don't look good sticking out of a roasted piglet's mouth. Gather all the old, tired, and even crabbed, apples of every kind together, and let them form the basis of a delicious wine. Call it applejack, or hard cider, or whatever you like; technically, it's really a wine. The apples have enough yeast cells in their skins to produce the alcohol, so you don't have to add yeast (though you *may* if you want quicker action). Or you can help things along by throwing in a few raisins, or even grapes. But let's pretend we don't know about that and see what we can do with just apples, not even adding sugar because the non-crab-apples are sweet enough in themselves. A fruit press would be nice to have, but lacking that, all it takes is a little time and patience.

CIDER
about 3 quarts

about 25 lbs. ripe apples (including some crabapples)
if they're not juicy enough, a little water

Be sure the apples are clean, but don't peel them. Cut them in quarters, and then pound or mash or grind them to a pulp. Core them or not, as you choose. Press out all the juice by passing the crushed apples through a jelly bag, letting it hang for some days and squeezing from time to time. Now put this liquid into your fermentation vat, uncovered, and let stand in a warm place for as long as it hisses. Adding some raisins will facilitate its turning "hard," while adding sugar will make it more properly apple wine. Then put it into the vat with air lock, if you have one, and proceed as though making wine. You can drink it any time after the second fermentation has stopped, but you can also store it up to 2 years, after which time real applejack fanciers say it is just right. (Another test, says one applejack maven, is to store it all in one barrel with a piece of raw beef thrown in. When the meat has entirely disintegrated, the cider is ready to drink. I don't know if this is Yankee leg-pulling or not, but I wouldn't advise it, as the beef might alter the taste of the apples in a dreadful way!)

You can make cider from pears, too. The procedure is the same, though the taste is novel.

Because we may have slighted berries in the chapter before this, let's make wine from berries. Try these two for size.

BLACKBERRY WINE
about 4 quarts

6 lbs. blackberries
rind of 1 lemon
4 lbs. sugar
1 3-oz. package yeast

Wash the blackberries, but try not to crush them in the process. Peel a lemon, and put rind and berries into your fermentation crock. Pour over one gallon of boiling water, and let the fruit stand in it for three days, stirring occasionally. Now strain out the fruit, stir in the sugar, and let it dissolve. Mix the yeast with a little of the warm liquid, and then add it to the vat. Cover, and leave for a day or two in a warm place. Then pour into jug with air lock, and leave to ferment for a week or two. Bottle, first loosely then tightly corked, and store for a month at least before drinking. This is a sweet, purplish-red wine.

GREEN GOOSEBERRY WINE
about 4 quarts

4 lbs. ripe green gooseberries
2 lbs. sugar
1 2-oz. package dry yeast

Remove tops and tails of gooseberries. Heat four quarts of water to boiling, and pour over the berries in your fermenting vat. Mash the berries when cool with a masher or your hands. Leave in place for two days, stirring from time to time. Strain through cheesecloth into fermentation crock, into which you have put the sugar. Stir to dissolve. Then sprinkle the yeast on top of the liquid, cover the vat, and leave it in a warm place for a few days more. Then transfer to air-lock fermenting situation, and leave for a few more days, until it has quieted down completely. Siphon into bottles, and cap loosely. Then, in a day or two more, cork tightly, and store for at least 3 months; 6 to 9 months are even better. The color of this wine is a surprising pale green; it is semisweet.

A countrywoman friend of mine, blessed with a small peach orchard, makes this wine every year, and it is delectable.

PEACH WINE
4 quarts

about 4 lbs. peaches
4 whole cloves
1 lemon
3 lbs. sugar
1 3-oz. package yeast

Don't peel, but stone the peaches, and cut them up. Cut up the cloves, and slice the lemon; add them to the peaches in fermentation crock. Heat a gallon of water to boiling, and pour it over the fruit. Stir, cover, and leave in a warm place for 3 or 4 days, stirring once or twice a day. Then strain out the fruit, and add sugar, stirring it in to dissolve. Soften the yeast in a little warm water, and stir it into the mixture. Transfer wine to the air-lock jug, and leave in a warm place for another few days. Siphon into bottles, cork loosely. A day or so later, cork tightly, and store for at least a month. A pale orange, medium-sweet wine with a spicy edge.

Quince wine could be made in the same way, though the hardness of the ripe fruits would dictate simmering them first to soften. But these lovely tree fruits, which you may have other plans for (like eating fresh or cooking into jam, jelly, or baked dessert dishes) aren't the only things to make wine from. Nearly any fruit, berry, or vegetable will suffice. Try making up a wine, substituting your chosen fruit or nut or vegetable, using the principles outlined above.

Make a wine from a grain, like wheat (use the whole grain, not polished). Or rice. You may think that Japanese favorite *sake* is beyond your occidental powers. Not at all. Here's how.

SAKE (RICE WINE)
about 4 quarts

2 cups white raisins
2 lbs. brown rice (unpolished)
3 cups sugar
1 3-oz. package yeast

Chop the raisins, and put them, with the uncooked rice, into fermentation crock. Add 2 quarts of cold water. Bring 3 more quarts of water to a boil; dissolve the sugar in it, then pour it into the crock. Stir well, and let the liquid cool to lukewarm. Then sprinkle yeast on surface, cover the crock securely, and let it stand in a warm place for 2 to 3 weeks. Stir, separating any clumps of rice, at least once a day. At end of first fermentation, strain the wine into airlock container, add a cleaned, crushed eggshell, and leave another 10 days. Siphon into bottles and leave, loosely capped, for another few days (this wine may take longer than fruit wines to finish fermenting completely). When you are sure it's become still, cork tightly, and store for about 10 months.

Drink this wine either warm or cold; warm is ceremonial in Japan. A colorless beverage that tastes like slightly sweetened rice.

Flowers, vegetables, fruits, and grains aren't the only media for good wines. Many weeds are used, and the leaves of some hardwood trees, the walnut, for example, or the oak. Here is a wine made from leaves.

OAK LEAF WINE
about 4 quarts

a tightly packed gallon of green oak leaves, some young, some older
3 lbs. sugar
rinds of 2 oranges, peeled thin
rind of 1 lemon, peeled thin
1 3-oz. package yeast

Pour a gallon of boiling water over the leaves, and let it stand for a day and a night. Remove the leaves from the liquid, and add the sugar and orange and lemon peels. Bring to a boil, and simmer for 20 minutes. Remove peels, and let cool to lukewarm. Sprinkle in yeast, cover container, and leave in a warm place for 2 or 3 days, stirring daily. Then strain into second container, and let second fermentation take place. When it has finished, siphon wine into bottles, cork loosely, and leave for some time, a few weeks possibly, until you're sure the wine is quiet. Cork tightly and leave for 5 or 6 months before drinking. The flavor of this rather dry, palest-orange wine is hard to describe: try it yourself and see.

Liqueurs

Liqueurs and cordials, which are distilled with the use of pure grain alcohol, present almost too much of a problem to the home winemaker to be worth it. Moreover, even if you could come by the proper neutral alcohol component (which is uncertain in this country), liqueurs would cost you more to make up at home than to buy already manufactured. Liqueurs are for the most part stronger and sweeter than the health-minded kitchen economist cares for —except for an occasional cooking use. The same is true of the fortified wines, such as sherry, vermouth, and marsala. My best advice in this subdivision of the spirit world is to save up your pennies, and buy one liqueur a year. Don't waste any dollars on big-name labels. If there is a house brand, buy it. And comparison shop. Macy's department store in New York City, for instance, carries a sherry that compares favorably with the much-vaunted Harvey's Bristol Cream at about two-thirds the price.

The house brand of vodka at my local Connecticut grog shop is in no way inferior to Smirnoff or Borzoi or any of the vodkas imported from Eastern Europe or wherever at highway-robbery prices. Which reminds me that vodka, being essentially tasteless and colorless, is probably the closest you can come to a pure (potable) alcohol. It therefore suffices for the base if you absolutely insist on trying your hand at some homemade liqueurs. So here are a very few suggestions that may fit in with your garden excess, your supermarket specials, or some other easy source of week-old or stored-in-the-cellar produce. Cordials, synonymous with liqueurs, are nearly always strong, sweet, and aromatic.

Start by making your own gin. Not in the bathtub, but in your very own wine-fermenting crock. Pick some very ripe juniper berries first.

JUNIPER CORDIAL
about 1 quart

3½ cups vodka
½ cup juniper berries
½ cup sugar

If you start with a quart bottle of vodka, from which you have used a little more than a half cup, you're ahead of the game. Just put the berries into the bottle, and recap it. Store in a warm place for a month or more, shaking it well every day or so. Now heat a half cup of water to the boil, remove it from the fire, and dissolve the sugar in it. Cool this syrup, and add it to the vodka bottle, first removing the juniper berries. Cork securely, and store for 6 months. What you will have after that time is a sweet drink that resembles gin in aroma and flavor.

Try an old European favorite made with nuts, whatever nuts you can get your hands on, bearing their flavor in mind. Let's say walnuts, though hickory nuts or almonds would probalby do as well. Gather them while still green and soft-shelled.

NUT LIQUEUR
about 2 quarts

2 dozen green walnuts
1½ quarts vodka
2 tablespoons minced lemon peel
4 cloves
2½ cups sugar
1 teaspoon cinnamon

Shell the nuts, and break up the nutmeats into quarters, roughly. You may have the vodka in its own 2-quart bottle; if not, put all the ingredients into a large bottle or jug, cork or cap it, and leave it in a warm place for 30 to 40 days. Shake it well every day or so. Strain the liqueur through several layers of cheesecloth, then bot-

tle it, corking securely. Store for 8 months to a year
before using. The nutty, spicy flavor of this liqueur will
please you.

Mint grows so crazily in many parts of the United
States that it's considered a pesky weed. If this is true where
you live, perhaps you'd like to make your own crème de
menthe. If you do, just don't expect it to be Kelly green
like so many of the commercial varieties, which are all
artificially colored.

MINT-LEAF CORDIAL
about 1 quart

2 cups fresh mint leaves, any variety
about 30 anise seeds
3 cups vodka
1 lb. sugar

Add the mint leaves and the anise seed to the bottle
of vodka, shake it well, and leave it in a warm, dark
place for 8 or 9 days, shaking every day. Now
make a syrup by simmering the sugar in 2 cups of
water. Strain the vodka into a larger-than-quart bottle.
When the syrup has cooled, pour it into the vodka.
(You can also add a few of the strained-out mint leaves,
for visual interest.) Cork tightly, and store in a cool,
dark place for at least 3 months. This colorless
cordial will have a licorice-mint flavor.

Here's where you fortunate people in some parts of the
country get to use up those fresh apricots that you have

growing in your backyards. Pick them ripe; or use them overripe from your larder.

APRICOT LIQUEUR
about 1 quart

about 1 lb. ripe apricots
1 cup sugar
3½ cups vodka

Put the apricots, skins on, pits in, in a large covered jar, pricking them all over first. Add the sugar, then the vodka, and seal tightly. Shake vigorously, then turn upside down and back a few times in the first few hours (about 24) of fermentation. Now remove the apricots. (Don't throw them away; crush them and use them in a fruit sauce.) Store the liquid in a warm place for about 3 months. Strain through cheesecloth into bottles, and store 3 months before using. A sweet, pale orange-colored libation.

CURRANT CORDIAL
about 1 quart

about 1½ lbs. red currants
2 cups vodka
1 lb. sugar

Wash, but don't stem, the currants. Add them to the vodka in a large bottle or jar. Shake vigorously, and let sit in a warm, dark place for 4 or 5 days, shaking from time to time. Now mix the sugar with a cup of hot water. Strain the vodka into a clean bottle, leaving the currants in the first jar. Pour the cooled-down sugar syrup over the currants, cork both bottles, put them back in the warm, dark place, and leave them to stand 3 days more. Now remove the currants from the syrup, and boil the syrup for 2 or 3 minutes. Cool it, and pour it again over the berries. Add the vodka, cork tightly, and leave 3 *more* days. Then filter the liqueur into a clean bottle, cork securely, and store for at least 2 months in a cool, dark place. The currants should also be stored, separately, in a small jar with a tight cover. When you serve the liqueur, you can add a currant or two to each glass.

This hard-won product is delicious: it has a bright red color and a rich, warm taste.

Note: Any one of these cordials makes a less fierce drink by combining with water or club soda, with or without crushed ice. So for that matter do the wines. Dress them up when you serve them to guests by putting them into a good-looking decanter.

SOFT DRINKS

Too many families are teetering on the brink of bankruptcy from buying bottled or canned soft drinks (and too many roadsides are littered with the empty containers). Making your own at home will save you a lot of space in your trash cans, weight in your shopping bags, and, over the long run, money.

If club soda is responsible for too large a share of your marketing dollar, it may pay you to invest in one of those carbonated siphon machines, into which you insert a carbonation cartridge from time to time. If you are a carbonated-drinks household, it won't take you long to save the price of the gadget.

Soft drinks can then be manufactured in a second by stirring a spoonful of some fruit syrup into a glass of this fizzy water. Where do you get the fruit syrups, nonalcoholic type? Collect them from the cans in which your canned plums, peaches, pineapple are packed. Or from the bottom of the dish in which you defrost those frozen berries. Steal a teaspoonful from your frozen orange-juice concentrate, and stir it up in plain water or soda water for a lovely orangeade. Soft drinks don't have to be bottled in the plant and sold to you at exorbitant prices; use your imagination.

Crushed ice you can achieve by whirling ice cubes in your blender or, lacking a blender, by putting ice cubes into a stout plastic bag (or two, one inside the other) and wielding a mallet or hammer. And crushed ice can make a prosaic fruit drink far more attractive in hot weather. Slice up some oranges and lemons in it, and call it Sangria.

I can't think of a more beautiful way to conclude a discussion of drinks, hard or soft, than by showing you how to make the princess of all fruit syrups, grenadine. True grenadine isn't alcoholic, and for the real McCoy you have to have a few pomegranates, a gorgeous fruit. (You can always add it to vodka or something similar to spirit it up.)

GRENADINE

pomegranates, several, if you can find them
sugar or honey

Remove the seeds from the pomegranates, together with the white substance that surrounds them. Discard the latter. Crush the seeds in a bowl, and strain the liquid into a bowl or crock. Cover this container, and let stand a day and a night, stirring every few hours. Then measure the juice, and add an equal volume of honey or a volume of once-and-a-half as much sugar. Bring the syrup to a boil, then simmer for 20 minutes, skimming foam from surface as it cooks. Pour into warmed bottles (so they won't crack as the hot liquid goes in) and let them cool, corked or capped tightly. Store in a cool, dark place. The syrup may be used immediately and will keep almost indefinitely.

VARIATION: Failing a quick, inexpensive supply of pomegranates, you can make a grenadine-like syrup by substituting red currants or raspberries, or a combination of the two. It won't be grenadine, but it will be a rich, red syrup that can begin your venture into making your own home-style soft drinks.

10

DON'T THROW IT OUT

What is this American mania for discarding? Some of my most successful bits of costuming for house or person have been items that someone else has thrown away. Some of my most delicious meals, too, have been made of things that in the hands of other people would have been destined for the garbage pail. Garbage-can soup may not be an enticing title, but it has saved many a penurious Yankee's life during the cold winter season.

You may have noticed through the previous course of this book admonitions not to throw out bits of this and that, but to put them into a rugged polyurethane bag in the freezer for when you have the time to thaw them out and convert them into a stock or soup-base. This applies to skins, peelings, scales, bones, outer leaves, cores, seeds, pulp, stems, stalks, and the less esthetically pleasing parts of any number of formerly living things that can be converted into food. I think now may be the time to say that possibly you should have as many as five such plastic bags in your freezer, if it can accommodate them, so you can keep the fish remains separated from the poultry carcasses from the meat bones from the vegetable leftovers from the fruits. (I have been known, by the way, to bag and carry home from a formal dinner party the carcass of a duck, which my host and hostess were about to consign to the trash bin. It's true that most of the flesh of a roast duck is easily consumed by a party of four—but what of the scrumptious soup that should follow?) Some savers would recommend a further division: the heavy-flavored vegetables from the less substantial, but that seems to me carrying things a step too far. As does sequestering in this way cheese rinds—they keep so very well attached to their cheeses, *not* in the freezer.

Generally speaking, food that is actually unsafe for you to eat announces itself by its noisome smell. Is there any mistaking a rotten egg, a spoiled piece of meat, a fish that has been out of water (or the freezer) too long? Fruits and vegetables, especially the low-acid ones, can spoil if left around unpreserved for too long before eating. (Interestingly enough, the very enzymes that cause them to grow and ripen are the components that ultimately rot them.) Usually, however, it is only the vitamin content of fruits or vegetables that declines somewhat before you get around to cooking and eating them. Cereals and grain products may mold; but mold is visible and can be removed. Fats and oils may go rancid, but the "stale" taste that results, though unesthetic, is not a danger to your life.

So stop throwing away day-old bread or cake and slightly hoary produce; subject them instead to the nose test, then to your oven or stovetop. Literal tons of edible food are wasted in this land every day because of the misconception that if it's more than an hour from its harvesting or purchase, it's not fit to eat. The animal foods—meats, poultry, fish, and seafood—are the items with which the most care and watchfulness should be exercised: don't keep them unpreserved or uncooked for very long, and chances are you will never have a case of food poisoning.

There is a school of thought that claims a decent chicken soup derives only from starting with a whole bird. But some of the best chicken soups I've ever made (or been served) have evolved from a carcass picked so clean you wouldn't believe it and then frozen *with* the peelings from vegetables and defrosted later for turning into soup. It's hard to remember exactly the ingredients, but I think that one of my prize offerings included the following:

1 chicken carcass plus seasoned bread stuffing adhering to the rib-cage

back and neck donated by a neighbor who cooks only chicken breasts and legs

peelings from 6 white potatoes, 1 eggplant, and 3 small zucchini

stalks from a going-to-wood basil plant

a few parsley stems

a few limp leaves of lettuce and chard

3 old carrots

half an onion, peel and all

the withering leaves from the top of a few stalks of celery

the peel of half a lemon

pinches of salt and pepper

3 quarts water.

Boiled for a half hour and then simmered for another hour and a half on the back of the stove. Then all the glop strained out, but the carrots sliced up and put back in the soup, along with the bits and pieces of chicken meat.

The duck soup, on the other hand, that grew from the destined-to-be-discarded bones mentioned above was, as I recall, made of:

1 duck carcass with a few grains of wild rice adhering

the outer, discardable leaves of 2 bargain artichokes

the skins of 4 baked yams

the shell of a winter squash

all the onion and garlic peelings from my freezer bag

some cucumber peelings left behind by a too-zealous houseguest who'd volunteered to do the salad

a pinch of dried oregano

3 tablespoons orange juice

2 quarts water.

It was marvelous, far more tasty a meal (or rather part of one) than the original roast duck served me by my friends, wild rice notwithstanding. Strained, of course, and served piping hot.

Do you remember the ham bone from Chapter 5? Here's what to do with it, along with the bones left over from your last rib roast of beef. Boil it in a couple of quarts of water, along with any leftover legumes you have in the refrigerator, or freezer bag. One of my best such soups grew out of:

half a can of chick peas that had been pushed to the back of the refrigerator

a handful of dried lentils

the pods (only) from a pound of shelled green peas

a pinch of dried mustard

the green shucks from 6 ears of sweet corn

stalk only from a fresh cauliflower

a bit of grated hard cheese (Romano, I think)

After I had strained it (through a coarse sieve this time, to preserve its thick texture), I threw in a half teaspoon of curry powder when heating it for serving.

That grape must (see page 292) from the chapter before this *might have* served for the making of a "small wine" or "second pressing" drink. But, as it happened, in my house it didn't. It got added to the other fruit remnants of that month and made into a cool, delicious fruit soup. The contents were:

purple grape pressings (white or red would do just as well; only the color of the soup would differ)

skins and cores from 4 Bartlett pears

6 peach *stones only*

a handful of beginning-to-ferment blackberries

skins, cores, stems, seeds, everything but pulp, from about 20 apples

a pinch of powdered clove

½ cup orange juice

½ cup sour cream and ½ cup yogurt

2 quarts water

Everything heated up together, simmered for a half hour, then strained and cooled. Served chilled for a summer lunch, accompanied by some whole-wheat crackers and cheese, it was divine.

But this was possibly not the absolutely best use of apple leavings. If you're making cider (see p. 297), applesauce, apple pie, or any number of delectable things from a variety of apples, you will have a good many peelings and cores to dispose of. Don't throw them away! They are full of pectin (that substance that is the basis of gelatin); you can boil them for a while, strain out the junk, and be left with a sort of loose apple jelly. You can also boil them in water and strain to get drinkable apple juice. Not to be confused with cider, which won't become tasty unless it's *not* boiled, but left to ferment.

You can also use these parings, et al., to make cider vinegar, which is a standard staple item in the economy kitchen. (Your apple wine or cider may *turn* into vinegar if you let lots of extraneous air-borne bacteria get into it by not covering it in the process of fermentation—but that's another story.) To make vinegar, take all these apple left-overs, add a handful of flat oats (raw oatmeal) or rye meal, and cover them with cold water in a wide container. Throw in a jigger of whiskey, or the last cupful of vinegar in your bottle from the grocery, and put the mixture in the sunlight, uncovered, for about a month, transferring to a warm, dry place nightly. What you should draw off in a month's time is apple cider vinegar. It's not exactly a tremendous saving since vinegar is still relatively inexpensive, but you can brag about having made your own vinegar. Don't discard that odd-looking, slightly gelatinous mass on top of the liquid, for that is the culture or "mother," which should be kept in the vinegar.

Making your own baking or brewing yeast is also not worth the candle—it's so obviously one of the great bargains in the supermarket. If, nonetheless, you do want to fool around with it, at least start with a bit of the commercial product. Then you can make it in the following way.

BAKING OR BREWING YEAST

1 large white potato
2 tablespoons flour
1 tablespoon sugar
1 cake yeast or 1 3-oz. package dried

Peel the potato, cover it with water, and boil it until it breaks apart a little. Take the potato out, and mash it with the flour, moistening with a bit of the cooking water. When this mixture has cooled to room tempera-ture, mix the sugar and the yeast together, and add to the potato batter. Pour it into a bowl (glass, earthen-ware, plastic—*not* metal), and leave it in a warm place.

When it has doubled in bulk, divide into small covered dishes and refrigerate, being sure there is room in each container for the batter to rise a little more. It will do this, even under refrigeration, though of course much more slowly than outside.

Some people would call this product sourdough starter. But all it is is yeast.

Here is how to make your own pectin, that substance so necessary in making jellies or jams from fruits (or from wines) whose pectin count is much lower than that of grapes, apples, and some citrus fruits. You must gather your apples green (underripe), though if some nearly ripe get in amongst them, it's probably not serious. Wash the apples (particularly thoroughly if the trees have been sprayed), and remove their stems and blossom corollas. Core and slice them, but *do not peel*. Now weigh them, and for every pound of apples add 2 cups of water to a saucepan. Then simmer the fruit until it is soft. Don't ever let it boil, or come anywhere near to boiling. Just barely simmer, for 15 or 20 minutes.

Now cool a bit, and strain the juice out through a jelly bag or several layers of cheesecloth. Put the pulp from the bag into a saucepan, and add just as much water as you used before. Simmer it again, for about 15 minutes.

Strain it once more, this time squeezing the pulp until it is nearly dry. Put the two juices together, stir to combine, and then store the liquid pectin in a cool place (not freezing) in clean jars or bottles.

You have your jelly-making agent all ready, awaiting your adventure into converting berries and fruits into jellies —which is one very good way of "preserving" them.

Throwing away all your not-so-fresh fruit is a sin against humankind. You could just keep adding it to a big crock in your pantry as it starts to go bad, mixing it together after each addition, and adding a little liquor at the same time. This is, basically, what some people call "Forever Fruit." It is used as a sauce for meats or fish, or a topping for desserts, or stirred into club soda or ginger ale for a fruity, refreshing drink. It doesn't matter what kind of liquor is used—nearly any will preserve the fruits for a long time and aid in their slight fermentation.

What other people call Forever Fruit is actually alcohol-less, more of an easy, loose jam, constructed without heating by just throwing the fruits into a crock and adding a cup of sugar with each addition. The favorite fruits of a friend of mine are pineapple, dark cherries, peaches, and apricots, in that order, preserved in nothing more than their own sugars plus the added cane variety. It can be used in the same ways as the alcoholized version.

Something else never to throw away is the detritus of baking or bakery goods: crumbs of crackers, cakes, and of course biscuits, muffins, breads. Gather them from your cake pans and cookie wrappers and store them in a container marked Sweet Crumbs; the crumbs from your table, cutting board, cracker boxes, and bread baskets in one not marked at all (or marked just plain Crumbs). These crumbs can combine with butter or margarine or grated cheese or what-have-you in wonderful toppings for casserole dishes, or can substitute as crusts for open pies. Bread crumbs can stretch eggs in an omelet or scrambled. Crusts and ends of loaves can either be converted into crumbs or used as chunks in meat loaves, puddings, vegetable casseroles. They can be diced and toasted to serve as croutons for soups or salads. Some Europeans even recycle their bread crumbs and crusts by rebaking them in a rising dough! And as we've seen in the chapter before this one, you'll need a crust or two of bread for the making of wines. I, personally, can't stand the waste of bread—something to do with its being the Staff of Life, I suppose. Most crumbs will last outside the freezer, or even the refrigerator, for a very long time, especially if they are salted or otherwise seasoned.

My next favorite food for not-wasting, I think, is dairy products. It just kills me to see people throw out milk that has gone a little sour, cheese that's got a bit moldy (cheese *is* mold, in a sense), a carton of ice cream with half a cup still sticking to the bottom. (Perhaps it has something to do with my fondness for nanny goats and cows, the chief pur- veyors of dairy products in this country—why should these gentle beasts have manufactured those good products only to use them profligately and then waste half of those we stock?) Possibly it's because the favorite homemade cake from my childhood was one my mother made from sour milk. She, in fact, was often persuaded by the rest of the family, suffering a sour-milk-cake drought, to leave a half-quart out of the refrigerator for a few days of a hot summer, specifically to sour it. Here is her recipe.

GRANDMOTHER PARKER'S
SOUR-MILK SPICE CAKE
6 to 8 servings

1 cup sour milk

1 cup margarine

2 eggs

2 cups flour (1 white, 1 whole-wheat is good)

1 teaspoon baking soda

½ teaspoon salt

2 tablespoons mixed spices: nutmeg, cinnamon, allspice,
clove

brown sugar (optional)

Preheat oven to 375°. Cream together the sour milk and margarine. Stir in the eggs. Then in another bowl sift together the flour, baking soda, and salt. Combine the dry with the moist ingredients, adding the spices at the same time. If you want a crispy, sweet crust on top, sprinkle the top of the batter with brown sugar before you bake it; if you're satisfied to enjoy a spicy flavor uncontaminated, omit the sugar. Bake in a buttered cake pan for 30 or 40 minutes. Test for doneness with a straw.

Yogurt, which has been enjoying such a spate of popularity in this country for the last few years, is essentially soured milk; although in the case of yogurt a very specific bacillus (or at the most two different species)—instead of anything that happens to be flying around in the air—has been introduced into the milk, which is then "cultured" at specific temperatures for a few hours. The economy-minded yogurt fancier should, of course, make his own yogurt at home, thus saving a goodly number of dollars a year over buying it in the market, where it's sometimes even hard to find *plain* yogurt not all glopped up with sweet, sugary fruits.

To get back to cheese, the hard or semi-hard kinds, if they have begun to get a little stale in your refrigerator or cupboard, can be brought back to health and longevity by simply cutting off the offending portions and wrapping the slightly smaller cheese in a damp cloth, then some metal foil. Bear this in mind when debating the saving represented by an economy-size wheel or block of hard (or semi-hard) cheese. Remember also that you will save money by not purchasing hard cheeses like Parmesan, Romano, Peccorino already grated. Buy a block and grate it yourself, thus knocking more than a few pennies off the price.

Soft cheeses such as ricotta or cottage or pot cheese can go bad even if kept refrigerated, especially if you've bought the large, economy size and then not had occasion to use

319

gobs of it. But they are not useless, to be thrown away, when this happens. Such slightly "turned" cheeses, though no longer tasty for eating cold, can be used with impunity in breads, cakes, cooked casseroles—anything that combines them with some grain, vegetable, or meat and then cooks them. Sour-ricotta griddle cakes are perfectly edible, even flavorsome. Likewise sour pot-cheese liver-and-vegetable casserole, or corn muffins. Slightly spoiled cottage cheese combines with eggs and flour into a lovely New England breakfast or supper dish called Humpty Does. Recipes for all these food-saving dishes follow.

CHANGELING-RICOTTA PANCAKES
breakfast for 2

1 cup souring ricotta
½ cup milk
1¼ cups flour
1 teaspoon baking powder
4 tablespoons melted shortening or oil
salt, to taste

Blend all ingredients together into a drop batter. Heat some cooking oil (or margarine) on a griddle until it crackles when you sprinkle a drop of water on it. Spoon the batter onto the griddle in serving-spoonfuls. As soon as bubbles appear on one side of the pancakes, flip them over and cook the other side. Keep the finished pancakes warm until you have used up all the batter, then serve them warm, with cold applesauce on the side.

If one of the "two" that are expected to breakfast on these (or any other) pancakes should suddenly rush out of the house on some emergency errand *after* the cakes have been put into the warming oven, don't throw away the uneaten portion. Pop them into the refrigerator, and use them to roll around a tiny frank-furter, a stalk of asparagus, a cup of dates plus some cottage cheese, or any dip or spread you have invented. Secure with a toothpick or skewer, and give them to him/her as a dessert, lunchtime snack, or cocktail accompaniment tomorrow. Or if you freeze the extra griddle cakes with a breakfast more than a day away in mind, you can just defrost them partially or completely, pop them into the toaster (run through twice if just out of the freezing compartment) and serve them as toast.

OLD POT CHEESE MUFFINS
about a dozen

½ cup sour pot cheese
½ stick margarine (or 4 tablespoons other grease)
½ cup flour (half and half whole-wheat and white
would be nice)
½ cup yellow cornmeal
1 teaspoon salt
2 teaspoons baking powder
¾ cup water or milk

Preheat oven to 400°. Rub the souring pot cheese and margarine together. Sift the flour, and combine it with the cornmeal, salt, and baking powder. Blend the dry ingredients into the cheese and margarine, adding the water or milk as you go along. Butter a baking tin, and spread the batter into it. Bake for 30 to 40 minutes, until the top is somewhat browned and is beginning to crack open. Cool, and cut into twelve square muffins. (Unless you own a muffin tin with twelve individual cups in it—in which case, butter each cup, and divide the batter up into the twelve cups, then shorten your cooking time a little.)

Should your elbow slip and you make too much of this (or nearly any other) bread batter, don't throw it away or feed it to the cat. Put it in a plastic container, and freeze it against the time you may want to deep-fry tempura, aging vegetables, fish cakes, or chicken. Then thaw it out, loosen it with a little milk or water—and coat your fryable food with it.

COTTAGE CHEESE HUMPTY DOES
breakfast for 2

2 small eggs
½ cup cottage cheese that has started to "turn"
2 tablespoons sour cream (commercial variety)
small handful raisins
salt, to taste
4 or 5 tablespoons flour

Beat the eggs slightly, then stir in the cottage cheese, sour cream, raisins, and salt. Sift the flour, and add it to the mixture, stirring until the batter is almost smooth. Then proceed as with pancakes.

While we're speaking of breads of a sort, I'd like to remind you that baking bread at home is, despite the higher prices of its ingredients, still far cheaper and more satisfying than making the Arnold, Pepperidge Farm, or other rich companies still richer. Baking your own bread is a sure method of knowing you have fresh-baked loaves (if that means something to you). *And* of impressing your dinner guests. You do, however, have to be on hand, not far from your kitchen, for a number of hours, so it presents something of a time problem to the fully-employed-outside-the-home.

If you're not going to turn into a home baker, go for the so-called day-old breads, and other bakery products as well, in the market. Freshening them up if they are harder than you think they should be is a simple matter: just sprinkle them with water and leave in your oven at 300° for 10 minutes or so.

If your excuse for not becoming a home baker is that you feel you're not up to it, put that idea out of your head immediately. To make risen bread doesn't take a high I.Q., a tennis champion's strength of hand, or James Beard's authority. All it takes is a leavening agent, some flour, and some liquid. And to prove this to you, here following are the two easiest breads in the world to make, either of which has it over your ordinary commercial product eleven ways. They are basic, white-flour breads; you can experiment with combinations of flours, the addition of herbs, eggs, sweetening (if you must), etc., after you've baked these successfully. The only difference between them is that one requires a certain amount of kneading and the other almost none. They should both be allowed to rise twice. First the "hard" one.

BASIC MILK-AND-SHORTENING BREAD
2 loaves

3 cups milk
3 tablespoons margarine
1 3-oz. package dry yeast
6 to 8 cups white all-purpose flour
1 tablespoon salt

Scald the milk (bring to a boil and then immediately remove from heat), and pour it over the margarine in a big bowl. When it has cooled to lukewarm (use the wrist-test if you don't trust your fingertips), scatter the yeast on the surface, and leave it there until the yeast has softened and begun to swell. Sift the flour if it looks lumpy to you. (I have a sifter that fits snugly on top of a one-cup measuring cup—I sift directly into that.) Add the salt to the first cup or two of flour as you stir it into the liquid. Then stir in the next two cups. And the next two. Until what you have in the bowl is a dough you can handle without too much sticking to your fingers. Now sprinkle some more flour on your bread board, pastry cloth, or other surface (directly on a Formica work surface is all right, or on a scrubbed wooden kitchen table). Turn the batter out of the mixing bowl onto the layer of flour, and start kneading: pushing, pulling, punching, folding over, turning around, and punching again. If it sticks to your hands, scatter a bit more flour in as you knead—there's no set amount that is sacred. When it stops adhering to the board or your fingers—that is when you can stop kneading. Grease the inside of a bowl or pan or little tub; shape the dough to fit, and drop it in. Turn it over once so a little of the grease is on top of the surface of the dough. Leave bowl in a warm place for a couple of hours or so, with a soaked, then wrung out, rag or dish towel on top. If it's the wrong season or climate for sunlight, then put the whole shebang into your oven, turn the temperature to the very bottom of the "warm" range, leave it on a few minutes, then turn it off without opening the oven door. Check every half hour or so to see if you need to repeat this warming procedure (it depends on how well insulated your oven is).

When it looks to you as if the dough has doubled in bulk (1 to 3 hours, again depending on the heat, the liveliness of the yeast, and so on), reknead the dough on a floured surface for a few minutes. Now grease two baking pans or glass dishes or loaf pans or whatever. (Coffee cans with one end removed and the insides buttered are favored by some home bakers—they make nice round loaves.) Divide the

dough into two roughly equal portions, and place one
in each baking container. Put back into the warm place,
and allow to rise again, using the same system as on
the first rising. (Omit the wet cloth this time, or you
may soon have a bread that's got a cloth for its crust.)
When the dough has doubled in bulk again, or nearly
so, it's time to turn on the high heat. Bake at 350°
for 50 minutes to 1 hour. Give it the straw or toothpick test for doneness, but not before 50 minutes have
passed. When it is baked, turn the loaves out onto
racks to cool before you freeze one (if you don't
anticipate eating both within a couple of days). If you
will want to defrost and eat a half loaf at a time, cut
the finished, cooled loaf in half before you freeze it in
two plastic bags or waxed commercial bread wrappers.

POOR PEOPLE'S WATER BREAD
2 loaves (or 1 large)

*This is the very simple one, the bread you don't need
to knead very much.*

3 cups water
1 3-oz. package dry yeast
6 to 8 cups white all-purpose flour
1 to 2 tablespoons salt

Heat the water to just lukewarm—or let hot tap water
cool a bit—and scatter the yeast over its surface in a
big bowl or heatproof pan or tub. Sift the flour if it
seems to need it, and add by cupfuls to the water (stir
in the salt at any point), stirring the dough at each
addition until you have achieved what looks to you
like a thick paste. Put the bowl of dough into a warm
place, covered with a damp cloth. Let it rise until it
doubles in bulk. Now flour your work surface or

bread board liberally, and dump the dough onto it. Knead or work the dough only long enough to be able to handle it. Divide it into two roughly equal parts, and shape them to fit the pans you are going to bake in. (The last time I made this bread I greased my 9 x 13 baking pan and made one big oval loaf in this. It looked very impressive and "peasanty.") Grease the pans and put the dough in. Now just leave it around the kitchen for a half hour or so (unless your kitchen is absolutely frigid) to do its second rising. This gives you time to fill a pan with water, and put it on the lowest shelf or floor of the oven, which is a good idea in baking this bread, though not absolutely essential. Turn the oven on to 350°. Sprinkle the top of the dough with water before you put it in the oven. And if you want an interesting texture on top, cross-cut the surface of the dough with a knife dipped in cold water. (If it's going to be one big loaf that you're going to let the family tear pieces off at suppertime, you can facilitate the tearing by cutting a bit deeper into the top of the dough.) Bake in the preheated 350° oven for 50 minutes to 1 hour. Test for doneness as above, and let cool before eating or freezing part of the bread.

This bread makes good French or Italian loaves if you get it floury enough to roll into long, skinny shapes. It could also be baked in one big oval or circular loaf, on a cookie sheet on which you have first spread a layer of cornmeal. If it is a flat cookie sheet with no upturned edges, just watch the second rising to see that it doesn't spread off the edges. Once it gets into the preheated oven, it won't spread very much farther.

Biscuit or muffin dough can also be frozen for future reference, if you decide midstream that you are making too much for your immediate needs. Some home bakers swear by empty round frozen-fruit-juice cartons for this purpose. Just line the little tube with waxed paper, and spoon the uncooked dough in with a bit of waxed paper between spoonfuls. Then waxed paper the top, and fix with a rubber band. Instant muffins all ready to bake when you thaw this out.

I'd like now to make a case for the saving of leftover vegetables of every description in a pot on the back of the stove. So to speak. The *pot au feu* of the French peasant can be the means of saving a good deal of money that would otherwise line the coffers of Mr. Campbell. Do you find at the weekend's conclusion a little bit of spinach, half a cupful of baked beans, a sprig of cauliflower with most of its flowerettes attached, several tablespoons of tomato sauce at the bottom of a casserole dish, one medium-sized roasted but not consumed potato? Into the pot on the back of the stove (or in the refrigerator if there's room—I'm not a purist)! Some poor, soggy-looking cubes of squash alongside the parsley with which you garnished last night's dinner plates? Into the pot for rescuing leftover, unloved portions of any vegetable. If you bring it to a boil once every other day, it can go on collecting for three weeks or so before it arrives at the stage where you think it's now or never—to be served as thick soup or thin stew. And it will probably be just as good as the mixed-vegetable peasant soups served in so many out-of-the-way restaurants in Europe, or in Mary Elizabeth's Soup Kitchen on East 36th Street, New York City.

Never, never throw away the pasta bits adhering to the edges of the baking dish from your last pasta concoction. They may look to you as if they are too hard and brown to enjoy a new life, but as chopped-up additions to your thick soup or thin stew, they will space out the vegetables nicely. And you won't even have to boil up a potful of rice to "go with"; the meal will achieve a nice balance with the addition of starch in this form.

What are you going to do with that one lorn frankfurter that you have left over from the cookout in the backyard the other night? Throw it out? Give it to the dog? Fie! Why, obviously it gets sliced up very thin and added to the creamed vegetable dish you're giving the kids for lunch today. (My sainted mother used to retread all the vegetables from the night before—when briefly she was feeding only herself and me school-time lunches at home. She'd throw in a little white sauce or leftover gravy, in two little individual-size beanpots, and announce Surprise Casserole. It was never a surprise, but it often included half a sliced-up commercial hot dog, which is probably all the hot dog a budding gourmet needed to be put off those creatures forever.)

Some pretty hot-stuff leftover cooks are willing to go along with all these things, inventing dishes by the thousands, as long as they pertain to meats, poultry, vegetables, or farinaceous dishes. But for some reason they draw the line at saving fruit leftovers. When, of course, fruits make some of the best concoctions around, for dessert, molded summer salads, and more. Fruits have other fascinating uses too. Lemon skins should be retained for a while and used to clean your fingers after you've done some particularly messy, staining domestic job. Even banana skins aren't a total loss: if you have run out of shoe polish some pre-stepping-out day, you can get a good shine on your toes (or handbag or belt or whatever) by rubbing it with the inside of a banana skin.

Coffee grounds may have struck you as one thing that no one could really find a use for—that damp little brown mess at the bottom of the pot that your mother used to wash down the sink to keep it drained—a practice that you may have learned is folly. Coffee grounds, left uncovered in a tin can or plastic dish and put into the bottom of a closet, will keep it cleared of musty odor, and in the refrigerator will combat sourness and rancid smells. So will an opened container of baking soda, but that you may have more primary uses for, like baking with it.

Don't throw away your vegetable-cooking water: pour it all together in a stockpot in the refrigerator or freezer for thawing out to become the first quart of liquid that you use when making a soup. You can even use beet-cooking liquid for a natural food coloring (freeze it in small amounts, for example in individual ice-cube containers, for quick and easy defrosting). I added some recently to an applesauce that was made from very pale-fleshed apples, to perk it up. I also had a good result when "coloring" yellow-tomato sauce with beet-cooking liquid. A little goes a long way (but it will go moldy if left in the refrigerator for more than a few days). Its taste is so bland that it seldom influences the flavor of whatever you add it to.

When you cook a soup with a fatty meat involved, what do you do with the fat that collects on the top? Skim it off and right into the garbage can, right? Stop this waste: save the skimmed-off fat in a jar in your refrigerator, and use it to sauté things in. It is nowhere written that you must sauté meats, fish, or vegetables only in virgin oil or first-time margarine. This recycled fat can serve nicely for frying.

When you peel an eggplant or squash for *ratatouille* or some such combined dish, what do you do with the peelings? If your soup bag has just been emptied and hasn't yet dried out to begin again, why not put the eggplant peelings into the refrigerator and use them to make a sort of crust or covering for a baked soft-vegetable mélange that you're going to make tomorrow to use up all those little half-cups of this and that left over from other meals?

The salad-vegetables bin in the refrigerator should be examined once or twice a week for spoilage. If you find in it some radishes (of any color), plus half a cucumber that is getting a touch slimy, and a handful of scallions (bulbs and greens) that have seen better days—don't throw them out for the rabbits: peel them and remove the really gooey parts, then stew them up together in just a little vegetable stock or water for an interesting new vegetable adventure. Radishes don't belong only in cold raw salads, as you'll discover. Limp stalks of celery, or carrots, can be refreshed quickly in ice water; but if that doesn't do the job, into the soup bag with them.

An important aspect of kitchen money-saving is the recycling of paper products. Our grandmothers did nicely without paper toweling, but the contemporary cook doesn't seem able to live without a roll or two of paper toweling a month. My own tendency is to bring home from un-posh dining out the paper napkins from the table, for my greasy-pan wiping out and the draining of some kinds of vegetables that have soaked in water. My salad greens get rolled up in an old turkish towel, which works fine.

There are two things you can do without much trouble to cut down on the number of rolls of paper toweling you have to buy in a year. First, let there be only one layer of paper toweling between your draining eggplant and a layer of newspaper underneath (everyone always has some newspaper around the house that's been read and not yet burned or collected for recycling by the local scout troop). And second, don't be too embarrassed to dry out your nongreasy paper toweling for use another day. By practicing these simple habits, I have cut down my toweling purchase to two rolls a year.

My wintertime cat-litter purchase has also just been eliminated from my marketing list. After years of believing that those claylike products that claim to be so absorbent and deodorizing really *are,* I recently put it to the test: I tore up half an issue of the daily newspaper in the cat's box and dumped this for fresh newspaper each day. The newspaper treatment actually smelled less than the commercial cat litter! No complaints from the cat, or the person who habitually cleaned up the scattered sand each morning, either. So don't throw away your daily paper after it's read. Instead, stop believing the advertising for the commercially produced cat litter.

While we're on the indelicate subject of toilets, do you

buy two kinds of tissue for the bathroom? Stop this waste immediately; start blowing your nose or wiping off excess face cream with toilet tissue. During the Depression days of the thirties, by the way, the toilet tissue in my home more often than not was demoted dressmaking patterns. And surely I don't need to remind some readers of the Sears Roebuck or Montgomery Ward catalog days. . . .

Now I want to tell you a saga of leftovers. Call it, if you will, The Liver That Had Nine Lives. It is a living demonstration of how never throwing anything away can not only save you many dollars but also save your life from utter boredom during a winter siege. My husband and I were recently snowed in for five days in the country with a cranky cat and a nonfunctioning automobile. Couldn't get to the market, and didn't want to in any case. Had enough work to keep us busy for ten twenty-four-hour days without having to interrupt ourselves for a two-hour marketing stint. Here's how a pound of beef liver stretched out to take on many guises, lend distinction to many dishes. It was, I think, a triumph of invention and kitchen economy—moreover, every evening meal was delicious, nourishing, and cheap.

The first night I cooked sixty-nine cents' worth of beef liver in beer (see page 127) and we ate it with boiled, then mashed, potatoes and a small green salad that finished off my fresh greens. No problem. Then the snows started falling. At this first sitting, we consumed about one third of the liver and onions. I put one third in the refrigerator and froze one third.

For evening number two I defrosted my final one-pint carton of yellow-tomato purée made last summer and frozen. I found in the vegetable crisper one last whole green bell pepper, and in a storage tin some uncooked rice. Let's see, if this were a leftovers cookbook, the recipe would read something like this:

LEFTOVER DISH I

⅓ of the recipe for Beef Liver in Beer
1 sweet green bell pepper
vegetable oil
a bit less than 1 pint yellow-tomato purée
salt and pepper, to taste
1 cup uncooked rice

Take the liver-and-onions-in-beer out of the refrigerator
and the tomato purée out of the freezer. Core, seed,
and cut up the bell pepper; soften it in a bit of vegetable oil. Add both the pepper and the liver-and-onions
to the tomato purée, as well as salt and pepper, and
simmer this sauce for half an hour. Meanwhile, cook
the rice in boiling salted water to *al dente* consistency.
Serve the meat sauce over the rice, hot.

Beautiful. We ate about two thirds of this dish. The
third day dawned cold and still snowy. A hard day's work
and then we peered into the slimming-down stores that night.
I found in the freezer a package of cut-in-strips zucchini
that I'd stored at the end of my swimming-in-squash period
in October. Also half a box of shell pasta, and some other
remnants. That night's dinner went like this:

LEFTOVER DISH II

½ lb. shell pasta
1 stalk celery, plus leaves, chopped
vegetable oil
⅓ of Leftover Dish I
1 cup frozen (and defrosted) zucchini strips
¼ cup yogurt

10 pine nuts (left over from making *caponata*)
½ cup cooked green peas

Preheat oven to 375°. Boil the shell pasta in salted water to *al dente* stage. Drain. Brown the chopped celery in a little oil. Mix all the ingredients together to blend well, add just a little water, and put it into a buttered casserole dish. Bake for 40 minutes and serve hot.

Not bad. Handsome and tasty. We ate all but about one-quarter of this casserole.

By the fourth evening, the orange color of the original tomato sauce had blended with other foods into a pale shadow of its former brilliance—and there was not much left of the liver but a sort of reminiscent flavor. No more onions in the house, but two cloves of garlic to mince into the dish. There were quite a few of the shells intact, and some beets for color. . . .

LEFTOVER DISH III

¼ of Leftover Dish II
2 cloves garlic
¾ cup sliced cooked beets, leftover
8 green olives
½ cup whole milk
2½ cups cooked cauliflowerettes, leftover
2 tablespoons grated Romano-Parmesan cheese

Preheat oven to 375°. Scoop the shells out of the left-over casserole, and chop them rather small. Peel and mince the garlic. Cut the sliced beets somewhat smaller. Slice up the green olives. Mix these ingredients with whatever else is left of last night's casserole dish, stirring in a little milk. Put it into a baking dish, arrange the cauliflower in a pattern on top, and sprinkle the cheese over. Bake for 45 minutes and serve, hot.

Nearly finished this one—only about a cupful of this strange mélange left. Don't throw it away though. Who knows what tomorrow will bring? We remember the third of a pound of liver-in-beer in the freezer, so start it thawing out for tomorrow.

The fifth day is the hardest workday of all, for both of us. Deadlines tomorrow and a practically empty refrigerator, the two remaining eggs and pint of yogurt being carefully hoarded for the muffins and hot breads that would spell the difference in our other meals (breakfast or lunch, or brunch). The certainty that the *next* day, surely, we could begin to fill in the empty spaces in our staples and stores. And there *were* still a couple of potatoes on the cellar stairway. Yet we didn't want to repeat dinner number one, with the one third of the original liver-in-beer and mashed potatoes (minus the green salad). Peering pessimistically into the kitchen cabinet produced only more pasta. But wait—lo and behold, behind the spaghetti boxes one can of Boston Baked Beans, bought, naturally, on a fantastic "special" and stuffed back there against a rainy day. Beside it, the last jar of pickles I put up when the cucumbers were flowing like water. So we combined the now-defrosted liver-and-onions with the beans, and then noticed that one of the two remaining eggs was hard-cooked. . . . This last, best dish of all went something like this:

LEFTOVER DISH IV

⅓ of recipe for Beef Liver in Beer
1 16-oz. can Boston Baked Beans (in tomato sauce)
¼ cup dill-pickled cucumber slices

Preheat oven to 375°. Combine the liver and onions in sauce with the baked beans, stirring to distribute evenly. Chop the pickles somewhat smaller, and add them to the mixture. Spoon the mixture into a casserole dish. Slice the egg, and arrange the slices on the top of the dish in a circle, then sprinkle it liberally with curry powder, over eggs and all. Bake, uncovered, for 40 minutes.

This one was so delectable, despite how it may sound, that we ate it all, thus saving ourselves from thinking up what to do the next evening. Each one of these dishes was an invention, a compromise, a making-do. All were quite splendid, with a variety of tastes and appearances. The cost was minuscule, but the nourishment was great. And the satisfaction this serial supper brought me was stupendous.

This narrative also demonstrates that the art and science of leftover cooking is no such thing—it is spontaneous innovation, which no one need be afraid of. You can do it. And the combinations that result from just such emergencies as my wintertime snowing-in make it a lot of fun, and show us how really inessential are some of the things we always thought we had to stock all the time.

The next time you fail to get to the market on your usual day, count yourself lucky: you're going to save a lot of food money that week. You may also invent some dishes that will become classics in your home. Just take a very hard look into your freezer, refrigerator, and grocery cabinet—and let your imagination do the rest.

P.S. I have just returned from my biweekly trip to the landfill area (alias the town dump), where I deposited some

scrap metal, a half pound of bargain cat food that my per-
snickety old feline refused, and some flattened tin cans; I
picked up some clay flower pots, a snowsuit that will see
one of my grandchildren through next winter, and some
choice gossip. While engaged in conversation with a neighbor, I also analyzed the garbage that three of my compatriots
were throwing out and came up with the following list of
admonitions. When you're reorganizing your garbage-can
philosophy and resurrecting the old notion of waste-not,
want-not, please study this modest collection of Don't Discards.

EGG SHELLS: Empty ones, of course. Use them to
clarify wines or to feed houseplants: water your
plants with water in which the eggshells have soaked
for a few days—an easy source of calcium, sulphur,
and a few other minerals that promote growth.

FLOUR AND OTHER MEAL: That bit in the bottom of
the paper bag in which you have dredged pieces of
meat, fish, poultry, vegetables. Even if seasoned, it
can be used to thicken your next gravy or sauce.

THE LAST OUNCE: Of cereals, crumbs, even sauces
or other liquids which remain in the corners or bottoms of the bag, carton, or jar in which you bought
them. Get it out with spoons, fingers, even with
water. You paid for it—don't waste it.

PICKLE AND OLIVE LIQUID: The stuff that remains in
the jars after you have fished out and eaten the
pickles and olives. Use it in place of vinegar (or
oil) for the next home-grown vinaigrette sauce you
make.

CONDIMENT CONTAINERS: The little covered plastic
cups of ketchup, salad dressing, etc., you're served
on some transportation (airplanes, trains, etc.) They
will save you pennies in postponing your next condiment purchase, and the empty containers themselves are very useful in a thrifty kitchen.

SALT AND PEPPER SERVINGS: Again, those little single servings in paper that come with your catered or

transport meal. Great to pack in lunchboxes or take on picnics.

SEEDS: Those you scoop out of vegetables like squashes before you cook them. Toasted on low heat in the oven, and salted, they make good-for-you snacks in place of sweets.

LEGUME PODS, NUT SHELLS, PIT SKINS: Boiled up together, these make natural, harmless food colorings.

PRESERVING JARS WITH NO TOPS: Good dry-foods storage containers. Or to keep already preserved foods. Fashion airtight seals from wax paper and foil, and high-acid fruits can also be kept in them.

PLASTIC BOTTLES, SQUARE: The sort some liquid bleaches come in make splendid birdfeeders or houses for wrens and other small birds. Cut an appropriate hole in the side and nail to a tree or the side of your house.

PLASTIC BOTTLES, ROUND: The kind you sometimes buy cider in are convertible to all manner of toy animals. See what different beasts are suggested to your imagination. For example, use the bottle cap for a snout, four corks for legs, pieces of felt or cardboard for ears, a twist of pipe cleaner for a tail, and presto! a pig. Cut a slit in his back and you have a piggy bank—to put your pinched pennies in.

11

EVERYTHING
UNDER THE KITCHEN SINK

Products for cleaning and beautifying the home and person represent, I don't need to tell you, a multimillion dollar industry. The ubiquitous advertising for these competing substances pollutes the media. We can hardly pick up a periodical whose pages aren't filled with the wondrous changes in your love life that toothpaste X will work, nor can we turn on the television without being bombarded by the miracles that household cleaner Y will perform in your home. The kitchen economist, however, is not the sort of person who will throw away countless dollars a week on a vast arsenal of spray-cans or fill the medicine cabinet with armies of skin creams, deodorants, shampoos, and cosmetics. To fall for every new product on the market that promises to bring a sparkle to your eyes, hair, windows, or dining room table is to be just as much a spendthrift as to buy a sirloin steak or live lobster for dinner every night. Or to throw away your new shoes after one wearing.

In the area of household cleaners, where too many hard-earned pennies are squandered needlessly, there is a staggering array of Name Brands, one of which is not very different in composition from another. But the most dramatic similarity from product to product is that, as with processed foods, what you are really paying for is the combining of elements—called "manufacture"—and their packaging, distribution, and *advertising*. In other words, the inflated price you're paying for a cleaning agent (money earned by the sweat of your brow) is shelled out to pay for the advertising that persuaded you to overpay for this over-priced item in the first place! What a vicious cycle! It doesn't make sense to reasonable people; why not fool the adver-tisers by refusing to buy any product whose advertising you object to, or whose jingle or trademark line makes the air-waves hideous? You will find that through this device alone —restricting your purchases to house brands or those that are advertised modestly or not at all—you will save quite a few dollars every week.

The second thing you can do is to find out what these preparations are composed of, and make your own at home. The basic ingredients, bought in bulk at your local grocery, hardware store, or pharmacy, always come to far less than the manufactured (and mass-produced) product. Moreover, we can *grow* some of the components. This is not always easy for the modern home operator: how many of us still slaugh-ter our own meat, thereby deriving a lot of animal fat with which to boil up some soap or candles? Or have access to a beehive from which to rob the beeswax? Or raise enough witch hazel to make ourselves a bottle of rubbing alcohol? Besides, the formulae of commercial products can still be carefully guarded by the manufacturers if the product is not something destined to be ingested. Hence it's our business to go back to some of the old-time literature to discover what the original household aids were, before the specialization and overproduction of the last century or so set in.

Actually, with a bottle each of vinegar, ammonia, and turpentine, a can of lard, a crock of salt, and a jar of baking soda, we could probably come up with essentially the same cleaning agents that we find in bewildering array underneath many a kitchen sink. Throw in some borax, and you've got it. We don't really *need* a different kind of preparation for the cleaning of every different variety of metal, for instance —oxidation is oxidation, and that's what makes copper dull and silver black. There is no excuse for the kitchen economist to stock ninety-three separate soaps. The soap that washes your sheets and towels is not wrong for your dainty lingerie; cake soap and soap flakes or powder are not basically diverse, and you can save more than a few pfennigs a week by creating soap flakes (if you're wedded to the idea of flakes) through scraping them off your cake soap with a swivel vegetable peeler. I suspect that if we threw a pinch or two of borax into the washing machine and turned it on to "warm water," our wash would be just as clean as if scalded "Rinso White."

One kind of plain cake soap will do for most of your laundering needs and for bathing as well. (I personally never buy any, as I manage to bring home, from the one or two hotel stays I spend each year, enough cake soap to see me through baths and face-and-hands washing for the twelve months. Proprietors of such hostelries tell me they expect the soap to be taken home by guests—that's why some of them advertise on the soap wrappers.) Fancy, scented, and colored soaps have no place in the penny-pincher's kitchen or bath. A special soap for washing dishes is another needless expense—the soap that's good enough for your skin is good enough for your dishes. In fact, hot water as it comes from the tap is really all you need (all I ever use) for washing dishes. Along with some plastic-mesh sort of scraper for cleaning baking dishes or casseroles (some kitchen economists draw the line even at this device, believing that fingernails were made for this process).

I still have under my sink the tail end of a bottle of bilious green liquid soap that a friend who lived in my house for a month five years ago felt she couldn't live without. Obviously it would have stretched for five years if she had used it only when nothing else would serve. Along about that time the whole phosphate-detergent matter came to decisive public attention (we are dirtying our waters with things intended to clean!), and I ceased using all questionable' soaps and detergents. No more harsh alkalines were going into the water system because of me! The box of all-vegetable biodegradable cleaning powder that I bought about the time my friend departed my house is still only half gone. It can be used to launder every kind of fabric that is safe in water—as well as the human pelt and skin. This "natural" product was not cheap, but I'll wager its price has been spent by most of my readers several times over each year on a variety of soaps, one for the dishwasher, one for the washing machine, one for cottons, one for silks and nylons, etc., etc. Stop this waste. If you must have a soapy soap for the Monday wash, one large box of Fels Naptha powder should last you for *months* if you scoop out about one third as much as your friendly appliance dealer tells you should go into every machine-load. (Save yourself some kilowatt expenditure, too, by washing in warm rather than hot water, which is absolutely unnecessary for all but the most grease-caked, filthy clothes.) Suds is the other misconception that is costing you money. Suds have never been proved essential in getting clothes clean—quite the opposite, they *waste* your soap. Stop worrying about the cleaning agent that doesn't result in a mountain of suds. Solvent is what gets dirt out, and that excludes suds. The most useful all-purpose solvent of all is water. H_2O. Just plain water. Hot for dishes, warm for clothing, and you're all set. Turn the television set off during the commercials—or use their duration to go out of the room to tend to a chore somewhere else.

Aerosol propulsion cans are another terrible ripoff. Do you know that in one of these cans you are paying anywhere from two to ten times the price for a product that is anywhere from one half to nine tenths propellants? Besides which, recent research indicates that these little dandies are responsible for messing up the earth's atmosphere in such a way that the incidence of certain types of cancer will proliferate. What makes it worth the extra cost and the medical risk?

You doubtless throw away at least a sixty-nine-cent cake's worth of people-soap a month by not gathering up your worn-down-to-a-nub soap ends, melting them together in a small pan, then letting them cool and harden into a new cake of soap. Or if, like me, you operate on a collection of small "guest" size soap cakes, they can be pressed together into a satisfyingly larger size by sandwiching some melted soap ends in between two cakes.

Here are some low-priced products to take the place of the myriad this-and-that cleaners beneath your kitchen sink or in the utility room. I think I have listed every sort of material needing cleaning that is found in the average house or apartment. (If there is something I've omitted, write me a letter.)

Then we'll go on to the cleaning—and beautifying—of the human substance. No more fortunes lost on separate tile cleaners, linoleum cleaners, etc., night cream, morning emulsion, noontime face cleanser, and so on, ad infinitum.

TILE: If plain old soap and water doesn't do it, try adding a little vinegar to the water. Terribly dirty tile will give way to kerosene (a whole quart for a few pennies from your local service garage). Then give it a protective film with any kind of wax— beeswax, paraffin, even the paste wax you bought (before reading this book) for your floors and furniture.

LINOLEUM: Good old soap and warm water. But be sure to dry it: one way is to spread newspapers over it to soak up the excess moisture (don't worry, the newsprint won't come off on the linoleum, unless you go over it with a hot pressing iron). Again, a good wax finish (see above) will save you having to wash it quite so often, and will save you soap as well. (Not too much wax, or you'll fall and break your neck.)

WINDOWS: Hot water, with perhaps a few drops of vinegar added, is still the best window cleaner going. The point about washing windows (and any other glass, like mirrors) is that, to avoid streaks, you must not let them dry on their own. A sponge in one hand that you keep dipping into hot water, and wadded-up newspaper in the other, is the answer. Do a small bit at a time, sponging wet, then wiping dry. (A drop of kerosene in the water will also serve to brighten.)

VINYL AND OTHER PLASTICS: Can be cleaned with hot water and a little gentle soap. If you want, you may add a little baking soda (sodium bicarbonate, and bought under that name cheaply at drugstores) to the water, 2 to 4 tablespoons to the quart. This is the best cleaner for the insides and outsides of refrigerators, whether plastic or metal-based, for stoves, for counter tops of Formica, too.

WOOD SURFACES: Hot water again, plus a bit of soap if you're not going to eat or prepare food on the surface. Cabinets or floors, whether painted or not, can benefit from scrubbing with soapy water. Then if they're unfinished, a mixture of equal parts turpentine and linseed oil (both very cheap at your hardware store) makes a good finish. Butcher blocks and other wooden table tops that may be eaten from directly should be cleaned by scrubbing with a clean brush and hot water. I always use a little bit of salt, too. And if you want to oil it, use a light vegetable oil.

WOOD FURNITURE: Unfinished: three parts boiled linseed oil, two parts vinegar, one part turpentine, rubbed with a soft cloth. Highly polished: rub with warm beer, dry quickly with a soft cloth. Lemon oil polish is a highly touted (and, I admit, delicious-smelling) product that many a householder has gone to the poorhouse over, after cleaning and polishing his mahogany table tops. Yes, it's good—but it's only that no-brand liquid mineral oil, to which a few drops of oil of lemon have been added. Can you manage to extract from the next half dozen lemons you buy all the oil in their skins? (Not lemon juice, which is too highly acidic, but the oil in the peelings) or perhaps you can purchase instead a small bottle of oil of lemon and mix your own very good fragrant furniture polish.

DISCOLORED WHITE FABRIC: You don't have to waste money on a dozen kinds of bleaches and whiteners if you add to the rinse of your white wash once in a while a tablespoon of turpentine. Or boil it in some water to which you have added cream of tartar, 3 or 4 tablespoons to the quart. If it isn't the sort of thing you can just dunk into a bath, try scrubbing at it with a cloth dipped in lemon juice.

MARBLE: No-brand mineral oil, bought for pennies from the drugstore or hardware shop. Make a paste of wood ashes, mineral oil, and vinegar. Leave it on for quite a length of time, then wash off with warm water and gentle soap. (If you lack a ready supply of wood ashes, try substituting tobacco ashes.)

PARCHMENT OR PAPER: Warm milk, a soft cloth, and gentleness.

BRICK: Plain hot water.

STRAW, CANE, SISAL: Salt and hot water (3 or 4 tablespoons to a quart)

ALUMINUM AND TIN UTENSILS: Baking soda and water (about 3 tablespoons to a quart)

IRON AND STEEL UTENSILS: Baking soda water, as above. Or scrub them with sifted wood ashes. Or let them turn black—the iron skillet, for instance, should never be washed with soap—after it has been "sealed" with oil, the only thing that should touch its cooking surface again is oil. Wash out with hot water under the faucet if you must, then dry immediately with a paper napkin or bit of paper toweling.

COPPER OR BRASS UTENSILS: Salt and vinegar, about 4 tablespoons to a quart, warmed up together, will do just as well as those fancy, expensive liquids and pastes under the brand labels. Linseed oil is a good polish for it too.

SILVER SERVICE, FLATWARE OR UTENSILS: Into a pan of hot water and soap put a teaspoonful or so of ammonia; then thorough rinsing and polishing-drying with a soft cloth, and you'll never need any of those jars of pink cream that dry up and get thrown away before you can use them up. (Keep the ammonia away from children and pets, of course, and tightly sealed. Don't let it get on your skin.) Less heavily oxidated silver will come clean in a solution of borax and water, or baking soda and water. Good for pewter too. *Very* blackened silver (also pewter and other metals) can be brightened by equal parts chalk and cream of tartar, and one fourth as much alum powder (from the pharmacy) with enough vinegar added to make a paste. Silver (and any number of other metals), according to one Old Wife, is best cleaned by sprinkling baking soda on the cut surface of an old half-potato and polishing it with that staple. If you can keep your silver wrapped, it won't tarnish so quickly. Or put a piece of camphor into your silverware drawer.

GOLD OR PLATINUM: Can be cleaned with a solution of ammonia and water; work out your own proportion.

STAINLESS STEEL OR PEWTER: Is best cleaned with soap and water followed by olive oil or other vegetable or mineral oil.

PEARL OR MOTHER OF PEARL: *Don't* use ammonia or vinegar or any of these high-acid compounds— only warm water and gentle soap.

OVENS: If you don't have a self-cleaning oven and your baking area is encrusted with guck and grease (left, naturally, by a previous tenant)—don't buy one of those special preparations at a highway-robbery price. *Do* leave an opened container of ammonia in your (closed) oven overnight. Then air out and sponge out your oven in the morning.

CLOGGED DRAINS: Good old baking soda and hot water, about 3 tablespoons to the pint, washed briskly down the drain every day or every other day should obviate the use of those commercial drain cleaners that contain lye. You can also flush baking soda and water down your toilet once in a while—

or add a few teaspoons of soda to the water tank. A half-cupful in your refrigerator, too, will keep it deodorized.

RUBBER, SOFT OR HARD: Gentle soap and water. Don't ever leave rubber surfaces damp or wet.

COTTON OR SYNTHETIC FABRIC RUGS: Can go into your washing machine if small enough, with plain soap and warm water.

FUR RUGS: Can't, obviously, be treated as fabrics. But can be cleaned by brushing or by rubbing in and brushing out cornmeal.

FIBER OR GRASS RUGS: Can be wiped occasionally with a damp cloth soaked in a half-and-half vinegar-water solution. Or brushed clean.

OTHER CARPETS AND RUGS (WOOL, ORIENTAL, ETC.): Should be brushed or vacuumed clean frequently, then shampooed with the same substance you clean your hair with. In other words, a shampoo you would use on your head can be used on your rugs, too.

LEATHER: Can be cleaned and kept flexible with an all-purpose oil like no-label neat's-foot, castor oil, or lanolin. Watch the color of the preparation to see that it won't change the color of your leather surface. Or use turpentine (which also could affect the color). Banana skins will add a nice sheen.

The subject of stain-removal is worth a book of its own, since each substance that puts unwanted stains into fabrics and other materials is of a different makeup and hence gives way to a different sort of remover. The dry cleaner (a misnomer if there ever was one, since the cleaning done in such an establishment is far from dry—it is only that it is not wet wash) uses something not dissimilar to the gasoline you put into your automobile. Kerosene, a related substance, is an efficient remover of some kinds of stains, but unfortunately it removes much besides stains from many kinds of surfaces. Alcohol, or alcohol-based beverages, can function as spot removers for some kinds of spots, not others. Hot water, milk, chalk, hydrogen peroxide, cold water—you have used one or all of these at one time or another, no doubt. It depends, variously, on whether it is a greasy or nongreasy thing that did the staining, the nature of the thing stained, how recently it happened, and what you have access to at the moment. Because of the complicated nature of this subject, I am limiting my suggestions to the removal of only two kinds of stains.

> MOLD OR MILDEW: Gives way usually to being wiped over with lemon juice, or vinegar, or baking soda and water. If it's a very stubborn case, and something portable is suffering it, then mix equal parts of salt, powdered starch (cornstarch, for example), and soft soap powder; rub this mixture into the surface, lay it in the hot sun, or in a hot oven. Repeat several times, brushing off in between.
>
> METAL RUST: White fabrics: lemon juice. Squeeze directly on, then hold fabric over steam from a boiling kettle for a few minutes, then rinse in cold water.
>
> Colored fabrics: dampen, sprinkle liberally with salt, then dry in the sun. Or boil in a solution of 1 tablespoon cream of tartar to 1 pint of water.

Another category of cleansers sometimes found in copious numbers and splendid array under the kitchen sink is the whole spectrum of house (or apartment) deodorizers. Things to clean the air we breathe indoors. Those that don't overpower us with a lusty, all-pervading smell of their own (which, the theory goes, combats the odor we want to get rid of), are largely made up of chlorophyll, that substance in plants that makes them green. So why not just buy a big bottle of chlorophyll from the cut-rate druggist and leave a cup of it in every room? Only trouble with that is that each plant makes its own chlorophyl, builds it into its own particular pattern, and doesn't easily give it up in its pure form. So such deodorants have to be made from the finished plants themselves. A lot of crushed fresh green grass soaked in a bit of boiling white vinegar will be as effective an air deodorizer (and cost a lot less) as any of the green commercial liquids sold at exorbitant prices as room deodorants.

For a more fragrant deodorizer, pour the boiling vinegar over one of the following herbs or flowers: rosemary, thyme, mint, rose, geranium, trillium, bee balm, violet, lily of the valley, lemon verbena, sage, tarragon, trailing arbutus, hyssop, marjoram, wormwood, and, of course, ambrosia.

It all depends on what's growing in your back yard, plant window, or kitchen-shelf garden. If you have a profusion of green things outside your window, but you don't know what those weeds are, crush a leaf or blade between your fingers, and see if a fragrance is released. If so, and you like it—use *that*.

Baking soda and water in a bowl will also function as an air refresher. So will bits of charcoal (be sure it's plain charcoal and not the commercially prepared product that has been treated with some sort of oil). And of course camphorwood, cedarwood, and sandalwood, if you can get them—chips from a cabinetmaker's or a lumberyard where they work with these woods can sometimes be picked up free, or gathered by yourself in your own plastic bag and taken home for pennies.

A good-smelling room is a clean one, and a clean house is usually—not always—free of bugs. So the next category of needless cans and dispensers one finds underneath the kitchen sink is antibug compounds. Get rid of the aerosol cans first—very expensive and to be boycotted for conservationist reasons. The small creatures that are interested in your food can be easily defeated by always and immediately transferring foods from the containers you bought (or made) them in to glass or metal airtight containers. Store them thus, even if you will surely finish consuming them the next day. (I was going to include wood and plastic in that short list of materials, until I remembered the adventure

I had with vermin recently in a rat-encouraging cellar, where an imprudent previous tenant had stored cans upon cans of meals, grains, and legumes in coffee cans with plastic tops!) The mealybugs that get into your flours may seem to have sprung from the very meal itself, but they didn't—unless their eggs were laid in it behind the grocer's back. You *can* guard against them by immediate transfer of the flour from the box or bag it came in. Or you can bake the mealybugs into your breads and cakes, where they add a touch of additional protein.

The tiny fruit flies that seem to have originated in the fruits themselves are not a case of spontaneous generation either. I don't know any way of avoiding them, except to keep your fruit in the refrigerator until shortly before eating it (this is fine for everything but bananas). If the lowly cockroach is one of your banes, you may as well try to work out a *modus vivendi* with him—he has survived for millennia longer than man, and despite airbombs of DDT, monthly sprayings with other deadly toxins, wars, famines, and pestilence of every variety, he is going to go on until the end of time. La Cucaracha thrives on such nourishment as glue or paste, paper, and cardboard, and if he can't get that, will get along for most of his life on a little moisture, duplicating himself by the trillions. Even so, I include him in the list that follows, a money-saving compilation of antipest substances, some of which you can derive from the garbage you didn't throw out, others of which come from your garden or woodland, and still others from the cut-rate drugstore, the herbalist, or the supermarket. None will cost you an arm and a leg under a TV-advertised label. They are all bug-discouragers, the merits of which may depend on the virulence of your particular strain of creepy, crawly, or flier.

COCKROACH (AND OTHER BEETLES): borax powder mixed half-and-half with cornmeal, plus a drink of water nearby plaster of Paris used in the same way as the borax powder

(These methods are said to be sure-fire against rats, too, as is chloride of lime.)

citrus fruit, whole,.placed near their access to your quarters

ANT: green sage, oil of citron, or kerosene

a trap baited with almond kernels or ripe fruit

MOSQUITO (OR GNAT): castor oil, oil of clove, or oil of pennyroyal

SILVERFISH: oil of lavender, sweet woodruff, or patchouli leaves

FLY: oil of sassafras, red clover blossoms, or plantain or fleawort dipped in milk

a Venus fly-trap plant

BEDBUG: Old Wives say there is no cure for an infestation except burning of the bedclothes followed by impeccable cleanliness of person and bed.

HEAD LICE (OR CRABS): kerosene or gasoline (be very careful—flammable and rough on the skin)

TICKS (AND FLEAS): kerosene or gasoline (and don't let the dog or cat near any fire for a while)

MOTHS: swat them on the wing; if they've already laid their eggs in your wool, fur, or feather storage places, lace those containers with

    camphor wood chips

    whole cloves

    tobacco leaves (or flowering nicotiana)

    wormwood leaves

    santolina leaves

    tansy leaves

or build yourself a chest of cedar, sandalwood, or southernwood

Any of these substances can be obtained cheaper than commercial mothballs or moth crystals, and you won't have to get rid of the odor by long airing when you take the woolens, etc., out to use.

GARDEN BUGS: are of as bewildering a variety as garden plants. Some can be kept from your plants by strategic placement of saucers of flat beer or ale—they crawl in, drink their fill and then can't crawl out. Also I've known some leaf-eating creepies to be discouraged by dusting the plants with flour, cornstarch, or detergent.

The pungency of tomato leaves must be good for discouraging something—bugs or bad-smelling air. I know that it has subtly perfumed the air in my dining room where tomato plants have prospered for nearly a year.

Marigolds are often planted near vegetable plots, for they are believed to discourage a wide variety of pests—something to do with the acidity of their flowers and leaves. Try it; you will undoubtedly benefit as much as the vegetables by having some pretty flowers around.

LADY BUGS: should *never* be discouraged. Like some others, they are a natural, ecologically sound encourager of plants. They dine on pests and blights.

Now for the cosmetics and other drug-counter items you can make in your kitchen, thus saving yourself enough money to eat that balanced diet that is the main road to health and thus beauty. A shockingly large percentage of American income is thrown away on such items as commercial cleansers for skin, hair, breath, teeth, armpits—even, by God, genitals, as if there were anything inherently different about the covering (called skin) in our intimate areas that dictates a cleansing agent especially developed for it. The bacteria that live on our bodily surfaces do need to be done in from time to time—but not too often, or we can throw the baby out with the wash, so to speak. Water is the best cleaner for human bodies and their parts. (If the truth were known, we'd probably find out that plain unglamorous water is the largest component of most of the little bottles, jars, and cans that clutter up our medicine cabinets and dressing table drawers.)

A gentle soap is the next essential ingredient of clean living, and, as mentioned earlier, it need not be "special" for taking baths or washing the face and hands. Too frequent bathing, however, with or without soap, can dry out your skin; then you waste tons more money on skin softeners with fancy labels and the endorsement of famous figures in the world of fashion, beauty, or sport! The hardness or softness (i.e., mineral content) of your bathing water has some effect on your skin and hair, too, so possibly the only addition to your water, if very hard, that is absolutely essential is something to soften it. The water softener that is put into household water systems at great expense, you'll perhaps be surprised to learn, is salt. Plain old sodium chloride, or rock salt, as it comes from the mines. There we are, back to that inexpensive general household-and-body cleanser, salt. Since its nature, unfortunately, does not lend itself to certain kinds of cleansing, we'll learn some others that are just as effective. A foot bath of salt water can make you feel good all over—also clean and not likely to "offend" with "foot odor," and less subject to the fungus growth called Athlete's Foot, which calls for more drastic treatment than a salty foot bath.

Next to the genitalia, the area of the human person that is probably responsible for more anxiety than any other is the mouth. Hence the massive fortunes made by the promoters of the latest dentifrice, mouthwash, or "breath deodorant." Again, health and cleanliness are the key: bad breath results only from poor digestion or decay in the mouth (unless you want to count eating pounds of raw onions or garlic). Tooth decay can best be avoided by cleaning the teeth each time you have eaten: the brushing is what does it, not the "dentifrice."

So here, starting with the mouth, are some cleaners from your kitchen or garden for all parts of the body.

(You may have to go to the hardware store, pharmacy, or even shoe repair shop for one or two of the ingredients: if you don't habitually keep neat's-foot oil, for instance, under the kitchen sink, your cobbler may be able to supply you with it. I guarantee that you won't have to order special items from mail-order pharmaceutical or herbalist houses.)

TOOTH POWDER: One part salt to one part baking soda. If you favor tooth *paste,* mix it up with a little warm water or cold milk of magnesia. And forget about fluoride content and all the other non-sense you hear on television commercials.
A drugstore product called oil of wintergreen is a good additive for tooth cleaners, mouth washes, even sun lotions—it has a cooling effect or refreshing taste. Use *very sparingly.* Ditto oil of spearmint.

TOOTH WHITENER: Burned eggplant, crumbled into powder, is also said to be a good tooth cleaner with a lightening effect. (I, personally, would much rather eat the eggplant unburned.)

MOUTHWASH: A teaspoon of salt in a glass of warm water is the very best mouthwash money can buy; gargling with it will do just as much to prevent colds and sore throats as things ending with "-ine."

BREATH DEODORANT: Nearly any fresh herbs, chewed slowly and not swallowed, will "sweeten" the breath if it's not a very hard case. Try sage, parsley, star anise, any kind of mint. Or green grass.

EYEWASH: All those drops for your eyes that are so heavily advertised are probably mostly water with a pinch of boric acid added. So why not make your own, and save dollars on those products that evaporate a lot every time you use them?

AFTER-SHAVE LOTION: No matter what it's named, it's doubtless mostly rubbing alcohol, so why not save money by simply using rubbing alcohol? Or witch hazel?

PRE-SHAVE LOTION: (That which makes the whiskers stand up and be counted—and reaped) Ditto.

UNDERARM DEODORANT: Equal parts cornstarch and baking soda make the best powder-type deodorant going—and cost very little. Apply as you would powder. For a liquid type, use rubbing alcohol or witch hazel. And wash frequently in hot weather.

Alcohol or alcohol-based liquids are astringent (the opposite of softeners, which are loosening). Astringents tighten the skin; they also have a drying effect. You have a number of efficient ones right in your larder: fruit juices, particularly citrus juices, are astringent. So is vinegar, which is highly alcoholic. Cut them with water for a lovely after-shave lotion, which can also be used to "clean" the morning face after it has been oiled with a cleansing cream or emulsion. Recipes for both tighteners and looseners will soon follow.

Here are the "cooking" directions for these preparations: Mix the ingredients together with your fingers or a mortar and pestle, at room temperature. If they don't seem to combine well with this treatment, then heat water in the bottom of your double boiler to simmering, and melt the ingredients in the top of the double boiler. Start with the hardest ingredient, then add the others in order of hardness, stirring them in with a spoon or hand eggbeater until the proper emulsion, suspension, or blend is achieved. (Of course, don't heat anything in which egg is an ingredient.) Study the nature of the separate ingredients first to decide which method to use.

Be extra cautious when dealing with any of the waxes or oils, as they are very inflammable. Where exact measurements are not given, use your judgment as you go along— if too thick, add a bit more of the liquid ingredient; if too thin, put in more of the oily or powdery. You will be working out your own formula, just as the highly paid chemists in the cosmetics industry do before they come up with a "new, revolutionary," and grand-larceny-price beauty aid.

Store all those preparations with a high organic content in the refrigerator, rather than the bathroom medicine chest. Keep tightly stoppered any that have an alcohol base.

ASTRINGENT LOTIONS: Equal parts rose water, orange flower water, plus a few drops lemon juice

Rubbing alcohol with a drop or two of oil of wintergreen, almond extract, or papaya extract

Vodka with a few drops of lemon, lime, or grapefruit juice

Straight gin

Drops of your favorite perfume or cologne can be added to any or all of these preparations if you don't care for their natural odors. They can all be used for cleaning a naturally oily skin, for an after-shave lotion, for removing cold cream, or just for tightening up the surface of the skin and promoting that wide-awake feeling. And you haven't thrown a week's wages down the drain for a cute bottle or a clever slogan.

SHAVING CREAM: A softening (as opposed to astringent) agent. You can make a very fine one from a cup of yogurt plus a folded-in beaten egg white.

DELUXE SHAVING CREAM: Equal parts lanolin, glycerine, and mineral oil, plus a pinch of borax and a drop of oil of wintergreen

STYPTIC PENCIL: Should you cut yourself shaving anywhere, you can cleanse and close the wound easily, quickly, and cheaply by applying a bit of powdered alum.

SHAMPOO AND HAIR CONDITIONER: Warm water is probably all the shampoo your hair ever needs, or can really use. That doesn't stop the "beauty" industries from trying to persuade you that at least three different kinds of soap are a must for Oily, Dry, or Normal hair types. The kitchen holds the ideal hair treatments, though, for those who don't believe that water alone can do it. Avoid detergent shampoos, and try treating your hair (oily, dry, or normal) with mayonnaise next time—wet your tresses, rub in the mayonnaise, and let it stay a while. Or use instead the whites of two eggs, beaten until fluffy. Rinse with warm water, then a solution of half warm water, half either vinegar or lemon juice.

DELUXE SHAMPOO: 3 tablespoons coconut oil, 2 tablespoons castor oil, ¼ cup glycerin

HAIR SET: Stop wasting your hard-earned shekels on this guck. Use flat beer or, if you don't fancy the slight odor of malt in your hair, egg white beaten slightly in a little water.

PORE CLEANER: Face masks that draw the dirt out of soiled pores in the face come very high from the cosmetics industry too. You can achieve the same effect for nothing if you have some clay in the soil around you. Wash your face in hot water, smear the clay on wet; let it dry completely, then peel it carefully off, softening in cold water if necessary.

OTHER FACE MASKS: 1 tablespoon powdered yeast mixed with 1 tablespoon warm water
half an avocado, puréed, 1 teaspoon skim milk powder, 1 teaspoon warm water
1 egg yolk, beaten frothy with 1 tablespoon lime juice

SKIN SOFTENER: Oh the dollars, pounds, lire, and marks that are poured down the drain under the names of Beauty Cream, Skin Softener, Moisturizer, etc. The softness of skin depends on the oils naturally in it, which are produced by the body decreasingly as we get older. Any emollient with an oil base is a skin softener. Why not then simply use natural oils to soften the skin that is harder or dryer than is comfortable or esthetically pleasing? Most preparations marketed in fancy packaging are basically one of these three: animal oil, plant oil, or mineral oil. If petroleum jelly or plain lanolin seems too "heavy" to you, try one of the following recipes:
½ cup safflower oil, ½ cup heavy cream, 1 beaten egg white

½ cup wheat-germ oil, ½ cup milk of magnesia,
1 teaspoon essence of almond
½ cup peanut oil, ½ cup yogurt or buttermilk,
2 tablespoons tomato juice

Animal oils range from neat's-foot oil (from the feet of cattle), to lanolin (from the wool of sheep), to beeswax (from the hives of bees), but include a number of others less savory. Plant oils, of course, are as various as plants, some coming from seeds, some from nuts, some from the actual flowers, skins, stalks, or leaves of vegetative matter. The term "mineral oil" usually applies to the liquid form of this petroleum by-product, and does so in the applications that follow. In its hardest form it is called (in the United States) paraffin wax. In between is petrolatum or petroleum jelly, which you can buy in drugstores a lot cheaper than trade-name products like Vaseline.

More cold creams or skin softeners follow. In them some unfamiliar pharmacy or health-food-shop products may crop up. Stearic acid is a stiffener; it can give "body" to a cream if your mixture seems too loose to you. Kaolin can make it whiter or more opaque, as can lecithin, which also acts as a binder. Some of these moisturizers will just lie on the surface of your skin, while some will seem to be more easily absorbed by the skin—I say *seem*, because actually your skin doesn't really eat any of these preparations; some do, however, sink into the porous top layer of your epidermis more readily than others. It's up to you to experiment and see which ones work best for your individual skin.

MORE SKIN SOFTENERS: ½ cup liquid mineral oil,
2 tablespoons beeswax, pinch borax, water to liquefy

equal parts glycerin, stearic acid
¼ cup liquid lecithin, ½ cup almond extract, 2 tablespoons lanolin, 2 tablespoons paraffin wax, 1 teaspoon boric acid powder

357

equal parts sesame seed oil, avocado oil, wheat germ oil, and kaolin

equal parts glycerin and rose water, plus ¼ oz. envelope plain gelatin

1 teaspoon honey, 2 tablespoons almond extract, ¼ cup glycerin

Myrrh is supposed to be one of the most luxurious oils going for a body rub. I think it is beyond either our geography or our pocketbooks—but you might try it on Christmas Eve.

Anything that changes the color of your skin is to be avoided at all costs, but that doesn't mean you can't treat yourself to some Vitamin D from the sun in easy doses, a little at a time. You're best equipped to take in the beneficial and strain out the harmful with a sun lotion whipped up in your kitchen. Try these.

SUN LOTIONS: Any vegetable oil (sesame is good), to which you have added some phenyl salicylate crystals

¼ cup petroleum jelly, 1 tablespoon mineral oil, 1 teaspoon beeswax, 1 teaspoon zinc oxide ointment

The same preparations can be used for healing if you have a bit of sunburn. Add a few drops of oil of wintergreen, or a few teaspoons of tea (tannic acid is very "cooling").

DOUCHE: You should never cleanse this inside part of yourself with anything more caustic than a four-to-one solution of warm water and vinegar. Unless it's an even weaker solution of salt or of baking soda (which, by the way, was called by our forebears "washing soda"). Avoid like the plague all commercial preparations sold under the rubric of feminine hygiene. I've known people who insist on douching with ginger ale or Seven-Up. I can always think of a better use for these liquids. (Contraception is another thing—and one I'm not going into.)

ENEMA: Likewise. Warm water and salt is the only solution that should ever be used

The "natural" look in cosmetics and face makeup is, I hope, still "in." We are not required to have green or orchid or white eyelids if our skin is by birth a lovely chocolate color. Or to stain our lips purply-red if their natural shade is a faint pink. Most cosmetics colorings are really dyes, made from lead and other metals that should not constantly come in contact with tender skin. If you insist that they do with yours, for reasons of fashion and style or just for feeling good about yourself, try to use creamy or oil-based colorings that are easy to remove. For the sake of those who work with you in the daytime, try to restrict the use of high-color makeup to your evening festivities.

If the good natural skin oils that pour out of your face in quantity and make the surface shiny embarrass you into powdering your nose, don't waste your money (and possibly endanger your health) by piling metal-based powders into the pores of your facial skin. Many powders for face or body contain very abrasive materials (asbestos fibers, for example). Don't be misled into using them if their labels say they are for babies. Plain talc, which you can purchase under no label at the drugstore, is the best and smoothest face or body powder around, for infants or adults. It is crushed and finely granulated soapstone, quite harmless to the skin.

You may prefer to revert to the ways of our forefathers and foremothers, who rubbed their shiny noses with a bit of powdered starch inside a square of muslin. Here are some wholesome shiny-nose aids.

FACE POWDER: 2 teaspoons boric acid, 3 teaspoons cornstarch, rice powder or potato flour equal parts arrowroot and whole wheat flour (fine-ground)

The color of either can be darkened with liberal additions of cocoa powder or carob flour. Or cinnamon, nutmeg, paprika, curry powder, or other mild spices whose shades you think will work. Don't try mustard, chili, or the very hot spices, for they may burn your skin

But do "deodorize" your hands after you've been working with fresh fish, onions, or other foods that may leave your hands redolent by treating them to some powdered or cream-style mustard for a few minutes, then washing it off. They will then return to the natural smell of your skin, which is perfume or cologne enough for most people.

Conclusion

When I was very young, I once walked into the parlor of a part-time farmer and saw on the table there a book entitled something like "Advanced Graduate Seminar in the Compost Heap." At the time I thought it hilariously funny—but no longer. Maintaining in your back yard a pit or a cage—or just a pile—where you can throw all your organic garbage may strike you as unsightly, but it saves you all sorts of things, most of all waste.

Waste not, want not is a viable philosophy that has never gone out of style. Recycling centers have sprung up all over our land, in cities and towns, at industrial centers, on the waterfronts and in the countryside, ever since our heightened awareness that plundering our planet can lead to famine and want of every sort. True, the communal recycling centers are usually devoted to the collection of glass, metal, or paper products; but there is no recycling center like your very own compost pit. In such a collection spot, all sorts of vegetative matter that has come from the earth can be left to decompose into material ready to return to the soil and promote the next season's vegetable growth.

A beautiful circle—and one that will save you money you might otherwise spend on commercial fertilizers. Composting will also save you energy in the form of trips to the garbage dump, or save you room in your refuse collection cans.

You can build a compost bin of wood, wire, cinderblocks, or stones, or some ingenious combination of these elements. Try to find a spot that is shady and not too windy, for optimum decomposition. Then put down layers in the following order:

1. green matter (grass, leaves, weeds, etc.)
2. organic garbage (fruits, vegetables, coffee grounds, etc.)
3. soil (the richest you can find)
4. manure (from cows or other animals)
5. lime or wood ashes

Once you have put down all these things in this order, repeat in the same order until you have filled up your space. Add a little water to each layer. And poke some holes in it. Turn it over about every three weeks, and in three months' time you will have good compost, ready to be worked into the soil of your garden plot. (You can achieve compost even faster if you happen to have a shredder among your tools and gadgets.)

Of course if you have followed all the advice in Chapter 10 of this book, you will have very little from the kitchen to add to your compost pit in any one day. Your non-composting neighbors, though, may be persuaded to save themselves an occasional trip to the dump; don't be ashamed to beg their garbage from them—they may be glad to get rid of it so easily. Don't forget that fallen leaves and all sorts of outdoor waste materials go in, too—anything organic that has served its primary function in garden or kitchen or fireplace is potential compost.

The humus of the forest floor is nothing more than natural compost—look what tall trees grow from this recycled fertilizer. You can have similar results in your garden. Composting is also a dandy way of disposing of horse and cow dung (which should never, never be thrown into the garden in its fresh, raw, unalloyed state).

I can't think of a better thing to wish you in conclusion than that your compost heap should grow by leaps and bounds, and become a goldmine in your back yard. Surely the ultimate in saving for Mr. and Ms. Pinchpenny.

GENERAL INDEX

363

364

RECIPE INDEX